Conjure

The Hoodoo Apprentice

Conjure

THE HOODOO APPRENTICE

LEA NOLAN

Entangled Publishing, LLC
2614 South Timberline Road
Suite 109
Fort Collins, CO 80525
Visit our website at www.entangledpublishing.com.

Edited by Liz Pelletier
Cover design by Alexandra Shostak

Print ISBN   978-1-62061-097-8
Ebook ISBN   978-1-62061-098-5

Manufactured in the United States of America

First Edition October 2012

For Gillian Raine, who loves her colored pencils.

Chapter One

The waves thrash against the shore in a rage. Last night's storm might be over, but St. Helena Island Sound is still angry. And I couldn't be more thrilled.

"Emma, how much longer is that sketch going to take?" my brother Jack calls into the wind. "You promised to surf with us before the waves die down."

An osprey squawks overhead, searching for prey in the churning water.

"Just a second." Squinting at the oil pastel drawing in my lap, I wiggle my toes in the cool sand. This beach is normally postcard perfect—sharp blue sky, shimmering teal water, and white talcum-powder sand—a never-changing snapshot of sunny South Carolina summer. But last night's storm switched everything up, if only for a few hours, and I'm determined to capture it. There's no telling when it'll be this dark and gloomy again.

Plus working on this picture gives me a good excuse not to stare at Cooper Beaumont, our best friend and sole heir to this beach and the rest of High Point Bluff Plantation. Cooper, whose golden-brown hair turns blond in the sun, and whose eyes switch from blue to green depending on his clothes. The same Cooper who smells like a perfect combination of summer and the sea. That Cooper.

The unrequited, secret love of my fourteen-year-old life.

After a school year away from each other—him at boarding school, me and Jack in Washington, D.C., with our mom—the last thing I need is for him to see me drool over the new, hard edge of his jaw or his etched cheekbones. Yup, that would definitely tip him off to my obsession and ruin the summer before it's even begun.

My heart flutters, so before I have a coronary just thinking about him, I force myself to focus on my sketchbook instead. I've got the waves right—thick and choppy, a deep, murky slate smattered with frothy white caps—but the sky is wrong. I've blended the alabaster, blue, black, and gray to match the platinum clouds, but something's missing. Holding my hand above the pastel tray, I clear my mind and breathe deep, knowing the right color will sing to me, beckon me to pick it up. As my hand passes over the greens, it stops over one in particular, just like always. My fingers tingle above chartreuse, a sickly combination of yellow and green. It's just the tint I need. I pluck it and blend it in.

"Heads up!" Jack calls as he flings his faded orange Frisbee at Cooper.

Glancing around, I see the disc is headed straight for him, but then it suddenly wobbles and dog-legs. Without losing speed, it bends in midair and arches toward me, whipping past my face. A whoosh of wind grazes my skin, and I tuck into a ball, pressing my chest against my sketchbook.

"Hey!" I yell.

Cooper charges up the beach from behind me and snatches

the Frisbee as he dives into the wet sand at my feet. "Got it!" He flashes that warm, easy grin of his. Holy hotness. Shivers race over my skin.

I gulp, determined to keep it together. "Thanks."

"No problem." He winks an emerald eye and picks himself up.

Jack rushes up to us, looking guilty. "Sorry, Emma, I wasn't aiming for you, I swear. That old thing is warped."

I peel the sketchbook away from my body. My white peasant blouse is smudged with grayish-blue and pukey yellow-green oil pastels, which probably won't come out in the wash. I sigh. "Maybe next time you should try to hit me. Then it might land in the water."

Cooper tosses the saucer at Jack, smacking him in the gut. "Works fine for me, bro." He laughs, then glances at the roiling sea on my lap. "That's really good."

My cheeks flush. "Thanks. It's not done yet."

"Really?" Jack asks, studying the now smeared image in my sketchbook. "Because it looks pretty awesome to me."

I drill my toes further into the damp sand. "Well, I'm not happy with the sky yet. It doesn't look…"

I bite my lip and search for the right word. *Mad* and *ill* aren't strong enough. I need something that means disgusted, furious, and nauseous all at once. As I concentrate, my feet burrow deeper into the coarse, cold grains.

"Ouch!" I wince and yank my left foot from the sand. Bright red blood streams down the pink skin of my arch. "What the heck?" Crusted with sand, the jagged cut burns.

Cooper kneels next to me and rests a hand on my bare knee. "Are you all right?" Normally his touch would make my heart race, but the pain beats him to it.

Blood trickles onto the sand.

Jack's eyes fill with alarm. "What happened?"

I grit my teeth. "I'm not sure but something cut me." My brow furrows as I bend my leg and peer at the dripping, inch-long wound. "I hope I don't need stitches." With a tentative hand, I probe the cut to see how deep it is, but it's bleeding so much, it's hard to tell. Ruby-colored streaks coat my fingers, and I try to remember whether I should flush out the cut in the Sound or if that will make it worse. "Whatever it was, it was sharp."

"There's only one way to find out." Jack drops to his knees, shoves his hand in the sand at my feet, and digs.

Cooper stretches his lean body and watches Jack. "Careful, bro." He picks up his discarded shirt and, without a thought for the designer brand, blots the blood as it drips toward my toes.

"Give me a hand, Coop." My brother scoops up sand.

"What are you doing?" My voice rises as I pull my other foot out of the beach. "You could get cut, too." I squeeze the wound together to apply pressure and stem the flow.

Jack shrugs. "Don't worry, Em. It'll be fine."

So says the boy who bawls over a splinter. I shouldn't be surprised, though. Jack's always the one to jump into things without thinking. Like digging for an unidentified, dangerous object.

"Hey, look at this."

I lean in, curious to see what attacked me.

Jack uncovers the top of what looks like a wax-covered bottle. The wax is dry and chipped in places, its sharp edges laced with my blood.

A queasy feeling swells in my stomach. I recoil and grimace.

Scraping away the rest of the sand, Jack frees the bottle. Its elongated neck and short, squat body look like the antique wine bottles on display at Cooper's house.

"That's cool," Jack says. Then quickly adds, "The bottle, I mean, not that it cut you."

"Yeah, yeah, I get it." The bleeding has finally slowed. The cut looks superficial, so at least I don't have to find a doctor.

"This must have been here a long time," Cooper says. "The storm probably eroded some sand and helped bring it to the surface."

Jack lifts the bottle to the overcast sky. "Look, there's something in it." A rolled piece of paper is nestled inside.

Cooper digs into his pocket and pulls out his Swiss army knife. "Let's see."

My head spins. Dizzy, I brace against the sand.

Jack grabs the knife from Cooper's hand and slides it around the bottle's neck, slicing through what's left of the crumbling black seal, then chips the wax away. A piece of cork is jammed into the top, but the knife's screw easily removes it. He fishes out the thick, yellow paper and tosses the bottle onto the beach. Then he unrolls the parchment and scans it. "Dang," he mutters.

Cooper reads over his shoulder.

Uneasiness crawls up my spine. Maybe it's a delayed reaction to the cut and all the blood, but I think I'm about to hurl.

"What does it say?" I ask, heaving a deep breath.

"See for yourself." Jack hands the letter over. Shaky, old-timey handwriting and scattered ink drops cover the page.

I squint to make out what it says.

St. Helena Island, Carolina Colony, anchored off High Point Bluff Plantation, April 1725

To ye who may find this bottle and the urgent missive it contains,

I, Bloody Bill Ransom, Captain of the vessel The Dagger, humbly request your most capable assistance. An old Gullah hag harnessed the wind and water to curse my ship and crew for plundering a flower, causing us grievous suffering. This abominable curse, The Creep, has taken half my sailors in the most heinous and gruesome manner and without your aid will surely ravage those who remain, leaving behind only a sorry bundle of dry bones to drift with the wind. We beg your assistance in removing the curse and will pay you richly, as soon as we are well enough to retrieve our treasure stolen by Edmund Beaumont, the Master of High Point Bluff Plantation. On my honour as a gentleman and an honest privateer, I pledge to share one half of the recovered treasure with anyone who responds to this plea and grants our fervent request.

Your most humble servant,
Bloody Bill Ransom
Captain, The Dagger

My stomach drops, and the hair on the back of my neck bristles. Shaking my head, I look at the guys. Before I can even process my reaction to the letter, a flash of color catches my eye and distracts me from the ancient parchment. Against the gunmetal sky, a figure in a crimson dress and straw hat approaches.

"Who's that?" I nod in her direction.

Jack's head snaps around. "No idea. I didn't think the locals ever came up to High Point Bluff." He jumps to his feet and turns toward the girl.

"Hey," Cooper calls to her and stands, but I stay put on the sand, squeezing my injured foot.

She tosses us a wave as her long, lean features come into focus. She removes her hat and shakes out her tumbling ebony waves.

Somehow I manage not to gasp. The air quiets, and time slows as I take in each of her exquisite features. My vision tunnels, focusing on her smooth, brown skin, petal-pink lips, and coal-black eyes, as my mind struggles to assemble them into one perfect human face. Even the six tiny silver ringlets that line the curve of her left ear are beautiful. She's about our age, but she's unlike anyone I've ever seen before in real life.

Jack must be thinking the same thing because his jaw hangs open for a second before he manages to speak.

"Hi." His voice is soft and breathy as he brushes his dark hair out of his eyes.

"Hello." She tilts her head as if she's waiting for him to say something else. Her flowery perfume fills the air. Sweet and cloying, it tickles my nose.

Jack stares, his baby blues vacant, so I help him out. "I'm Emma Guthrie." I flick my thumb at him. "He's my brother, Jack."

Without even a glance in my direction, she grasps his hand. "Hello, Jack Guthrie. I'm Magnolia Akan." Her accent is a weird cross between British, South Carolina Lowcountry, and Jamaican.

Jack's brows rise in a mixture of rapture and disbelief. His lips move, but no sound emerges. I'm just wondering why she is using his full name.

She smiles at him and nods toward Cooper. "Who is your friend?"

"C-C-Cooper. Cooper Beaumont," Jack manages.

Her smile slips as she gives Cooper the once-over while keeping a firm grip on Jack. "May I ask when you'll come of age, Cooper Beaumont?"

"Huh?" he asks.

She looks up and off to the right, as if she's searching for a word. "When will you come into your manhood?"

Cooper chuckles. "Um, I'm not sure what you're asking, but I turn sixteen next month, at the end of July."

She grins and extends her free hand toward Cooper. Except it's not like a regular handshake. Instead, she holds her hand out flat like a princess and grasps his fingers when he reaches to touch her.

Jack snaps out of his daze and frowns at Cooper. "Emma and I will be fifteen soon."

Um, only if he thinks four months is "soon." Which it's not.

Slipping her hand out of Cooper's grasp, Magnolia finally acknowledges my presence and wags an elegant finger between Jack and me. "You two are the same age. How can that be?"

"We're twins," I answer, anticipating the inevitable explanation to come.

Her lips twist into an over-sweet smile. "But you don't look the same."

I resist rolling my eyes at her revelation that my strawberry-blonde hair and Irish-pink skin are different from Jack's jet-black mane and olive complexion. As if we hadn't realized it ourselves or heard it a million times. Yes, we're twins who don't look alike. We've noticed. But we're fraternal, so it's not that big a deal.

Jack laughs. "Yeah, no one ever believes us, Maggie—you don't mind if I call you that, do you?"

She arches her brow but smiles and shakes her head.

He grins. "Oh, good, because I'm kind of a nicknamer. Plus

I'm not really down with calling you the name of the Mississippi state tree. Don't ask me how I know that. It's just one of those things I learned in school, I guess." He squeezes his eyes shut and tries to shake off whatever's making him babble like an idiot. "Anyway, no one ever believes we're twins because I look like our dad, and she takes after our mom. Thanks to my dad's genes, I never burn in the summer, but she's a total French fry."

Maggie giggles, probably because Jack is acting like such a dork. "That is excellent. It is good to have family. Very good, indeed." She squeezes his hand.

Why is she still holding his hand? I mean, it's not that Jack is hideous—he's actually pretty decent looking—but let's face it, he's no Cooper. Not that I'm suggesting she should switch her attention. I don't need to compete with a supermodel.

"So, Maggie, are you from here?" I try to sound casual. "I haven't seen you around any of our summers on the island."

She nods, slow and easy, brushing her bare toes over the sand. "Sa'leenuh is my home." She uses the local Gullah term for the island. Unlike a lot of the other Sea Islands, St. Helena still has a large Gullah population, the descendents of enslaved Africans who grew cotton and indigo for their masters.

I'm confused. She doesn't sound like any local I've ever met.

Cooper rubs his chin. "Hmm, Akan. I don't recall anyone with that last name on St. Helena."

She narrows her gaze at him. "Small as it is, I doubt you've met everyone on this island."

She finally notices the scarlet smears on my hand and foot. For just a moment, she goes still and pale. "You are injured, Emma Guthrie. You should cleanse that in the water."

"I was going to, but—"

Jack cuts me off. "We found this cool letter in a bottle." He wriggles free of her grasp, bends down, and takes the letter from my hand. "It's about a treasure right here at High Point Bluff." He thrusts it under Maggie's nose.

Itchy unease creeps up my scalp.

Giving the yellow paper a cursory peek, she bats her eyes. "That sounds exciting."

"Well, even if it's real, it was written a long time ago," Cooper says. "Any treasure is probably long gone by now."

The chill spreads down my arms and spine, prickling my skin. "But it's not just about a treasure."

Ignoring me, Maggie strokes Jack's shoulder. "There are many strange and unknown things in the Lowcountry. Who is to say a treasure couldn't exist?"

Cooper shakes his head. "I don't know. It seems like a story this good would have been passed down through my family."

Jack persists. "But don't you see? If you've never heard about it, maybe it was hidden."

"Perhaps it is lying under this very ground." Maggie flashes doe eyes at Jack. "You'll never know if you don't search." She slips her hand back into his and entwines their fingers.

The tingling intensifies, and my heart races. What is wrong with them? "Um, am I the only one who noticed most of the letter is about a curse?" My chest is tight, making it hard to speak.

Jack scoffs. "Please, Emma, there's no such thing. People were just superstitious back then."

My stomach clenches. "But what about the bone thing? It says it's gruesome."

Jack looks at me like I've lost my mind. "Seriously? They probably had scurvy or something."

Crossing my arms, I glare at him. "Uh, they were pirates. I think they'd know the difference between scurvy and whatever this was—what did he call it?" I hobble to my feet, and Cooper rushes to help me. Leaning on his arm, I look at the letter in Jack's hand. "The Creep. That doesn't sound like scurvy to me." Another chill rushes through me.

"Give me a break. Why would anyone get cursed for stealing a flower?" Jack waves me off and turns to Cooper. "What do you think, Coop?"

Cooper scratches his temple with his free hand. "Honestly, I don't know. This area is full of stories that sound crazy but are based on a little bit of truth. I don't know what The Creep was, but Emma's probably right."

Maggie shrugs. "Perhaps. Perhaps not. But a treasure might be enough of a reward to try."

"I say we do it." Jack holds his free palm up for a high-five, but Maggie's lids stretch in surprise, and she leaves him hanging. He chuckles and shrugs it off, drops his hand, and turns to Cooper. "Come on, what do you say? It'll give us something to do besides sit on the boat. Plus it could be fun. We'll start by poking around the Big House."

Cooper takes the letter and reads it again. When his lips curl into a half-grin, I know he's decided to give in to Jack and this ridiculous idea. "I guess there's no harm in taking a look. But we should start at the ruins instead," he says, referring to the remains of the original plantation house. "This letter was written before the first Big House burned down. In a hurricane, I think."

The prickling eases, allowing me to think straight. "Burned in a hurricane? How the heck did that happen?"

Cooper shakes his head. "I don't know. Maybe the wind knocked over some candles. Or maybe it was Captain Bloody Bill's revenge. Bwuhaha." He waves the ancient letter at me and laughs.

Maggie stiffens and glances over her shoulder. Shuddering, she releases Jack's hand and rubs her arms like she's freezing, even though despite all these clouds, it's at least seventy-five degrees. "Forgive me. I must go."

"Aw, really?" Jack asks, almost whining.

"Yes, my grandmother is calling me." I quirk my head, listening for an old lady or a cell phone, but there's only the sound of the endless, churning waves. Maggie backs up to leave. "Good-bye, Emma and Jack Guthrie. Good-bye, Cooper. Good luck finding your treasure." She spins on her bare heels and saunters down the beach.

"Bye," Jack calls, unable to peel his eyes off her. "See you... soon." Only it comes out more like a hopeful question than a fact.

When she's out of earshot, I clear my throat. "Wow, she was... different."

Jack sighs, still transfixed. "She can be anything she wants to be. She's hot." He shakes his head to clear the Maggie-induced fog, then narrows his gaze at me. "What about you, Em? You in?"

I know what he's really asking: will I spend the summer with him and Cooper, searching for the dumb treasure, or by myself, sketching at the nearby wildlife preserve?

Put that way, I don't have a choice. Jack's sucked Cooper in to this scheme, and I can't be without Cooper. I sigh, shaking my head in defeat. "Fine. But just remember, I told you so."

Chapter Two

Cooper plants his shovel in the rich soil and wipes the trickling sweat from his grimy brow. "Jack, you know I love you, bro, but this is so not going to work." He's surrounded by a bunch of holes and unearthed clumps of vegetation.

It's been a long three days. The searing South Carolina sun is back, wearing us down. And so is Jack. He's turned into an overlord, bossing us around, pointing at the ground, and ordering us to dig wherever his new, Internet-ordered metal detector tells us to. So far we've found a few iron nails, some spare change, and a crappy old charm bracelet. This is a colossal waste of time. And it doesn't help that my twin sense is getting super weird vibes from Jack. Part of me wants to confront him about it, but he is being such a jerk lately that I don't even want to bother.

"We can't quit now. I'm telling you it's here. I can feel it." Jack winces and pinches the bridge of his nose. "Dang, this heat's making my headache worse."

I sigh. "Are you kidding me? Look around." I jab my muddied hand at the mounds that litter the clearing surrounding the ruins.

"There's nothing here." I tug my clingy T-shirt off my soaked chest and fan my scorching face. "And if your head hurts so bad, we should quit."

A warm breeze blows off St. Helena Island Sound. Its cool water beckons just a couple hundred feet away at the bottom of the bluff. We should be on the beach or floating in a boat, our legs dangling in juicy, delicious wetness. Anything besides being stuck here in pothole hell.

"It's *here*." Jack strides toward me, his shoulders looming since I'm still knee-deep in my own pit. He grinds his teeth. His normally cool blue eyes have darkened like slick little pools of oil. "You just haven't dug deep enough." He plants his hands on his hips and growls. Like, literally. His nostrils flare, and for a second, I think he might hit me. But that would be insane and totally unlike my brother.

Cooper tosses his shovel, jumps out of his hole, and rushes to Jack's side. Grabbing his arm, Cooper drags Jack back a few steps away from me. "Take it easy, bro. Emma's only trying to help."

Jack spins around and glares at Cooper. His hands ball into tight fists, and his body quakes.

I gape, wondering what the heck he's thinking. Last summer, they were both lean, lanky, and the same height, but over the school year, Cooper changed. He's taller, bigger, and way more muscular. He could flatten Jack without trying.

Cooper broadens his chest. "I don't think you want to go there, bro." His voice is deep and firm.

Jack shudders and blinks a couple times. The hard edge to his face softens. "Yeah." He nods and rubs his forehead. "Yeah. I guess you're right." He looks around, bewildered. "I'm sorry, dude."

My pulse charges. I don't know what's gotten into my brother, and I don't care if Cooper wants to stay. I'm sick of Jack's epic weirdness. Not to mention the mosquito bites, sweating, stinking, and scraping dirt from my nails. I'm done.

Thrusting my shovel to the side, I stomp out of my hole. "Enjoy your obsession. I've got better things to do." Wiping my hands on my crusty shorts, I shake out my flip-flops. Considering I'm caked with crud, it's a total waste of effort. The stupid bandage on my foot has come loose—again. I just wish it didn't hurt to wear sneakers.

Pushing past them, I scoop up my messenger bag laden with colored pencils and the other art supplies I've neglected over the past three sticky and pathetically unproductive days. Shuffling around the other holes and piles of unearthed fill, I head toward our golf cart and sweet freedom. Now that we're done playing Indiana Jones, I can get back to sketching. After I shower.

"No! Emma, you can't go." Jack breaks free of Cooper's grasp and charges after me, his voice panicked.

I stop short and whirl around to face him.

Jaw tight, he rubs his temples. "Look, I'm sorry." His words are soft and full of pleading. "I know ever since we found that bottle, I've been a little—"

"Psychotic?"

"Driven." An embarrassed smile inches across his lips. "And I haven't exactly been the easiest person to get along with, but I know we're close. Trust me, I can feel it. Please stay and help?"

Jack's ever-changing moods are giving *me* a headache now. I sigh. "Look, it's too hot to dig anymore today, anyway. You need a break, some water, and definitely something to eat. Sub sandwich sound good?"

He shakes his head. "The only thing I need is the treasure."

My ears prick. *Need* it? Before the other day, he'd never even heard about it. And since when has he ever passed up a meal?

I peer over Jack's shoulder at Cooper, who looks as confused as I feel. Reading my silent call for backup, he steps over to Jack and slaps his shoulder. "We can search again tomorrow morning when the sun isn't so high. But for now, let's get out of here, grab some lunch, and go for a sail. We haven't been out on the boat this summer, and I'm itching to get on the water."

I nod and grab Jack's hand, guiding him away from these godforsaken holes. "Yeah, that's a great idea. We can sail over to Hunting Island, and I can sketch the lighthouse."

Jack takes one last look at the clearing. "Okay. That sounds good."

I sigh with relief.

A figure in a bright yellow dress and straw hat makes her way up the bluff toward the ruins. My stomach drops. It's the girl from the other day. I want to get out of here before Jack sees her.

Cooper spots her, too, and points in her direction. "Hey, Jack, look! It's…" He turns to me. "What is her name?"

"Maggie," I answer, thrilled she didn't make an indelible impression on him.

I can't say the same for Jack, though. He rubs his hands together. "Oh, yeah. I wonder where she's been." Elated for the first time in days, he sprints toward her.

Stunned by yet another head-spinning change in Jack's mood, Cooper and I watch him plow down the bluff to greet Maggie halfway. They exchange a few words. He points to us. She slips her arm through his, and they climb the sandy hill together.

"She is pretty, isn't she?" Cooper remarks under his breath. His words crush my heart. She and I might be around the same height and have similar builds, but that's where the comparisons end. If she's his type, there's no way I can compete. Biting my tongue to distract from the ache welling in my chest, I try not to whimper like a puppy caught underfoot.

I glance down at my filthy flip-flops and crusty bandage. "Yeah, gorgeous."

When they get to the top of the bluff, Jack's beaming. "Maggie was walking on the beach when she heard our voices and decided to come see us."

I don't know if it's the heat, my hunger, or the fact that her unexpected arrival has delayed our departure, but queasiness rushes over me. I don't want to be here anymore. My skin flares as a strange impulse takes hold. I want to race away from them all, escape down the bluff, and throw myself into the cool Sound. But to avoid looking like a crazy person, I resist.

Maggie unhooks her arm from his and waves. "Hello, Emma Guthrie," she says in that odd accent. "Hello, Cooper Beaumont." Her flowery perfume hangs in the air.

"Hi." I nod, avoiding her ebony eyes, which are so deep and dark, they look like they go on forever.

Cooper nods. "Hey, how are you, Maggie?"

"She's fine," Jack answers for her and casually takes her hand in his, as if he's done it a thousand times before, which is totally weird, since he was never touchy-feely with his ex-girlfriend, Katie. What is with these two? They've only known each other for a total of maybe ten minutes—since when did they start dating?

Jack points to the clearing. "We've been searching for the treasure."

Maggie quirks her brow. "But you haven't had much luck."

Thank you, Ms. Obvious. Frustration swells, and my hands itch. I don't need her commentary. I need to leave.

"We haven't found it because it isn't here," I cross my arms and concentrate hard, battling the antsy feeling once again. "Which is why we were just leaving." I incline my head toward Cooper and

Jack to get us moving again.

Maggie tightens her grip on Jack, holding him in place, and tilts her gorgeous head. "Why haven't you dug within the ruins?" She leads Jack to the edge of the excavation and points to what's left of the original Big House. Made of ancient tabby concrete, an unstable mixture of oyster shells and sand that crumbles to the touch, the foundation's footprint is still intact, but the walls have been whittled down by wind and rain. It's hard to imagine what the house looked like back in the day. Based on what's left, though, it must have been a palace.

I groan. The last thing I need is her getting Jack worked up again. We'll never get out of here.

Cooper grunts. "We promised my dad we wouldn't go near them. He doesn't want us wrecking the remains."

"But it would be easier to hide a treasure inside a house than in the yard, no?" Maggie smiles and bats her lashes.

As much as I hate to admit it, she does have a point.

Jack smiles. "You're a genius, Maggie!" He slips from her grip, grabs the metal detector, and launches himself over a low tabby wall.

Cooper follows. "What are you doing? You promised not to touch the concrete!"

"Relax, I'm only scanning the ground." Jack crouches to stare at the base of the foundation, then stands up and inches the detector along until he's made it all the way around the base. "Dang," he mutters, squeezing his eyes shut and rubbing the bridge of his nose. A moment later, he shakes his head and scans the dirt again. He spins and looks at the center of the ruins, then cocks his head and moves across the vegetation. "Hey, Coop, come here. I got a strong reading. And the dirt in this section seems different than the rest."

"What are you talking about?" Cooper jumps inside and kneels beside Jack. Finally, he lifts his head and calls, "Hey, Emma, could you hand me a shovel?"

What? Now Cooper, too? I thought he was on my side. Against my better judgment, I hand him the nearest shovel.

Maggie adjusts the brim on her hat. "I must be on my way, friends."

Jack pops his head up from behind the fragile concrete. "So soon? You just got here." His eyes turn down, crestfallen. "Can't you stay awhile? Maybe even help?"

She shakes her head. "I am sorry. My grandmother is waiting for me. I will see you tomorrow morning, Jack Guthrie. Good luck." She turns and heads down the bluff.

Biting back tears, I plop down on the golf cart's rear seat and sink my head in my hands. It's going to be a long day.

• • •

Six hours later, after two food and water runs, Cooper and Jack have managed to dig out a six-by-eight-foot hole in the ground. It's an old root cellar where people stored food to keep it cool. The two of them are standing waist-deep, scraping out earth and tossing it over their shoulders in a huge pile next to the hole. I sift through the rich, loamy soil with my bare hands, just in case they missed anything. But there's nothing.

Jack's shovel clangs against something solid.

"Whoa, what was that?" I crane my neck around the dirt pile.

Jack bends over to dust the ground with his hands. "I'm not sure."

Cooper leans in. "It's tabby." His jaw drops in amazement.

I stand and step to the opening. "Like a hunk of it?"

Cooper shakes his head. "No, it's smooth and more yellow than the ruins."

Jack's eyes gleam. "I told you we'd find something. I could feel it." He feverishly scrapes at the dirt like a dog worrying for a bone.

Cooper helps, suddenly as driven as Jack, and soon they've uncovered a flat, rectangular piece of concrete about two feet long and a foot-and-a-half wide. A few more shovelfuls reveals it's not just a slab, it's the top of some sort of tabby box wedged into the corner of the root cellar. They dig and scrape until they uncover the whole thing.

Cooper slaps Jack's back. "I've got to hand it to you, bro. You were right."

The hair rises on the back of my neck. "Why would someone put a tabby box in a root cellar?"

Jack shrugs. "Maybe it was a kind of safe." He hooks his fingers around the top and strains to lift the lid. "Let's see what's inside this baby." He grunts, unable to yank it loose. "Help me, Coop. This is really stuck."

Cooper bends over and pulls, flexing his sculpted arms, but the top refuses to budge.

My pulse quickens. But it's not from excitement. That weird anxious feeling has crept back again.

Jack stands, panting and gnawing his bottom lip, glaring at the uncooperative lid. "Crap!" He kicks the top, his fists clenched.

"Maybe we can try leverage." Cooper shoves the tip of his shovel into the crease below the front corner of the lid. He pushes down, leaning into the handle with his chest. His jaw clenches as the top creaks, but the shovel's blade bends, and he tumbles to the ground. Heaving for air, he says, "Sorry, Jack. It's not coming off."

"It has to." Jack jumps out of the hole, snatches my shovel off the ground, and hands it to Cooper. Then he jumps back into the pit, grabs his own shovel, and jams it into the other corner of the box. "Come on, move over a little. If we push together, I'm sure we can lift it."

Acid swirls in my stomach. Something doesn't fit. Why would something that's been buried four feet in the ground for three hundred years need to be sealed? If this was a root cellar, people would want to get to their stuff, not lock it up.

Cooper wedges the shovel's blade into the crease under the tabby slab.

The words from Bloody Bill's letter flash across my mind. He said the curse was abominable, heinous, and gruesome. My heart gallops. This is a mistake. We shouldn't open the box.

Jack and Cooper bear down on the handles, their faces flushed with effort.

A wave of nausea rolls over me, leaving my skin clammy and coating my mouth with hot saliva. I have to stop them before it's too late. "Stop!" I cry, my voice echoing across the clearing.

Jack and Cooper spin around. Cooper drops the shovel and lurches toward me, deep creases etched into his brow. "What's wrong?"

I'm breathing hard, in through my nose and out my mouth, hoping I don't throw up in front of him. Or into the hole next to him. I shut my eyes, swallow hard, and will the nausea away.

Jack's voice, tense and impatient, cuts through the clearing. "What's the matter with you, Emo?" He lobs his favorite insult, intended to make me feel bad for listening to indie emo music instead of the hip-hop he loves.

I ignore him, and the lump in my throat eases enough for me to speak. "It doesn't make sense that it's sealed." My voice is thick and raspy. "There must be a reason you can't open it."

Jack rolls his eyes. "Oh, don't start with the stupid curse again. Dirt and gravity pushed it down for hundreds of years. That's the only reason it won't open." His lips crack into a crazed smile. "But it will when we're through with it." He thrusts his shovel into the air, and his eyes narrow and darken.

"No, Jack," I plead. "It's not closed. It's *sealed*."

Cooper turns to him. "Maybe she's right. That feels like a concrete bond to me."

Jack points the blade end of his shovel at Cooper. "She doesn't know what she's talking about. We've come this far. We're not stopping now."

"But bro—"

"But nothing." Jack's eyes flash like lasers. "I'm doing this with or without you. What's it going to be?"

I can see Jack standing before me, but this crazed lunatic is nothing like my brother.

I lean toward Cooper. "Please don't." But it comes out in a hushed whisper as shivers—definitely not the good kind—shoot up the back of my neck.

His gaze meets mine. He knows I'm right. I can see it in his jade-green eyes. He places his hands on the edge of the pit to boost himself out.

Cool relief spreads through my chest. Now that Cooper's given up, maybe Jack will, too.

"I've never asked you for anything, Cooper," Jack says. "I'm your best friend, the closest thing you have to a brother. Help me with this."

Cooper squeezes his eyes shut, and his lips form a tight line. He doesn't have to look at me or say a word. I know I've lost the battle. He looks up at me and mouths the word "sorry" before turning around and picking up the shovel he'd tossed to the ground.

Together they slide the shovel blades into the crease between the top slab and the tabby box.

"On my count, we lift on three, okay?" Jack asks.

Cooper nods. "Got it."

Jack draws a deep breath. "One, two, three."

They press hard on the shovels, biceps flexing and veins straining, forcing the blades farther into the crease. The muscles in Jack's neck strain, pulling like thick cords, contorting his throat into a rectangle, while Cooper's face flushes crimson, and the skin at his temples throbs.

My stomach clenches, and my chest constricts. No matter what Jack thinks, deep down in my bones, I know this is wrong.

The slab grinds against the tabby box, wiggling back and forth until a loud crack cuts the silence, popping the slab off the top and propelling Jack and Cooper to the ground.

A howl, long and mournful, bellows in the forest surrounding the ruins.

An electric jolt shoots up my spine. I gasp. "Did you hear that?"

Jack pumps his fist and erupts in giddy laughter. "We did it!"

Cooper stands, shaking out his arms. "Heck, yes. There better be something in there to make it worth our while."

Caught up in their excitement, they don't answer me. Either they didn't hear the sound, or they're ignoring me. "Hello? Am I talking to myself?" I scan the woods for the source of the sound. Nothing's there. I whip back around to the pit.

Jack crawls over to the tabby box. He peeks in, then turns to Cooper, an almost maniacal smile on his face. "It's not empty." Reaching in, his eyes glaze over as he pulls out a carved wooden box about the size of a large loaf of bread.

Goose bumps rush over my arms and legs.

Cooper's jaw hangs open. "I can't believe it."

Jack tucks the box into his chest and runs his fingers over the carving. "You guys doubted me, but I knew it was here all along. Look, it was Bloody Bill's." He holds the ornate box up just long enough for me to see the words "The Dagger" engraved over an etching of a three-mast ship. A black iron latch connects to a metal plate with a keyhole. Jack strokes the box like a lapdog. "I found you, treasure, and now you're mine," he murmurs, sounding an awful lot like Gollum.

"What do you suppose is in it?" Cooper asks.

Jack sets the wooden box on the edge of the tabby one. "Let's see." He flips the lid with his thumb and reaches for the top.

The nausea roars back, flooding over me like a tidal wave. My stomach seizes as if clamped by a giant vise. I grab my sides and double over in pain. "Don't!"

He cracks the lid and screams as a flash of fire explodes in his hand.

Chapter Three

Yelping, Jack drops to the ground and curls into a ball, cradling his body around his arm. The acrid scents of sulfur and charred flesh fill the clearing.

"Jack!" I jump into the pit while Cooper lunges toward him.

Jack shrieks and grinds his head against the packed dirt floor.

"Are you all right? Answer me." Cooper's voice is tight and strained as he reaches for Jack's back. Jack screeches again. Cooper's face turns ashen and slack.

Oh, my God. Jack's hand. Could it have blown off? It's the only way to explain his reaction. My eyes dart around the pit, but I don't see blood anywhere.

Jack babbles and rocks as Cooper crouches over him, offering words of reassurance.

My stomach drops as I gape at my still-screaming brother, and I try to keep my voice calm. "Jack, I need to see your hand."

Cooper steps aside to let me get close, his eyes wide with fear.

"No!" Jack tucks his legs closer to his midsection.

"Jack, please." I squat next to him and place my hand on his shoulder, bracing for the metallic scent of his blood. But there's only the rich smell of musty earth and sweat.

I examine his abdomen, expecting his T-shirt to be covered in slick red-black liquid, but there's only a thick smear of dirt. I blink, trying to make sense of it.

Jack falls over onto his side, his arms tucked against his chest, and writhes in pain. His face is maraschino red and swollen from all the screaming, but at least I can see his hands. They're clenched into fists. And clearly still attached. There's no blood. Not one drop.

Goose bumps rush up my arms. What the heck's going on? I stand and step back, unsure of what to do next.

Cooper steps toward Jack and grasps his shoulders. "Bro, get a hold of yourself." His voice is loud and firm.

Jack shakes his head and rolls over onto his other side, turning his back to us. He's still screaming, but now that he's facing the dirt wall, his cries are muffled.

"What's wrong with him?" Cooper shouts.

I hunch my shoulders and search his panicked jade eyes. "I have no idea. But we can't stay here. We've got to get him home."

My nose burns as a putrid scent wafts across the clearing. It's bitter and rotten, threatening to choke off my throat. And then as quickly as it appeared, it's gone.

Cooper grips his shoulder. "Can you stand, bro?" Jack wails and shakes his head. Cooper sighs. "We'll have to lift him out of here. But what do you want to do about that?" He points toward the wooden box that slammed back into the tabby vault with the explosion.

A high-pitched yowl echoes in the distance. It's almost… happy, like a wolf baying at the moon.

A chill zips up my spine. I spin around to face the woods. "What is that?"

Over my shoulder, Cooper calls, "What's what?"

"That sound, some kind of howl." I rub my arms, which have gone cold and prickly.

"The only hollering I hear is coming from your brother."

The forest is quiet and empty. I don't even see any birds. Jack screeches again. I turn to watch him roll up on his knees again and tuck into a ball. We'd better get out of here quick.

But first we've got to take care of the so-called treasure. Afraid to get too close, I crane my neck toward the tabby vault to see inside. The wooden box is intact and somehow, despite the explosion, isn't burned. My stomach churns. This is too weird.

"I don't want anything to do with it."

"Me, neither," Cooper says. "It's probably a booby trap. For all we know, it could explode again. But we can't leave it like that. It's not safe. We've got to cover it."

We each take an end of the tabby lid and groan as we lift it off the ground. It's heavy and brittle. The concrete crumbles under my fingers as we set it in place.

Jack's wailing quiets, his stomach shuddering with each hitched sob.

"Okay, bro, think you can you stand now?" Cooper asks. Jack whimpers and shakes his head. Cooper sighs and turns to me. "If you help me get him out of the pit, I think I can carry him to the golf cart."

I haven't tried to lift my brother in five years. He might be tall and lanky, but he's no lightweight. We roll him onto his side, and I grab his legs while Cooper gets his shoulders. The first couple feet aren't too bad, but pushing his midsection out of the hole isn't easy, especially since Jack's shaking and so freaking heavy. But after tugging and pulling, we finally manage to roll him over the lip.

Hoisting ourselves out, we try to pry him off the ground. This time I reach for his hands, which are still balled into fists.

Jack clutches my fingers with his left hand, clawing into my skin, and stares into my eyes, almost boring a hole straight to my brain. His face is drawn, and fear etches his brow. "It hurts, Em. It really, really hurts," he manages. He's a total mess, eyes swollen and bloodshot, face muddied from all the tears. Dirt and snot run out of his nose.

My stomach twists. I've never seen him so bad. Even though he's five minutes younger than me, he's always been my bossy big brother. But now he's lying crippled in the dirt, unable to drag himself to the cart.

I swallow hard, forcing back the lump in my throat. "I know, Jack. We'll take care of you. I promise." I reach for his right hand, the one he used to unhook the latch, and turn his fingers over in my palm to examine the tender flesh.

A nasty, puckered welt slices across his four fingers.

That's it? I expected it to be blistered and oozing. Or worse. All I see are a few swollen red marks.

Cooper examines Jack's hand and quirks his brow. "That's pretty ugly, bro, but I'm betting you'll live." He chuckles. "And I think you can walk to the cart by yourself."

Jack bites his lip and swallows hard as he rolls onto his side to push himself up. As soon as he places his hand on the ground, he howls and flops onto his back. Tears flood from his eyes, cutting fresh rivulets through his dirt-caked face. Cooper and I exchange confused glances. Jack's carrying on as if he's dying. Can it really be this bad?

Cooper stares at Jack, whose shoulders quake with each new round of sobs, and drags his fingers through his hair. "We're going to have to carry him."

At first we try to split Jack's weight, with me at his legs and

Cooper taking his arms, but with all Jack's convulsing, it's nearly impossible. Finally, Cooper slings him over his shoulder and carries him fireman-style to the cart.

It's a miracle Dad isn't there when we get back to the house. Normally he's slouched on the couch with a beer, watching the six o'clock local news, but the driveway's empty and the house is quiet, even though it's eight o'clock. I'm just glad we don't have to explain to him what happened. Because we couldn't even if we tried.

Knowing how much of a neat freak my dad is, Cooper throws Jack, clothes and all, into the shower. While they're busy upstairs in the bathroom, I race to my room to change my clothes, then sprint to the kitchen sink and scrub with the dishwashing liquid. Cooper and I don't get many chances to be alone, and I'm not spending this one filthy.

Just as I'm blotting my face with a dishtowel, Cooper plods down the stairs, stretching his neck and rubbing his shoulder with a freshly rinsed hand. Judging by his soaked head and T-shirt, which, by the way, clings at just the right places, he must have taken a dunk, too. "Well, he's in bed and clean enough not to wreck the sheets. I figure he'll sleep it off."

Distracting myself from the way he rakes his fingers through his golden-brown hair, I attempt to focus. "Hey, our Internet's down. Do you mind if we go over to your house to use yours? I want to research how to take care of a burn." Accidentally on purpose I neglect to mention that, as the caretaker of High Point Bluff Plantation, my dad's got a fully stocked first-aid kit, and I know how to use every ointment in it.

He smiles. "Of course. Let's go." He takes the dishcloth from my hands and tosses it on the counter.

A few minutes later, we park the golf cart and plug it in to recharge its battery, then sneak up the steps of the Big House, creak open the shiny double doors, and try to make a stealthy getaway to Cooper's room. As we're ascending the stairs, his dad, Beau, stops us in our tracks.

"Cooper? Is that you?" he calls from down the hall, his southern accent as thick and goopy as maple syrup.

"Uh, yeah, Dad. Emma's with me."

"Emma? Well, come on in and set awhile."

Cooper grunts as we backtrack and head through the grand foyer to the library.

Beau and Missy, his very blonde and very young fourth wife, lounge on the two oversized red silk sofas that somehow look small in the enormous oak-paneled room. Beau's chewing on an unlit cigar, reading a business newspaper, and she's leafing through a gossip magazine, cracking her gum.

Even though he's the same age as my dad, Beau strains to push himself off the couch to stand. "Emma! It's always a pleasure to see you, darling." His jowls shake with every syllable, and a faint whiff of something rotten wafts through the air. It's pungent, sort of like cold cuts that have been in the refrigerator too long. Even though it's always the same, the smell still takes me by surprise. He gestures toward an empty club chair next to the sofa.

Keeping my eyes down and my breath shallow, I sink into the plush leather. I've always hated this room because of the creepy portrait of Lady Rose Beaumont, the original mistress of High Point Bluff, mounted above the fireplace. I'm sure she was considered beautiful a few hundred years ago, but today that high, bald forehead and gray-white skin are just plain scary. And worse, no matter where you go, her bug eyes follow you. Nothing made of paint and canvas should be able to do that.

Missy peers over her magazine. "Hey, Emily." She chews her

gum in a slow circle.

Cooper stares hard as he leans against the arm of my chair. "It's Emma."

I resist the urge to lean over and hug him.

"Oh, that's right." Missy shrugs. "Sorry. Any idea where your daddy is, *Emma*? I sent him on an errand to Charleston this afternoon and I haven't seen him since."

I shake my head. "No clue." Not that I'd tell her if I did.

She sighs. "I hope he isn't wasting my time. There's plenty of stuff for him to do around here."

I force a smile as I swallow my response. My dad's been High Point Bluff's caretaker for eight years, ever since he and Mom divorced and he moved south from D.C. He doesn't need a twenty-two-year-old new plantation mistress to tell him how to do his job. As much as I'd like to tell her off, I don't because Dad doesn't need any trouble.

Beau plops down on the cushion, shaking the sofa with his girth. "Now, Missy, you don't have to worry about ole Jedidiah. We were boys together, just like our daddies, and their daddies before them. He's practically family. Besides, you can't run him off. He's the only decent help I can find." He swigs some scotch from a glass on the side table. "So, Cooper." He chuckles and eyes his son's mud-stained shirt. "What have you kids been up to?"

Cooper shoots me a sideways look before answering. "Oh, nothing much." His voice shakes.

Beau leans forward. "See to it you don't get into any trouble." His gaze then shifts over to Missy as he grinds the soggy cigar between his yellow teeth. "Doesn't that necklace look spectacular around her pretty little neck?" he asks nobody in particular and gestures to the giant ruby pendant every Mrs. Beaumont has worn since Lady Rose.

It's mounted like an enormous red camellia blossom, surrounded by thick, pointy gold leaves. It's even in Lady Rose's spooky portrait, but back then, it hung low on her chest on a thick gold strand that appeared more like a bicycle chain than a piece of jewelry.

"It's beautiful." I can't help wonder why she's wearing it with cutoffs and a tank top.

Beau sucks his teeth. "Eighty carats of pure fire."

Missy strokes the ruby's face. "It sure is."

"Enjoy it while you can, baby, because thanks to my trusty prenup, that bloom's basically a loaner." Beau turns to Cooper, who's grinding his teeth. "And one day it'll be yours, son, to lend to whichever little filly, or fillies, you decide to harness."

Cooper nods stiffly.

Missy glances at Cooper, her eyes narrowed and jaw set, then releases the ruby, slapping it against the hollow at the base of her throat. "Well, I'm bored." She gets up, stretches her arms up over her head, and yawns, then baby steps over to Beau in her stilettos. Leaning down, dangling the ruby in his face for a moment, she drapes her arms around his neck.

How can she be that close and not gag? Either she's madly in love, or her nose doesn't work.

Missy nuzzles his ear. "I'm going out to the hot tub. You coming?"

"In a minute."

She kisses his flaky bald patch. "Don't make me wait." She sashays to the door, swaying her hips with each exaggerated step.

When she's gone, Beau licks his lips. "So, Emma, I've been meaning to mention something." He rolls the cigar over his tongue with his stubby fingers. "You sure have matured, haven't you?"

My stomach seizes. I slump into my seat and tuck in my

shoulders, hoping he's referring to the extra inch I grew this past year and not the reason I graduated out of a training bra. Just in case, I drape a long hank of hair over my chest.

"Um, yeah, thanks. I guess," I mumble into my lap.

Cooper groans. "Come on, Dad."

Beau scoffs and waves him off.

Cooper holds his hand out for me to grab and pulls me out the chair. "Emma and I have something we need to do."

Upstairs? With Cooper? Away from his creeper of a dad? I'm totally there.

Chapter Four

I flip on Cooper's computer and tap my fingers on his desk, waiting for it to boot.

"Hey, Cooper," I twist and call over my shoulder, about to ask him for his password, but the words freeze in my throat.

He's tugged off his shirt and is standing in the middle of his room, bare chested.

I swallow hard and avert my eyes. But that doesn't stop the flitty somersaults in my belly.

"Sorry, I couldn't stand the stink of that shirt." He laughs, balls up the dirty fabric, and tosses it in the hamper.

A rocket of red-hot embarrassment flushes my cheeks. I gulp and turn back to the computer.

"Oh, here, let me get that for you." He leans across me, poking the keys with one hand, entering his encrypted code. Not that I'm even looking at what he's typing. I'm too busy reveling in his Cooperness—which just happens to be the perfect mixture of sun and salt—and trying not to faint. He might claim to stink, but that couldn't be further from the truth.

He pulls a fresh shirt and shorts from his dresser. "I'm going to take a quick shower and will be right back, Emmaline. You should be able to search whatever you need now."

Um, yeah, if I could think straight and my hands weren't shaking.

He used my real name. Finally. I've waited a whole school year to hear it, and it sounds just as good as I remember, slipping easily off his tongue. No one besides my parents calls me that, and that's only when I'm in serious trouble. I've banned its use by everyone else because no one can get it right, always mangling the "line" to "lynn" or even "leen," and that drives me crazier than Brillo on a chalkboard. But Cooper has always known how to pronounce it, almost singing it in that silky southern accent of his. It was worth the wait.

The bathroom door clicks closed, and I stare at the blank search engine, trying to remember what I'm doing here. Oh, right. Burn remedies for Jack.

Even though I already know how to treat the burn, I do a few searches anyway, just in case Cooper checks. A few clicks later, I've seen pretty much all I need to know. Compared to the nasty burn pictures splattered across the screen, Jack's wound is a joke.

Bored and alone in Cooper's room, I go through the stuff on his desk. The edge of a glossy photo sticks out of his school agenda. My pulse pounds. Maybe it's a picture of him and a girl from school. Even though I know I shouldn't look, and he's totally free to date whoever he chooses, I can't resist. I peel the corner of the agenda back and sneak a peek.

My heart cracks. It's a picture of Cooper and his mom, probably taken just before she died. He looks about five and is nestled in her lap, gazing at her in adoration. She's beyond beautiful—golden-blonde with a kindness in her eyes and a warmth to her smile that reaches right off the paper and wraps around you. I've only seen this picture once before, by accident, when I was looking for a sweatshirt on a cool summer night, and it was tucked inside one of his hoodies. Just as I did then, I slip the photo back in its hiding place, vowing never to mention it. Her sudden death hit him hard—apparently he stopped speaking, got left back in kindergarten, and suffered years of nightmares. Beau wasn't much help, either, stripping all her things from High Point Bluff. Aside from Cooper, this picture's pretty much the only proof she ever existed.

The bathroom door opens, and Cooper steps out, freshly showered and smelling of sandalwood soap. "Sorry to keep you waiting, but whew, that felt good." He plops down on his bed. His eyes look baby blue now to match his new, clean shirt. "So what'd you find?"

Not a hidden picture, that's for sure. I swivel to face him. "Pretty much what I thought. Ointment, bandages. He'll be fine."

Cooper laughs. "Good, because I don't think I can take much more of his crying."

I snicker. "Yeah, he's the biggest baby on the planet. But still, that was weird, wasn't it?"

"Totally." He scratches the small patch of stubble on his chin. "You know, with all his hollering, I expected that burn to be much worse."

"Me, too. But I guess the booby trap freaked him out. It was scary."

He shakes his head. "But that's the thing that keeps bothering me. My military history teacher said those traps were used in war against enemies. That letter doesn't say anything about that. I mean, why would a pirate ask for help and then lead someone to an explosion? It doesn't make sense."

An odd, almost pinging sense of foreboding crawls around the base of my scalp. "I don't know."

"Let's take another look at that letter." He bounds off the bed, pulls a geometry text off his bookshelf, and opens the front cover. I don't know what he's thinking, but this isn't the time for math. He must read the expression on my face because he chuckles. "It's the perfect hiding place. No one would ever voluntarily open this book." He lifts the letter from behind the front cover.

I laugh. "You've got a point."

He plops down on the bed and motions me over. "Come here." He waves the thick yellow parchment.

As if he needs to ask. I spring from the office chair and ease down next to him, willing my heart to stay in my chest.

But the giddy tingles stop as soon as I start reading. Just like the first time, the words make my gut sink. Sure, Bloody Bill offered to share his treasure, but only after someone helped him break *the curse*. The one an old Gullah hag imposed after his crew plucked a flower. The same curse he said was heinous and gruesome and ravaged that crew. How can something called "The Creep" be anything but bad, especially if it leaves behind a bundle of dry bones? An eerie, unsettled sensation fills my chest.

"I don't care what you and Jack think. That letter freaks me out."

"Hey, I wasn't the one who was all gung ho. That was Jack."

My brow crinkles. "Are you kidding? You guys saw the word 'treasure' and totally forgot about the curse part."

"Listen, I don't want to argue, Emmaline." The creases on Cooper's face soften, soothing all the weirdness I'm feeling. "I don't understand what Bloody Bill wrote any more than why that box was booby trapped. Nothing makes sense. All that matters is Jack is safe."

He's probably right, but that spooky feeling clings. Cooper flashes his easy grin, shooting a fresh set of goose bumps over my skin. The good kind.

I look out his bedroom window and notice it's pitch dark. My dad's probably home by now. "It's late. I've got to go." I suppress a sigh.

He pops off his bed. "Let me take you home."

There's no way I'm turning down a personal escort. We tiptoe down the stairs, hoping to avoid Beau and Missy. We're nearly at the front door when Beau's voice carries down the hall into the grand foyer. "Cooper? Emma still with you? Bring her on in here."

Cooper rolls his eyes. "I'm taking her home. Be back later."

Even though the cut on my foot still twinges, we sprint for the door and race down the porch steps into the steamy June night. Laughing, Cooper veers away from the still charging golf cart and instead slows down to walk toward the wooded path that leads to the caretaker's cottage.

The woods are thick with tall, spiky cabbage palms, leafy cypresses dripping with resurrection ferns, and small, scrubby post oak shrubs. It's so dense, it's nearly impossible to glimpse the sapphire sky and its silver constellations. Cooper and I grow quiet, walking in time to the sounds of summer, supplied by the rattling cicadas and croaking toads.

Suddenly Cooper breaks the silence. "I'm sorry my dad's such a jerk."

Truer words have never been spoken. But Beau's the last person I want to think about right now, so I wave it away. "That's okay."

"No, it's not." He sighs. "I guess it's just one of those things."

"What things?" When it comes to Beau, I'm almost afraid to ask.

He stares at the path, avoiding my eyes. "An example of how not to act when I'm older. He's given me lots of those lately."

"Maybe he'd be different if your mom was still here." My words are soft to lessen the blow.

"As much as I'd like to think that, even though I was young, I remember things weren't great between them. Before she, well, you know." He mashes his lip, swallowing years of regret and pain.

There's so much longing in his voice, I want to reach out and hold his hand, or hug him—anything to share the burden. A year ago I might've been able to. But now, even though it's exactly what he needs, I can't. I don't want to just be his friend anymore. I want more.

But he's not interested. So I keep my hands to myself and offer a few useless words instead. "I'm sorry, Cooper."

He shakes his head. "Nah, it's in the past. Nothing you can do about it."

A snap, loud and cracking, ricochets in the woods.

My heart seizes, and I stop short. "What was that?"

Cooper shakes his head. "I didn't hear anything."

"Are you sure?" The echo of the sound still rings in my ears. I stand stiff, straining for any sound. Night creatures sing, filling the night air, but theirs are the normal sounds of summer. Crickets and toads aren't big enough to crunch things in the forest.

He grasps my arm and smiles. "Trust me, Emmaline. There's no boogeyman waiting to eat us."

Warmth fills my quivering chest, easing my tense shoulders. I'm being silly. It's been a long day. Between Jack, his burn, and that creepy letter, I must be going nuts.

I start down the path again, passing sedge brooms and saw palmettos. As crazy as the day has been, I don't want the night to end. Maybe I can get Cooper to stay awhile, watch a movie or something. It's not like he's dying to get back home to hang with Missy and Beau in the hot tub.

Another snap, sharper than the first, slices the night.

My pulse charges. Cooper and I freeze.

The night critters suddenly stop mid-song, leaving a heavy silence in the sultry air. My heart threatens to leap from my chest.

Dead leaves rustle just a few feet away. It's right behind us.

Forgetting to breathe, I sink my nails into Cooper's arm. Together, we pivot on our heels.

Two enormous, glowing yellow eyes flash in the pitch black.

Chapter Five

I scream.

Cooper snatches my hand and bolts down the path, dragging me behind him.

Twigs break and crack in the woods behind us. Heavy, quick footsteps pound. Whatever it is, it's keeping pace, following us.

"Run faster!" Cooper yells and tugs on my hand, navigating us around the thick roots that cut across the path.

I try to keep up, but my flip-flops and flapping bandage trip me up, and my short legs struggle to match Cooper's long stride.

"I'm going as fast as I can!"

The footfalls gain speed and draw closer.

"Not fast enough! Come on, dig in!" He yanks hard on my hand and flings me in front of him, launching me farther down the path. Still running, I gape. He has taken my place, wedged himself between me and whatever is out there. "GO!" he yells, and I do, tapping into an unknown reserve of adrenaline, speeding toward the caretaker's cottage. Cooper is right behind me.

The porch light glows up ahead. I pump my legs and zoom

toward home and safety. The woods thin, and the path widens. Charging up the porch steps, I yank the screen door and hold it open for Cooper.

A six-point buck blasts out of the woods next to the cottage and sprints across the front lawn, then down the gravel driveway.

Chest heaving, Cooper roars in laughter. "Nothing but a dumb deer!" He doubles over and grips his side. "But Lord, you had me spooked there for a minute."

There aren't enough words to express how supremely stupid I feel. "Well, it sounded scary." My cheeks burn as my pulse rages. "And you saw those yellow eyes."

He rolls his baby blues. "Uh-huh, a real monster."

"Bucks have been known to attack people during their rutting season."

Cooper just shakes his head.

The front door yanks opens. Dad's scowling. "What's going on? What've y'all been up to?" He looks exactly like Jack plus twenty-five years and a whole lot of manual labor.

Still sucking for air, my mouth opens to answer, but my brain is empty—how can I begin to explain what happened today? Instead, I laugh, releasing pent-up fear, panic, and exhaustion. It must seem like I've lost my mind.

Dad isn't amused. When I stop to take a breath, he says, "Emmaline Claire, I just got back from Charleston searching for some nonexistent parts for the weather vane Missy wants restored. I'm tired. Just tell me, are you okay? And why's your brother in bed already?"

Cooper saves me. "We're fine, Uncle Jed. Just wiped after a long day. Jack was so tired he crashed early."

Dad quirks his brow. "Oh-kay." He shifts his gaze between the two of us. "It's late. I'm packing it in. Best you two do the same."

I find my voice and reply, "Be right in."

"You do that." Dad shuts the door.

"It's been a crazy day," Cooper says.

I smile, his new height making me tilt my head back more than normal. "You can say that again."

He grips the screen door handle but turns to face me. "I'm so glad we were together, Emmaline. I couldn't have gotten him home without you."

I shake my head. "Well, you carried him—" My cheeks fill with heat.

"Yeah, but you still helped."

He bends down and wraps his arms around me, pulling me close in a tight embrace.

I melt against him. "No problem," I manage, clinging to him as my heart races, and wishing he'd never let me go.

• • •

"Dang, Em, that hurts." Jack jerks his right hand from the ointment I'm squeezing onto his fingertips and scoots away from me on the couch.

I clamp his wrist and yank it back. "Well, what do you expect? It's a burn. It's not supposed to tickle." After all his whining this morning, he's exhausted my patience.

He stares at the ceiling, tears welling. "You can't imagine how much this hurts."

I sigh. "What else do you want me to do? I've followed all the burn-care instructions. Unless you want to go to the hospital, I'm out of options."

His eyes flash. "No, no hospitals. They'll ask how it happened, and then we'll have to tell them about the treasure. I don't want anyone to know." He inches his hand back toward me and winces, anticipating the pain. I hold his palm as gently as I can and dab a tiny bit of cream on his middle finger. He bites down on his tongue and lets out a high-pitched moan.

"Can we at least ask Dad to take you to his doctor?" I apply the ointment to his other fingers as quickly as I can.

"No," he grunts. "Can't tell Dad. He'll tell Beau."

"Fine." I loosely wind a strip of gauze around his tender fingers and tape the end down.

"Thanks." He exhales and collapses back onto the couch. "We have to get back to the ruins to see what we found."

"For real? After what happened yesterday, I figured you'd want a break." I return the ointment and other medical supplies to Dad's first-aid kit. "There's no rush. The ruins are in the middle of nowhere. No one's going to steal it."

He shakes his head. "I'm not leaving it out there."

"Jack, the box isn't safe. It could blow up again." I bring the kit to the kitchen and fill a large glass of water to keep him hydrated.

"There's no way it'll explode again. Eighteenth-century gun powder only gives you a one-time blow."

I hand him the water. He's the history genius, but something still bugs me. "Yeah, but I don't remember smelling gun powder, do you?" There was that momentary putrid scent, but Jack was probably too spazzed out to notice before it disappeared.

His eyes shift upward as if tracing his memory. "I'm sure I did. At least I think I did. But even if I can't remember, it's probably because I was busy freaking about blowing my hand off." He tips the glass to his lips and downs it in one long gulp.

"Which is why we shouldn't chance it again." I sigh. "Your hand's already hurt."

He tilts his chin. "I'm fine, Emma. Besides, we have to go back. Maggie said she'd meet us this morning."

Ugh, Maggie. The hand-holding, sort-of girlfriend with the overprotective grandmother. I bite my bottom lip. "Jack, don't you think she's a little weird? I mean, you hardly know her, but you two are all over each other."

"Wow, jealous much?" He arches his eyebrow.

I scoff. "Of course not. Don't be ridiculous."

He winks. "Sure. It couldn't have anything to do with the fact you've basically thrown yourself at Cooper and he hasn't noticed, yet I can get a girlfriend without even trying."

I open, then close, my mouth. Has it been that obvious? Does Cooper know, too? I was sure I'd done a good job of covering. If we were a normal brother and sister, I could lie to him and deny it, and maybe be convincing, but our stupid twin sense ruins everything.

I spit out the only response that comes to mind. "You're a jerk."

He laughs. "Awesome comeback."

The doorbell rings, and he springs from the couch to get it, awkwardly reaching across his body with his good hand to open the door.

Cooper smiles when he sees Jack. His pale yellow T-shirt turns his eyes royal blue today. "Hey, bro!" He slaps Jack's shoulder. "It's good to see you up and about. After all that crying, I was afraid you might not make it through the night."

Jack holds up his bandaged hand. "Yeah, well, this hurts like a mother, so thanks for the sympathy."

Cooper chuckles. "No problem. Seriously, I was worried, though." He nods in my direction and smiles. "Hey, Emma."

I exhale in relief. He's acting totally normal. There's no way he knows. Plus there's no way he would have hugged me last night if he suspected anything. As much as that hug meant to me, I know it was only a mutual-support thing for him, a gesture of thanks for sharing the weirdest day ever.

Jack steps in front of him to slip into his flip-flops and conveniently breaks our eye contact. "No worries. I'll live. We're headed back to the ruins. You coming?" He jams his baseball cap onto his head.

Cooper cranes his neck around Jack. "Really?" he asks me.

I push off the couch and walk over to them, wiggle my still bandaged foot into a flip-flop, and snatch my messenger bag off the floor. The cut has formed a nice scab and is nearly healed, but I still want to keep it covered. "He doesn't want to keep his girlfriend waiting."

Cooper nods. "Hmm, I see."

Maggie's already there when we arrive, sitting on one of the ruins with her sea-grass hat. Her long black hair is twisted into thick spirals that drape down her shoulders.

She hops off the ruin wall and sprints to Jack. "You've had success, Jack Guthrie! I saw the open pit. Did you find something?"

"Oh, we found something all right, and I had to take one for the team." He lifts his gauze-wrapped hand for her to see.

Her brows arch. "What happened?"

He puffs his skinny chest and lowers the pitch of his voice, trying to impress her. "Oh, just a booby trap that burned my hand. But it'll take more than a little explosion to wipe me out."

I shift my gaze to hide my expression. Too bad she didn't see him sobbing last night like a gigantic infant.

"A burn? Let me see it." She lifts his hand and picks at the tape holding the gauze.

I lurch toward her. "Don't. It needs to stay covered." The last thing he needs is to get it infected. If I have to listen to Jack blubber any more, I might kill him.

She levels her gaze at me. "I want to see it." Then she smiles at Jack, softening her voice as she strokes his shoulder. "Please unwrap your hand."

I glare at the pair of them. "Whatever."

He slowly unwinds the gauze and gently tugs it from the ointment coating his skin. She cradles his hand in hers and stares closely at his fingers. "You must have this looked at."

He waves her off with his good hand. "It's nothing. Emma took care of it."

She shakes her head. "No, that is not enough. It is blistered."

"What? No, it's not." My eyes snap to his hand.

She lifts his hand toward me. "Yes, it is."

I gape. She's right. Four slick yellow blisters have risen across his fingers. Blisters that weren't there a half hour ago. "What the heck?"

Jack attempts to appear unaffected.

Maggie re-wraps his hand. "You must go to a Grannie."

Cooper tilts his head. "You want us to meet your grandmother?"

She laughs. "That is not possible."

He scratches his temple. "I don't understand. Whose grannie do you mean?"

She shakes her head. "You need a Gullah Grannie with powerful medicine. And I know just the one."

Chapter Six

"It's too far to walk." Maggie points at Cooper. "Go get a car, and I'll meet you on the main road." Although she says it with a smile, it's not a request. She walks to the wall and grabs her hat, then turns toward the forest, away from the Big House.

Jack's brow crinkles. "Wait, we can't leave the treasure here. Let's grab it, and then we'll go."

She stops and walks back to him, cupping his cheek in the palm of her hand. "The treasure is unimportant now. You must see the Grannie."

"But—"

"There is nothing more important than your health, Jack Guthrie." She clasps his free hand and stares into his eyes for a long moment. "Now, go fetch a car. I'll see you in a few minutes."

His shoulders relax, and he smiles. "Okay."

Wow. That was impressive. I wish I could make him do things that easily.

We head back through the woods to the Big House to climb into the only car Beau will let Cooper drive—a safe, boring beige station wagon. Cooper's had his conditional license for two months now, so he's finally allowed to drive us legally. Not that we let the legal aspect stop us last summer.

Cooper punches in the key code to open one of the doors on the five-car garage. "Who do you think this Grannie is, anyway? Seems kind of strange."

When the lock clicks open, I step into the freestanding building, which, with its glossy polymer floors and shiny sport cars, is more like a new-car showroom than a private garage. "I have no idea, but if Jack's hand is really that bad, maybe we should find a doctor."

"No." Jack's voice is firm. "Maggie knows what I need, so let's do what she says."

I glare at him and feel the space between my eyes pinch. I barely even know her, but I'm sick of Maggie. The words burst from my mouth unchecked. "You know what? I've had about enough of what Maggie wants. She wasn't the one who had to deal with you yesterday or drag your sorry butt home. We did that. Cooper and me. For you. It's about time you start actually listening to us."

Jack steps close, into my personal space, and leans down to stare into my eyes. "It's my hand, and we'll go where I say we go." He sets his jaw, and his eyes narrow into tiny slits.

I rise up on my tiptoes to meet his gaze. "You mean where *Maggie* says."

He clenches his good hand into a fist, and his olive skin turns a shade of magenta I've never seen. His nostrils flare, and he snorts like a bull, shooting air on my face. Then he starts to quake. What the heck does he think he's doing? I should back down, or at least step away, maybe even apologize—anything to make peace, but I can't.

Cooper whistles and steps between us, shoving us apart. "Easy, Guthries. Calm down." He walks Jack back several feet, so I'm out of arm's reach.

Jack stares at him, his lips mashed in a crooked line. "Will you take me to meet Maggie? Or are you siding with her?" He nods his head in my direction.

"I'll take you anywhere you want to get that hand looked at."

"Fine. Let's go." Jack steps toward the car and grabs the handle of the front passenger seat. "Shotgun." He plops onto the front seat and slams the door.

I shove my hands on my hips and glare at Cooper. "You do realize how stupid this is, right?" Am I the only sane person in this garage?

He leans toward me and whispers. "We'll take him to this Grannie. If she can't help, we can always take him to my family doctor. We've just got to get him in the car and into town." He smells as clean and fresh as a sea breeze, and his royal-blue eyes are so calming, I can't resist. I drop my arms and cave. But I'm still mad at Jack.

Jack opens the door and calls out to us. "I'm waiting. And so is Maggie."

"Come on, Emmaline, what do you say?" Cooper smiles and nudges me in the ribs, completing my defeat. The only thing left to do is climb into the car.

But I don't have to be happy about it. I sigh. "Okay. But if this gets any weirder, I'm out of there." I toss my bag onto the car floor and slip into the backseat behind Cooper, then cross my arms and lean against the window.

We travel the mile-long, oak-lined driveway and find Maggie waiting at the end. When we pull up, she flashes Jack a triumphant smile before opening the back door and taking her place next to me. Her enormous hat hogs the empty seat space between us, and the rim scratches my leg. Plus the overwhelming scent of her flowery perfume burns my throat. Smoothing her bright red skirt over her lap, she bats her super long eyelashes at me. As if that'll win me over. I nod, pull my lips into a phony half-smile, and turn to stare out the widow.

"So where to, Maggie?" Cooper asks.

She pops her head between the two front seats. "Go straight down this road. I'll tell you when to turn."

We pull out onto Coffin Point Road. Jack switches on the radio, spinning the knob from Beau's favorite country station, and stops on a hip-hop song. He turns his baseball cap backwards and sings along, pumping his head and jabbing the air with his bandaged hand. I guess he's trying to impress Maggie with his killer MC skills, but he's only humiliating himself. Cooper laughs and joins in, slamming his hand against the steering wheel, and punctuating Jack's lyrics with an occasional, "Yeah, boy." I cringe, embarrassed for them both, but especially for Cooper, who, despite his general all-around perfection, is not hard-core enough to rock the mike.

Instead, I focus on the view outside the car as we pass a thick forest of towering willow oaks, longleaf pines, and the dwarf palmettos that grow between their tall, skinny trunks. The sunlight hits the trees at just the right angle, illuminating the bright green canopy in dappled sunlight that streams down to the forest floor. It's a watercolor begging to be painted. One I can't do because I'm wasting all my time with my idiot brother. I take a mental photograph, memorizing each detail in case I ever get a chance to get back to my artwork.

Maggie's cheery voice interrupts my concentration. "Aren't you excited, Emma?"

Annoyed by the unwelcome distraction and her cloying flower smell, I sigh and turn to her. "About what?" I almost have to yell to hear myself over the pulsing bass.

"The Grannie. She will help Jack." Her smile is radiant. "Of this I'm certain."

"I hope so." I pull out my iPod from my messenger bag, select my favorite emo playlist in a silent protest against Jack, then turn back to the window.

Maggie guides Cooper onto Sea Island Parkway, which is more of a sleepy two-lane road than a highway.

Several miles later, she sticks her long, elegant arm between the two front seats and points to something up ahead. I yank out my earbuds to hear what she says. "You will need to slow down," she directs Cooper. "A dirt road lies beyond that house. That is where you'll need to go."

He hangs a left at the dingy gray tract house and starts down the dusty dirt road. Maggie shuts off the radio. "Please stop the car." Cooper pulls over and cuts the ignition. He looks at her in the rearview mirror, waiting for further instructions.

She grabs her hat off the seat. "Her house is located at the end of this road. You will need to walk the rest of the way." She steps out of the car and places her gigantic hat on her head.

"Why can't we drive?" Cooper asks.

She smiles. "Because the road is not fit for your car."

Jack leans out his open window. "Aren't you coming?" His voice breaks, full of longing.

Maggie reaches in and strokes the side of his face with her graceful fingers. "Not today. I have something else I must do."

"Dang." His shoulders slump.

Cooper flashes me a look in the mirror. His hitched eyebrow tells me he's just as confused as I am. What the heck is she trying to pull? Before I can stop them, words lurch from my mouth. "Let me guess, your grandmother's calling you."

Maggie whips her hand away from Jack and turns to me, tilting her head. "My grandmother is none of your concern, Emma Guthrie." For a second, her eyes flash with something dark and angry, but she recovers, fixing a sugary smile to her lips. She turns to Jack and squeezes his forearm.

My face burns as she gazes down in total admiration and paws at him. If she likes him so much, why doesn't she want to come? "Really? Then what else could possibly be so important? You're the one who wanted to come here." My voice is strained because I'm resisting the deep need to go medieval on her.

"My business is just that. I don't have to explain it to you." Somehow she manages to say that without dropping the ridiculous grin from her face. Maybe I should remove it for her.

Jack twists around. "Relax, Emma. She never actually said she'd come with us. Only that she'd take us to the Grannie."

Cooper shakes his head. "Uh, I'm not sure that's entirely true, bro. It did seem like she'd come with."

Jack brushes him off with his good hand. "Look, she brought us here, that's what's important. We don't need her to walk us down the road like babies. We'll find it on our own."

I realize Maggie's a local, but I can't help but be suspicious of her "help," especially when it seems so obvious we should be headed toward the hospital instead of an unpaved road. Maybe I can convince Jack and Cooper this is a bad idea. I lean toward the front seat. "We don't even know this Grannie lady. What are we supposed to say when we get to her door?"

Maggie sinks her hand on her hip and flits her lashes. "Introduce yourselves and ask for her help. It is really that simple."

"But—"

"See? No problem." Jack winks at her. "Come on, Coop, the Grannie's waiting, and my hand's not getting better on its own."

Cooper sighs. "All right. I suppose it doesn't matter who comes with us. We just need to get you better." He peers at Maggie. "Do you want us to meet you somewhere after we're done? I don't want to leave you stranded."

"No. I can make my own way home, but thank you for asking." She strokes Jack's cheek once again. "Be well. I'll see you soon." Then she walks back toward the main road.

We climb out of the car and head down the lane that narrows as it curves toward the right. It's covered in pocked holes, stones, and overgrown vegetation. No wonder Maggie didn't want us driving the station wagon down here. In fact, I doubt anyone's driven here recently. Enormous live oaks draped with long gray-green plumes of Spanish moss line the lane and block out most of the sunlight. But there's one definite plus: all this shade provides a pretty decent refuge from the sweltering sun. The air is cool and damp, infused with the scents of honeysuckle and wildflowers.

How could we be so stupid to let her dump us here? I'm not sure who's most to blame—her for telling us to come, or us for listening to her. We should forget this and go to Cooper's family doctor. With each step, my mind tries to convince my feet to halt, to turn around and run to the car, but a quick glance at Jack and Cooper makes me wonder if I'm just being a baby. They're totally unfazed, laughing as they trudge through the overgrown weeds and kick at loose stones.

A breeze blows through the forest, billowing the moss as it passes and carrying a low, moaning sound. My stomach twists, and I freeze, scared to take another step.

"What's wrong, Emma?" Cooper asks.

"Did you hear that?" I eye the bend in the road up ahead.

"It's just the wind," Jack says. "Stop being so dramatic."

"No, really, Jack. This place is weird." The breeze blows again, but this time it brings a high-pitched, hollow wail. "What about that?"

Jack grins. "There's only one way to find out." He sprints down the road, rounding the corner in less than thirty seconds and disappears from sight.

Cooper and I bolt after him, running as fast as we can in flip-flops and trying not to trip or fall into a hole.

When we catch up, a gasp leaps from my throat.

Chapter Seven

It's the most beautiful thing I've ever seen. A hulking live oak, decorated with thousands of glass bottles, each dangling off a cord suspended from its branches. Most of the bottles are blue, but there are red ones, too, and some green, yellow, and brown as well, scattered throughout to add dazzling flashes of color. It's like an enormous southern Christmas tree, glistening in the dappled sunlight that filters through the canopy. The breeze blows again, releasing a low moan as it passes over each bottle's opening. The colored glass gently sways in the wind, but somehow none of the bottles crash into each other. I burn every detail into my memory so I can paint it later.

Beyond the tree, nestled in a clearing, sits a tiny ramshackle clapboard house with peeling indigo trim and a cockeyed front porch. Judging by the style and degree of deterioration, the place has to be at least a couple hundred years old. I'm surprised it hasn't fallen down by now.

My brow furrows. This is definitely a mistake. There is no way anyone lives here.

Just as I'm about to plead that we leave, I notice the lush garden of wildflowers and herbs that surrounds the house. It's gorgeous and abounds with life. My forehead smoothes as I inhale its fragrance. Although the building may have been neglected for a century, the garden sure hasn't. Whoever tends these plants has more than a giant green thumb. They have a nurturing spirit.

Against my better judgment, I sense this is where we belong. I want to stay. And I want to meet the gardener.

The faded blue front door opens, and a little old woman peeks out. Her brown skin is smooth and thin, and her hair is snowy white. "Can I help you folk?" Her voice is high-pitched and scratchy with age, and her accent is pure Lowcountry, peppered with dropped consonants and abbreviations.

Cooper clears his throat. "Yes, ma'am. We're here to see the Grannie."

She cocks her head. "Grannie? You *buckruh* ought to recognize I can't be your kin. Run along now and find your own relations."

Jack's brow furrows. "What'd she call us?"

I huff. "It's the Gullah word for white people. God, haven't you learned anything after eight summers down here?" I whisper.

Cooper flashes his warm and honest smile. "Yes, ma'am, we know you're not our grandmother, but our friend sent us here to get some help."

The old woman gingerly steps out onto the porch in a floral housedress and thick orthopedic shoes. "Who sent you here?"

Jack steps forward and lifts his bandaged hand. "Maggie. She said you could fix my hand."

The woman crosses her withered arms in front of her chest. "I don't know no Maggie. You best get a move on, and don't mess with my bottle tree. Don't think I don't know about you *comeyah*, trying to steal my bottles for a vacation keepsake. Though I should let you and watch what happens." She cackles and turns back toward her door.

No! She can't leave. For some reason I can't explain, I need her to stay. Lurching forward, I stand next to Jack. "But ma'am, we're not *comeyah*." I call, repeating the Gullah word for a newcomer. As much as I doubted Maggie for dragging us here, now that I've seen this lady's kind face, I'm sure she's the one to help us. Now I've just got to convince her.

She stops and turns, hitching a gray brow.

"Cooper's family has lived on St. Helena's forever, so they're as close to *binyah* as you get," I say, thumbing my hand in his direction. Her face softens, so I continue. "Our dad's family is from here, too. We visit him every summer. My brother Jack's hurt, and we really need your help." I lift his bandaged hand again.

The woman grips the doorjamb to stabilize herself and calls across the yard, "What's wrong with him?"

"I've got a burn, and it seems to be getting worse," Jack answers.

She narrows her gaze. "Worse?"

He nods. "Yes, ma'am. It's blistered and pretty painful."

She sighs and waves us up to the rickety porch. "Well, come on up here and show it to me. And be quick about it. I'm ninety-seven years old. I can't stand here all day."

I'm shocked. I mean, it's obvious she's old, but I'd never guess *that* old. She seems way too full of spunk to have lived for almost a century. But then again, maybe it takes a lot of spunk to get that old.

We follow the path to the house and bound onto the porch, which is probably a dumb move, seeing as the floorboards are likely to crumble under our feet. The woman settles into one of the old wooden rocking chairs and points her crooked finger toward the one next to her, directing Jack to sit.

"Thanks so much for your help, ma'am." He sits on the cracked seat and holds out his hand. Grateful that Jack knows how to be polite and drop his attitude when it's important, I place my messenger bag on the porch and sit in the third chipped chair, while Cooper sits on the splintered floor next to me.

She takes his hand in hers and slowly unwraps the bandage with her gnarled fingers. "So you're Jack?" She squints up at him through a cloudy blue cataract in her right eye. Her veiny hand shakes as she unwinds the gauze, but it's clear she's done this a million times.

"Yes, ma'am. Jack Guthrie. And this is my twin sister, Emma."

"Twins, eh? You don't look alike. My name's Cordelia Whittaker, but you can call me Miss Delia."

Cooper leans toward her, extending his hand. "And I'm Cooper Beaumont."

Ignoring Cooper's gesture, she tenses and grips Jack's hand instead. "Beaumont?" she asks, staring at Cooper. Jack whimpers, but she doesn't seem to notice, focusing only on Cooper. "Beau is your *farruh*, your pa?"

Cooper's lips turn down. "Yes, ma'am. But we're not very close."

She shakes her head and sucks her yellow front teeth. "No, I expect you're not. At least not now. How old are you, son?"

Cooper shoots me a quick sideways look, and I know he's just as perplexed as I am about why the locals seem so interested in his age. "Fifteen. But only until the end of July."

Her mouth pulls down in a sorrowful frown, and she shakes her head. "So soon."

Cooper and I shrug in confusion.

Miss Delia unfurls the last of the bandage. Maybe my eyes are playing a trick, but I swear the blisters are bigger than they were a half hour ago. "You say this is a burn?" She holds his fingers in the palm of her hand and gently spreads them apart.

Jack winces. "Yes, ma'am. And it hurts a lot."

She traces a blister with the tip of her crooked index finger. "This isn't like any burn I've ever seen." She purses her lips. "This will need powerful medicine. You sure you don't want to see a doctor in town? Most *buckruh* don't like to mess with hoodoo medicine."

Cooper's eyes expand. "You're a root doctor?"

She cackles. "Of course, boy, what did you think I was? You came to see a Grannie, didn't you?"

Cooper scratches his temple. "Ugh, I guess I didn't give it much thought."

Jack snaps his head around to us. "What the heck is hoodoo medicine? Is it like voodoo?"

Miss Delia drops his hand in her lap, making him yelp. "They are not the same. Hoodoo is for healing. It's not my religion."

"But do you use spells and stuff?" He pulls his hand back and cradles it to his chest.

She laughs and rocks in her chair. "When I need to. But that burn of yours doesn't need any more magic than a few roots and plants. It's up to you. Take what I've got, or get on out of here and find yourselves a doctor."

"No doctors." Jack's voice is firm. Miss Delia raises her brow at his insistence, but he smiles and turns on the charm. "Because then, you know, our dads will find out about the burn, and they'll worry about me."

She smirks. "And you'll have to tell them what you were doing when you got hurt in the first place."

Jack actually blushes and nods. "Plus my friend Maggie said you were the best, so I don't want to go anywhere else."

She throws her head back and laughs. "Be careful, Jack. Sweetmouth me like that, and you don't know where it could end up. I haven't had a gentleman suitor in a long time." She winks her milky eye at me and tries to push herself up out of the seat, but the strain is too much. "Give me a hand now, boys, and we'll go inside and see what I can fix up for that hand of yours."

Cooper and Jack gently pull her out of the chair while I push open the front door. We follow her inside to the front room, a neat but sparsely furnished combination dining and living area. An old television with a big, fat dial runs in the background next to a slipcovered couch. The walls are tilted and cracked, but they seem sound.

I drop my messenger bag next to the door and am hit by one of the most heavenly scents on earth—fatback and collard greens must be simmering somewhere on a stove. My mouth waters as I take a deep breath. I can almost taste that salty, vinegary goodness. I love southern food. It's one of the best perks of visiting my dad in the summer. Aside from seeing Cooper, of course.

Miss Delia reaches for a cane tucked next to the front door and slowly crosses the spring-green area rug on the way to a swinging door that leads to the kitchen at the back of the house. "Emma, could you give me a hand?"

"Sure." I follow her toward the collard greens while Cooper and Jack make themselves comfortable on the couch.

My eyes pop. It's a kitchen, all right. There's an antique white porcelain stove, refrigerator, and sink, but there's so much more. It's got a wraparound butcher-block countertop, marred with at least a century's worth of stains, gashes, and cuts, and a huge prep island in the middle that is just as worn. The walls are lined with shelves filled with earthen apothecary jars that look ancient, their glazes aged and cracked, each etched and painted with the name of an herb or spice. There are hundreds of them, some as common as salt and cinnamon, and others with weird labels like boneset, galax, kidney weed, and sassafras. But my favorite has to be sticklewort. What could you possibly do with something like that?

"Normally I'd treat a burn with cow dung and spittle, but I doubt your brother would like that." Miss Delia cackles as she washes her hands at the sink.

"Too bad, because I'd love to see his face when you put those on him." Although considering his recent behavior, maybe that's exactly what she should use. But she seems too nice to go through with it.

She dries her hand on a dishcloth. "Not to worry, I've got plenty of other remedies. We're going to make us a poultice for those ugly blisters. Fetch me that pot from under the counter and put it on the stove." She points her warped finger at a cast iron saucepan.

I reach for the long, textured handle, but it's so heavy, it takes two hands to lift, and crashes against the gas burner with a thud. She squints up at the jars with her good eye. "I'll need the American senna, elderberry, and sweet gum bark. And don't forget the balm of Gilead buds, either." On tiptoe, I search the labels, then reach for each of the items she asked for and carefully place them on the center island. Meanwhile, she drags a small marble mortar and pestle across the counter.

"I'll need your help crushing these since I don't have the strength." She pulls a thick wad of wound cloth from a drawer. Humming to herself, she draws some water from the tap, pours it into the pot, and turns on the flame. Then she opens each jar and places some of their contents on the counter. Pursing her lips, she stares into the elderberry jar.

"What's wrong?"

She sucks her front teeth. "It's empty."

"Is that a bad thing?"

"It's not good." She shakes her head. "It's the best medicine for boils."

"Do you want us to run to the store for some?"

She laughs and replaces the lid. "Child, you can't go to the store to pick up elderberry leaves. You got to pick them in the wild. I suppose I could do without them, but he said that burn was getting worse. I wanted to brew the strongest medicine I could."

"What do they look like? I'm sure I can find some."

She pats my arm. "Bless your heart, but you'd probably get confused by the wild cherry. Their leaves are pretty similar."

"No, I wouldn't. Wild cherry's a tree, and the other's a shrub, right?"

She cocks her head. "How do you know that?"

I stare at the counter and mentally trace the shape of a deep brown scorch mark. "Um, well. I don't have a ton of friends back home, so I spend a lot of time in the woods sketching."

I'm not sure why I feel so comfortable telling her the pathetic truth about my life, but I can't hold back. At home, I'm generally recognized as the art freak with a bag of art supplies. With Jack busy playing soccer or baseball or working on the school paper, and Mom at work or with one of her boyfriends, most of my free time is spent at the Arboretum or the National Zoo, reconstructing their gardens in my sketchpad.

Summer is my saving grace. When I'm with Cooper and Jack, I feel like I belong, like I'm part of a team. And even though we usually spend our time sailing Beau's boat or fishing and swimming in the Sound, there's plenty of time for drawing or painting—that is, when we're not obsessing over an exploding treasure.

But all that time in nature has its upside, too. Like being able to recognize the difference between a wild cherry tree and a shrub. I meet Miss Delia's cloudy eye. "It's amazing how much you notice if you take the time to look around."

A small smile bends her lips. "That's true, child, that's true. Well, go hunt down some elderberry leaves. They'll be shaped like feathers with jagged edges, like a bread knife. It's done flowering by now, so you might see the beginnings of some small, dark berries."

I'm pretty sure I know exactly what she's talking about. "Hang on a sec." I bolt from the kitchen and run to the door to grab my bag.

Cooper and Jack turn from the grainy TV screen. "Everything okay?" Cooper asks, his brow furrowed. His eyes are so sweet and full of concern that I stare for a second and get lost in their bright blue beauty.

Jack's voice breaks through my Cooper-induced fog. "Aren't you supposed to be in there helping?"

Ignoring the impulse to smack him, I reach into the bag for a small sketchpad. "Everything's fine." I try not to blush and turn to Jack. "You can thank me later after I help fix your stupid hand."

I jog back to the kitchen and place the book on the counter. Flipping through the pages, I search for one of the sketches I did on Hunting Island. "Here, this is what you're talking about, right?" I turn the book around for Miss Delia to see.

She bends down and peers over the sketch with her good eye. "That's it." She grins. "Find one and tote back some leaves."

I bolt out of the kitchen, passing Cooper and Jack again, and out the front door into the thick woods that surround her house. A few hundred yards in, past some scattered tupelo, mimosa, and wisteria trees, I find the bush. Miss Delia's right, the berries are a dead giveaway. I strip a handful of serrated leaves from the branches.

My scalp tingles. Someone's watching me.

I whip around, but no one's there.

Silence, deep and penetrating, fills the woods. Even the birds have stopped chirping. I don't see anyone, but I swear, someone's eyes are on me.

My eyes skitter from tree to bush, making sure no one has slipped behind one of them. An eternal minute passes. Still nothing.

I sigh, sure I'm losing my mind. First I freaked out about a deer last night, and now, for all I know, I'm doing it again over a chipmunk. Feeling dumb, I turn back to the elderberry and strip another branch of its leaves.

A foul odor wafts through the air. Chemical and squalid, it's like rotten eggs and burnt plastic mixed with decay.

I've smelled this before—at the ruins after Jack opened the box and got burned.

My spine stiffens. Maybe it's not a chipmunk, after all. Gulping hard, I try not to inhale while shifting my gaze from side to side, peering for its source.

A loud crack, like the snap of a dead tree limb, booms behind me. That was definitely *not* a chipmunk. Adrenaline surges. Without bothering to look back, I spin on my heels and race through the woods, careening around shrubs and trees and leaping over roots, shooting toward Miss Delia's.

My chest heaves as I charge up her porch steps. Nothing followed me back. I'm safe.

Then, as I'm congràtulating myself for evading the unseen evil, it suddenly dawns on me that a much more likely explanation exists: I was in the forest, where lots of wildlife lives and dies, and that smell probably emanated off the rotting corpse of some unfortunate beast. And the thing that sounded like a dead tree limb was probably just that—a branch that broke off a tree and crashed to the ground.

I've got to stop doing this to myself. I'm going to have a stroke.

Shaking off my wacky paranoia, I calm my breath and head back in. Miss Delia's bark chips have boiled down to a soft, mushy lump, and the kitchen smells way more earthy than it did before. She's got the rest of the ingredients lined up, ready for me to crush in the mortar before she tosses them into the gently boiling water. While the buds and leaves cook down, she asks me to grab a crock of lard from the old refrigerator and place it on the counter.

I gag a little as she digs a butter knife deep into the congealed white substance and plops a thick glob onto the cotton strip.

Her hand quivers as she drags the knife across the grease, trying to smooth it out. But her hand and the knife refuse to cooperate. Shaking her head, she slips the smooth metal handle into my fingers and steps aside so I can spread the lard across the cloth.

A chill hangs in the air as we wait for the mush to cook down and cool, which is weird because Miss Delia doesn't have air conditioning. But maybe it's a natural consequence of the huge live oak that dwarfs her house. Miss Delia doesn't seem to notice the change in temperature as she busies herself flipping through my sketchbook. She practically knows everything about each of the plants I've drawn—their names, where they grow, when they bloom, what parts are poisonous, and what can be used for medicine.

"I can't believe you know all this stuff." I jot notes next to each plant.

She laughs. "Child, I've had ninety-seven years to learn."

"Yeah, but who taught you? You couldn't have learned it on your own."

"My *maamy* taught me. And she learned from my gran, who learned from my great-gran. This is old medicine passed on from mother to daughter." She looks off, out the kitchen window onto the enormous herb garden.

"Did you teach it to anyone?"

She turns back to me and smiles, but it seems sad and empty. "Oh, I taught my daughter and even my own granddaughter, but they moved off Sa'leenuh a long time ago to work in the north. They don't use hoodoo anymore, ever since my granddaughter became a doctor in Chicago and decided it's bad medicine." She shakes her head and eases herself off the stool.

I frown as I watch her check the temperature of the mush. Her regret is almost another scent in the room.

When the mixture is cool enough, we spoon it on the lard. I help her spread it over the cloth, and she calls Jack into the kitchen. "Lay your hand here."

Jack gulps. "What is that stuff?" He grimaces at the mushy brown layer of cooked bark, leaves, and balm of Gilead buds.

She raises one eyebrow. "It's what you came for, boy. Now put your hand on the poultice." For once, Jack does as he's told. She wraps the strip snug around his hand.

His shoulders release, and the creases in his forehead smooth. "Wow, that feels good."

She laughs. "Of course it does."

He stares at his re-wrapped hand. "No, really, this stuff is so cool and mushy, the burning's completely gone. I guess I didn't realize how hot my hand has been."

She shrugs her thin shoulders. "It's the strangest burn I've ever seen, but I gave you an extra strong mixture just in case." She puts some lard and what's left of the mush in a small glass jar and hands it to me, along with another cotton strip. "Change his dressing tonight. It should be a whole mess better in the morning."

We walk her to the front door, where Jack and Cooper each slip her a twenty-dollar bill.

"Thanks, Miss Delia." Jack's happier than I've seen him in days. Now maybe his attitude will improve, too. He stares at his hand with amazement. "Maggie was right. You're a lifesaver."

She pats his shoulder with a liver-spotted hand. "I wouldn't go that far, but you're welcome." She watches as we make our way down the porch and through her herb garden. "Take care of yourselves, and don't get into any more trouble!"

Chapter Eight

"Emma, wake up!" Jack looms over my bed and shakes my arm.

"Huh?" My eyes are fuzzy, and my brain is clouded from sleep.

"Emma, I need your help. You've got to get up." Jack's face comes into sharper focus. His skin is drawn, and his brow is etched with deep lines.

I rub the sleep from the corners of my eyes, relieved to see that at least the sun is up, and he didn't wake me in the middle of the night. "What's going on? Is it Dad?"

"No, he's fine. He already left for Charleston looking for Missy's stupid weather vane part. My hand. It's gotten worse."

I yawn. "How's that possible? Miss Delia said it would be better."

"I don't know what that quack did to me, but see for yourself." He thrusts his palm into my face.

"Ah!" I wince and scramble to sit up, totally awake now. His fingers are red and swollen like uncooked Italian sausages, too engorged to bend. And the blisters have grown, stretched into huge, pus-filled boils that literally throb with his pulse. But the rest of his hand is normal—toned and muscular—and strangely unaffected by his engorged fingers.

"That's totally gross. Does it hurt?" I gingerly tap his index finger. Suddenly I get a whiff of something I can't quite place, but it reminds me of vinegar, or maybe something I've smelled in Dad's workshop.

He shakes his head. His eyes betray the panic he must have suppressed until now. "That's the weird thing—it doesn't. And it's freaking me out because I think it should." With his lips turned down, he stares at his fingers, and it looks like he might throw up. "Dang."

I run my hand through my ratty strawberry-blonde hair, dragging it up off my forehead and behind my shoulder. "We've got to get you to a hospital. I know you didn't want to tell Dad, but we don't have a choice now."

Jack pushes himself off my bed and paces across my bedroom floor, massaging his temples with both his healthy and swollen fingers. "Okay, but first we've got to stop by that crazy lady's house to find out what she did to me. Maybe she poisoned me. We need to know what she used to tell the doctors."

I shake my head. "No, I helped her do everything." I toss off the covers and jump out of bed. "I know what plants she used so I can tell them." I grab some clothes from the dresser and head to the bathroom to get ready.

He follows me down the hall. "But Em, you weren't there the whole time. Remember? You left in the middle of it." My trip to the elderberry bush suddenly flashes across my mind. "How do you know she didn't slip something into that concoction she cooked up?"

I can't help but think of Miss Delia's kind face and gentle demeanor. There was something so, I don't know, *good* about her that makes me doubt Jack's right. We only met yesterday, but I can't imagine her deliberately hurting him.

"Jack, I don't think she did anything to you on purpose. Maybe you're having an allergic reaction?"

His shoulders ease a little. "Yeah, I guess so." Closing his eyes, he pinches the bridge of his nose. "But we still need to find out what she used." He rests his head against the bathroom door. "I'm scared, Em." His voice breaks.

I grasp his forearm and muster the most reassuring smile I can. "I know. But we'll take care of it. I promise. Now go call Cooper while I get ready." I shut the bathroom door and let the smile slip from my face as a wave of dread washes over me.

• • •

Within an hour, we're standing on Miss Delia's porch. I knock on her door and wonder how to get her help without accusing her of hurting Jack.

The door opens, revealing Miss Delia in a pale orange housedress. Her brow crinkles with confusion. "Emma? I didn't expect to see you this morning."

Before I have a chance to answer, Jack steps forward and thrusts his hand at her. "Look what happened." The boils are even larger now, stretched taut over the fluid encapsulated inside, and throbbing.

She recoils. "What did you do, boy?" Her voice is suddenly at least an octave lower, deep and gravelly, and frankly, kind of scary.

"I used the stuff you gave us, just like you said," he says.

She narrows her cloudy eye and sets her jaw. "That didn't come from what I gave you. You best be on your way. Now."

Cooper pulls Jack back and tries to smooth things over. "Miss Delia, we don't want to bother you. But we're taking Jack to see a doctor, and we hoped you'd give us a list of the poultice ingredients, in case he's got an allergy."

She huffs. "No doctor can cure what he's got. I know bad magic when I see it."

Jack's lip curls. "What?"

She sets her hands on her hips and glares into his eyes. She's a foot-and-a-half shorter than he is but seems twice as powerful. "You messed with something you shouldn't have. Something dark and evil. Probably something belonging to Beau Beaumont."

Jack's head jolts back as if she's punched him across the jaw. "No, you're wrong." He shakes his head and sounds dazed. "There was a treasure…and a booby trap."

I jump in, eager to explain. "There was an explosion. That's how he got burned."

"I don't care how it happened. I don't want any part of what you got, boy." She flicks her wrist, shooing us off her porch. "Get on now, before it's too late."

Jack's gasp draws all of our gazes—to his hand. The boils pulse now, enlarging with each beat. The skin thins under the mounting pressure like a balloon filled with too much air. After one final, massive pulse, there's a sickening ripping sound, and all four boils erupt.

Jack screams as a fluorescent yellow liquid seeps across his fingers, bubbling against the skin. The scent of battery acid, tart and bitter, hangs in the air as Jack's flesh disintegrates, starting at the center of the boils, then spreading to cover the length of his fingers. The top layer of skin fizzles away, revealing several thin, clear layers below, which, along with his fingernails, quickly give way, exposing the ivory-colored fat and crimson muscles beneath.

It only takes a few moments for the tissues to dissolve, exposing milky white bones connected only by a few remaining ligaments.

The sizzling suddenly stops, and the remaining liquid drips onto the porch, scorching the wood and leaving Jack with skeletal fingers.

My stomach seizes, and I blink, trying to make sense of what I've just seen. But it's impossible. Jack is shaking, gawking at the bony fingers cradled in his good hand. He flexes them, and the bones curl inward toward his perfectly normal thumb and palm, forming a tight ball.

Cooper leans over the porch railing and hurls his breakfast into a giant purple salvia bush.

The low moan I'm hearing is coming from my own mouth. What the heck is going on? I turn to Miss Delia for an explanation.

She purses her lips and glares at Jack. "You are cursed, boy."

The pieces click into place. I gasp and turn to Jack. "It's The Creep."

Miss Delia's milky eye whips around to stare at me. "How do you know about The Creep?" Her gaze bores into me, singeing my skin.

I struggle to answer in a complete sentence. "It was…in a letter…the one about the treasure…I tried to warn him, but Jack didn't believe in it."

She peers at Jack, who's whimpering now, and points toward the yard. "Go sit under the bottle tree. Maybe it'll soak up some of the bad spirits." Then she turns to Cooper and motions toward his puke. "And you better clean up that mess."

Jack stands there, his mouth hanging wide enough to catch a swarm of flies. I don't think he heard a word Miss Delia just said.

She pokes his chest with a crooked finger. "Move. I don't want that curse seeping into my house."

Cooper gently takes him by the shoulder and guides him off the porch. "Come on, bro, we're going to move over to the bench under that tree."

Forget about the hospital and Dad. This is way beyond them. There's only one person who can fix this.

"Can you help him, Miss Delia?" I pray she's got some amazing secret magic up her sleeve that'll *poof* this all away.

She crosses her arms. "I don't want to fiddle with what he's got."

"Please?" My voice sounds as desperate as I feel.

She turns toward me. Despite how young and vigorous she seemed yesterday, she suddenly appears to have lived every one of those long ninety-seven years. Her shoulders slump, and she grips the doorjamb for support. "I don't know, child." She sucks her teeth, then turns around and shuffles into her house.

I'm not sure if I'm invited to follow, but I do, anyway. "Isn't there something we can do?"

Leaning hard against her cane, Miss Delia heads into the kitchen and pulls out a metal spoon before settling on one of the stools at the island. "I need to know what we're dealing with. Scrape up some of the pus that dripped on my porch. Mind yourself now, and don't touch it. Just put it on the spoon."

I bolt to the porch and grimace at the already thickening bright yellow goo, then scrape some up and race back to the kitchen. Miss Delia tells me to get her mortar and pestle and a large earthenware jar that's tucked away at the back of one of her cabinets. Next she asks for a scoop of dirt dug from the yard under the bottle tree and a small glass of water.

Once I've collected everything, she empties the dirt into the mortar, along with an equal amount of water, and mixes the substance into a dense, muddy paste. Then she rests the spoon in the bowl and reaches into the jar, retrieving a pinch of a fine gray powder. She chants a few words in a language I don't understand—probably Gullah—and tosses in some powder as she blows a puff of air on the spoon.

The wind whips up in her backyard, shaking the trees and rustling their leaves.

A flash of fire erupts in the mortar, sizzling the gooey substance clinging to the metal surface. First the yellow fluid hardens, darkening until it looks like a shiny nugget of onyx. But then the burning intensifies, condensing and dulling the black blob until it fades to a dull gray and implodes on itself, crumbling to dust. It looks like an old charcoal briquette after a barbecue.

The wind dies down as suddenly as it arrived, leaving an eerie calm.

Miss Delia shakes her head. "This is a very ancient and powerful curse. It must be The Creep."

"Is that a good thing? I mean, since you know what it is, you can reverse it, right?"

She leans on the butcher-block counter top. "Until this moment, I didn't know if it was real or a story my great-gran told me."

I bite my lip. "What'd she say about it?" I'm almost afraid to find out.

She rests her head in her hand. "As far back as anyone can remember, folks said a powerful doctress used the elements to work a revenge curse." She points to the mortar. "This is an elemental curse."

My forehead crinkles. "What does that mean?"

"It can only be broken with wind, fire, water, and earth. It's almost impossible."

"But if it isn't, what will happen to Jack?" My voice cracks because I'm pretty sure I already know.

Her face softens to deliver the bad news. "It will spread, little by little, until he is consumed."

A surge of fear, anger, and power shoots through me. I pound my fists on the counter. "We can't let that happen. You have to do something."

She reaches her withered hands to grasp my own. "Child, I'm an old woman, and this is an evil curse. I don't have the strength to fight it."

An idea pops into my mind. "Could I do it?" My voice rises with hope. "You could teach me what to do, and I could do it for you."

She stares at me like I just announced I'm running for president. Her face fills with pity. "Child, I know you mean well, but I've never seen a *comeyah* or *buckrah* who could work hoodoo, at least not as well as you must to break this curse."

Tears well in my eyes. She can't say no, at least not that easily. Jack might be a total jerk, but he's my jerk, and I can't let him go without trying. "But I can learn, especially if you teach me. He's my only brother. He's my *twin*. I can't lose him."

She pulls back and assesses me for a long moment, chewing on the side of her lip. "You said your father grew up on Sa'leenuh?"

I sniff away my tears and nod. "Yes. So did his father and grandfather. And I've been here every summer for the last eight years."

She purses her lips. "Then I suppose you're not really a *comeyah*. And you do know your plants." She strokes her chin with her crooked fingers, and I clasp my hands in prayer, sensing she might be willing to go along. "There's no official rule against *buckrah* working hoodoo. I could pass the mantle to you and take you on as an apprentice."

I exhale as relief pours over me. "Thank you, Miss Delia. I won't let you down."

"It's not me you should be worried about. Your brother is the one who needs you." The lines around her eyes seem deeper now, chiseled into her frail brown skin. Her good eye looks cloudier than before.

"I'll do whatever it takes. Just tell me where to start."

She reaches a liver-spotted hand across the counter once again. It lies heavy against mine, as if she doesn't have the strength to pull it back. "For now, you best get him home and be sweet to him. I need some rest after all this so I can figure out how to break the curse. You, too, while you're at it. We're going to need all the energy we can get."

Chapter Nine

I tap on Jack's bedroom door for the hundredth time today. "Jack?" I wait for him to respond, determined not to leave until I at least know he's okay.

He's been holed up in there ever since we got back from Miss Delia's yesterday. No matter what Cooper and I have tried, including begging and threatening to break the door down, all we've gotten is silence. At least my twin sense is telling me that he is alive.

After another long minute of silence, I knock again on the hollow maple door.

"Yeah." His voice is so flat and deep, I almost don't recognize it.

"Can I come in?"

"Yeah." He sounds cold and colorless.

I turn the brass handle, and the door squeaks open. Jack's lying on his bed in the same clothes from yesterday, staring at the ceiling. His arms are propped behind his head on his pillow, and his hand is tucked under his jet-black hair.

I slink toward his bed. "You okay?"

He doesn't bother to look at me. "I'm dying." His voice quivers. My stomach wrenches. "No, you're not."

"Yes. I am." He says it with surety and conviction, like he's lost all hope.

I sit on the side of his bed. "I'm not going to let that happen. I promise. Miss Delia's teaching me how to reverse this curse, and we're going to fix you."

His eyes are like two pools of ice—frozen dead zones of doom. "You can't fix me. And neither can she. This thing is going to spread until it kills me."

"Don't say that, Jack. I won't let it take you." I bite my tongue to keep from crying.

He shrugs. "Whatever. I know what's going to happen." He pulls his unwrapped hand from behind his head.

It's different than yesterday. Now the flesh at the edge of his bones is exposed and frayed, though somehow not bleeding, and his palm is swollen and red, even though his thumb still is normal.

Oh, my God. It *is* spreading.

He wiggles his bony fingers in front of his face. "Soon the blisters will come, and they'll get bigger until they finally burst, and my whole hand will be like this. And then little by little, it'll spread until I'm a walking, talking skeleton." A long, rolling laugh escapes his lips. But it's not his normal laugh. It's hollow and empty and sends a chill up my spine.

"What's so funny?"

He quiets. "It doesn't even hurt. You'd think dying would be painful, but I can't feel a thing." He thrusts his hand into my face. "Here, touch it. I won't feel it."

I get a whiff of something chalky and gag, realizing it's his bones. "No, I can't."

"Sure you can." He pushes his hand closer, and his eyes glisten with maniacal insanity.

Recoiling, I cry, "Stop, Jack!"

His face falls. "You want to save me, but you can't even touch it."

Ugh, he's right. I draw a deep breath and inch my finger toward his, bracing myself for what has to be the most disgusting thing I've ever imagined. Or anyone's ever imagined. My fingertip grazes the smooth bone before my reflex kicks in and I jerk my hand away.

His face is grim. "Dang, Em. Touch it for real. It's not going to kill *you*."

I stare into his steely blue eyes and realize I have to do this for him, to build his trust, and convince him I'm serious about breaking the curse. With a gulp, I reach out and grasp what used to be his index finger. It's cold and moist, like a piece of sidewalk chalk that's been left out in the rain. The three joints hang together by only a thin piece of stretchy tissue, which is probably a tendon. I run my finger over the top bone that's curved in the middle and rounded at the tip. It's like a chess piece, a tiny ivory pawn at the end of his finger.

He hikes up his eyebrow. "You know what it's called?"

"What?"

"That bone. It's the distal phalange. I looked it up in one of the old encyclopedias in the middle of the night. And this one's the intermediate." He points to the middle section with his good finger. "The bottom is the proximal."

"I'm so sorry," I whisper, lowering my gaze to my nearly normal foot. It's surreal that I could heal so quickly, but he's only getting worse.

He swallows back the welling tears, but one escapes and trickles down his cheek. "Nah, don't worry about it." He brushes it away with the back of his good hand and sniffs. "At least I'll be the coolest living anatomy lesson ever, right?" He forces a smile, but I'll take it, because it means he hasn't totally given up. At least not yet.

I reach over and grasp his knee. "We're not going to let it get that far."

"I want to believe you. I just don't know if I can." His eyes get glossy again, and he rubs them with his healthy hand. When his tears are under control, he tucks this arms behind his head and changes the subject. "So what's your plan to save me?"

I bite my bottom lip. "Um, Miss Delia needed some time to think on it. But she's got some ideas." I decide not to mention how difficult, if not impossible, she said the curse was to break. He needs all the hope he can get.

"That's good. I guess Maggie was right about her."

"Yeah, that's weird, right? I mean, how did she know we'd need a root doctor? Don't get me wrong, I'm glad she took us to Miss Delia, but it just seems really coincidental."

Jack rolls his eyes. "God, Em, when are you going to get off her case?"

Heat flushes my cheeks. "I'm not on her case. I'm just saying it's strange she got us to the exact right person to deal with this. I mean, seriously, what would have happened if we went to the hospital? They'd have you locked up in intensive care or zipped behind one of those plastic biohazard barriers."

"It's not weird at all. She's my girlfriend, and she cares about me. And she's a local. I bet all the *binyahs* know Miss Delia and her freaky hoodoo magic."

Since when did she become his girlfriend?

"But that's not what I mean—"

"Stop trying to make this into something it's not."

It's clear I've gone as far as I can with this.

I sigh and give up my need to be right, especially if it keeps him from going all reclusive hermit again. Plus it doesn't matter what he says or thinks. I have my own opinion, and he can't change it.

His face softens. "Have you seen her?"

"Who? Maggie?"

"Yeah." He picks at the thin patchwork bedspread with his distal phalange. "I was just wondering if you or Cooper ran into her. Or maybe if she stopped by to check how I am."

"We haven't exactly been hanging out at the beach the last couple days, you know. Plus she doesn't know where we live."

He stares at the ceiling. "I know, I was just wondering." He tries to act tough, but his voice is tinged with sadness.

Ugh, he's such a *guy*—thinking about his "girlfriend" when his hand's rotting away. But then again, maybe he just needs something positive to distract himself from The Creep.

I peer out the small window into the tall pines that surround the house. "I was thinking I'd head down to the ruins today. Maybe I'll run into her."

He lurches up onto his elbows. "Are you crazy? You can't go down there."

"Why?"

"Because that's where it all started."

"Uh-huh, exactly. I need to get the treasure box for Miss Delia."

He grabs my arms. His cold bony fingers wrap around my bicep and dig into my flesh. "Emma, promise me you'll stay away from that box."

His forcefulness takes me by surprise, as does his total change in attitude, but I remain calm so maybe it'll rub off on him. "Relax,

Jack. I'll be fine. I won't open it."

He grips even tighter, and his eyes bore into mine. "No, you won't be fine. I don't want this to happen to you, too. You can't touch it. Ever. I don't care what's inside, even if it's an antidote. It's not worth it." He shakes his head, and his chest shudders with another sob. "I should have listened to you in the first place."

I appreciate his sort-of apology, but that's not what's important—fixing him is. "But Jack, the curse is in that box. How else are we supposed to find a way to stop this?" I peek at his skeletal hand and gulp.

Suddenly aware of his actions, he releases his bony grip and slides away from me. "You'll have to find another way."

I understand his fear, but he's totally tying my hands here. Staring off into his room, I try to figure out what else I can possibly do to help Miss Delia besides waiting around for her to have a giant brainstorm. And then it hits me, because it's literally staring me in the face. There, on the desk next to his laptop, is the squat brown spirits bottle we dug up last week with Bloody Bill's letter rolled inside. It's what got us into this mess in the first place. It's not as good as the treasure box, but it's the next best thing.

I hop off the bed and grab it. "Okay, we'll do it your way for now. But I'm taking this."

Chapter Ten

"Emmaline, do you really think this is going to work?" The uncertainty in Cooper's voice echoes the silent fears that have rumbled through my brain all morning. He tightens his grip on the station wagon's steering wheel as we drive to Miss Delia's, his brow creased with worry.

Normally I'd be ecstatic to be alone with him, but things are different now. Jack's cursed and probably dying. Fear and worry trump everything else, even the giddy shivers.

"I hope so. It has to." I'm not entirely sure I believe it myself, but I don't have a choice. It has to work. My fist tightens around the neck of the thick brown bottle, as if I can will it into revealing a cure. I'm not even sure what I want it or the letter Cooper took from his geometry book to do, but they have to help us save Jack.

We park the car off the main road and walk the rest of the way to Miss Delia's, rounding the bottle tree and making our way through her front herb garden. Miss Delia is seated in a rocking chair on the porch. "I've been wondering when y'all would get here," she says as we climb the front steps. She must have gotten some rest because she seems a lot better this morning. The color's back in her cheeks, and there's a hint of a smile on her lips. Even her good eye seems clearer.

Cooper waves. "Morning, ma'am. I'm sorry again about yesterday." He thumbs his hand toward the now-clean salvia bush he hosed down before we left.

She smiles, then cranes her neck around us to squint into the clearing. "Where's your brother?"

"Home in bed." I press the bottle against my side. "He's not dealing with this whole situation very well, especially since the rest of his hand is swollen now."

She shakes her head. "It's going to make working the charm much harder."

Cooper and I exchange troubled looks. Jack won't even get out of bed. How were we supposed to drag him all the way here? Cooper rakes his fingers through his hair. "Uh, I could drive us all back to High Point Bluff. We've got a huge kitchen. Can you work the charm there?"

Her shoulders stiffen, and her mouth hardens into a straight line. "I'm not setting foot on that plantation. Never have. Never will. Not even if the Lord himself is waiting on me."

Wow. That's a pretty strong stance. "Why?"

She eyes Cooper before answering me. "I got my reasons."

"But—"

She cuts me off with a raised hand. "I'm not going. Besides, I'm too old to go traipsing up there, anyhow."

Panic swells in my gut. Why does she have to make this so difficult? Doesn't she realize how important this is? We're talking about my brother's life. Does it really matter where she works the spell? My fists tighten, and I suddenly remember the bottle in my hand. "You said his not being here makes it harder to break the curse, but not impossible, right? Maybe this will help." I extend the bottle toward her.

She squints with her good eye. "What is it?" She reaches for the bottle, and it nearly drops to the floor. Cooper springs forward and catches it before it crashes.

"Lord, that's heavy."

Cooper gently rests it in her lap. "We think it's from the 1700s."

I nod. "Remember the letter we told you about? The one that warned us about The Creep in the first place?" I flip up the cover of my messenger bag and fish out the piece of parchment. "This is it. We found it rolled up in that bottle and buried in the sand at the beach. I thought maybe it could give us a clue or something."

"Well, let's see it." Miss Delia fiddles with the reading glasses hanging around her neck, hooks them around her ears, then takes the letter from me.

I stifle a giggle. The lenses are so thick they make her look like a google-eyed fish. And now that it's magnified, I can't help but notice the cloudy splotch on her bad eye is shaped like Australia. If she needs this much help to see, she's got to be almost blind.

Unrolling the letter, she holds it out the full length of her arm, sucks her teeth, and mumbles, "This is good."

Cooper exhales. "Really?" Smiling for the first time in days, he squeezes my hand. His relief flows into me.

"Hold on now. I didn't say I found the exact cure." Miss Delia removes her glasses, returning her eyes to their normal size. "It's still going to take some doing."

My joy deflates like a balloon pricked with a pin. I slump against the porch railing, feeling the weight of Cooper's warm, muscular hand in mine. Oh. We're still holding hands. Normally that would probably make my heart explode, but Jack's life is still at risk. I can't pretend it doesn't feel good, though. Actually, way better than good—more like awesome. But now's not the time. I need to focus. I let go and act casual as I pull my hand back to my side. "But you said the letter was good."

"Yes, because it says she used the wind and water. That proves this is old elemental magic, and it gives me a better idea of where to start." She rubs her chin as if calculating something in her head. "Can you get me a piece of his clothing? Something that's got his sweat on it?"

I snort. That's about the easiest thing she could ask for. "That won't be a problem. Pretty much everything he owns reeks."

"Actually, I think he left his cap in the car yesterday." Cooper juts out his thumb toward the path. "That ought to have plenty of sweat in it."

Miss Delia flicks her wrist to shoo him off the porch. "Then go get it, boy. I don't want to wait any longer to work this spell."

Cooper springs off the porch and bounds into the front yard, jogging down the path through the herb garden.

Miss Delia leans toward me, her good eye glistening. "Help me to the kitchen. There's something we need to do before he gets back. And leave the letter and bottle out here. I don't want you dragging their bad mojo into my house."

I set the bottle on the wide plank floor, roll up the letter, and shove it back in the neck. Then I gently grasp her forearm to lift her out of the chair. "Okay, but Cooper's a good guy. You can trust him." I hand her the cane and support her other arm as we head into the house.

Leaning hard against the cane, she steps inside and hobbles along, shuffling her orthopedic shoes across the nubby green carpet. Despite how refreshed she appeared sitting in the chair, she's definitely not as strong as she was the other day. I clutch her elbow as gently as possible and guide her across the living room.

She shakes her head. "Maybe now, while he still has his childhood. But soon he'll come into his manhood."

That's the same phrase Maggie used when she met Cooper for the first time. Even though Miss Delia said it, I'm still confused. "What does that mean, come into his manhood?"

"Why, becoming a man, of course." She looks surprised I don't get it.

"But he won't be eighteen for two whole years."

She chuckles. "Child, being a man doesn't have anything do to with when the law says it's so. Take a look at that boy of yours. He looks nearly like a man, don't he? You know, in years past,when a young man turned sixteen, he could marry and start a family of his own. You watch—soon after that birthday of his, he'll start acting as corrupt as his father."

Her words sting like a slap across the face. His father is revolting—ogling young women and constantly recycling wives, eating like a hog, and tearing down every forest he can find to build crap nobody needs. Not to mention that disgusting rotten bologna smell of his. Cooper couldn't be more different from his dad. "You're wrong, Miss Delia. I've known him almost all my life. Cooper's the kindest, sweetest guy I've ever met. He's nothing like his father and never will be." My cheeks flush, giving away a lot more than my defense of him, but I don't care.

She stops, lifts her arm out of my hold, and pats me on the back of the hand. "Child, every Beaumont starts and ends the same way. It's an unbroken cycle that will never change."

I shake my head. "No. Not Cooper. He's different."

She chuckles and grips my forearm again. "Okay, Emma. Enjoy him while you can. Just don't plan on spending your life with him." She wags a gnarled finger at me. "And don't say I didn't warn you." My scalp tingles, and I reach up to scratch at the strange sensation.

We make our way to the kitchen, and I stop short when I see the island counter. It's covered with glass vials, beads, an ancient-looking book, and a box of white candles. She's been busy. I help her to a stool and plop down on the one next to her. "Where do we start?"

"First I need to initiate you as my apprentice. Normally I'd have you take a bath first, but we don't have much time before he gets back."

"Oh, don't worry, I'm clean. I showered this morning." I resist the urge to lift my arm and sniff my pits. I used deodorant this morning, but it's summer in South Carolina, after all, not exactly a cool, sweat-free place.

She smiles. "I'm talking about a different kind of clean. Before you work a strong spell in hoodoo, you should always cleanse your body with minerals and herbs to purify your soul, protect it from evil spirits, and fortify you against the effects of working magic."

Even though it makes sense, those last two parts surprise me. I've been so wrapped up in saving Jack, I hadn't considered that I might need protecting. And what does she mean about the side effects of casting magic? This is more complicated than I thought. "But I didn't do that purification thing. Will that ruin the spell?"

"No, I'm working the charm. You're just assisting. Besides, I've got a little something to help cheat when time's short. Give me your hands."

I extend my fingers toward her on the countertop. She flips them over so my palms face up and reaches for a small green bottle then works to unscrew the top, but it doesn't budge. Without a word, I gently take it from her hands and push down hard, twisting to the left, and open it. With a grateful smile, she lifts it from my hand and drips oil on my wrists. She rubs it in, releasing its citrus scent, and dabs a bit of the residue behind my ears and down my neck.

"Hmm, what is this?" I can almost taste the lemon, butter, and grassy notes that swirl around my head. I know I've smelled it before, I just can't remember where.

"It's citronella, one of the basic cleansing essential oils. We use it to repel evil."

That's it. The patio candles at Cooper's house. So now not only will I be free of evil spirits, but I shouldn't have to worry about mosquitoes, either. Bonus!

She reaches for a small white ceramic pot with a top that's sort of like a sugar bowl. "This is a *pot de tête*," she says in a French accent. If my ninth grade translation skills are correct, it means "head pot." Thankfully it's not big enough to literally hold my head. Not that I think Miss Delia's into that sort of magic. "Every apprentice gets one when they're initiated. I'll keep it here for as long as I need your assistance. When our work is finished, you'll get it back." She grabs a pair of scissors by the sharp end and points the handle toward me. "Snip off some of your hair and put it in."

Ah, so that's why it's called a head pot. I stare at the scissors, unsure of what to do. It's not that I'm vain, but my hair is probably the nicest thing about me. "Um, how much do you want?" I twist a long strawberry-blonde strand around my finger.

"Not much, but enough to know it's yours." She must sense my hesitation because she arches her brow. "Child, you've got plenty enough that no one's going to notice. Cut it."

I reach back to the nape of my neck and separate a small section. Draping it over my shoulder, I snip off a piece about ten inches long and drop it into the pot.

Miss Delia nods. "Now clip your fingernails and add them. too."

That's easier to do. My nails are usually on the short side, anyway, since they get pretty filthy from my charcoals and pastels. I snip the few nails long enough to peek over my fingertips right into the ceramic pot.

Miss Delia places the lid on top then removes a long, multicolored beaded necklace from around her neck and wraps it around the jar, several times, crisscrossing the strand. "Now you're under my protection." She grasps another, much shorter beaded strand from the counter and holds it out to me. "And this here's your necklace. It's a *collier*, and shows you've been initiated into my house."

The tiny beads are grouped together in blocks without an obvious pattern. Although the colors might ordinarily clash, there's something powerful in its simplicity. I slip it over my head. "Thank you. It's beautiful. Are these your colors?"

"The order is mine. But the colors, and even the number of beads, represent the powers we need to work hoodoo. You see these red and white beads? They'll give you the power of spoken word and prayer. And these clear and white beads? They're for seeing spirits."

Seriously? What kind of a charm are we working here? Do we have to see spirits to break this curse? Anxious to push the possibility out of my mind, I spin the necklace around to the block of purple, white, and black beads. "And what about these?"

"They're for communicating with the dead."

I gulp. That's so much worse. "Let's hope we don't have to do much of that."

She cackles, and her good eye twinkles. "You never know when it comes to hoodoo. Best to be prepared."

The last section is the widest, a group of light blue and pink beads. "What are these for? And why are there so many of them?"

"Ah, those are the most important. They'll help you listen to your spirit guide." She places her hand on top of mine to emphasize her point. "Never ignore the voice of spirit. She'll always help you make the right decision."

I roll the smooth glass beads between my fingers and consider what she said. I'm not sure if these tiny, round pieces of glass will do everything she says they will, but she obviously believes in them. And since she's my only hope to save Jack, I've got to believe in her.

The front door slams, alerting us that Cooper's back with Jack's hat. Miss Delia starts and pushes the head pot toward me. "Put this in the back of the cabinet over there. And remember, it's our secret." She lifts her crooked finger to her lips to seal the deal.

"You got it." I stow it just as Cooper steps in the kitchen.

"We're in luck. This thing's covered with dried sweat." He tips the Washington Nationals hat toward us, revealing the previously navy-blue brim that's faded to a dull gray from all Jack's stinky perspiration. He smiles at me. "Nice necklace, Emma. It looks good on you."

My stomach dances at the compliment.

Miss Delia takes the hat from him, puts on her glasses, and peers at the cap. "This'll work." Something catches her eye, and she squints at the inside again. "But that hair is even better." I peek inside to see a stray jet-black strand tucked alongside the brim. She sets the hat down, reaches into a drawer in the island, and grabs a long piece of twine. Without looking up, she extends her hand. "Cooper, could you grab that bottle from the porch and hang it from my bottle tree? The other bottles need to soak up its bad spirits. And when you're done, busy yourself in the living room with a television program. Emma and I need to work."

Cooper glances at me, but I shrug, because after what she said before about the Beaumonts, there's no way I'm going to ask her to let him stay, even though she's totally wrong about him. He seems to catch my drift because he grins when he takes it from her. "Sure, no problem. Holler if you need me." He winks and heads out of the room. As much as I resist it, a warm, tingling wave floods over me, heating my cheeks until I'm sure they're bright red. *Focus, Emma. You've got a brother to save.* The kitchen door swings closed, and a few seconds later the screen door slaps against the jamb.

"Watch your heart, Emma. Don't wade too deep into the fire. You don't want to get burned."

I bite my tongue to distract myself and gaze down at the counter. "I don't know what you're talking about."

"Sure you don't." She reaches for the thick-spined book, then shoots me a deadly serious look. A shiver runs down my spine. Laying her veiny hand on the faded black leather cover, she says, "Before we start, you've got to understand something. This is an evil curse, as dark a magic as I've ever seen. If I was still young and strong, it would take everything I have to break, and even then, I might not have recovered from its power. Now that I'm old, I can't do it alone. I need you. But taking you on as my apprentice means you're going to see and hear things most people never get to know. I've got to know I can trust you."

I nod. "Yes, definitely. I totally understand."

She hitches her brow. "I don't know if you do. This book is filled with strong magic—roots and spells handed down from mother to daughter for as long as anyone can remember, from even before we were brought to this country. I started writing them down while I was teaching my own daughter. It's one of my greatest secrets. No one outside my kin knows about it."

The importance of her trust ripples over me, raising the hair on my arms. Although I can't totally understand what she means, I realize she's talking about hundreds of years of knowledge squished into one single hand-written book. And I'm smart enough to realize the responsibility is enormous. "You can count on me, Miss Delia. I promise I won't tell anyone about it." I don't think I've ever meant anything more.

Her lips part into a wide, yellow grin. "Good girl." She thumbs through the handwritten pages, showing me how it's divided. There are lists of hundreds of plants, herbs, and roots, and each includes a physical description, where it grows, and what it can be used for. There's also a section on spells, broken down into the different types of magic: white for protection and blessings, red for drawing love, green for money, and black for controlling others or placing a curse on someone. The last section is a list of Miss Delia's ancestors, each one a hoodoo root doctor that goes back fifteen generations.

She flips back to the section on spells. "I believe we can break this curse by working a few of the charms at the same time. The trick will be to combine the ingredients to get the maximum strength from each, while making sure they don't cancel each other out." Her thick fingernail runs down a list of white magic charms.

I'm totally confused. "The curse is black magic, right?"

"It sure is, which is why we're using white magic to break it."

"Why wouldn't we use black magic instead? Shouldn't we match the spell to the curse?"

She sets the book aside. "The first thing you need to learn is that we only use black magic when there's no other choice. And never, ever add it to a black magic curse, unless you want to create something even more evil. Only white magic can fight black. Just like only light can defeat darkness."

"Oh, so it's like a yin and yang kind of thing?"

She squints. "How's that?"

"It's Chinese philosophy. It describes how there can be two opposite sides to everything, but they're really two halves of a whole. Sort of like male and female, or hot and cold." It feels kind of nice to teach her something. "Together they keep everything in balance. Which is why a white magic spell is the only thing that'll break a black magic curse."

She nods. "Yes, that sounds about right. That balance is essential. It's one of the fundamental laws of hoodoo."

The screen door slams, and the television fires up in the living room, blaring the local public station. Cooper lowers the volume and switches the station. He must be watching something sports related because there's a lot of cheering. Or maybe it's static. I'm pretty sure she doesn't have cable.

"You ready to brew up a *Break Jinx* curse?" Miss Delia's voice pulls my attention back to the kitchen. I nod. "All right, then." She points to one of the kitchen cabinets in the far corner. "I'll need you to fetch me a roasting pan. Pick one that's burned." She opens one of the earthenware jars and spills some of its contents. "Wouldn't want to light a fire in one of my good pans."

I yank it out from the others and bring it to her. "Did you say you're going to light a fire? In the house?"

She plops a heaping tablespoon of dirt into the bottom of the pan. "How else do think we're going to break an elemental curse? Can't do it without fire."

"But shouldn't we light it outside? Wouldn't that be safer?"

She spreads the soil evenly in the pan. "Nah, the windows and back door are open. Besides, we're not building a bonfire, just enough to smoke some roots. Now pay attention, child. This represents the earth in this spell, but it's not just any old dirt." She raps the spoon against the side of the pan. "It's special."

"Is it blessed or something?"

She waggles her brows. "It comes from a graveyard."

"And that's supposed to be a good thing?"

Her good eye sparkles as she chuckles. "Sure it is. It repels evil. Believe me, we need plenty of help." She tosses a handful of dry charcoal chips on top of the dirt, then grabs one of the white candles from the counter and hands it to me. "Turn this upside down and whittle a new end with that knife over there. Then carve your brother's full name down the side."

The blade on the old paring knife is dulled with age, but it's still sharp enough to scrape down the wax. When the new end is pointy and the wick is exposed, I bear down on the blade and keep the letters small enough to fit his whole name. Until now I've never noticed how many letters it takes to write Jackson Sawyer Guthrie. My hand feels like it weighs ten pounds as I whittle his name. When I'm finally done, Miss Delia opens a vial labeled "Uncrossing Oil" and drips some liquid on the candle, then strikes a match to light the new end. She hands the flickering candle to me and points to the charcoal.

I dip the candle into the pan and run the flame along the chips, watching as they slowly ignite, their edges glowing orange and red. A faint hickory scent rises in the air. "So we've got fire and earth." I blow out the candle. "What about the wind and water?"

She points to a clear vial with a glass stopper. "The holy water comes at the end to douse the flames. In the meantime, you're supplying the air. My lungs aren't what they used to be. Blow on those coals to get them to light, but not so much you put them out."

Pursing my lips, I lean over the roasting pan and focus my breath toward the chips. A smoky barbecue smell wafts up. Soon the charcoal is enveloped in tiny, crackling flames.

Miss Delia sucks her teeth and smiles. "It'll be ready in a few minutes. In the meantime, I'll need you to fetch me some of those crocks so I can make up the smoking potion." She puts her giant reading glasses on and flips through the pages of her spell book, peering closely at a number of white magic spells. As she reads, she mumbles to herself, debating each ingredient. Then she motions toward the earthenware jars on the shelves and rattles off the list of things she needs. "I'll need some holy ghost root, patchouli, verbena, sandalwood, and sticklewort."

There are so many jars, it's hard to keep the list in my head and locate the ones she wants at the same time, especially since they're not organized in any obvious order. I'm sure she knows why the wormwood is sitting next to the frankincense, because it's definitely not alphabetical order.

She scoops a small amount from each crock into her mortar and hands me the wooden pestle. "Grind these up nice and smooth."

The dried herbs crush easily, breaking down into a smooth powder that, well, stinks. Each of the ingredients has its own strong fragrance, but added together, their spicy scents merge into something truly funky. It's sort of like potpourri on steroids. And not one you'd want to put in your living room.

"Wow." The thick stench burns my nose. "This stuff is pretty strong." I know exactly what Jack would say if he was here to smell this, and I can't help but think the word in my head—*dang*.

My eyelids grow heavy. I blink hard, resisting the urge to close them.

She winks. "It's where the real magic is. Each of these is potent enough to turn back a regular curse. Burning them together will increase their power and should cure your brother." The flames in the roasting pan settle, and the chips glow a deep orange. "Now shake this mixture over the coals."

Stifling a yawn, I sprinkle the powder over the glowing chips. Last night with Jack was rough, but this is ridiculous. I shake my head to clear the fatigue.

The herb mixture ignites as it hits the hot charcoal, spitting and crackling like tiny beads of gunpowder. A cloud of gray-green smoke billows up from the center of the pan.

The sky darkens as the clouds shift and converge, blocking out the sun.

Miss Delia thrusts Jack's baseball cap at me. "Quick, fish out your brother's hair and add it to the pan."

I tug the jet-black strand from the inside of the brim. It's straight and coarse, almost like a strand of wire, and way thicker than mine. Definitely Jack's. As I toss it onto the coals, Miss Delia grasps my hand and chants, "As dawn breaks night, and heat melts ice, turn back this curse and restore Jack's life."

A blast of wind barrels across the backyard, whipping the rear of the house and rattling the windows. A ghostly moan surrounds the bottle tree.

A flash bursts in the pan, and a fireball leaps into the air, blowing the powdered mixture all over the kitchen and us. A split second later, the flames collapse on themselves, retracting back into the pan with a loud sucking sound that smothers all the heat. Even the charcoal has stopped glowing.

Miss Delia starts, then leans toward the quiet pan, holding her hand above the coals that blazed just a second ago. Her eyes are fixed in stunned confusion. I lift my hand and hold it next to hers. There's no residual heat. It's completely cool. Miss Delia pokes a tentative finger at a charcoal chip. It disintegrates into a heap of ash.

Suddenly a loud and ferocious bark booms from outside Miss

Delia's kitchen window. Deep and gravelly, it's almost more of a roar than a bark. The yowl repeats, brutal in its persistence, filling my stomach with dread. I spring off my stool and race to the window to see what's outside.

A giant black dog with long, glossy fur and electric yellow eyes stands in the middle of Miss Delia's herb garden, howling its enormous head off. It's at least as big as a pony, but I'm sure it's a dog.

Some kind of crazy-eyed, half-Newfoundland, half-Doberman beast.

Now I'm awake.

The raw, bitter smell of rancid eggs seeps into the kitchen.

My mind races to comprehend. Miss Delia slips off her stool and joins me at the window. When it sees her, the dog bares its jagged teeth and seethes, growling so deeply the floorboards rumble.

Cooper charges into the kitchen, slamming the swinging door open into the wall. "Y'all okay in here?" His eyes bulge as he peers into the yard. "What the heck?" He sprints toward us, shoves the back kitchen door shut, and encircles us with his long arms.

The dog barks again, the sound so vicious, I can almost feel the cutting edge of its teeth on my flesh. My hands shake. Even though the door's closed and I'm enveloped in Cooper's strength, I don't feel safe. Not with that beast around.

Miss Delia's face is drawn as she clutches my hand. "This is more serious than I thought. We need the ancestors."

Chapter Eleven

The creature narrows its yellow eyes and curls its lips up on one side. If it wasn't a dog, I'd swear it was sneering at us. I mean, how can a dog *smile*? On second thought, it's obviously psychotic, so maybe that's exactly what it's doing.

"Holy crap," I mutter. "I think it wants to kill us."

"Not while I'm around." Cooper grabs a metal pot off the stove and rushes to the back door. Yanking it open, he darts across the side porch, pushes open the screen door, and launches the pot at the dog. "Get!" The metal bounces in the grass at the monster's feet.

It crouches as if it's about to pounce, then snarls and barks again.

I rush to the cabinet and find another, heavier pot. Dashing onto the screened porch, I slap the iron handle into Cooper's waiting hand and retreat back to the safety of the kitchen.

"I said, 'GET'!" He launches the pot at the dog, which springs to the right at the last second, dodging the incoming missile. The dog howls, long and low. It's not English, but we understand nonetheless. It doesn't like us. Not one little bit. The dog pivots and barrels into the woods behind Miss Delia's backyard.

Miss Delia whimpers and slumps against the counter. Her legs give out, and she slides toward the floor, but Cooper scoops her up, carries her to the living room, and sets her onto the sofa. Her forehead and upper lip bead with sweat, and she reaches for the tissue box on the coffee table with a shaking hand.

"Are you all right, Miss Delia? Should we call a doctor or something?" My voice is strained as I hand her a tissue. The dog was horrifying, but it didn't actually attack us, so I don't understand why she's so overcome.

She blots her lip. Her eyes are unfocused and glazed, but she waves me off. "No, child, I'll be fine. I just need a little breather, is all." I doubt it. She's flushed and flustered like she's about to have a stroke, and there's no way I'm prepared to handle that. And neither are the ancestors she mentioned—whoever they are. She needs a hospital.

"We need an ambulance." I step away from the couch to grab my cell from my bag. I haven't seen a landline anywhere in the house.

"No!" Miss Delia grips the cushions and tries to lift herself up. Her glossy eyes grow intense as she shakes her head with as much conviction as she can muster. "No hospitals, no doctors. They can't treat what ails me. I can handle it myself." She collapses back onto the sofa, and her frail body quakes. Oh, jeez, she's going to die right here in front of us.

"But—"

"I said no doctors. I'll fix myself as soon as I've gotten some rest." Despite how feeble she appears, fire still lights her eyes. I won't push it, even though she's being ridiculous. Her eyes roll to the back of her head, and her teeth chatter.

Cooper squares his shoulders. "I'll get her some water." He jogs to the kitchen.

"And maybe a cool, wet cloth," I call after him. Kneeling, I pull the afghan off the back of the sofa and drape it over her, hoping it'll stop her shaking. I'm willing to play it her way, at least while she's conscious, but then I'll do what I think is right. Until then, since I am her apprentice, maybe I can help cure her. "Um, Miss Delia, what the heck was that out there?" I take her limp, clammy hand.

Her shivers begin to quiet. "A warning," she manages. "Our spell didn't work. The curse doesn't want to be broken, and it's telling us so."

"What do you mean? You're describing the curse like it's a living thing or something that can make its own decisions."

Her eyelids sag, and she strains to keep them open. "I told you this is a strong curse. It's been working for almost three hundred years. It's not going away easily."

Cooper comes back with the water and a cool, damp dishcloth. "Here, Miss Delia, take a sip." He slips his hand behind her shoulders and lifts her head so she can drink. Grasping the glass with trembling fingers, she lifts it to her lips, but some of the water slips past the rim and dribbles down her chin. I reach and steady the glass so she can get enough into her mouth to swallow. When she's done, she hands the glass to Cooper and wipes her chin with the tissue, which is disintegrating in her hands.

"Thank you, son. That was very kind of you." She lays her head back down on the cushion and shuts her eyes, which roll behind her lids.

"Miss Delia, I know you don't want to go to a hospital, but I'm worried about you being all alone with a wild dog on the loose." Cooper dabs her forehead with the moist cloth. "Did you see the froth around its mouth? I'm pretty sure it's got rabies. If you've got a shotgun, I could go after it, maybe put it out of its misery."

She forces her eyes open. "That dog isn't sick, boy. It's evil." Her words are barely audible as her lids close again.

Cooper's brow crinkles as he hunches his shoulders.

I mouth, "I'll explain later," then stroke the back of her hand, her moles and wrinkles rough beneath my fingertips.

In a weird way, her skin is tough and fragile at the same time. Almost translucent, it's thin enough to see clear through to her raised blue veins but strong enough to encase her hardened and twisted knuckles. These hands have spent nearly a century working with roots and herbs—planting, harvesting, and converting them into medicine and magic. If anyone knows what we're up against, it's her. I'm just not sure if she's up to facing it.

I don't know if she's asleep, but I can't just leave her here, especially if I don't know what the heck that dog wants from us. I gently nudge her shoulder. "Miss Delia, do you think it'll come back? I'm afraid to leave you by yourself." Because if it hasn't killed her by now, it will the next time.

Her eyes slide open, and she nods. "Maybe. It depends on whether we try to break the curse again." Her voice is weak. I don't think she'll be able to talk much longer.

My brow knits, and anger bubbles in my stomach. So this is some kind of supernatural ultimatum: give up trying to reverse The Creep, or it'll take Miss Delia. It's an impossible choice. There's no way I'm abandoning Jack, and I don't want to lose Miss Delia, especially to something as nasty as that electric-eyed creature. Neither option is acceptable. I'll have to find a way to help them both.

I set my jaw.

Cooper must read my thoughts because he places his hand on

Miss Delia's shoulder. "It's not safe for you to stay here. Is there somewhere we can take you?"

"I'm not leaving," she whispers, not even trying to open her eyes. "I just need another *collier*." After a long pause she continues. "It'll protect me."

I glance at her bare, wrinkled neck, and remember she used her necklace for my *pot de tête*. Is that why I'm okay and she's not? A chill runs up my spine, and I reach up to stroke the smooth glass beads hanging around my neck. I'm embarrassed for doubting their power earlier. Clearly she needs them more than I do. I pull the strand off my head. "Here, Miss Delia, you can have mine."

She shakes her tired head. "No, child. Keep it. The curse knows about you now, so you'll need its protection. I'll make my own when I wake up."

I doubt she'll last that long. She needs a *collier* now. I pull the necklace back on and push off the floor, sprinting for the kitchen. "I'll be right back."

Using my own necklace as a model, I use the beads and elastic cording still lying on the counter to string together a new *collier* for Miss Delia. Then I remember how she blessed the upside-down candle earlier and figure I should do the same with the necklace. Unsure if the uncrossing oil is the right thing to use, I flip through her spell book for something better. Recalling her rule about not mixing different kinds of magic, I scan the white magic section, sure it's the only way to protect her from that psycho dog.

The entry for *Four Thieves Vinegar* looks good. The description says it's supposed to offer personal protection from disease and magical attack and can be sprinkled on stuff and even taken by mouth. We've got a winner. I search her shelves, examining each vial until I find it, unstopping the top and taking a sniff. Whew, the garlic, pepper, and minty scents instantly clear my sinuses. I sprinkle a little on the new necklace, then grab the bottle and a teaspoon and run back to the living room. Cooper moves over to give me some space.

Crouching next to the now-sleeping Miss Delia, I arrange the necklace over her head and pull it down past her snowy hair to rest on her neck. Then I pour some of the vinegar mixture on the spoon and bring it to her lips. "Miss Delia," I say softly in a singsong-y voice to rouse her, "I've got some medicine for you."

Her lips part slightly, and I tip the spoon, drizzling some of the mixture into her mouth. She swallows and stirs a little, just enough to open her eyes and grip my wrist. "*Four Thieves,*" she whispers. "Good girl." Her lips turn up in a faint half-smile.

Relief floods through me. I'm not sure what I'm happier about—that she'll probably be okay, or that I didn't kill her myself with that concoction. Plus since she seems to be responding, I don't need to call an ambulance, after all. I sigh, feeling the stress slip off my shoulders. "Is there anything else we can do?"

She tightens her hold on my hand. "Find the mortar. We can't break the curse without it."

Oh, my gosh, it's bad enough the dog-monster sapped her strength, but is it possible it took her memory, too? I lean close. "The mortar is in the kitchen, Miss Delia. On the counter, remember? I used it to crush all the leaves and roots before we worked the spell." I'm speaking loud and slow as if she might also be deaf now, too.

Even though she's practically still at death's door, she looks at me like I'm a moron. "No, not *that* mortar." She shakes her head and clears her throat. "My gran's mortar, handed down by all my great-grans. It's old magic, and the only way to call the ancestors. We need their help."

That's a relief. At least she's still mentally with it. Although I think she just said we need to contact a bunch of dead people.

Cooper leans in close. "Where is it? We can get it right away."

Her lids droop again as she shakes her head. "I don't know."

Cooper juts out his square jaw, begging for my help in prodding her.

"Think hard, Miss Delia. Where did you put it?"

She grips my wrist. "The missionaries stole it when I was a girl. I haven't seen it in more than eighty years."

Chapter Twelve

Cooper and I race down Miss Delia's driveway to his car. The path is clear and quiet, and we slip into the car in one piece. But as thrilled as I am to be on my way home, dread wells in my throat.

What are we going to tell Jack? We didn't reverse the curse, but we can't even try again until we find something that's been missing for more than eighty years. God knows how long that's going to take, or if the magic mortar still even exists. And if by some miracle we do find it, how will we get it from its current owners? And what about the devil dog?

Jack's situation doesn't look good.

When we arrive, Jack is sitting on the front porch steps, waiting for us. I blink to make sure I'm not seeing things. He's smiling. No, that's not right. He's beaming.

That's…unexpected. The last time I saw him, he was miserable and convinced he was about to die.

"Hey!" He waves. His decaying hand is covered by one of Dad's work gloves, and he's plastered with dirt.

Cooper and I exchange looks, and he shuts his car door. "Hey, bro. It's nice to see you up and about." He strolls to the porch and sits down on the steps next to Jack. Speaking softly, as if he doesn't want to agitate Jack, Cooper asks, "How're you doing? We were real worried about you."

"I'm all right." Jack swats his gloved hand in the air and giggles as if the trauma of the last few days never happened. That's right, he actually *giggles*.

Have I stepped into a parallel dimension? The guy wouldn't come out of his room for a day because his hand is disintegrating, but now he's "all right"? And when was the last time he giggled?

A chill runs up my spine. Is it possible the *Break Jinx* charm took hold before the beast showed up? But Miss Delia seemed convinced we'd failed. I try to steal a peek, but there's no way to tell with the glove on his hand.

Suppressing all hope, I bite my nail and search for a polite way to ask if he's still falling apart. "Um, Jack, did something happen to your hand while we were gone?"

"Yeah," he answers with a nod. The grin is still plastered across his face.

Joy surges through me. Cooper's eyes light up. Maybe we did it. Maybe all it took to defeat The Creep was to toss a few crushed herbs and a piece of hair over a fire. And even better, now I don't have to give Jack all that bad news.

I lurch forward, filled with excitement. "So what happened? Is it better?" My voice raises at least an octave as I resist the urge to yank off the glove.

"See for yourself." He lifts his hand and tugs at the glove, but it sticks on the puffy heel of his hand. He pulls a few more times, and it finally slides off, revealing his bloated and now-scarlet palm and thumb, and four ivory bones. That bizarre smile is still in place.

My stomach sinks. I stare at his ruined hand, simultaneously transfixed and freaked by his odd expression. It's not better. If anything, it's worse. Way worse. Judging by the swelling, that skin probably doesn't have more than a day before it explodes and burns off. So why is he so happy? I catch a whiff of something fetid, sort of like a pond filled with decaying plants.

The smell of death. I take a giant step back.

Cooper gags and turns away, managing not to hurl.

Jack pats him on the back with his good hand. "It's all right, Coop. I know it stinks." He breaks into full-throated laughter.

Um, Earth to Jack. I set my hands on my hips. "What the heck is going on? This morning you thought you were going to die, but now you're Mr. Excited? And you're okay with that stench? I don't get it."

He straightens his spine and flashes a serene grin. "I know I'm not going to die, at least not from this—" He lifts his half-distended, half-bony hand. "—so there's no reason to get all bent."

He's happy because he's *not* going to die? Does he really have that much confidence in Miss Delia and me? For real? I'm touched. I had no idea my pep talk this morning was that persuasive.

But there's no way we can live up to his expectations. Even before these new developments, Miss Delia said it wouldn't be easy to break the curse, but now I know it'll be dangerous, maybe even impossible. I force a deep breath in my constricted chest. "Jack, I'm glad our talk this morning helped, but—"

He scoffs. "What? It wasn't you. It was Maggie."

Oh, her. I should have known. She's the only one who can make him that delirious. Or despondent when she takes off to find her grandmother.

Finally over his queasiness, Cooper spins around toward Jack. "You saw Maggie?" He tries to be discreet as he covers his nose with his hand to escape Jack's smell.

Jack sighs and gets that dreamy expression again. "Yeah… she's so great."

My eyebrows knit as I stare at my brother and try to make sense of his erratic mood swings. He's gone from ecstasy to snapping at me and back again in about two seconds flat. It's weird. It's obvious Maggie makes him happy, but I've never seen him pine over anyone like this before, not even his ex-girlfriend Katie, who he practically drooled over. I set my hand on my hip. "Wait, I didn't think she knew where we live."

"I brought her here, and she made us lunch. It was awesome." He rubs his stomach.

Cooper's brow crinkles. "Where'd you find her?"

"After you two left this morning, I got to thinking about that treasure being out in the open. I know you said you put the lid back on the chest, and no one but us would probably go down there, but I just didn't feel right about it." Jack turns to Cooper. "I mean, what if your dad decided to check up on us and ended up opening that box?"

Um, I understand Jack's concern, but for the record, I'm not sure Beau could actually make it down to the tabby ruins without a forklift. I wonder if Cooper's thinking the same thing because for a split second, I'm sure he smirks. But it must be my imagination, because a moment later, he mashes his lips into a straight line, and his eyes drop to his feet.

Jack doesn't seem to notice and continues. "It wouldn't be hard for him to find. And if he got to the treasure inside…" He focuses on his hand and scowls as he clenches his bony fist. "Well, let's just say I didn't want to take that chance. This can't happen to anyone else." He scuffs his flip-flop against the porch step.

After a long, painfully quiet pause, I have to ask, "So what'd you do? And how does Maggie fit in all this?"

Jack's head snaps up. "Oh, I took a shovel down there and filled the holes. All of them. It looks just like it did before we started."

So that explains why he's so dirty. And why he was wearing Dad's glove. I can't blame him. It would be pretty gross to get dirt on that hand.

Cooper prods. "And Maggie?"

"She met me there. I guess she was walking on the beach and must have heard me shoveling." Squinting, Jack scratches the side of his head and stares off to the right, as if he's trying to remember how everything happened, but after another long pause shakes his head and gives up. "Anyway, she kept me company, and then we came back here after I was done." He gets that faraway look in his eyes again. "Man, she made the best sandwiches. And she mixed up some punch for us, too. She was right—it really did make me feel better."

Cooper laughs, but it sounds strangled because he's still avoiding Jack's odor. "Well, that explains a lot. What'd she put in it, rum?" He elbows Jack in the side.

Jack shrugs. "How am I supposed to know what she used? She was feeding me. I wasn't going to interrogate her. Anyway, she said I'm definitely going to be fine, because Miss Delia is a hoodoo ninja master who'll blow this curse away. I wasn't sure I agreed at first, but Maggie knows what she's talking about, and she can be kind of persuasive." He turns to Cooper and winks. "If you know what I mean."

Cooper chuckles.

I huff and kick at a clump of grass, my mind chewing on Jack's words. What exactly went on here today? She's gorgeous, so I get why he'd want to be with her, but what's in it for her, especially

with that nasty, smelly hand of his? I try to let it go, telling myself
it's none of my business, but I just can't. "Did she see your hand?"

Jack's lip curls. "Yeah. Why?"

"Just wondering whether it bothered her, that's all." I shrug
and motion toward Cooper. "I mean, it grosses us out, but we love
you, so we're not going to turn our backs on you. But she's only
just met you."

Jack sighs. "Wow. You're so jealous, it's sad. I should pity you
because you don't know what real love is." He hitches his brow
and tosses a quick sideways glance at Cooper. "But I'm not going
to waste my energy because Maggie and I have too much to look
forward to."

I gasp. "What the—" I should tear him a new one, but I
stop myself before I reveal too much about my true feelings for
Cooper. How could Jack go there, especially when he knows—
even though I haven't admitted it—how much I like Cooper? Jack
doesn't need twin sense to know how mortified I'd be if Cooper
found out. My hands ball into fists so tight, my short nails dig into
my palms. Creep or no Creep, I'm about to pound him in his face.

Cooper sits up straight, squaring his chest. "Hey, bro, I'm glad
you're happy with Maggie, but you've got no call to talk to Emma
like that." His brow creases with anger.

My heart leaps. I didn't think I could love him any more. I was
wrong.

Jack shrugs. "Sorry. I didn't mean anything by it. I only meant
that Maggie promised everything would work out, and I believe
her because she hasn't steered me wrong yet."

He's full of crap, but Cooper's intervention has helped quell
my rage, so I unfurl my fists and decide to let it slide. This time.

Dad's truck rumbles up the driveway. Jack shoves his hand
into the glove as Dad parks in the gravel at the side of the house.

Dad gives us a tired wave before he steps out of the cab. Here under the bright summer light, he seems older than usual. Last year he had a full head of thick jet-black hair, but now it's thinning at the crown, and his temples are streaked with gray. He works too hard. A quiet desk job would be much less of a strain, but he feels indebted to Beau because they were best friends when they were kids, kind of like how we are with Cooper, and because Beau took him in when Mom and he split. Since Beau can never find anyone else to work at High Point Bluff, Dad will never abandon him.

"Hey, y'all." Dad's eyes are droopy as he rubs the back of his neck. He stops short when he sees Jack's filthy clothes. "Now what do we have here? Is it too much to hope you did a little landscaping for me up at the Big House?" His expression is deadpan, so it's hard to know if he's serious or not.

Jack freezes. "Uh, no, I was out at the tabby ruins again. Did you want me to do something?" He looks at his gloved hand and swallows hard. "Because we'd be happy to do whatever chores you need."

Dad laughs. "Are you kidding? You two would tear up those rose beds, and I'd get stuck replanting a whole new row. I've got enough trouble on my hands building Missy's silly free-range chicken coop." He looks at Cooper. "No offense, son. I didn't mean to disparage your stepmother's coop."

Cooper scoffs and waves him off. "No problem, Uncle Jed. I didn't know she had you working on a new project."

Dad chuckles. "She's working me, all right. Been at it all week. First we sited it under a big oak so the chickens would have shade, then she wanted it moved so they'd have a view of the Sound." He rolls his eyes. "She read some article that claimed the waves help chickens meditate and lay better eggs. Personally I doubt it, but she's the *mistress*." He yawns. "Excuse me, kids. I've been at it since six-thirty this morning, and I'm bushed. There's a cold beer in that refrigerator with my name on it." He brushes past Jack on the porch step and stops, sniffing the air. "You notice anything dead lying around here?"

"No," Jack and I snap in unison. It's not really a lie, but I tuck my fingers behind my back and cross them anyway.

Dad eyes Cooper. "You sure you didn't hit anything with the car? Maybe a skunk?"

Cooper shakes his head. "No, Uncle Jed. I promise I haven't hit anything."

Dad sniffs again. "Maybe I'm just tired, but something stinks. You ought to have that car washed anyway, just in case." Dad's cell phone rings. "Hello? Oh, hi, Missy." He shuts his eyes and shakes his head as he listens to her. About a minute later, she finally stops talking. "I understand, but I'm not sure it's the best idea. We can talk about it in the morning."

She goes off on him, yelling loud enough that I can hear her squeaky voice from several feet away. She says something about being the mistress and getting what she wants. Then Beau's voice comes on the line. Dad nods his head as he listens. "Yes, Beau... I understand... But we've already framed in two big picture windows and some smaller ones on the sides. Adding skylights is liable to turn it into a greenhouse. Those chickens will roast... Yes, of course you're right... I will... All right. I'll be there in a few minutes." He snaps his phone shut and heads back down the steps, his shoulders slumped.

I hate to see him treated this way. And that he seems so willing to take it. "Where are you going?" I ask.

Dad mashes his lips. "To frame out a few skylights. I'll be back later, kids. Don't hold dinner for me."

Cooper's brow crinkles. "You've done enough today. Why can't it wait until tomorrow?"

Dad sighs. "Because Missy wants it done now. And Beau wants what Missy wants."

Cooper's lip curls. "But what she wants is stupid. And it's going to kill her chickens. You shouldn't let them talk to you like that."

Dad jiggles his keys as if he's weighing whether to tell Beau to stick it. But that would probably get him fired and kicked out of the caretaker's house. He shakes his head. "Beau's my boss, son, and the boss is always right." He climbs in the truck and backs out the driveway.

Cooper kicks the dirt. "Things will be different when I'm in charge." He sounds like he's speaking more to himself than us.

Jack shakes his head and spits. All that giddiness from before? Gone. I almost wish Maggie would stroll by to lighten Jack's mood. Almost. But even she can't mix a punch strong enough to wash away the bad taste in our mouths.

Jack juts out his jaw. "So what happened today with Miss Delia? I was kind of expecting some results." He waves his cursed hand in my direction.

Anxiety, fear, and guilt grip me all at once. This is the moment I've dreaded all afternoon. Maggie's visit and my dad's scolding offered a merciful distraction, but there's no more stalling. This is it. Once I tell him, he'll realize how hopeless this is, and that Bloody Bill's note will come true—he'll be ravaged by The Creep and eventually become a bundle of dry bones. That's what he's *really* got to look forward to. He'll be crushed.

Cooper and I exchange pained glances, and I gnaw my lip, searching for the words. "Jack, I'm sorry, but we tried—"

Jack's eyes flash with dark anger, and his face contorts. "What's that supposed to mean? Either you fixed it or you didn't." His voice is deep and gravelly.

Cooper reaches for his arm. "Easy, bro. She's working hard."

Jack jerks out of his reach. He winces and squeezes the bridge of his nose. "Ow. Stupid headache is back."

I huff. Shaking my head, I take a step forward, trying to explain. "No, you don't understand. We were working the spell, but there was this dog—"

"A dog?" He glares at me through his long black eyelashes.

Cooper's bright green eyes widen as he nods in agreement. "Not just any dog. I swear it was as big as a hog."

The words tumble from my mouth. "It was evil and had these horrible yellow eyes, then Miss Delia collapsed, and now we need to find some kind of special mortar to call her ancestors."

Jack shakes his head. "Whatever." He stands and grabs the screen door handle to retreat back into the house. "Just find the frigging thing and cure me."

Cooper rises to face him. "It's not that easy, Jack. It's been missing for more than eighty years."

I lurch forward, willing him to see how hard this will be. "It was stolen by some missionaries, and we have no idea where they put it."

Jack winces, grabs his head, and rubs his temples. Then he shoots us his I-can't-believe-you're-such-idiots glare. "When are you going to stop being so dramatic, Emo? Of course we can find it. The answer is up at the Big House."

Chapter Thirteen

Up in Cooper's bedroom, Jack strides toward the desk and rips off his glove. Waving his mangled hand at the laptop, he says, "This is a computer. It connects to something really cool called the Internet."

Cooper stares at him hard. "You know what, bro, I know you're dealing with your hand and all, but your sarcasm sucks."

Nodding, I set my hands on my hips. "Yeah, and considering you need us to help you, I'd think you'd be acting extra nice instead of being a giant jerk."

Jack blinks. The sneer slides off his lips. He rubs his forehead with his phalanges, then stumbles over to Cooper's bed and collapses in a heap.

Alarmed, I reach for his arm. "Are you okay?"

He nods. "Yeah, it's just a stress headache." He pinches the top of his nose. "Look, guys, I know I haven't been myself lately, and I'm sorry. I guess I'm just freaked by this curse thing."

When he puts it that way, it's hard to stay angry with him. I sigh. "Just try to be more like the jerk I know, okay? Because it's hard to love this extreme version."

His lips pull into a half-smile. "I'll try."

Cooper chuckles and slaps him on the shoulder. "Good. I'm glad that's out of the way because I didn't want to have to kick your butt." He jerks his thumb at the computer. "You want to explain how the Web's supposed to help us find the mortar?"

Jack shakes his head as if the answer is lying right there on the desk, and we should be able to see it. Cooper and I look at each other, clueless.

Jack grunts. "Jeez, you two are thick." He gets up and mashes the on button with his bony index finger. I guess he's already forgotten his promise. He plops into Cooper's desk chair, clicks onto the Web, and taps his phalanges against the track pad.

The sound is beyond nauseating, not to mention the putrid stench wafting through the air. Sour saliva pools in my mouth, and I gulp it back, trying not to puke.

"Um, Jack could you possibly stop doing that?" I ask, swallowing hard.

Cooper winces. "Yeah, bro, it's all kinds of wrong. Can't you at least put that glove on again?"

Jack grumbles something I can't understand. "Tough. It's what you get when you two screw up and leave me to fix everything."

That's it. I'm out of sympathy. "That's totally unfair." I cross my arms. "We didn't screw up, and I certainly haven't been sitting around braiding my hair." Nobody asked him to fix anything. While he was busy crying, I became a hoodoo apprentice to help save his nasty self—cutting off a hank of my hair and being terrorized by a demonic monster—not exactly how I planned to spend my summer vacation.

Jack ignores me as he types "South Carolina St. Helena Island history" into the search engine. His bony phalanges click against the keys with each stroke. So. Gross.

"Hello? Are you going to clue us in here? What's your amazing plan?" I ask.

"Research," he answers as he twists around toward us. "Listen, this is just like any other research paper or one of my journalism investigations. The answer is out there. We've just got to find it. And we've already got the first clue."

Clue? I don't get how searching the island's history is going to give us what we need. Jack clicks a link and scans the page.

"So you think we need a history lesson?" I ask, plopping down on Cooper's bed. Cooper does the same, sitting so close I feel the heat emanating off his skin. I fight the urge to rest my palm against his tan leg or lean my head against his broad shoulder. Or both.

Thank God Jack doesn't take his eyes off the screen. He'd totally skewer me if he saw what was going on behind his back.

Oblivious to my Herculean effort not to paw Cooper, he scans different pages and drones, "That's the problem with you art students. All you want to do is draw and paint. You don't realize how important history is." As much as I want to tilt his chair back and watch him crash to the floor, I don't because I'd have to step away from Cooper to do it.

I grunt. "Ugh, spare me. Now you sound like Ms. Darling." Our history teacher's pretty cool, but she's always going on about how the present couldn't exist without the past. Well, duh. But that doesn't mean I have to waste my time studying useless facts about a bunch of dead guys. Especially when I could use that time to create something beautiful.

"See, that's what I mean. Ms. Darling's the smartest teacher at our school. Maybe if you paid attention more, you'd do better in her class."

"Whatever, butt-kisser. I did fine."

"Yeah, a B- is stupendous."

"Um, I'm not an art student," Cooper adds unhelpfully.

I gawk at him. He shrugs, then flashes that adorable grin that melts my irritation.

Jack snorts. "Yeah, well, being into maritime and military stuff probably won't help us, either."

Cooper pushes off his bed and strides to his desk. I hate him for making Cooper leave my side. Crossing his arms, Cooper asks, "Okay, genius, why don't you tell us what will." His voice is tinged with annoyance.

Oops. Jack's done it now. It takes a lot to tick off Cooper, and busting on his love of the water is the best way to do it. I haven't seen his brow furrow like that in a long time. I don't like how the deep creases squish his light green eyes, making them appear smaller, or how his lips pull into thin, straight lines.

Jack is too engrossed in what he's reading to notice Cooper's reaction. He clicks on a new link and skims halfway down the site. A broad grin spreads across his face as he highlights a section of text and points to it. "See, here it is. All the missionary organizations that came to St. Helena's to work with the Gullah. Our mortar thief has to be one of them." He clicks the print button.

Cooper's face brightens. "How the heck did you find that?"

Dang, why can't he keep a grudge?

Jack shrugs. "It's from a dissertation on Gullah theology." He works to sound unimpressed with his find, but I know he wants to squeal like a happy little girl.

I peer at the list. There are at least twenty organizations, all with religious-sounding names like Salvation Sisters, Women of the Word, and The Lord's Prayers. "Um, Jack, I don't want to be a downer, but there are a lot of groups here, not to mention they're eighty years old."

He nods. "That's the whole point of doing research, Em— tracking down leads and seeing where they take you."

I hunch my shoulders. "But how do you know if these groups still exist, and if you do manage to contact any of them, who's going to admit stealing the mortar?"

Jack grimaces, then grabs his head with both hands and massages his temples. "Can't you just go with me on this?" He sighs. "I know I'm right about this. I can feel it, just like when I knew the treasure was buried under the ruins. I bet whoever took it still has it, or maybe they know what happened to it." His blue eyes plead. "Let me do this. It's what I'm good at."

Tears well in my eyes. Finally, I'm not the only one trying to save Jack. He's as much a part of this as I am or Cooper is. Suddenly I don't care if he thinks I'm emotional, or that he's a jerk. I can't hold back how I feel. Wiping away the tear rolling down my cheek, I nod. "Okay, find the mortar. Your hand's getting worse, and I don't want to lose you."

He reaches over with his good hand and squeezes my fingers. "I will." He winks. "See? I told you to pay more attention in class. History saves lives."

• • •

"Thank you, child. You're very kind." Miss Delia reaches her shaky hands to grasp the teacup and saucer.

"No problem. I think you'll like this batch better than the last. I added some mint this time."

She blows on the steaming cup and bends her head to take a sip. "Mmm, that's good. Your blending skills have definitely progressed." I settle into the rocker next to hers and gaze at the herb garden and bottle tree. She sets the cup on the saucer. "Thanks to you, I'm doing much better. You sure you wouldn't rather be at home with those boys, hunting for that mortar?" She reaches up to stroke her *collier.* "I'll be all right on my own."

"Nah. They'll call if they find something. Besides, I like coming here."

There's no way I'm leaving her. It took me four days to get her out of bed to eat a decent meal and another two to come out onto the porch. There's no telling what might happen if I leave her alone, especially if that dog-beast shows up again. And it's not like I'm of any use at home, what with Jack tearing through the list and bossing Cooper around like he's his research assistant. I'm staying as far away from that mess as possible.

Despite Jack's cockiness, the mortar hasn't been easy to find. It turns out most of the missionaries were on St. Helena's around the same time, so he's got to investigate them all. So far, he's managed to get through more than half, calling a bunch of churches and talking to little old ladies who remember visiting the island with their parents. Just as I feared, none of them recalls taking anything from the Gullah, just handing out a lot of Bibles.

Miss Delia smiles. "I enjoy your company, too." She points her crooked finger at me. "You're a good girl, Emma. I could see that the moment I laid eyes on you."

"Really?" My cheeks flush.

"Uh-huh. That's why I asked for your help in the kitchen that day." She narrows her cloudy eye at me. "You think I'd have you back there if I didn't think I could trust you?" She cackles for the first time in days. It feels good to hear that high-pitched ring in my ears. I was afraid I'd never hear it again.

"No, I suppose not." I chuckle and sip the hot honeysuckle tea, noting how much better it tastes with the mint. The last cup

I brewed had way too many bark chips and tasted like steeped mulch.

She nods and sucks her teeth. "Not to mention taking you on as my apprentice. Saving your brother is one thing, but when we're done, you'll know my secrets and have tremendous power. I wouldn't pass the mantle to just anyone."

I haven't thought about what will happen after we save Jack, but I doubt it'll include more hoodoo. I figured everything will just go back to normal.

As much as I'd like to, I doubt I'll be able to erase the terrible image of Jack's bony hand from my mind, especially now that The Creep has progressed, stripping him of the remaining ragged and festering flesh that clung to his palm and thumb. It exploded the other day while he was using the computer, dissolving most of the keys on the right side and frying the motherboard. Since I was with Miss Delia, Jack got to clean up while Cooper ran to the office supply store to get a replacement. Even though I knew his hand would burst—it started to throb before I'd left that morning—it was almost impossible to see his stripped hand when I got back. Now the tiny bones hang together by the faintest layer of connective tissue but somehow still manage to bend and flex as if they were wrapped in muscle and skin. The swelling has moved on, too, encircling his wrist like a scarlet watchband. So far Jack's been able to hide it from our dad by wearing a glove wherever he goes—Dad thinks it's some weird fashion statement—but that won't last long when the curse moves farther up his arm.

I bring my attention back to Miss Delia. "You know I'd never tell anybody your secrets." I sound as solemn as I feel.

"Of course I do." She rocks back in her chair. "I'll tell you something else I know." Her voice is deep and serious.

"What's that?"

"You've got a touch of the Sense."

I choke on my tea. "The what?"

"Sense. You know what I mean." She states it like it's an indisputable fact.

"Um..." I don't. I search my mind, trying to figure out what she's talking about. But as usual, I'm clueless. "Do you mean I make sense, like I'm a logical person? Or that I've got sense, like I'm street smart?" Because while I might be the first, I don't think I'm the second, even though I'm from D.C.

"No." She takes another sip. "You've got *the* Sense. You're sensitive."

I sigh, thinking of Jack's favorite insult. I'm tired of defending myself against being emo. "I guess I'm a little emotional. But isn't everyone?"

She laughs. "You're not hearing me, child. Having the Sense means you know things. Like when something's bad, or when it's good. Everyone has the ability, but it comes easier to some folk than others. You're one of those people who can hear your spirit guide. It's what's going to make you an excellent root doctor someday."

Oh. Well, when she puts it that way, it doesn't sound half bad, but I'm not sure I agree. "I don't know about that. I mean, it's not hard to see when things are obviously evil, like that crazy dog last week. I'd say you'd have to be pretty dense not to get that."

She nods. "Sure, there's no mistaking that evil. But I'm talking about things that aren't so clear. Tell me, you knew it was a mistake to go after that treasure, didn't you? But you didn't just know it in your mind." She points to my head. "You felt it in your gut." Her hand tilts down toward my stomach.

Memories rush over me. The chills the first time I read Bloody Bill's note, then nearly hurling in the root cellar before Jack and

Cooper opened the tabby box. They thought I was being dramatic, but it turns out I was right all along. I nod. "Yeah. I knew we should leave it alone. I tried to tell them, but they wouldn't listen, and the further we went, the sicker I felt. So that was my spirit guide, huh?"

"It sure was. Some call them guardian angels, others spirit guides, some even say it's your conscience. Either way, it's all the same thing. They try to talk to us, let us know what's going on, but some of us are too jaded or scared, or just too plain dumb to listen. Normally that'd be fine, but sometimes, when a spirit guide has something important to say, she won't be ignored. If you don't listen, she'll take it out on your body until you do. We're going to have to help you hear her better." She smiles. "I don't want you heaving off my porch and ruining my salvia like your boy did."

I can't help but laugh. "You don't have to worry. My stomach's a lot stronger than his." My cell phone goes off, blasting a ring tone by my favorite emo band, specially selected to annoy Jack. I reach over to my messenger bag and grab it. It's him. "Hello, freak." It's so much easier to insult him over the phone.

"Cooper's on his way over to pick you up. I think we found it."

Chapter Fourteen

Cooper gave Miss Delia and me only the vaguest details. It seems Jack thinks the ancestors' mortar is at the King Center, the local Gullah museum, and if so, he's come up with a plan to use Beau's donor status to borrow it. But Cooper's acting all fidgety and avoiding Miss Delia's gaze, so I'm sure he's not being completely honest. Maybe he's waiting until we leave Miss Delia's to spill his guts, but that only makes me wonder what he's hiding, and why.

He nudges my arm. "Well, Emmaline, we better get going. Jack's waiting on us."

"Wait, before y'all go, let me mix you up some charms. You're going to need all the help you can get." Miss Delia strains to lift herself out of her rocking chair.

Cooper gnaws his lip as we grasp her hands and help her up. "Yes, ma'am. Although I think we're planning on scouting things out at first, just to make sure they have it."

Miss Delia narrows her hazy eye at him. "Boy, I've lived five times longer than you and seen every scheme there is. Don't think I haven't figured out what you and her brother have cooked up.

Trust me, if it is there, you'll need the charms."

Cooper's eyes widen—today they're pale blue to match his T-shirt—and he gulps. He looks…guilty. "Uh, I don't know what we're going to do, at least not exactly." Sweat beads along his forehead, and it's not because it's July in South Carolina and Miss Delia doesn't have air conditioning.

Miss Delia chuckles. "Don't ever play poker. You'll get cleaned out." With a sigh she adds, "At least it means you're honest, which is more than I can say for the rest of your kin." With our help, she takes the few cautious steps toward the screen door.

Cooper mashes his lips into a sad, thin line. He's wrestling with something, but I'm not sure if it's her crack about his family or whatever he and Jack have planned. He holds the door open so I can guide her into the living room. "But you said you need the mortar to save Jack, right? So we don't have much of a choice."

Miss Delia pauses and removes her hand from mine. "Don't misunderstand me, son." She grips his fingers and pats the back of his knuckles. Her withered brown hand looks small and fragile against his. "You get what I need, and you'll get no judgment from me. It belongs with me, anyhow."

My stomach thuds. What the heck are they talking about? And how much trouble are we going to get into? Is this a message from my spirit guide, or am I just freaking myself out?

Miss Delia grabs my arm again. "Help me to the kitchen, Emma. We've got a few spells to cast." She turns toward Cooper. "See if you can't find yourself another program to watch on the television." Her thick yellow fingernails dig into my skin as she steadies herself. I bite my tongue to diffuse the pain as we baby-step across the living room carpet, through the swinging door, and into the kitchen.

Miss Delia settles onto a stool, and we purify ourselves with citronella. She calls out a bunch of ingredients almost faster than I can assemble them. Before long, the island counter is covered with crocks, and we're measuring out small quantities of herbs to make *gris-gris* bags, which are small pouches filled with powder and other items.

The breeze picks up, swaying the trees that stand beyond the garden. Within moments, the temperature drops, raising goose bumps on my sleeveless arms. The normally crystal-blue sky turns a dull steel gray, and a gentle summer rain begins to fall.

Miss Delia still hasn't told me what she thinks the guys are up to, and it's driving me insane. I could ask, but then she'll think I couldn't figure it out myself. Instead, I decide to start with the charms and work backward, figuring they might give me a clue to the big picture.

While Miss Delia works to fill one brown leather bag with her quaking fingers, I've already made up two sets of my own according to her instructions. Though it's a challenge, because I'm suddenly overcome with a maddening fatigue that makes it hard to concentrate. I don't understand. The first three yellow pouches contain a mixture of yarrow and nettle, which unfortunately smells like cabbage but shouldn't make me drowsy. According to Miss Delia's spell book, they're supposed to increase courage and bravery, not sleep.

I yawn. "I know this is going to sound weird, but is it possible I'm allergic to some of these plants?"

She gazes at my skin. "I doubt it. You haven't broken out in hives, and you're not sneezing."

"Then why am I suddenly so tired? It happened last week, too, before that crazy dog showed up. I feel like I could crawl into bed and sleep all day."

Miss Delia chuckles. "It's been so long since I trained as an apprentice, I forgot to warn you of the effects."

My lids droop, and I shake my head to clear the fog. "You mean this is going to happen whenever I work a spell?"

She pats my hand. "Only at the beginning or whenever you're working a very strong charm. You see, magic is basically energy which is used to influence people or events. That energy has got to come from somewhere, usually the root doctor. But don't worry, you'll build up a tolerance eventually."

Eventually? How long is that going to take? And how many naps will I have to take between now and then? "Let's hope so, because I'm not sure I can deal with this." I yawn again.

"You can do anything you put your mind to," she says matter-of-factly and hands me an empty white *gris-gris* bag. Evidently she's done sympathizing over my condition. Shaking her gnarled finger at me, she admonishes, "Never, ever allow yourself to be defeated by negative thinking. That kind of energy is just as destructive as dark magic." She reaches for the crushed sea spirit seaweed powder and sprinkles some in the bag.

Nodding, I bat my eyes to keep them open and get back to business. "I don't remember reading about seaweed in your spell book. What's it supposed to do?"

"That's because it's listed under agar-agar, the name for the crushed powder. If you hold some of it in your hand and walk around slowly, it'll give you semi-invisibility. I'm sure you'll need it."

As bizarre as that sounds, after seeing Jack's hand and that hellhound, not to mention this bone-crushing weariness, I've learned not to doubt anything about hoodoo. Rather than ask about why we need it or make a big deal of getting quasi-super powers, I keep my mouth shut and concentrate on blending the last potion while trying to stay awake.

Miss Delia cinches her pouch and hands it to me. "This one's just for you."

I drop the pestle and take it from her. "Thanks. What's it for?" I sniff at the bag, inhaling its sweet, buttery flavor, then hang the long cord around my neck.

Her good eye sparkles. "It'll help you get a little bit of what you want." She turns her attention toward the potion I'm working and changes the subject. "That mixture's just right." She points her crooked finger toward the counter behind me. "Now fetch three blue flannel bags from that drawer and drop three bark chips in each before you add the rest."

I follow her instructions and spoon the oregano, fennel seed, and black mustard seeds into each bag. I'm sure I've never come across a charm with these ingredients in her book, and I'm tired of acting like I understand what's going on. "I give up. What's this spell for?"

She hands me a tiny bottle of oil to drizzle on top of the mixture before sealing the bags. "To keep away the law." She winks.

The rain stops, and the clouds part, revealing a perfect cerulean sky.

I swallow hard. "The l-l-law?" My voice rises.

She hitches her brow. "Don't tell me you believed that boy's story about asking the King Center to loan out my ancestors' mortar?"

Up until now it seemed like a perfectly reasonable plan. "Sure. Why not? Beau's one of their biggest donors. Why wouldn't they?"

She sucks her teeth. "There's not a museum in the world that would loan you kids an artifact, no matter how much you claim Cooper's daddy will pay."

My forehead crinkles as I cock my head, trying to figure out what she means. "So how are we going to get it, then?"

She levels her good eye at me. "You're going to steal it."

• • •

Despite the *gris-gris* bags, Cooper's scared. He grips the steering wheel like he's trying to choke it. "Maybe we should rethink this, bro. If that thing is in there, I'm sure my dad really could send a letter asking to borrow the mortar." He wipes at the sweat beading on his brow.

We're parked in front of the King Center. One of their main exhibits features three hundred years of Gullah root medicine. Long before it was a museum, the building was a missionary school for Gullah kids. If the mortar isn't here, we're lost.

Jack pinches the bridge of his nose and grunts, then sneers as he whips his coarse black hair off his face. "Are you kidding me? I'm sitting here, losing chunks of skin practically by the minute, and you want your dad to write a letter?"

I lean forward from the backseat, completely sympathetic with his point but nearly paralyzed by the impossibility of this task. "But Jack, you want us to steal from a museum. How the heck are we supposed to do that?"

Living in D.C., I've been to every Smithsonian a million times and seen how much security they have. Everything is held down by trip wires, tracked by motion detectors, or recorded on videotape. And that doesn't include all the guards posted in every room. You can't get within a couple feet of an object, much less come close enough to touch it. There's no way we're going to pull this off. With or without the *gris-gris* bags, we're so going to get arrested.

Jack cranes his neck around to face me, his gaze narrowed into snake-like slits. "Okay, so who's going to explain to Beau why we need the letter, and who'll make sure Dad doesn't have a heart attack when he sees my hand? And then, if by some miracle we convince them not to send me to a hospital, and they actually believe an ancient magic mortar will fix me, who's going to make sure the museum gives us the mortar before I'm dead?" He drops his face in his hand and squeezes the top of his head. A low moan rises from his lips.

"You okay, bro?" Cooper asks.

Jack shakes his head. "It's the headaches. They're getting worse. It's all the stress from The Creep. I've taken pain meds, but nothing seems to work. We've got to end this curse before my head explodes."

"We're doing everything we can. We're in this together, remember?" I rub his shoulder. "You're right. Compared to all that stuff you just laid out, stealing the mortar sounds a lot easier." I sigh, sounding as defeated as I feel, knowing that although stealing is wrong, we have no choice but to try, even if it means we end the day in a jail cell. I sink back into the soft leather seat. "I'm just afraid we won't be able to take it if we do find it. What if it's bolted down or something?"

Jack slaps his forehead with his good hand. "This isn't the Air and Space or Natural History museum, Em. Compared to those, this one's got to be rinky-dink. Besides, you don't have to take it now. Just go in there and check things out. If everything's good, grab it and run. If not, come back out, and we'll switch to plan B."

Plan B? We've barely got a Plan A.

I'm so busy worrying about our impending incarceration that I miss one important point, but Cooper doesn't, turning to Jack with fear etched into his face. "You're not coming with?"

Jack rolls his eyes and shoves his gloved hand in Cooper's face. "Hel-lo, have you not noticed my hand is falling off? No? Well then how about this?" He tugs on the end of the glove, releasing a hint of that revolting scent, and revealing the inch-wide strip of bulging flesh that encircles his wrist and pulses like it's about to blow. Oh, man, I hope it doesn't explode in the car. Getting a new laptop was easy. Replacing the leather in Beau's car, not so much.

Cooper blinks, shifting his gaze between Jack's hand and his snarling face. "But you've got the glove." He lifts his finger to point out the obvious.

Jack tosses me his best can-you-believe-this-guy look.

Cooper gulps, panic filling his eyes as he tries to reason with Jack. "I don't think we can do this without you, bro. I've never stolen anything in my life, and I don't have the first idea where to start. It's not that I think you're some master criminal, but I figure we've got a better chance if the three of us work together. And this is a museum, for cripe's sake. One my father gives a lot of money to. If we get caught, he'll kill me." His shoulders slump in desperation. He's right to fear his dad's temper. It isn't pretty. "If we're just scouting things out, why can't you come in with us? Then at least you'd know what it looks like in there, and you could help us come up with a plan to take it."

Rather than convincing him, all Cooper's words do is make Jack angrier. Combing his fingers—gloved and ungloved—through his hair, he grips the sides of his head and speaks into his lap. "Don't you think it's a little suspicious for me to walk around a museum with one glove on? Especially in the summer?" After a few moments of chastened silence from Cooper and me, Jack lifts his head. "Besides, someone needs to stay in the car to be the getaway driver in case you do grab it."

I bolt forward again. "But you don't know how to drive."

He huffs. "I *know* how to drive. I just don't have a license."

Um, I've been in the car when he's practiced with my dad. That's an exceptionally generous assessment.

Cooper clenches the door handle, psyching himself up. "Okay, let's do this."

He's obviously too freaked to realize he just agreed to let Jack drive Beau's car.

Chapter Fifteen

Cooper and I walk across the nearly empty parking lot and pull open the front door. After paying our admission, we stop at the information desk, pick up some maps, and then sit on one of the lobby benches to plan our attack.

The one-story museum is laid out in a big T, with the main entrance, lobby, and gift shop at the bottom, and the two permanent exhibits anchoring either end. Smaller rotating exhibits on the art of sweet grass weaving, agricultural methods, music, and the unique Gullah language fill the spaces in between. The exhibit on Gullah medicine takes up the back corner of the African Legacy Wing, but rather than run straight there, we decide to take our time, pretending to study the whole collection, while we're really taking an inventory of all the cameras, motion detectors, and security guards instead.

"We're really going to do this, aren't we, Emmaline?" Cooper whispers as we explore the lobby. Despite the air conditioning, a bead of sweat trickles down the side of his face, and I can't help but notice how quickly his pulse throbs at his temple. If he wasn't

too young and so jaw-droppingly fit, I'd think he was on the verge
of a coronary.

"If we can find it, and it seems easy to do, then yeah. We don't
have a choice. It's the only way to save Jack."

He nods. "And it's even kind of okay to do this, right? I mean,
it was stolen from Miss Delia's family, so it's only just to give it
back. Right?" His voice cracks on that last word, so I can tell he's
grasping for some justification to make our larceny acceptable.
The whites of his eyes are tinged with pink, enhancing today's light
blue tint, and it almost breaks my heart. His nervousness rubs off
a little on me, making my gut churn, but I don't have the luxury of
giving in to fear. We need that mortar.

We head out of the lobby and down the main corridor toward
the wing labeled "The Gullah Today." The building is quiet. Aside
from the old guy at the counter, a security guard sitting on a stool
at the front door, and a teen picking her nails in the gift shop, I
don't see too many other people. Just a family with a tired mom
and four bored kids who were obviously dragged here by their
overly enthusiastic dad.

We pass the weaving exhibit, which is chock-full of antique
sweet grass baskets and hats. The two video cameras mounted to
the ceiling watch every object in the area. I guess it makes sense
because those baskets are pretty expensive, and practically every
tourist wants one.

A second security guard walks out of The Gullah Today
exhibit at the end of the hall. Judging by his scowl and gray hair,
he's much older and crankier than the guy at the door who smiled
when we first came in. Grumpy watches from the corner of his
eye as he passes us, as if he can sense we're here for more than a
little culture. Instinctively, Cooper steps toward me, right into my
personal space, as if he might be able to hide in my shadow. Don't

get me wrong, I welcome this closeness—the sensation of his taut abs pressing against my arm, the warm of his skin, even the piney scent of his deodorant melding with the musk of his panic-induced perspiration. But we've got an agenda to accomplish. So since he's clearly lost his mind, I've got to stay focused and get us back on track.

"Come on, Cooper." I grab his hand and try to ignore the tingle that rushes through my body. "You've got to focus. If you act too weird, we're going to get caught."

His eyes turn down, and his brow crinkles as he leans into my ear to whisper, "I'm trying, Emmaline." His fingers entwine with mine, clutching tightly. "But I'm not exactly used to this sort of thing." His warm breath on my neck makes my knees buckle, and I catch myself before I crash to the floor.

We leave the sea grass exhibit and head for the agricultural diorama, where my eyes skitter around the brown-skinned mannequins planting plastic rice seeds as I locate the motion detectors and cameras. Preoccupied, I don't realize Cooper is still holding my hand until my palm gets clammy. My heart jolts. I steal a quick glance at him, hoping for a smile, or some hint as to why he's picked this of all moments to return my silent—but if Jack's right, embarrassingly obvious—affection.

But one look at his fear-etched face crushes my hopes. He's so freaked out, he can't possibly notice my hand is in his. I wonder whether I should let go, act casual and pretend it never happened, or if I should cling to his sweaty hand and hold on for as long as I possibly can.

Who am I kidding? There's no way I'm letting go.

We leave the area and peek into the last exhibit on this side, which describes the recent history of St. Helena Island. There's only one camera at the front entrance, and surprisingly, none above the door at the back of the building. Hopefully the security on the other side of the museum is equally lax.

We work our way back down the corridor, past the agriculture and weaving exhibits and toward the lobby. The guards have switched positions. Now the nice young guy is on foot patrol, smiling as he passes us in the hall, and Grumpy has taken his stool at the front door. He scowls as we go by, sending a not-so-subtle warning that we'd better behave. Considering we're here to rob them, that's out of the question. Instead, I turn my lips up into a non-threatening half-grin and hope it's enough to throw him off. And I've got bigger things to think about. Along with auditing the museum's surveillance capabilities, I'm totally engrossed in the sensation of Cooper's strong hand in mine, the curve of his palm, and the rough calluses on the tender side of his fingers that are no doubt the result of heaving miles of sailing rigging. Thank goodness Jack didn't come in. His glove would definitely have alerted that cranky guard, and there's no way Jack could have resisted a snide remark about Cooper and me holding hands.

The music and language exhibits are small and equally unprotected. There's only one ceiling camera in each to guard the few artifacts and video screens that play on-demand videos of Gullah spirituals and storytelling. Rather than moving on, we hang out to get a sense of how long it takes Smiley to make his rounds. Judging from the clock on my iPod, one loop takes just under ten minutes. And so far, he's made three, nodding or winking at us each time he passes.

I'm not sure what takes that long, since it's a small building and there are hardly any people here, but after three loops, I'm fairly confident that's the pattern. This might be easier than I thought. Ten minutes should give us more than enough time to take the mortar. That is, if it's sitting in the next room, waiting for us.

The African Legacy room is next, the one with the section on Gullah medicine. This is it. With any luck, everything we need to break The Creep should be in the next room.

"You ready?" I ask.

Cooper nods and slaps on a brave face. "Yes. You?" He squeezes my hand.

We step into the African Legacy exhibit. Adrenaline shoots through my veins, making my pulse rush. The room is cordoned into several sections, each showing Africa's influence on American culture. The area at the back corner, under the Medical Arts banner, seems to glow under the fluorescent lighting. Our pace quickens as we make our way through the exhibit, hoping we might find what we've come for, the only way to save Jack.

I stop short. The entire history of hoodoo medicine is laid out among the many artifacts, photos, and placards. Normally I'd bypass this, find the mortar, and try to get out of here without getting nabbed, but after all my training with Miss Delia, I can't pull myself away. There are tons of plaster root replicas and fake floral plants and herbs, each with an accompanying description of how it was used in Africa and later in colonial South Carolina as well as how it's used in pharmaceutical drugs today. Compared to Miss Delia's enormous spell book, this is only a tiny sliver of what the root doctors who were brought to this country knew. And of course, there's a section on hoodoo magic, explaining how it's not a religion like voodoo but a unique melding of Christianity and African spirituality, which, along with root work, is used in spells and rituals to bring good luck or make people fall in love.

Whoever wrote that doesn't understand the full power of hoodoo, and isn't acquainted with The Creep.

"Emma, we've got to move on. That guard's bound to come

back soon." Cooper pulls my hand. Reluctantly, I step away, but I can't wait to tell Miss Delia how little this museum knows.

And then I see it. There, next to the side exit, at the far side of a display of early medical tools and equipment, is a huge stone mortar. It's nearly two feet tall, and although its outer surface is rough and dark and covered with deep cracks, its insides are smooth and almost slick from ages of near-constant grinding. The mortar's wide, flat lip contains crude etchings of scrolling, rounded symbols that look African. Just as Miss Delia described, the symbol for harmony, a sun over a crescent, is next to what looks like an upside-down eye, the symbol for the universe.

Cooper releases my hand and nudges me with his elbow. "That's it, isn't it?"

"It has to be," I whisper back, sad to lose his hand but grateful for the cool air on my palm. As much as I enjoyed it, that clammy feeling was getting to be kind of gross. "Now we've just got to figure out if we can grab it and get out of here." I wipe my damp hand against my shorts.

The most obvious obstacle is the Plexiglas barrier that separates us from the artifacts. It shouldn't be much of a problem, since it's only three feet tall, and the mortar is within arm's reach of the railing. We should be able to lean over and grab it as long as Smiley's in another part of the building. But there could be other pitfalls.

Glancing around, I check for motion detectors but don't see any. As far as I can tell, the mortar isn't bolted down to the pedestal it's sitting on. This might just work. Hope swells in my chest, and tension drains from my jaw and shoulders.

A quick scan of the ceiling reveals one surveillance camera at the main entrance, just like the other exhibits, and another at the side emergency exit door beside the medical display. We can easily avoid the front camera, but we're smack in front of the second. I can't let one camera stop us, especially with the mortar so close. We've come too far, and Jack's getting worse by the day. Biting my lip, I survey the room, silently asking my spirit guide for help, figuring this is as good a time as any. Who knows, maybe she'll answer. I just hope I know how to listen.

Suddenly I realize there's no red plastic warning sign attached to the push bar on the metal emergency exit door. Is it possible it's not alarmed? That would make this infinitely easier.

A plan springs to mind: we'll grab the mortar, cling close to the wall, and stay behind the camera's field of view, then bolt out the door and run to the waiting car, praying no one sees us. Granted, Cooper's not tiny, so it might be difficult to remain unseen, but by the time anyone catches on, we should be long gone.

Feeling almost confident, I step closer to Cooper. "I'm pretty sure that door doesn't have an alarm, and I'm thinking we can grab the mortar and run."

He nods, seeming more secure than before. He's not sweating anymore and appears to have control over his jitters. "That's what I was thinking, but what if the railing has some sort of internal pressure detector or something? I'm going to have to lean against it to get at that thing, and I'd hate to set off some kind of siren. I bet I can outrun that skinny guard, but the old one is kind of scary. You never know what he might do to us."

A tiny note of dread pings in my stomach. I hadn't even considered whether the railing was rigged. That's why we need each other. I sigh. "You're right. We've got to test it."

At that moment, the four kids from before charge into the exhibit, whirling around like little Tasmanian devils, dodging behind display cases, and pretending to blast each other with imaginary finger-guns. They've outrun their parents and created their own indoor shooting gallery. And the perfect distraction to test the railing. If we do set off any alarms, we can always blame the wild ones when the security guards come running. Sure, it's not very nice, but neither are those bratty kids.

Cooper smiles and waggles his eyebrows, letting me know he's got the same idea. Pressing his hip lightly into the banister, he waits to see if there's any reaction. Nothing happens. No bells or high-pitched wails blare through the hall.

Two of the boys tackle each other and fall into a heap on the ground. They wrestle, rolling on the burnt-orange industrial carpet, and come dangerously close to knocking into one of the displays. The girls are bobbing around the installations, playing laser tag without the lasers. Normally I'd put my babysitting skills to work and intercede in this mess, but this is the best break we've gotten all day.

Cooper leans even harder into the railing, eventually pressing his entire weight against the Plexiglas, and extends his fingers toward the mortar. The hellions' mother and father rush into the exhibit hall, yelling their kids' names. The mother screams when she sees the boys spinning on the floor, crashing against a glass case of decorative gourds. Their father, the history buff, snatches both boys by the back of their shirts and strains to yank them apart and up off the floor.

Cooper's fingers extend, stretching toward our prize. He's *this* close to grasping the mortar when both security guards bound into the African Legacy room. Smiley runs right to the kids, doing whatever he can to contain them in his friendly way. Cooper pulls back, away from the mortar, but he's still leaning into the railing, his arms slightly outstretched.

"Hey!" Grumpy's bark booms across the exhibit. "What are you two up to?" If the shivers crawling up the back of my scalp are any indication, his cold glare is boring into us.

My heart pounds. Panicked, I stare up at Cooper and try to think up a reasonable excuse for the security guard. Before I can think, Cooper's lips are locked on mine.

Chapter Sixteen

What the heck is he doing? My lids pop, searching his face for some explanation, but his long, soft lashes are sealed. Before I can react, he wraps his arms around my waist and pulls me close, leaning in. My heart trips, then takes off at a gallop. Fireworks explode in my brain and body, short-circuiting my senses and shooting tingles over my skin. His bottom lip is soft and yielding, plumper than I ever imagined. Grumpy bellows again, but it hardly registers. My brain is so preoccupied with Cooper's warm breath and his amazing velvety lip that Grumpy's words sound mashed and distorted like the teacher in a Snoopy cartoon.

I've dreamed of this for more than a year, imagined where we'd be, what I'd be wearing, how it would happen. This is so *not* how it went down in my mind. We were supposed to be on the beach, in the moonlight, and I was supposed to be wearing an effortlessly gorgeous sundress, my sandals dangling from my fingers as we walked hand in hand in our bare feet. But I'm in a museum, on the cusp of committing what's probably a major felony, and I'm pretty sure my deodorant isn't as fresh as it was before we sat in a roasting car.

A war wages in my brain over what was supposed to be and what is. One half of me wants to pull away, change the setting, and get a do-over, while the other wants to smack that first half, relax, and enjoy this unexpected but definitely squeal-worthy development. I inhale all that's Cooper—his crisp, clean cotton shirt, that pine-scented deodorant, even the salty tinge of his skin—and concede the battle as I swoon and my knees sink under his intoxicating spell. His lips part slightly, and the tip of his tongue grazes mine, jolting me with an electric charge. If this is a slice of heaven, I want to die right here.

Grumpy rushes toward us, bellowing louder as he approaches. "You two, stop! This isn't some make-out joint!"

I try to pull myself away and address the advancing threat, but I'm powerless. Finally, just as the mean old guard is about to pounce and physically separate us, Cooper breaks the kiss. Stunned, I stand there like an idiot, waiting for my heart to stop pounding as I blink at Grumpy.

Cooper clears his throat. "Sorry, sir, we couldn't help ourselves."

Grumpy glares. "I knew you two were up to something. And here I find you hiding in a dark corner, trying to get the jump on each other." He grabs us by the elbows and guides us to the front of the exhibit area. My feet move on autopilot as my brain tries to sort out what just happened between Cooper and me. Grumpy keeps jabbering. "It makes me sick what you teenagers do today." He shakes his head. "Babies having babies. Well, not on my watch. Let me tell you something: you want to play house, you do it somewhere else, on your own time. This here's a respectable place."

One of the girls kicks Smiley's shin, and he loses his grip as she squirms away and runs deeper into the exhibit. The mother gasps, and the father screams his daughter's name as they take after her, followed closely by Smiley, leaving the other three kids un-chaperoned. Free from their father's grasp, the boys battle again, and the girl chases after her sister, mother, and father.

Grumpy has no choice but to give up lecturing us and face the real menace. Granted, we were planning on stealing an artifact, but these little monsters could destroy the place. He grunts and releases our arms. "I've got to deal with these here little cretins, but I want you two out of my museum. You got that? I don't want to see y'all in here again!"

Cooper and I nod and answer at the same time, "Yes, sir." The old guard leaves us at the front of the exhibit to give Smiley some much-needed backup.

Even though we're supposed to leave, I'm still so dazed, I can't go farther than the hallway just outside the exhibit. I slump against the wall, shaking my head to regain some clarity.

Cooper laughs. "That was pretty quick thinking, don't you think?" He taps his temple. "That old buzzard totally bought it. There's no way he knows what we were trying to do." His smile's a mile wide as he nudges my arm.

My chest sinks. Of course, it was only a trick. A little ruse to throw off the guard. I should have known. There's no way Cooper would kiss me for real. That would be too much to hope for. And so is my fantasy about the beach and the moonlight and the stupid sandals.

The little wishful-thinking voice niggles at the back of my brain, reminding me how well we fit together when we were kissing. Like he was comfortable with me in his arms. Like he actually enjoyed it. But that voice is as dumb as I was a few minutes ago. The kiss was all for show. And now I'm mortified for thinking otherwise. My stomach lurches, and I'm sure I'll throw up on the industrial-grade carpet. How could I be so incredibly brain dead?

"Emmaline, it's all right. He didn't catch us." Cooper leans down and gently grasps my arms. "Are you okay?" He strokes my jaw with the back of his hand.

Jeez, is he trying to kill me? I suddenly realize I'm hyperventilating. If I don't snap out of it, I'll faint and end up splayed on the floor. So I shake it off quick, because really, how much more humiliation can I take?

I nod and will my chest to stop heaving. "Yeah, I'm fine. Just a little scared, that's all. That guy was pretty fierce." Forcing a brave face, I try to sound convincing when I add, "Seriously, that was really smart of you. Faking all that, back there, with the kissing thing." I jab my thumb toward the exhibit and state the obvious as if he might have forgotten what happened. "Maybe you should give up sailing and join the drama club or something, because you're an awesome actor." I purse my lips to keep them from trembling. Excellent way to play it cool, Emma.

The guards have finally corralled the kids and their inept parents. Saving me from Cooper's reaction to my "compliment," the entire pack approaches on its way to the front entrance. Panicked, I search for a place to hide. The hallway is bare, but the women's room is just steps away. I grab Cooper's arm, drag him through the bathroom door, and run right for the roomy handicapped stall.

Cooper's eyes fill with panic as I latch the door behind us. "What if that guy finds us in here? He'll kill us."

I shake my head. "He won't come in. Judging from his sermon back there, he is obviously too prim and proper to come into the women's room, much less break down a stall door. We're safe."

"Okay, I'm confused. What are we going to do?" Cooper shrugs. "Are we staying in here all day? Because that guy wanted us out of here by now."

I set my hands on my hips. "I'm not leaving without that mortar. It's right there. We've got to take it."

He scratches his head. "But as soon as we step out of this room, he'll catch us and toss us out. Next time we won't have another bunch of brats to hide behind."

I sigh and clunk my head against the cold yellow tile wall. We need a plan.

Then I remember Miss Delia's *Semi-Invisibility Powder* and *Law Keep Away* potion. Duh. They've been hanging around my neck, tucked under my peasant blouse the whole time. How could I have forgotten them? I notice Cooper's not wearing his.

"Where are those *gris-gris* bags I gave you when we left Miss Delia's?" I tug my own out from under my shirt.

"They're in my pocket. Why?" He pulls them out of his khaki shorts.

"Because they might be just what we need. See this one?" I slip the white pouch filled with crushed sea spirit seaweed off my neck. "It's supposed to make us semi-invisible." He hitches his brow in disbelief, but I wave it off. "Okay, I realize it sounds crazy, but based on everything we've already seen, I don't think we're in the position to doubt Miss Delia. I mean, if Jack can walk around with a bony hand that still moves, then I'm pretty sure anything's possible."

Cooper nods, but his crinkled forehead tells me he's not entirely convinced. "Okay, how's it supposed to work, because judging from before, it didn't. There's no way we were semi-invisible to that guard. He gave us the hairy eyeball the first time he laid eyes on us."

I open the pouch and dump some in my hand. A few grains spill onto the stall floor. "Miss Delia said you have to walk real slow and drop the powder as you go."

He stares at me for a second. "Uh-huh. And what are the other bags for? X-ray vision and shooting spiderwebs from our wrists?"

I frown, disappointment with his unusual Jack-like response squeezing my stomach, and shake my head. "No, the yellow one is for courage and bravery, and the blue one is for keeping the law away."

Cooper snorts. "Right, because it worked so well with those guards."

Maybe I'm still mad about the fake kiss, but his pessimism is really getting to me. Okay, there's nothing *maybe* about it. A burst of stress, fear, and anger explodes in my brain. I set my hands on my hips and cock my head. "Listen, it's the best we've got. Either we stay locked in this stall forever, or we give it a try. So unless you've got a better idea, decide which it's going to be."

His jaw drops, probably because he's not used to Angry Emma. Too bad. "Uh, I guess we'll try."

"Good. Loosen the top of your blue pouch. Maybe the *Law Keep Away* potion needs to breathe a little in the air." Cooper drapes all three *gris-gris* bags around his neck. The yellow one lies on top of the others, and I can't resist a tiny dig. "While you're at it, open the yellow one, too. You could use some bravery and courage so you don't freak out like before." His expression slips, and his eyes soften as he nods and tugs at the drawstrings. Dang, now I feel bad, which is totally unfair considering I'm the one with the crushed heart.

I pick at the blue pouch around my neck, trying to loosen the knot, but it's difficult because my hand's still filled with the *Semi-Invisibility Powder*. Cooper notices my struggle and steps closer, taking the bag from my fingers. His lips curve into that sweet, gentle smile of his as he gazes at me through his crazy-long eyelashes. "Here, let me help you."

My heart skips a beat, softening my resolve. To be fair, I don't really have a right to be angry with him, anyway. It's not like I confessed my undying love to him—how embarrassing would that be?—so, he couldn't possibly have known how much planting that kiss would hurt. And he was just trying to distract the guard and save us.

Tapped out of reasons to stay mad, I sigh, and the last residue of my resentment melts away. "Thanks," I murmur and offer an apologetic half-grin.

His pale blue eyes brighten. "No problem." He pauses for a moment, gazing at me as if he might say something else, but then shakes his head and tips the seaweed powder into his palm. "You ready to do this?"

Forcing myself not to wonder what he was thinking, I nod. "As ready as I can be."

We exit the handicapped stall and walk to the bathroom door, cracking it open just enough to peek into the hallway. Neither guard is in sight, so we slip out, walking slowly and trailing a thin line of powder as we go. My heart thuds in my chest. As much as I believe in Miss Delia's magic, it's hard to accept this powder's going to make us almost invisible. Maybe it'll conceal us from living, breathing humans, but what about all the cameras mounted everywhere? There's no way we can hide from the video. Our only hope is that no one's watching the monitors until we're gone.

My mouth goes dry as we plod down the hall and into the African Legacy exhibit. With each careful step, the powder slips from my hand in a steady stream onto the museum rug. After what seems like forever, we finally make it to the back corner. I don't know if we're semi-invisible or not, but we're alone and apparently undetected by either guard. The mortar is right where we left it, waiting to be plucked and brought home with us. It's now or never.

Cooper pokes me in the ribs with his elbow, breaking my concentration. "Emma, take a look at that." He nods toward a display of ancient tools laid out just to the left of the mortar. "Doesn't that seem familiar?"

I lean closer to see what he's talking about. Amid the rough-hewn spoons, measuring scoops, tweezers, and a few other medieval-looking things I can't imagine how to use is a knife with an ornately carved handle. But it's not your average vegetable-chopping blade. It looks an awful lot like a dagger. The knife's grip is embossed with the same familiar scrolls, swirls, and flower reliefs that adorned the treasure box we found in the tabby ruins. The one that gave Jack The Creep. My stomach clenches. I peer even closer and see that some of the scrolls aren't just decorations—they form the initials BBR.

I gasp. "Cooper, look at these letters." I point to the rounded engraving that runs down the handle. "I think this belonged to Bloody Bill Ransom."

He leans over my shoulder. "You're right. But how did it get in here with all this stuff? And what does it have to do with hoodoo medicine?"

I shake my head. "I have no idea. But there has to be some connection." I stand there for a moment, transfixed, forgetting the ancestors' mortar. My right palm tingles, then itches. I reach over with my seaweed-filled left hand to scratch it, but the itching only intensifies. An irresistible urge takes over, willing me to reach out and snatch the dagger. But I try to ignore it because one theft is enough for today.

"We should take it," Cooper whispers, prodding me toward further criminality. My eyes widen with disbelief that he'd want to take anything besides what we absolutely know we need. He shrugs. "Listen, if it was Bloody Bill's, it could be connected with The Creep. Maybe Miss Delia can use it to cure Jack."

The itching increases, progressing well past an uncomfortable or even irritating sensation. Now it burns, and as crazy as it sounds, the polished knife handle seems like the only thing that will cool it. Even though the grip is covered with designs, my gut insists it will feel smooth against my flaming skin. I want the knife. I need it.

Biting my lower lip, I extend my shaking red hand over the Plexiglas barrier. A cooling tingle flows down my fingers, prodding me forward, assuring me that everything will be better once I have the knife in my grasp. Inches away, my hand lurches as if out of my control and scoops it up. The burning ceases, replaced by a tranquil wave that floods over my body. Even though we didn't plan it, I'm sure this was the right thing to do. I tuck the knife deep into my messenger bag, hoping I just figured out how to listen to my spirit guide. Although she could have been a little more subtle.

With the knife in my bag and my single-minded focus satisfied, I suddenly remember the mortar and the reason we're here in the first place. Stepping away from the medical instruments, I point to the mortar. "Okay, now it's your turn. But don't get any ideas about taking anything else. I'd like to limit our criminal charges if possible."

Cooper empties his palm of the remaining *Semi-Invisibility Powder*. He leans over the Plexiglas barrier, grabs hold of the mortar's lip, and strains to lift it off the pedestal. It tips slightly but then falls back with a clunk. "That thing weighs a ton. I'm not sure if I can lift it."

The space between my eyes pinches. "You have to. This is our only chance. Just get it over the barrier, and I'll help you from there."

He rakes his fingers through his golden-brown hair and sighs.

"All right, I'll try." He leans over the railing once more, his *gris-gris* bags dangling, and grips the mortar at its base this time. He struggles to lift it. His shoulders broaden, and his arms tense, accentuating his thick forearms and round biceps as his face flushes like a cherry with the effort. With a grunt, he manages to lift the mortar off its stand and draws it toward us. His arms shake under the weight. Tiny blood vessels rise under his skin at his temples. The mortar inches closer, nearly reaching my extended hands when Cooper loses his grip and it knocks against the barrier. I lunge forward, adding my comparatively feeble strength to his, and together we lift the mortar enough to rest it on the barrier's edge.

"Holy crap, you weren't kidding. This thing is heavy." I keep a firm grasp on the mortar to keep it from tipping off the banister.

Cooper's chest heaves. "I'm pretty sure it's solid granite. This isn't going to be easy."

"I can help you carry it from here. That should make it a lot easier."

His lungs have calmed, and his face has returned to its normal shade. He shakes his head. "No, it'll be too clumsy. I'll carry it on my own." He nods toward the side exit door, the one we're gambling doesn't have an alarm. "You just be ready at the door."

I nod and wait for him to lift the mortar again. A moment later, he inhales deeply and yanks it toward him, resting it against his abdomen. He takes a few slow steps and groans, then braces himself and moves toward the door. I stand at the exit, my hand poised on the push bar, waiting until the very last second to open it. If there is an alarm, we don't want to risk it going off until we're able to run. Cooper ambles close. Two steps, and he's near enough to tap the door with his foot. He nods, giving me the signal to push it open.

My heart races as my hand connects with the cold steel, and I push it open into the bright afternoon sun. I burst outside and hold the door for Cooper.

The silence feels strange. No alarms, no screaming guards, no police waiting to catch us red-handed. It's almost too easy. But this is exactly what we hoped for, so I'm not going to second-guess it. Miss Delia's hoodoo magic must be working.

Cooper shuffles through the doorway with the mortar, the muscles in his arms on the brink of bursting. The door shuts, and I search for Jack, anxious to get into the car and away from here as fast as possible. But my stomach drops when I remember he's parked at the front of the building. There's no way Cooper can carry this to the car. First, it's way too heavy, and second, we can't risk being seen by the guards. I dig into my bag, carefully avoiding the sharp knife's blade, and fish out my cell phone, pushing the speed dial to ask Jack for a pickup.

A familiar low growl rumbles from the woods behind the museum, which is more than a football field away, shooting chills up my spine. This time the growl is heavier, thicker and deeper. I swallow hard. Cooper's gaze whips to the tree line. Despite the fact that his face is red from the weight of the mortar, he somehow manages to look ashen.

"We can't just wait here." Cooper's voice is tight and strained as he hitches the mortar higher on his hips.

"Emma?" Jack calls through the phone. "It's about time. Do you realize how hot it is out here? Where are you guys?"

The growling intensifies. Two giant black dogs emerge from between the slash pines. Like identical twins, each has the same long, glossy fur and eyes that gleam with fluorescent yellow light. As if programmed, they bare their jagged teeth at the same time, curling their lips and snarling as gooey white froth drips from their mouths. I lift the shaking phone to my ear. "We need you, Jack," I whisper. "Around the side of the building. *Now.*"

He huffs. "Do you have the mortar? Because I don't care whether you think it's safe or not. You better get back in there and get it. While you two were playing tourist, that strip of skin exploded all over me and burned through my shorts. You're lucky I managed to keep it off the leather, because Beau—"

"Jack!" I interrupt his monologue. "Get your butt over here *now*!"

"You didn't answer me. Do you have—"

"Now!" I yell and hang up.

The gigantic demon dogs stalk in unison, approaching the edge of the parking lot.

How could Jack not hear the panic in my voice? I jam the phone into my bag and turn to Cooper, who's braced against the museum's exterior wall, trembling under the weight of the granite mortar.

A car engine starts in the distance, and a moment later, the dogs snarl in eerie harmony, their deep, ferocious voices melding in gravelly resonance. Their yowling boomerangs across the nearly empty parking lot, bouncing off the building wall, and echoing through the still summer air. They crouch low, their eyes narrowing into electric slits. Like spring-loaded fiends, they quiver, waiting to pounce.

"Emma, they're coming," Cooper's voice shakes. His eyes skitter around, frantic, searching for Jack and the car. Tires screech somewhere on the other side of the building.

Where is Jack? He should be here by now. But then I remember he doesn't know what he's doing behind the wheel of my dad's truck, much less a car he's never driven before.

The dogs lurch forward in a full gallop, pounding the ground as they charge toward us.

Chapter Seventeen

I reel and collide against Cooper and the outside wall. We're trapped. My pulse pounds. The woods aren't an option—there's no telling how many other psycho dogs are in there, waiting to pounce—and we can't run to the front of the building where we'd get caught with the mortar. We're stuck, and we're about to be eaten.

The station wagon hurtles around the back of the museum, careening straight at us. Jack went to the wrong side of the building. My mind screams *hurry, hurry, hurry*!

The dog-beasts close in, gaining yards with each tremendous stride of their enormous legs. Their massive jaws snap open and shut, exposing their sharp teeth in a terrifying demonstration of what they'll do when they get here.

Speeding toward us, the station wagon swerves at the last moment, wedging itself between the demons and us. The brakes squeal, and Jack stretches toward the open passenger window. "Get in!" His eyes are wide with fright.

I yank the back door open and whirl out of the way so Cooper can heave the mortar across the backseat. It bounces once against the far cushion, then ricochets off the opposite door. I dive in after it. Cooper follows close behind, his heaving chest smashing into me, as he throws out his arm and slams the door.

The dogs howl and launch their gigantic bodies against the back half of the car. The station wagon rocks under their weight.

"Drive, Jack!" I yell, scrambling to right myself, but I'm sandwiched between the stone mortar and Cooper's almost equally hard abs. But Jack doesn't take his foot off the brake or step on the gas. Instead, his mouth is agape, frozen.

Vicious barking assaults the air with staccato bursts of bloodthirsty hate. Intent on tearing us apart, and undeterred by the closed car door, the dogs stand on their hind legs and furiously claw at the back windows. I cringe and scream as thick white foam spews from their colossal mouths, caking the glass and their dirty paws. Up close, their strange yellow eyes are even more frightening. Although they crackle with energy and promise a deadly electric charge, they're hollow and expressionless. Dead.

Cooper reaches forward and slaps Jack's shoulder. "Go!"

At the same moment, one of the dogs slides toward the open driver's-side window. Its sharp nails breech the cabin and just miss scraping Jack's face. Jolted out of his paralysis, he screams and punches the accelerator. The car jerks forward, and Cooper and I slam against the backseat. Jack's hands quake as he steers, turning the wheel too far to the left and carves a doughnut hole in the parking lot blacktop. The dogs snarl and lunge as we loop around.

"Cut it straight!" Cooper cries. For once, Jack obeys without hesitation, fishtailing as he speeds toward the exit and skids into the turn onto Sea Island Parkway.

The dogs give chase, but we're going so fast, we leave them in our dust. In the distance, two uniformed figures round the corner from the front of the museum and stop short where Cooper and I were standing just a few moments ago. But we're long gone, and so are the dogs, and that's all that matters. With a shuddering sigh, I slump into the seat, my arm wedged against Cooper's. My heart's racing, and for once, it's not because of him. After stealing the knife and mortar and escaping those hellhounds, we're lucky to be alive. I shut my eyes and try not to imagine all the things that could have happened.

Cooper grabs my hand. "We did it, Emmaline!" His voice is bright as he stares for a second, then squeezes me in a tight hug.

Uh, okay. Since I don't get many chances, I'm not about to miss this one. I wrap my arms around his broad back and embrace him, nuzzling against his neck. He grasps me tight, overloading my brain with ecstasy. A long moment later, he pulls back and flashes that amazing, blissful, gorgeous smile of his. I'm not sure if he's proud of our larceny or if he's just happy we eluded jail or death. Either way, I have to agree with him.

I nod and find myself slipping into one of those huge, apple-cheeked grins, too. "Yeah, we did. And we didn't get eaten." I laugh.

Jack stares at us in the rearview mirror. "What the heck happened? And what were those things? They could have killed us." The car swerves sharply to the right, onto the thin shoulder on the side of the road.

"Hey, pay attention!" Cooper yells, then sinks back into the seat when Jack rights his steering. Cooper's still got a firm grip on my hand, which is, of course, all right with me. "They're the psycho dogs we tried to tell you about."

I lean forward enough for Jack to hear, but not so far that I'll risk losing Cooper's grasp. "Yeah, remember the day we tried to break the curse but couldn't, and Miss Delia collapsed, but you didn't care why? Well, that day there was only one of those disgusting creatures. Today he brought a buddy. Aren't we lucky?"

Jack gulps and clenches the wheel. "And Miss Delia thinks the mortar will get rid of them?" His speech is slow and methodical as he concentrates on the road ahead.

"Something like that." I settle back into the seat, jammed gloriously close to Cooper because the giant mortar takes up most of the seat next to me.

Cooper laughs. "You should have seen it, bro. Just as we were about to take the mortar in the museum, a pack of kids started tearing up the place, and two guards rolled in, so we had to create a diversion to fool them. And then we hid in the bathroom, and Miss Delia's magic powder kept the law away and made us semi-invisible so we could steal the mortar."

Jack hitches his eyebrow and glances into the rear mirror. "What kind of a distraction?" Of all the things Cooper just ticked off (hello—we were *invisible*!), he's got to zero in on the distraction, the one thing I don't want him to know. Curse our freaky twin sense.

The station wagon swerves again, this time into the opposite lane. Jack yanks the wheel hard with his gloved hand, turning back to the right. But he overcorrects and tosses us straight through our lane, past the shoulder, and off the road. He slams on the brakes, and the car lurches to a halt on the grass at the edge of the woods. My heart pounds in my chest. Thank goodness this "highway" really isn't, and we're the only ones on the road. If there had been any oncoming cars, we'd have been toast.

Cooper lunges forward, letting go of my hand. "Jeez, bro. Watch what you're doing. You could've gotten us killed! Not to mention if you wrecked my dad's car doing it, he'd kill us again."

Jack *thunks* his head against the wheel as the engine idles.

"I'm doing the best I can. In case you haven't noticed, I've only got one good hand. And I haven't seen Maggie in days. Why hasn't she visited?" His voice breaks, and his chest heaves silent sobs. A minute later, he lifts his head, sucks up the snot dripping from his nose, and wipes the tears from his eyes. "Look at me. I'm a frigging mess." He laughs, sounding more embarrassed than amused. "If you don't like my driving, you can do it yourself."

Cooper sighs. "I would, but after carrying that rock, I can barely move my arms. They feel like Jell-O, or maybe stretched-out spaghetti. I'm sorry, but there's no way I can steer." He slips his hand back into mine and rubs the edge of my thumb.

Um, what's going on? Don't get me wrong, I don't mind all the hand-holding, but this doesn't make sense. We're clear of the museum, so there's no reason to keep up the charade. Plus it isn't like Cooper not to help Jack when he's down. Or to let him keep driving Beau's car.

But the selfish part of me, the one that's dreamed of Cooper's affection for an entire year, refuses to ask the questions looping through my brain out loud. For now, I'll enjoy this moment and keep quiet.

Jack grinds his teeth. "Fine. I'll drive, but keep your criticism to yourself."

Cooper chuckles. "So long as you keep your mouth shut and your eyes on the road."

• • •

We drive straight to Miss Delia's. Normally we park the car on the side road, just outside of the dirt lane leading to her house, and walk the rest of the way. But not today. There's no way Cooper can carry the mortar by himself. My puny arms aren't much help, and since Jack's bony hand is missing its muscle, he's useless, too. Plus we can't risk a stroll through the forest in case those maniacal dogs show up again. We're driving. And praying we don't wreck the suspension.

Jack does a fairly decent job steering the car through the minefield that leads to Miss Delia's house. He only hit three holes, which is really not his fault because they were camouflaged by some serious overgrowth. For the most part, the car's intact, although after all the monster dog drool, dirt, and plant material, it needs a total wash down. I've got to admit, this excursion has sharpened Jack's driving skills way more than our trips to abandoned parking lots with Dad. Maybe it's the fear of getting caught driving without a license, or the life-threatening demon ditching, but after today, I'd say he's graduated to almost-menace on the road.

We park the car next to Miss Delia's bottle tree. Cooper and I roll the mortar across the backseat toward the open door. With a grunt, Cooper scoops it into his arms and wobbles across her lawn and through the herb garden, while Jack and I run ahead to alert Miss Delia. She opens her door just as Cooper climbs her steps.

Her hands fly up in excitement. "My mortar!" She's so happy, I'm afraid she might try to jump for joy. "Bring it straight to the kitchen." She steps aside to let Cooper through. Jack goes to follow, but she puts a gnarled finger on his chest and stops him. "I'm sorry, son, but I can't let you bring that curse in here. You'll have to go sit under the bottle tree."

Jack's face flashes with apprehension. He's probably just as worried as I am about more devil dogs showing up. Out here, on her lawn, he'd be a sitting duck just waiting to be gobbled up. But she must sense his concern because she waves him off. "Pshaw, ain't nothing going to happen to you under that tree."

"Uh, if you say so." He nervously eyes the enormous oak.

"I do." Miss Delia's face softens. "I know it hurts, but it's for the best. If we're going to cure you, my home needs to stay purified. Now I know those bottles don't seem like much, but they'll help soak up some of that evil in your hand."

"O-okay." Jack turns to leave.

"Hold up. Let me see it while you're here." She points to his glove. Without a word, he slowly pulls it off, revealing the newly exposed area at his wrist and the bare bones in his palm and fingers. And, of course, the rancid scent of his rotting flesh. She winces. "This is truly an ugly curse." She reaches out and touches the tip of his index finger. "And now it's drying." Shaking her head, she sucks her teeth. "We are running out of time to make you whole."

Jack's brow creases. "What do you mean?" He grips the top of his phalanges with this good hand.

She cocks her head as if she's surprised he doesn't already know. "The bone will dry and turn to dust, then blow away in the wind. When that happens, it'll be too late to repair, even if we do break the curse. If you're lucky, you'll keep these fingers, but you'll likely be left with a stump or two. Haven't you heard the prayer, ashes to ashes, dust to dust? It's what the preachers say when your soul has departed your body and moved on to the Great Eternal. That's exactly what The Creep means to do."

He staggers back, and I grasp his shoulder. "Don't worry, Jack. We won't let that happen."

Cooper returns from the kitchen, wringing his hands. "I set it on your island counter. I hope that's okay, because I don't think I can lift it again." He notices the sick expression on Jack's face. "You okay, bro?" Jack nods, then shakes his head. Tears well in the corner of his eyes as he jams his hand back into the glove.

Miss Delia pats Jack's other shoulder. "He's just adjusting to a revelation. One he won't have to worry about if that mortar does its job. But you'd better sit with him under the bottle tree. It'll make him feel better." Cooper gulps. "What's got you boys so spooked? I thought you were big and tough." She laughs.

Cooper shrugs. "Well, it just feels so, I don't know, out in the open."

Miss Delia sets her hands on her hips. "Do you think I'd put you in harm's way?"

"No, ma'am."

"Of course not. I've worked charms all over this property."

As much as I trust Miss Delia and her spells, I'm sort of with Cooper on this one. We've already been chased by hellhounds today; we don't need another round. Her magic should hold, but if it doesn't, the tree is just yards from the car and front porch. If another dog does show up, Cooper and Jack will see it and have plenty of time to sprint to safety.

Cooper may be thinking the same thing because his shoulders ease as he switches his gaze between Miss Delia, the tree, and his car.

Miss Delia claps her hands. "Now get on before you ruin my good mood."

Without another word, Cooper guides Jack off the porch and through the garden while Miss Delia and I make our way to the kitchen. Holding her arm to keep her steady, I figure I have to tell her about the beasts that nearly killed us. It's the only way to explain Jack's and Cooper's fear. But I try to keep the news casual so I don't upset her. Now that we're so close to breaking the curse, the last thing I want is for her to wind up back in bed, or worse. "You know, we ran into two of those devil dogs on our way over here."

She grips my hand, scanning me for signs of damage. "They didn't hurt you, did they? I didn't give you anything to fight them off."

I smile and reassure her by omitting a majority of the facts. "No, we're fine. We outran them with the car. To be honest, it was so easy to get away I debated whether to even mention it at all, but then I thought you should at least know."

She pats the back of my wrist. "Good girl, although I'm sure it wasn't as easy as you're pretending, especially with two at your heels." She takes another step toward the kitchen. "I expected another *plateye* to show up sometime, but I thought it would be here. Don't worry about your boys. Thanks to all the protection charms I've worked, the *plateyes* won't be able to get into the house. And that tree's filled with protective magic."

"That's good to know." I sigh with relief. "So is that what they're called, *plateyes*? We didn't have much time to talk about them when you were, you know, recovering." I hate to bring up that frightening week of her near-total incapacitation.

"Yes, child, that's what we Gullah call them. Sometimes they show up as a dog, other times it's a bear or even a horse. However they appear, they always mean evil. And now that they're multiplying, we know they mean business. They don't want that curse ended."

I gulp. A giant psycho dog is bad enough. I don't want to imagine how frightening a horse or a bear would be. But rather than dwell on those horrific possibilities, I choose to be positive. "Well, then they're going to be very disappointed when we break it." I force a laugh, mostly to convince myself that we will.

Pushing the swinging door open, I see the mortar in the center of the counter. It looks…at home. Miss Delia nearly sprints to the counter to inspect it. Her lips quiver as she runs her hands over its rough outer surface. "I haven't seen this since I was a little girl. I don't care how you got it." I open my mouth to explain, but she puts her hand up. "I don't want to know, Emma. All that matters is it's back where it belongs." She stares at it lovingly, then runs her arthritic finger over the crude scrolls etched into the rim. "See these markings? This one means hatred and this one divorce. But of course, to balance those energies, on the other side we've got the symbol for love here, and this one is for unity. This one means, 'the earth has weight,' which reminds us of Mother Earth's divinity. And this here is my favorite. It means, 'help me and let me help you,' a reminder of how interconnected we all are."

Now that I know what they mean, the markings are so clear. And even though the carvings are simple and uneven, they're beautiful. I reach up and touch the symbol for love. "This one's pretty special." Maybe stroking it will bring me a little luck with Cooper. Before I can prevent it, a wistful half-grin works its way up my cheek.

Miss Delia hitches her brow. "You thinking about your boy?"

There's no use lying to her. I bite my lip and remember how soft and velvety his felt on mine. My face flushes. Even though it wasn't real and was only to throw off the guard, I can't pretend it wasn't one of the best moments of my life. And then there was all that hand-holding in the museum and afterward in the car. As much as the rational side of my brain tells me to forget that, too, the hopeful side pleads to believe I might have a chance. "Yeah. Aside from getting the mortar, let's just say I've had a pretty excellent day." The smile spreads until I'm beaming like a lovesick fool.

She sucks her teeth and winks. "That *Follow Me Boy* charm works every time."

My heart stops. "What?"

"The leather pouch I gave you. It's filled with the *Follow Me Boy* spell. Guaranteed to work. Have as much fun as you can with him for now, but you'll want to toss out that *gris-gris* bag before he turns sixteen. Remember what I told you about those Beaumont men."

My hand flies up to the extra bag she gave me before the museum heist. The special one she mixed for me alone and said would give me a little of what I want. I figured she meant the mortar, not Cooper. So all his extra attention wasn't for mutual support, or even because he kinda, sorta, might possibly like me. It was because she bewitched him with hoodoo magic.

I've loved Cooper for more than a year, but I don't want him this way. I want him to like me for who I am: the awkward art freak who listens to indie emo music and sketches in the woods, and who knows enough about plants to become a hoodoo apprentice to save my brother from a vicious curse, but who wouldn't think about using magic for anything else, especially not to manipulate someone into loving me.

I suddenly feel sick. Lifting the leather bag off my head, I toss it on the counter. "I understand why you did it, but no thanks."

Miss Delia's face turns down. "Oh, sugar, you don't understand—"

But I cut her off because I don't want to prolong this humiliation. "Forget it. Really, it's fine. I don't want to talk about it." I look down at my feet and see my messenger bag lying on the floor next to the counter. Amid all the super fantastic news about Jack's fingers drying up and turning to dust and my ill-fated and secret love charm, I've completely overlooked our other stolen object, Bloody Bill's knife. "Oh, I almost forgot this." Holding my lip tight to keep it from quivering, I bend down, pull the dagger out of my bag, and hand it to Miss Delia, handle first.

Her eyebrows pinch together. "What is this?"

"Cooper saw it in the medical equipment display in the museum, but it doesn't look like any of the other Gullah tools."

She shakes her head. "It doesn't look like anything my folk would make."

"But it does look like the treasure box we found. The one that exploded and gave Jack The Creep. It was carved exactly the same as this one. And look at this." I grab the magnifying glass off the counter and hold it over the handle, then run my fingers over the etching. "This isn't just a design. It says BBR, which are the initials for Bloody Bill Ransom, the pirate who wrote the letter we found in the bottle. We figured you might know what to do with it. And since we were already stealing the mortar, we kind of figured one more crime wouldn't matter. Much."

She closes her eyes and rubs the handle. "This knife has great energy in it." She takes a deep breath. "If it did belong to your pirate, it could give us important information about how The Creep was cast and how to break it."

My forehead crinkles. "How's a knife supposed to tell us anything?"

Her eyes gleam. "Would you like to see into the past?"

Chapter Eighteen

"We'll be working a *Psychic Vision* charm." Miss Delia settles into her stool, as pleased as a kid at a carnival with a giant wad of cotton candy. "But first we need to purify this knife. If it did belong to your pirate, there's no telling how much of his taint could be left on it, even after all this time." She pours some citronella on it, then instructs me to gather a list of ingredients, which I pile on the counter next to the dagger.

"I haven't seen a *Psychic Vision* performed since I was a girl. My gran cast it before they stole her mortar." She hands me the purifying oil to cleanse myself. "Make sure you use plenty of this. After casting those spells this morning, you're likely to be extra tired when we're through."

Oh. Good to know. Dabbing some of the oil on my wrists and neck, I scan the assembled crocks and wonder what the heck she's talking about. Granted, there are a few ingredients I've never heard of, much less used before, but for the most part, they're ordinary roots and herbs, not a time machine. "Um, I think I'm missing something. How are these things supposed to help us see into the past?" The teapot on the stove squeals as it comes to a boil. I lift it off the burner and shut off the gas.

Miss Delia spoons dried herbs into two small pieces of cheesecloth. "Each of these plants has its own purpose. When mixed in the right concentration they form the perfect blend to open our minds." Her fingers shake as she works to fold the cloth into neat squares. But the thin fabric won't cooperate, so I reach over and help complete the makeshift tea bags. When they're done, she hands them to me and points to the mugs I've already placed on the counter. I drop the bags in and add steaming water to steep her psychic tea. She gazes at the mortar and strokes its stony surface. "But no matter how open we are, only a deep and ancient power will reveal the past. That's where this mortar comes in. It's bursting with old magic. Here, lay your palms against it. Can you feel its energy?" Her eyes crackle with excitement. Even the cloudy one.

All I feel is the mortar's cool, rough surface. I shrug, obviously missing something.

"Close your eyes and quiet your mind." Her voice is slow and soft. I quirk my brow, unsure what she means, but she prods me on. "Go on, child, it's not going to bite. You've got to learn to tap into these places in your body and soul. It's the same way you'll hear that spirit guide of yours."

Judging from how my spirit guide basically forced me to steal the knife in the museum, I'd say I hear her just fine, thank you very much. But since Miss Delia doesn't want to know the details of how we came to possess either the mortar or the knife, I decide not to get into it. Instead, I shut my eyes and think of a big black hole. A low, tingling vibration hums beneath my palms. My eyes fly open.

The mortar is a block of solid granite. I'm no geologist, but I'm pretty sure rock is not supposed to vibrate.

Miss Delia cackles. "There you go! You did it. Good girl. That's the magic I'm talking about. It's strong enough to rip those memories right out of that knife."

I drop my hands. "Wait, the knife has memories?"

She nods. "Everything has a memory, child. You just have to know how to coax it out."

"That doesn't make sense. People have memories. That knife's an inanimate object made of metal and wood."

She smiles and hitches one brow. "Yet you're both made of the same thing, aren't you? Aren't we all?"

Based on a vague memory from science class, I think Miss Delia's right, but it's still hard to believe. "Okay, so let's say the knife has memories, just like people do. How do we get them? I mean, it's not like it has a mouth to tell us what happened back then."

"That's where the root blend comes in to open the *Psychic Vision*. But there is a limit. You see, people recall what they want, from whatever happened over the course of their lives. Objects aren't the same. Their memories happen in a straight line according to how they're used. We're going to ask this knife to tell us what happened the last time it cut, and hope it had something to do with The Creep."

I sit on my stool and prop my feet on the brace near the bottom. "But what if it didn't? That was almost three hundred years ago. How do we know your ancestors didn't use it before it ended up at the museum?"

She shakes her head and glares at the dagger on the counter. "None of my kin would use that knife for hoodoo." Her voice is deep and gravelly. "It's filled with bad mojo no root doctor could miss. I don't know how it ended up where you found it, but chances are, some doctress was keeping it hidden so it wouldn't be used for evil."

A shiver runs up my spine. If it's filled with so much dark energy, why the heck are we messing around with it? "You're freaking me out. Are you sure it's safe to do this?" My voice cracks. Between The Creep and those scary *plateye* dog-monsters, I've had enough bad mojo for one summer. Actually, for my whole life.

She cackles and pats my hand. "It's just a memory, child. Something that already happened in the past. It can't hurt you."

As sure as she seems, it's not enough to calm my jitters. "But you said it's evil." I glare at the polished, carved handle and wonder if some of that bad mojo tainted any of the stuff in my bag. My sketchbook's in there, and so are my pencils and watercolors. They're my only source of true joy, and I don't want anything messing with them. "Why shouldn't we just toss it in a fire and destroy it?"

Her eyes flash with alarm, as if I might be serious, which I totally am. "Because we need the information it contains. Besides, the knife itself isn't evil. It's been used for evil. There's a difference. We're not doing this to hurt anyone. In fact, we're doing the opposite, helping your brother. It's like I told you before about the importance of balance. If our hearts were dark, this knife would help us do great harm, but since we've got love on our side, its bad energy gets canceled out. It can't harm us. Now are you ready to blend the burning incense? It'll help lift up that memory."

I steel myself for the inevitable fatigue and remind myself Miss Delia hasn't been wrong yet, so I don't have a reason to doubt her now. But still, it can't hurt to rub my *collier* for a little extra luck and protection. "Sure, why not?" The glass beads' smooth texture is reassuring.

She drops a handful of charcoal chips into the bottom of

the mortar and lights them. As soon as the flame dies down, she carefully shows me how to layer all eight ingredients. The acacia leaves and buchu go first, filling the air with soft meadow florals and warm cherry currant. The weariness sets in. My arm feels like it's made of lead as I sprinkle a little anise powder on top. As it heats, its licorice scent blends with the others and transforms the kitchen into a candy shop. My head bobs, desperate to drift off to sweet sleep. But thankfully Miss Delia adds the celery seed and dragon's blood. Their pungent peppery scents jolt me awake enough to help add the myrrh, frankincense, and mint. Combined, these roots and herbs make Miss Delia's kitchen smell like an ancient and very stinky cathedral.

A smoky gray cloud rises from the incense and floats out the back windows and over the herb garden.

Thunder rumbles in the distance, which is totally weird because the sky is a bright cobalt and nearly cloudless.

"So now what?" I yawn and wave a tendril of smoke away.

"We drink our tea and let the show begin." She waggles her brows and points to the two mugs that have cooled. "You've got to drink it all at once, no sipping. The vision should start right away."

I remove the cheesecloth tea bags and peer into the reddish-brown liquid in my cup. "Um, are you sure this isn't going to make us hallucinate? I mean, how do we know we're having a *Psychic Vision* and not tripping?"

She scoffs and rolls her eyes. "Please, child, I'd never give you any drugs like that. And it's not a hallucination if we both have the same vision." She shakes her head. "Just drink your tea."

I can't resist a sniff. For the most part it's sweet, but there's a hint of something I can't place. But Miss Delia made it, so I'm sure it's safe. Right?

*Clink*ing the side of her mug with mine, I raise a toast. "Here's to a fun hoodoo adventure!" Then, before I give myself another second to think about it, I tip the mug to my lips and let the lukewarm liquid flood my mouth. Thankfully, I'm too busy gulping to taste anything until the last swallow, when I'm struck by a two-fisted flavor punch of sour cherry and bitter spinach. Ugh, it must be the buchu and dandelion greens. I swallow hard, willing myself not to hurl.

Miss Delia finishes her tea as quickly as I do, then holds the knife over the burning incense with one hand and grabs mine with the other. I close my eyes, expecting the vision to play out in my head, but she gives me a squeeze. "You'll want to look into the smoke if you don't want to miss anything." She laughs. "And I'll need you to grab hold of this knife with me. It's heavier than I thought." She slides her fingers up the handle to make room. I wrap my hand just below hers and rest my forearm against the African symbols carved around the mortar's lip. But I don't know how she thinks I'll be able to hold it, either, since it suddenly feels like a concrete block in my tired hand. She clears her throat. "Smoke and mist reveal the past and how this object was used last. Reveal the truth about this curse, so we may find a cure to reverse."

Another clash of thunder rumbles, still far away but closer than before. The water faucet suddenly gushes at the sink, distracting my attention.

"Ignore it," she commands. "Focus on the spell."

The incense smoke thickens and condenses, creating a floating canvas for the vision. A bright light flickers in the middle of the gray haze, followed by a quick succession of images that sputter like the beginning of a movie reel. My head swoons, and I blink, training my eyes on the vision before me. That was some powerful tea.

The pictures speed up and come into focus, revealing a vast, oak-paneled bedroom warmed by candlelight. A four-poster bed sits across the room, its drapes pulled back to reveal a woman writhing in agony under the covers. A tall, slender African woman leans over her, patting her face with a wet cloth.

The image zooms closer. The woman's long, bedraggled hair hangs wet and matted over her face. She's moaning and crying. One hand reaches up to squeeze the African woman's fingers. "It's agony, Jemy. I shan't withstand this pain any longer." Her accent reveals her status as part of the English aristocracy.

"It won't be long now, Miss Lady Rose. This baby's coming." The woman with almond-colored skin tries to sound reassuring, but her strained voice reveals her concern.

Lady Rose? I peer at the woman in the white dressing gown soaked with perspiration and see her ghostly white skin, giant forehead, and freaky bug eyes. Even though she's in the middle of childbirth, the giant ruby necklace is slung around her neck, the gold leaves clawing at her chest. I gasp. It *is* Lady Rose Beaumont, the first mistress of High Point Bluff.

Lady Rose screams and doubles over onto her side. When the contraction passes, she catches her breath. "I need Sabina."

"But Miss Lady Rose, Master Edmund made us promise not to mess with her." Jemy quivers with fear.

Lady Rose pulls her scraggly hair off her face and glares, her eyes bulging more than I thought humanly possible. "How dare you speak his name!" Lady Rose screams. "You are not worthy to tend his grave. Now do as I command, and bring me Sabina!" Another contraction slams through her body, and she cries out.

Jemy cowers and takes a step back toward the door. "But Miss Lady Rose, I gave him my word on his deathbed. She's dangerous. Especially after, well, you know." She wrings her hands in worry.

Lady Rose gasps for air, tears streaming down her face. "I know I am the mistress of this plantation." Her words are stilted, grunted out as she fists the sheets in pain. "And now that my Edmund is gone, I am the only master you have left. Fetch. Me. Sabina."

Jemy nods. "Yes, ma'am." She scurries from the room.

Lady Rose weeps alone in her bed.

Finally, Jemy returns with Sabina, a small but stocky woman whose ebony face is scarred with a floral design. She's dressed in coarse, dingy white clothes, and her hair is wrapped in a turban. A stubby, dark-colored root is clenched between her crooked teeth. She smiles when Lady Rose twists in pain.

"Well, now, ma'am. Looks like you in trouble." Her accent is thick and foreign, making it harder to understand.

Lady Rose's head lolls to the side. "Please help me." It's barely a whisper through her dried, cracked lips.

Sabina snickers. "Yes, Miss Lady Rose, anything for my mistress."

Jemy grabs Sabina's arm. "Don't you hurt her, Sabina."

Sabina wrenches free from the much-taller, younger woman, then leans toward her, her eyes narrowed into menacing slits. "I know my place and don't need you to tell me how to work my healing. I've delivered nearly all the children on this plantation since I came—you included—so you best get out my way." She grinds the crushed root between her teeth and walks to the foot of Lady Rose's bed. "Now, ma'am, let me have a look at you."

Lady Rose heaves a sigh. "Oh, Sabina, I knew you could do it! I've pleaded for you for days, but they wouldn't listen to me." She turns to Jemy and blasts her with scorn. "You nearly killed me and my child. Begone. I'll deal with you later."

Jemy is stricken by panic as her body stiffens. "No, Miss Lady

Rose. You're mistaken."

Another massive contraction hits. Lady Rose clenches her bloated belly and shrieks. When it passes, she glowers at Jemy. "Get out, vermin!" Jemy bursts into tears and flees.

Sabina shuts the door, then goes to the sideboard, spits the root out onto the floor, and washes her hands in the dry sink. Then she sits on the bed next to Lady Rose. "This won't take long. Before you know it, your babe be in your arms." A wry smile inches across her lips as she reaches her hand under Lady Rose's dressing gown. Lady Rose shrieks. Sweat pours from her already-soaked head, and she's even paler than before.

"You're ready, Mistress," Sabina says. "Wait for the next squeeze, and give one good push. Then it'll all be over." She licks her lips.

Lady Rose strains with the little energy she has left. A moment later, she howls, then collapses on the bed, her chest heaving for air.

Sabina lays her hand under the newborn infant's head and wipes it with a nearby sheet. It snorts and coughs, then makes a mewing sound.

A deep, rolling laugh bubbles from Sabina's chest as she slips her hand into the pocket of her skirt. "Well done, Mistress. You have a son. Exactly as I hoped." She withdraws the dagger—the one Miss Delia's holding over the mortar right now—and grabs the infant's umbilical cord.

Lady Rose lifts her head off the pillow and manages an exhausted smile. "Thank you, Sabina." Her voice is soft and ragged. "Thank you for saving me and my child. I knew you would redeem yourself. I will never forget this."

Sabina's lips curl at the corners. She looks like a psycho killer. "I know you won't, Mistress, not after what I'm about to do." She runs the knife's blade up and down the cord but not hard enough to cut it.

Lady Rose tenses and strains to pull herself up as she eyes her newborn with grave concern. "What are you doing?"

Sabina cocks her head. "Repaying what you done to me and mine. Master Edmund got his for what he done." She quirks her brow, and a giddy laugh slips from her lips. "His dry bones up and walked around till they turned to dust. Now he hears the mighty word of the Lord. Too bad it's too late to save him."

Lady Rose shudders. "Sabina, I had no part in what happened between Edmund and those dreadful pirates. You must believe me and spare my child."

Sabina halts the knife's menacing slide along the cord. Her gaze hardens, and she jabs the shiny blade at Lady Rose. "I might have believed you, but you're wearing that blood stone. Even now. So I know you were involved." She sneers and twists the knife in the air. "You and the master think you rule over us Africans, but you don't know who I am. I am a queen in my homeland." She beats her chest with her knife-wielding fist, then points the blade at Lady Rose. "You spilled royal blood. So you must pay, too, and here's your punishment."

She scoops the baby up with her free hand, nestling him in the crook of her arm, and reaches for the cord, looping it around her fingers. "I'm not going to take this boy now. No, I'm going to let you have him for a little while. Let him grow big and strong, happy and bright till he comes of age and becomes a man. Full of potential. That's when I'll steal his soul. And when you see how corrupt he becomes, you're going to know it's because of the evil you and the master did for a red rock." The baby cries. Sabina rocks him gently and makes shushing noises. "And the best part is, this cycle's going to repeat, for his son, and his son after that, for as long as the Beaumonts live." Sabina erupts in peals of deranged laughter.

Lady Rose's eyes flash with anger. "You don't have the power."

"Don't I? The master learned different."

Lady Rose scoffs. "You claim credit for Edmund's pestilence. And though you may have convinced some of your fellow ignorant slaves, I know it was nothing more than the plague, certainly not the work of a madwoman. You are a charlatan, and I'll see you hanged before you threaten my child again." She screams, "Jemy! Cato! Jupiter! Come here at once!"

Sabina chuckles. "They'll never catch me. And even if they do, it'll be too late." She slips the blade into the umbilical cord loop. "As you took mine, I take yours and all of theirs." With a flick of her wrist, the knife severs the cord. The candle flames sputter. Sabina tosses the infant at Lady Rose, who screams and fumbles to catch him. Sabina throws the knife on the bed, reaches into her pocket and lobs a handful of powder on the mother and child, and bolts for the door. Even though the window and door are shut, a massive gust of wind whips around the room, extinguishing the candles and leaving the room in total darkness. The door opens a crack, then slams shut.

Sparks shoot up in the mortar, then suddenly cut off, stifling the incense screen and dissipating the smoke. I shake my head to clear the hazy fog that still hangs in my brain and turn to Miss Delia, who's doing the same. She releases my hand. Beyond tired, I'm drained and lose my grip on the knife, which drops on the counter with a clatter.

I'm totally confused, and it's not because of the psychic tea's lingering effects. The vision showed the knife's last cut, all right, and confirms that Edmund died from The Creep, but it certainly didn't show us how the curse was cast.

My addled brain grapples with all the information revealed in the scene, ruminating over Sabina's words.

Oh, my God. I gasp. *It can't be.*

The blood drains from my skin, and a wave of nausea crests over me. My ears ring. It's got to be my spirit guide, screaming at me, confirming what I already suspect. But I have to know I'm right and not misunderstanding. I clear my throat and force the words through my constricted throat. "What did that mean?" My voice cracks.

Miss Delia's mouth turns down. "Your boy is doomed."

Chapter Nineteen

The kitchen is suddenly scorching, filled with dense, humid air that stinks of stale incense. My mouth dries, and my tongue hangs like a piece of old shoe leather. Another wave of nausea rises. I've got to get out of here before I throw up all over Miss Delia's counter.

Despite my exhaustion, I spring off the stool, charge through the kitchen and side porch, then bolt out the screen door into the garden. Tipping over, I brace my hands against my knees. But it doesn't stop the queasy jolt of electricity that rushes over my body and dumps my lunch on a sweet lavender bush. Another, more powerful charge grips me, emptying the rest of my stomach. I catch a whiff of the mess and stumble backward to keep from dry heaving. My foot catches on something, tossing me on my butt, smack in the middle of another scratchy lavender plant.

High above, the endless crystal-blue sky looms, mocking my insignificance. I suddenly realize how vulnerable I am—outside by myself, just steps from where the *plateye* retreated after it attacked Miss Delia and me. Normally that would be enough to send me straight back into the house, but not now. It was bad enough that my brother—my *twin*—contracted the most horrific curse imaginable. But now I know that my Cooper—my sweet, adorable, kind Cooper—is destined to lose his soul in a matter of weeks. And then he'll morph into a dark-hearted, egocentric, repulsive glutton. Just like his father. The Cooper I know and love will be gone forever.

Hot, stinging tears pour from my eyes. The scrubby lavender scratches my bare skin, but I don't flinch. I'm too overwhelmed by the knowledge that the two most important people in my life are doomed. Maybe Jack's got a chance, thanks to Miss Delia and the magic mortar, but assuming we do reverse The Creep, how will we live without Cooper? He's Jack's best friend. He's my summer, the golden sunlight that warms my otherwise cold and lonely year. I won't be able to face him when he turns. And I know Jack won't accept his change. We won't be like our dad, who's taken a lifetime of Beau's crap out of a perverted sense of loyalty.

Anger boils in my gut, giving me a boost of energy to fight the hoodoo-induced fatigue. It's not fair. Jack and Cooper don't deserve this, and I don't deserve to lose them. Sure, Jack was greedy wanting the treasure, but that doesn't mean he should lose his skin and bones, and maybe even his life because of it. And Cooper shouldn't be punished for something some random ancestor did almost three hundred years ago. I sniff and wipe the goopy mixture of tears and snot from my face. There has to be something we can do. If the *Psychic Vision* was right, and Sabina really did curse the Beaumont men with black magic, then Miss Delia and I should be able to counteract it by working a white magic spell.

The thought quiets my throbbing head. I sit up straighter.

The knife is the key. It knows what happened and why Sabina cursed Cooper's family. Maybe it knows how she cursed them, too.

We need to pull another memory. I push myself off the ground and fly back to Miss Delia's kitchen with my fists clenched, determined to get the information I need and force both curses to obey my will. They're not going to steal Jack and Cooper from me.

Miss Delia starts when the back door slams behind me. "Lord, child, you scared me." She has shut off the faucet and is wearing her giant goggle glasses while poring over her spell book. "You feeling better?"

I plop down on the stool next to her and hope she doesn't smell the puke on my breath. "Yeah. Listen, we can't just let this happen to Cooper. There's got to be something we can do. I've got an idea."

She runs her gnarled finger down the page. "Shhh, I'm way ahead of you. There ought to be something in this here book that'll help us." She taps the yellowed page. "See this list of my ancestors? The very first name my great-gran could remember was Saba. I'm wondering if she's the Sabina we saw in the vision. You know, names handed down for fifteen generations are bound to get mixed up a bit. The old stories claimed Saba worked a powerful black magic revenge spell. From what I saw in that vision, Sabina was getting back at a whole bunch of people."

"She was pretty psychotic—cursing a whole family and turning people into skeletons. What could they have done to make her so angry?"

Miss Delia removes her glasses and pats my hand. "People are capable of unspeakable things. At my age, you'd think I'd have seen it all by now, but I'm still surprised by our evil." She purses her lips and shakes her snowy head. "I don't doubt Sabina had cause to do what she did. Root workers don't turn to black magic easily."

"But all we have to do is work some white magic to reverse it, right?" My voice rises with hope as the lessons from my hoodoo training fall into place.

She nods. "Yes, white magic is what we need. But it's got to be the right spell."

"So let's fire up the mortar again and pull another memory." Defying the extreme weariness that threatens to overwhelm me, I reach for some charcoal chips to create another fire.

She gently lays her hand on mine. "Not today, child."

My brow creases. "What? Why not? It knows the answers we need."

"The knife needs to rest. So does the mortar. And so do we. We've worked a bunch of charms today. It's too much."

Fury bubbles in my stomach once again. "That's ridiculous!" My voice rises, and the space between my eyes pinches. I know it's not her fault, but I'm so mad at Sabina and her stupid curses, I can't help it. "I'm sick of waiting. It's just a knife and a hunk of stone. They don't need to rest. They need to tell us how to save my brother and Cooper *now*." Forcing my eyes to stay open, I add, "And I'm fine. I'll just sleep in tomorrow."

Her brow softens in sympathy. "I know you want your answers, child. But we must wait."

"Why?" Tears sting my eyes.

She sighs. "Because even if we were both at our top strength, ripping a memory from an object is traumatic, especially if it's filled with as much anger and hatred as that one was. That knife needs time to settle and regroup, cleanse itself of all that negative energy. If we take another memory before it's ready, it's liable to break apart, and we'll never get what we need."

"Okay, then forget Cooper's curse for now. We can still use the mortar to break The Creep, can't we? That's what we brought it here for, right?" I reach for the charcoal chips.

She grasps my wrist with more vigor than I thought she had. "Emma, you're not hearing me. The mortar was disturbed by the dark energy in that vision, too. It needs to set awhile." The crinkles in her forehead smooth, but her eyes are still serious. "It's already cracked. I won't have it split apart now, not after I just got it back." She places her palms against the stony mortar, then flinches as if she's been shocked. "If you don't believe me, you can feel for yourself. It's crackling with anger. If you push it, it'll be destroyed."

My shoulders sink, and I rest my aching head in my hand. She's right, but I don't have to be happy about it. "No, I believe you."

She puts her glasses on and turns back to the spell book. "Besides, you're getting ahead of yourself. Sabina said she cast The Creep. And we know she had that knife. When it's ready, we'll sort everything out. You just need a little more patience. In the meantime, I'll work on figuring out what was in that powder Sabina tossed on that poor woman and child. Whatever it was, it was mighty powerful. Maybe I can come up with an antidote."

I pick at a crescent-shaped scorch stain on the counter with my other hand. Normally the idea of a possible antidote would perk me up, but it barely registers now. I keep replaying the vision in my head—Sabina's scarred face and the glint in her eye as she cursed an entire family for eternity. "Lady Rose was pretty surprised when Sabina threw that baby at her. Although I don't think she believed in Sabina's magic."

Miss Delia scoffs. "I'm sure she changed her mind when the babe became a man. Sabina's power was strong. He must have caused a mess of trouble." She shakes her head. "You said you knew the mother?"

"Oh, not really. I've only seen her freaky portrait in the drawing room at High Point Bluff. Believe me, those scary bug eyes and giant forehead are impossible to forget. Beau makes everyone look at it and tell him how beautiful she was."

She shakes her head and chuckles, but her laugh has a sad, pitiful ring. "We Gullah knew there was something wrong up there. Something dark and depraved. That's why none of us have set foot on that plantation since we were set free."

Something niggles at the back of my brain. "Miss Delia, how can someone live without their soul?"

She shrugs. "I don't know, child. The Gullah believe we have both a soul and a spirit. When we die, the soul moves on to heaven, but the spirit stays behind to help our loved ones who are still alive. Perhaps it's possible to live with only one of these, perhaps not. Maybe it's a mystery we're not meant to understand."

My mind races, thinking of Cooper and how he'll change. Hot tears well in my eyes once again.

She reaches out and pats my hand. "We'll see what we can do to spare your boy. Now I need some time to rest and think on this antidote. Why don't you take those young men of yours home and come back in a few days? The mortar and knife should be ready for another go 'round by then."

A few days? For real? By then the tips of Jack's fingers could be dried out, and he'll have lost more flesh. Not to mention, Cooper will be that much closer to sixteen. My shoulders sag, and my stomach churns. But it won't do me any good to argue with her. Once she's made up her mind, it's locked solid. Plus she's right about needing to rest. I'm so wiped, I bet I could sleep for a month.

I inhale and suppress the tangled knot of fury and despair that chokes my throat. "Okay. I'll see you then." A sob threatens as I slip off the stool and slink toward the swinging kitchen door. "You have my cell phone number in case you need me before then." When she was sick, I found her only phone hooked up in her bedroom.

"Uh-huh," she murmurs without lifting her eyes from the book. "Take care now."

I cross the living room and pause to regroup before opening the screen door. Jack and Cooper are sitting on the bench under the bottle tree, just as Miss Delia told them. They're laughing, elbowing each other in the ribs and chucking pebbles into the woods. Cooper must have convinced Jack we'd fix him before his bones turned to dust and floated away with the wind. As far as they're concerned, it's only a matter of time before Miss Delia and I break The Creep and set everything right.

They have no idea what she and I just saw, what we know, and how bad things are about to get. I doubt I can even find the words to explain it all. How do you tell your best friend, the unrequited love of your life, that he's about to lose his soul? And even if I do find a way to tell him, I'm not sure I can handle the aftershock. Because I know one thing for sure: Cooper would rather die than turn into his father. And to be honest, I'm not sure Jack and I could survive watching that happen, either.

As much as I wish I could, I can't hide this from him. He deserves to know the truth.

I gulp and step out onto the front porch and let the dark blue doorframe slam behind me. Forcing one foot in front of the other, I make my way down the steps and through the herb garden.

Cooper stops mid-chuckle when he sees me, and his eyes turn down. "Are you okay?" His voice is soft and caring. Someday soon it'll be callous and indifferent.

Dread oozes over me, trickling from my scalp all the way down to the tips of my toenails. I have to keep this simple and straightforward. Just stick to the facts. I can't wallow in all the gory implications. He'll figure them out on his own.

I gulp back the welling tears.

Before I can form any words, Cooper pushes off the bench and rushes to my side. "What's wrong, Emmaline?" He wraps his hand around my shoulder and rubs the top of my arm. Even though I tossed the *gris-gris* bag, he's still obviously stricken by its effects. "You look like you've been crying. Is Miss Delia all right? Did we get the wrong mortar?"

Ugh. My face is probably as puffy as a pincushion. I should have splashed it with cold water before I came out here. I've got to tell him now. I shake my head and try to force the words from my locked throat, but it's no use. They're stuck and lodged deep in my burning chest. My mind races as I grope for something to say. This is so not how I wanted this to go. I was supposed to downplay the catastrophe, not emphasize it.

Jack rolls his eyes. "Come on, Emo, knock it off and just spill it. It's obvious you haven't broken the curse yet." He lifts his gloved hand in my direction.

"I...um...well, you see..." I gnaw my bottom lip and twist away from Jack's piercing stare, only to be caught by Cooper's tender gaze. His pale aquamarine eyes are so sympathetic, so gentle, I'm not sure I can bring myself to tell him and shatter everything he thinks he knows about himself and what the future holds. How can I darken that light?

An odd, electric tingle flutters in my chest. Maybe there's a chance I won't have to. There's still time before he turns sixteen, and Miss Delia could come up with an antidote.

Maybe I'll wait to tell him when I have to. If I have to.

Chapter Twenty

I couldn't tell him. At least not the truth. Instead I chickened out and fumbled a lame excuse about working on an antidote, then blamed my freak-out on how guilty I felt for taking so long to break the curse.

I bit my tongue when Jack agreed, saying I should feel even worse for not saving him by now, but Cooper's reaction nearly killed me. He tucked me into his warm embrace, cradled my head against his broad chest, and whispered soothing, shushing noises into my ear. All I kept thinking as I inhaled his spicy freshness, was that I am the worst fraud in history. Okay, maybe that's an exaggeration. I mean, I'm not a murderer or an embezzler or anything like that. But there's no debating I'm a horrible friend who'd keep a life-changing secret just to spare herself the hurt of telling the truth.

So as penance, and since I can't stand to be near him without crumbling under the crushing weight of my epic guilt, I've exiled myself to the beach with my art supplies. If nothing else, the meditative waves of St. Helena Island Sound will give me a chance to figure out how to tell him the truth.

In the meantime, I'm having trouble with his face. I've worked this sketch three times already, ripping the thick drawing paper from the pad and tossing the crumpled ball into the fine white sand every time Cooper's features turn heavy and dark. I don't want to draw Dark Cooper, the soulless being I imagine he'll become when Sabina's curse takes hold. I want to capture the light in his eyes, his bright energy, and that loose, easy smile of his. But the charcoal pencil has a mind of its own, carving deep creases around his mouth and across his forehead, and pinching his lids in an angry glare. This is not my Cooper, and he can't stay in my sketchpad. I grab the page to tear it from the spiral binding.

"Emma Guthrie."

My heart skips, and I yelp in surprise, then twist around to see Maggie looming over me, her bright red skirt billowing in the balmy sea breeze. Her flowery scent dances around my head.

I exhale a gust of relief. "You scared the crap out of me. I didn't hear you come up." Dang, how long has she been there? Was she snooping? I flip the cover on my pad, hoping she hasn't seen this frightening version of Cooper. Because if she did, she's going to think I'm a pretty horrid artist. Which, humbly, I am not.

She laughs. "You did not hear me because I meant to surprise you." She settles herself, uninvited, on the sand next to me and smooths her crisp cotton skirt over her lap. Then she slips her leather sandals off and wiggles her bare toes. Of course, her feet are beautiful. Just like the rest of her. Sickening.

My lip curls, and an involuntary grunt leaps from my mouth. Oops, that wasn't supposed to be out loud. I scramble for the words to cover it. "It's not nice to surprise people like that. You could give them a heart attack."

"True, but it is entertaining nonetheless." She chuckles. "Besides, you are still young and have no need to worry about your mortality. At least not yet." Maybe it's just her strange Jamaican-British accent, or the formal cadence of her words, but she really sounds weird. I still haven't figured out why she always calls me by my full name. And so is everything else about her, including her bizarre attraction to my brother.

"If you're looking for Jack, he's not here. He's somewhere with Cooper. You should check our house, but they could be up at the Big House, too."

She nods. "Oh, I know where he is. I check on him regularly and have been watching your progress."

"Uh-huh. Well, then you know we haven't gotten very far."

"Nonsense. You have accomplished much in a short time. You will achieve much success with the Grannie, I am sure of it." Her smile is dazzling.

Sure, now that we've met Miss Delia and knocked off a museum, maybe we'll break The Creep before Jack's bones dry up or he loses so much flesh he collapses dead in the street. Maybe. But there's a new wrinkle that only Miss Delia and I know about. One we're not sure we can iron out in time.

My brain throbs, reasserting the headache I've had for the last two days, ever since I lied to Cooper, and we left Miss Delia's to recuperate and let the knife and mortar rest. I rub my eyes with my thumb and forefinger, then squeeze the bridge of my nose to get some temporary relief.

"What is wrong, Emma Guthrie?" Maggie's voice is soft and sympathetic.

I watch the red and yellow sparks zoom behind my closed lids. Everything is wrong. Devastatingly, earth-shatteringly, horrendously wrong. But I couldn't even tell Jack and Cooper the truth, why should I confide in her? It's none of her business.

"Everything's hunky-dory. Couldn't be better, in fact." I force a smile and hope it's enough to shut her up so she'll move on and leave me to get rid of Dark Cooper in peace.

"That is a lie." She doesn't even try to sound nice about it or turn it into a question. The ugly accusation hangs in the air, absolute and definitive. Her face is blank as she waits for me to fill the uncomfortable stillness. The only sound comes from the waves lapping at the shore and the osprey squawking overhead.

I feel like I'm locked in an interrogation room, under the relentless glare of a high-wattage spotlight. I set my jaw and stare, debating whether to tell her to go screw herself, or shove her down into the sand and run away. She hitches her brow and smiles, as if she's daring me to do one or the other, or maybe both. My fingers clench, tightening into a fist around my charcoal pencil. I know which option would make me feel better.

She clears her throat. "Why don't you try speaking the truth? Perhaps it will lead to the answers you seek."

An exaggerated sigh escapes my throat. I glare out at the rolling waves. As if she knows anything about what I'm dealing with and can offer even the slightest bit of help. I don't think so.

Her smile softens, and she nudges my arm with her elbow. "Please, Emma, I am just as interested in your success as you are. We both want the same result. Confide in me. Sometimes just talking about a problem helps reveal its solution."

I don't like being cajoled into doing anything, especially by her. I'm so angry, I'm ready to throw that punch, but something about her eyes catches me off guard. For the first time, there's a depth and genuine sincerity to her gaze that makes me believe she might actually be worried about Jack. Maybe she really does care about him. He's definitely gaga over her. Who am I to judge their relationship, as peculiar and unfounded as it may be? She's probably just scared for him, and my lying has only increased her worry.

I swallow hard. "Listen, I'm sure Jack's going to be fine." I bolster my voice with more certainty than I actually have to reassure her. "Miss Delia and I are working on it, and based on some of the...complications we've encountered"—I figure it's best not to try and explain the devil dogs—"we're getting there. So don't worry. I'm not concerned about him." It's not entirely the truth, but it's close.

She leans in. "But you are anxious about someone else." Once again, it's a statement. Can't she at least pretend this is a real conversation where we tell each other things we don't already know? Her head tilts, begging me to continue.

I stare, my lips pursed, debating whether to spill the beans. She certainly seems to care. Maybe I can confide in her, just a little bit. I don't have to go into all the gory details. Plus it's probably the only way to get her to stop staring at me.

I nod. "Yeah, I'm worried about Cooper."

She pulls back in surprise. Finally, something she didn't expect. Ha, victory is mine! Her perfect brow crinkles. "What could possibly trouble you about Cooper Beaumont?"

This is exactly what I was trying to avoid. I blow out my cheeks, wondering how far I want go with this. Normally I wouldn't expect anyone to understand what hoodoo is or how curses work, much less to believe that all this stuff is real. But Maggie's different. She was there at the beginning when we thought Jack only had a burn. Right away, she knew otherwise and sent us to Miss Delia. And she's stuck with Jack even though he's turning into a rotting, stinky pile of bones. But her believing me isn't the problem. I'm just not sure I can trust her.

Her dark brown eyes bore into me, beckoning the words that

are locked deep in my throat. She seems famished, desperate for any crumb of information I'm willing to toss her way. Which is weird, considering this has nothing to do with Jack, and until now, she's barely seemed to notice Cooper exists. Her gaze deepens and grows so warm, so needy, it's hard to remember why I didn't want to tell her in the first place. Her eyes soften and turn down, overflowing with compassion and sympathy. My chest aches to see her so sad, especially since I've got the answer that will make her happy again. There's no reason to keep it from her. I want to tell her.

"Cooper's in trouble." I stroke the cover of my closed sketchbook. "Like, really bad trouble."

She scoffs. "I doubt that is the case."

Jeez, what's with her? She practically drags it out of me, and then doesn't believe me? I set my jaw. "Trust me. He's cursed. He's going to lose his soul when he turns sixteen."

The smirk slides off her face. "How did you learn that?" Finally I've gotten her attention.

"Miss Delia worked a *Psychic Vision* charm on this knife we, uh, found, and it showed us its last memory." There's no need to get into all our felonious details. The fewer people who know what we did, the better. "It was from a few hundred years ago when this African slave lady helped Lady Beaumont give birth, but then she turned around and cursed the baby and all the future Beaumonts for the rest of eternity."

Maggie's brows stretch upward. She looks like she's been struck by lightning. "She was a root doctor?"

"Yeah, they called her Sabina. She said she was a queen in her country and was cursing the Beaumonts for spilling royal blood or something."

She nods, her face vacant. "She avenged a despicable act."

"Apparently. But come on, what could be so bad that a whole family should be cursed for centuries? It's not fair."

"That is precisely what it is. The Beaumonts have always been unscrupulous. They deserve what they've got." Her mouth puckers as if she's tasted something bitter.

My cheeks flush red, and it's not because the midday sun is beating down from the sky. "How can you say that? Granted, Beau's disgusting, and maybe his father was, too, but how do you know it wasn't because of this curse? Sabina said she'd take their souls when they come of age so they'd do horrible things. So how can anyone know what they'd have been like if she'd just left them alone?"

She shrugs. "Their depravity goes back further than the recent occupants of High Point Bluff. It is legendary."

"You know what?" My neck cranes to the side, and I jam the charcoal pencil in the sand. "The Gullah tell their stories and think they know everything, but they don't. Things handed down over generations get mixed up and distorted. Maybe the stories about the Beaumonts are the same. Maybe they really weren't that bad."

Maggie glares. "You *buckrah comeyah* think you know everything. You don't know what the Beaumonts did to my people here on this island. What they did when they purchased human beings to grow rice and indigo. They sowed a dark legacy in this soil, on this very shore, for which they must pay."

I mash my lips into a tight line. Okay, slavery was indisputably bad. Evil, even. But how can she be so callous about Cooper? He's never done anything to anyone. "So Cooper should pay, too? Is it fair for him to lose his soul?"

Maggie swallows whatever words she seemed poised to utter. Her shoulders sag, and she stares at her feet for a long moment.

"Hello? Maggie? Are you going to answer me?"

Her long eyelashes flutter. Is it the wind blowing off the Sound, or is she batting back a tear? "No, it would not be fair. Cooper has a good heart."

"Exactly. But we're running out of time, and that's precisely what's going to happen if Miss Delia can't work some miracle to stop it."

"She is very capable. I am sure she will discover a cure."

My throat constricts, and a familiar sob wells in my chest. But I swallow it because I'm tired of crying. I've moved on to anger. "It's not that easy. The vision didn't give us any clues about how she cast the spell. All we know is she threw some crushed-up powder on Lady Rose and the baby, then ran away. Miss Delia's trying to figure out what was in it. But in the meantime, I can't bear to tell him the truth."

She leans close. "Surely you saw more than you think. Perhaps there were other details you didn't recognize as important. Think, Emma, what did S-s-"—she trips on Sabina's name then gives up, probably because she doesn't remember it—"the root worker say to the mistress when she cursed her."

I bite my lip and search my memory for something that might make sense. So much happened in the vision—a lot of it super scary—it's hard to keep track of it all. "Um, well, besides the royal blood-spilling thing, Sabina said she created The Creep, but that wasn't much of a surprise..." I scan the images stored in my brain. "Oh, yeah, she was really mad that Lady Rose was wearing a necklace. Which, I've got to agree, was kind of strange. I mean, seriously, who wears a fancy ruby like that when they're giving birth?"

Maggie's eyes flash with interest. "A ruby? What did it look like?"

"Oh, it's giant. A big, round flaming ball set like a blooming camellia with gold leaves. Sabina called it a blood stone, but Beau says its 'eighty carats of pure fire.'" I do my best Beau impression, mimicking his exaggerated good-old-boy accent. "Of course back then, the chain was really long and thick. Now it's on a much shorter necklace."

Her jaw drops. "Beau Beaumont still has the necklace?"

I snort. "Yeah. It's like his most precious possession. He loves to flash that thing around and tell everyone how it's been passed down to every mistress of High Point Bluff since Lady Rose. But none of them ever owns it for keeps. It always stays in the family. So far, four of his wives have worn it, but the latest, Missy, wears it every day. At least the others had some class and only took it out on special occasions."

She nods. "It certainly seems like an important piece of Beaumont history."

"Yeah." I grow quiet, revisiting the vision and scouring my memory for details. Then suddenly, disparate pieces click together in my mind like tumblers in a lock. I gasp, struck by a bolt of mental lightning. It's so obvious, I don't know why I haven't realized it until now. I grab my sketchbook and pencil, and shove them into my bag.

"Sorry, I gotta go." I jump to my feet. "I know how to save Cooper."

Chapter Twenty-one

Cooper scratches his head. "So let me get this straight. You want us to steal my stepmother's ruby pendant?" The porch swing creaks under his weight as he leans forward.

Jack snorts. "Dang, Em. One museum heist and you're going hard-core. What's next? A bank robbery?" He laughs, delighted with himself, then squeezes Maggie, who insisted on following me home from the beach. She snuggles into him, tucking her knees up on the cushion, and strokes his temple with her elegant finger. I'm working to be more accepting of their relationship, but their coziness is a little hard to take, particularly as I'm leaning against the door, the only one standing because plopping next to Cooper on the swing would feel too much like a bizarre double date. I wish I could be that giddy and carefree. But I can't because I know what's at stake.

I glare at Jack. "Don't be a jerk."

He shrugs. "Hey, I'm not the one pursuing the life of crime, Gangsta." He pounds his chest with his gloved fist and flashes me a sideways peace sign. He's an idiot, but now that he's wearing

Cooper's brand-new, bright white golf glove, he's an idiot with style.

"I doubt that is the case," Maggie purrs, tracing the curve of his ear. "Perhaps we should hear her out."

Despite the fact I'm totally grossed out by their uncomfortable PDA, I forgive her because she's on my side. I think.

I turn to Cooper. "I didn't say we should steal it, exactly. I just said we need it."

Cooper hitches his brow. "But why? I don't understand what it has to do with The Creep."

Well, neither do I. And in all honesty, I don't completely know how it fits in with the Beaumont curse either. But thanks to my talk with Maggie, I do know two things: the curse started with Lady Rose's son and has affected every generation since, and every mistress of High Point Bluff since Lady Rose has worn that ruby. It can't be a coincidence. Somehow, they're connected, and the necklace is central to undoing the curse. But I can't exactly explain all that right now, unless I want him to hate me forever for lying to him. It would be better to get the ruby, give it to Miss Delia, and let her figure out how to combine it with the antidote. Maybe we can take care of this on our own, and he'll never even need to know. But for now, I've got to come up with a good story to convince him.

"Uh, I can't really explain how they're connected, but they are. You just need to trust me."

Cooper shakes his head. "I'm not sure about this. Missy really loves that necklace. I doubt she'll just hand it over." He crinkles his forehead. "Why are you standing over there by yourself, Emmaline? Come sit down. You're making me nervous." He scoots over, making room on the swing.

Great, now I have to sit, otherwise I'll look like a total dork.

I cross the porch and ease into the cushion, trying not to sit too close. Just being near him makes the temperature rise at least ten degrees, which is saying something because the thermometer's already pushing ninety. Despite the heat, I'd love to imitate Maggie and nestle next to Cooper, draping my arms around his neck, but that's an impossible fantasy since I threw away the *gris-gris* bag. It's probably just as well, anyway. Jack would make a nasty crack, and after all the drama of the last few days, I'm not sure if I'd punch him or cry.

Jack sneers and leans forward. "That's total crap, Emma. We're in this together. You can't go all top secret on us now."

My head snaps in his direction. "I'm not keeping anything from you." Technically it's true, since I've only directly lied to Cooper. "We've got a curse to break, and we need the necklace to do it." I try not to sound as defensive as I am.

Cooper twists toward me and rubs his worried brow. "I'm not trying to be dense here, but I don't get the connection. I mean, the necklace has been in my family forever, but no one until now has gotten The Creep. How do you know it'll help find a cure?"

My mind sputters to answer.

Maggie quirks her brow. "Miss Delia needs it. Isn't that enough?"

Jack narrows his eyes, unconvinced. "But how does Emma know that? She hasn't been over there for two days." He glares at me. "Don't think I haven't noticed you've been doing your artwork instead of trying to save my life. I'm only dying over here, but it's okay, you work on those pastels."

He tugs on the long sleeve of his rash guard and reveals the new swollen and blistered ring around the bottom of his forearm. The all-too-familiar stench of rot floats through the air. I can't help but wince. When this strip bursts, it'll reveal both his radius and ulna, which will be a lot harder to hide than his hand. It's a good thing he's got a couple of those surfing shirts because they've become his new uniform. The long sleeves are uncomfortable to wear in this heat, but at least they provide camouflage.

"Shhh, Jack Guthrie." Maggie smoothes the deep creases in his forehead. "Your sister loves you. She would not neglect you. I am sure she has her reasons for waiting to see the Grannie."

Jack crumbles under her amazing powers of pacification, but I can tell he's resisting them, desperate to stay angry with me. "Yeah, and what are those? Because I can't think of anything more important than keeping my skin."

Cooper nods. "I'd like to know, too, because after we went through all that stuff to get the mortar, I don't understand why we haven't been back to her house."

Hey, what's going on here? I expect the inquisition from Jack, not Cooper. Maybe I need that *Follow Me Boy* charm, after all.

No, I can't think like that. It would be wrong to force someone to like me, even if it would make it easier to save his doomed soul.

I sigh as a pointy headache whittles a hole between my eyes. All this deceit is making me a little nuts, and it's clear it's made them suspicious. I have to tell them something, just not too much.

I huff. "Fine. Miss Delia worked this special kind of curse that let us see into the past."

Jack and Cooper lean forward. "Huh?" they blurt in unison.

Jack laughs and slaps his leg. "Dang, hoodoo is cool."

"Yeah, she created this *Psychic Vision* that let us see way back to when The Creep was started. I can't get into the details because it's sort of a hoodoo secret, but the necklace was there." I've got to hand it to myself, that was pretty good—not exactly true, but not an outright lie, either.

Jack looks like his head's about to explode. "Wait, you saw

how The Creep was started? What happened? Who did it? And why? Did they make an antidote?" He's on a roll, pelting me with so many questions I can hardly keep track of what he's asking.

"Jack, hang on! The vision cut out before we saw everything. But I'm sure we'll learn all that stuff the next time we work it. We just have to wait a little while before we do it because the equipment has to rest." Their eyebrows hitch, and I raise my hand, anticipating their question. "Don't ask me why, it just does. Miss Delia thinks we'll be ready to try again tomorrow."

Cooper's lids widen, and he leans in close enough for me to smell the fabric softener on his shirt. "What did you see? Besides the necklace, I mean?"

There it is, the question I've feared all along. His gaze—today it's the color of green sea glass—is so earnest, so innocent, my heart seizes. He doesn't realize what he's asking. "Uh, I can't tell you."

Jack scoffs. "That sucks. I'm only the victim, but I'm not allowed to know. Nice loyalty, Em."

Cooper cocks his head. "But you told us so much before." He lays his hand on my knee, shooting a jolt of electricity straight to my brain. "Remember all the charms we used at the museum? You told me what they were for. Are you sure you can't tell us anything? Is it really a hoodoo thing?"

I gulp, stunned by the ecstasy of his touch and the agony of his question. Sweat trickles off my forehead, and my overloaded brain locks. I glance at Maggie, pleading for a little help. Thankfully, she receives my distress call and jumps to the rescue.

"I am sure Emma will divulge all she knows when the time is right. But for now, we must respect the rules of hoodoo. We wouldn't want her to lose her apprentice position, would we?" She brushes Jack's jet-black hair off his face.

He shakes his head, but it's obvious he's not satisfied. "No, I guess not." He winces and rubs his temple.

Cooper lifts his hand and sinks back into the swing. "Me, neither. I guess we've got to trust Miss Delia. There's got to be a reason Emma can't tell us what she saw."

I heave a sigh of relief and send Maggie a mental note of thanks. She must read the gratitude in my eyes because she nods and flashes a smile before turning her attention back to Jack. As grateful as I am for the save, I can't ignore the pain that's twisting in my gut or the tightness creeping across my chest. I've lied to Cooper, again. Sure, there's a good reason I can't tell him, but it's still a lie of omission. I've got to wrap this up before I get myself in any more trouble. Or he touches me again.

"Okay, so then you'll get the necklace, right?" I hop off the swing and head for the door to the house. There's air conditioning in there, which should make it easier to breathe.

Cooper sighs. "Sure, I'll try."

My brain throbs. Didn't he hear what I've been saying? I stop and turn around to face him. "Cooper, you can't *try*. You have to get it." Dang, I sound a lot like Jack, which is never a good thing.

"I know, Emma, but it's not going to be easy," he snaps. "She loves that thing. It's not like she's just going to hand it over. Especially to me." He picks at the metal chain suspending the swing as his eyes cloud with something dark.

Jack tears himself away from Maggie's gaze. "You know, thanks to your dad's prenup, it's not really hers. Why don't you just ask your dad to borrow it for a while?"

Cooper glares. "I'm not asking my dad for anything."

Jack shrugs, totally oblivious to Cooper's reaction. "Actually, when you think about it, it's technically yours, since you'll get it after he dies. You should just take it."

Cooper's lip curls. "And how am I supposed to do that?"

I massage my temple, hoping to rub away the mounting headache, and work to contain my emotions. But my cheeks flush with irritation, anyway. Why can't he understand how important this is? Granted, I haven't explained everything, but he knows we need it to break the curse, not for some personal gain. He needs to get creative.

I cross my arms. "She doesn't wear it twenty-four hours a day, does she? Grab it when she doesn't have it on." Hmm, maybe I am getting a little too comfortable with crime. I'll have to work on that when all this curse stuff is over.

Cooper wrenches his jaw. "I thought you didn't want me to steal it."

His moral compass is killing me. I know this isn't easy for him, but it'll be way harder to lose his soul. Despite his principles, I'm going to save him whether he likes it or not. Anger and frustration boil in my chest as my patience wanes. It's too hot for this crap.

My hands fly to my hips. "Listen, we all know stealing is wrong, but I wouldn't ask you to do it if we didn't really, really need it. Plus we'll give it back. Eventually. And Jack can help. It's not like he's doing anything else." I jab my thumb at my brother, who's nearly hypnotized by Maggie's stroking. His jaw hangs slack as her hand glides across his back, lightly tickling his skin through his rash guard.

Jack snaps out of his pleasure haze. "Hey, I didn't agree to that. Maggie and I have plenty to do on our own."

I narrow my gaze and shoot him a mental laser beam. "Are you kidding me? You're the *victim*, remember? This whole summer has been about us saving your sorry butt. You're going to help him, all right, and I don't care if you have to follow Missy around all day to do it. Get that necklace." Wow. I've never gone after Jack like that. But dang, it felt good.

Jack sneers. "Unclench a little, will you?"

Maggie nuzzles Jack's ear. "Emma is correct. You must help your friend. It is the only way to set things right. We will have our own time, Jack Guthrie." She winks at me.

With a shrug, Jack laughs. "Sure, why not? Beats sitting around waiting for another chunk to fall off."

"You have made the right decision." She pats his leg, then hops off the settee. "Now I must be going. I am certain my grandmother is searching for me." She chuckles to herself as she walks toward the screen door.

Jack's face falls. "I thought we'd spend the rest of the afternoon together."

She smiles. "You have a job to do with your friend, do you not? Now is as good a time as any to start." Jack and Cooper stare at her, unsure what to do. She tips her head toward the door. "The afternoon is still young. Do not waste this valuable daylight."

Without another word of protest, the guys get up and march off the porch.

Holy impressive persuasion. This moment is so priceless, I can't help but stand with her, watching them jog down the path toward the Big House. Her perfume tickles my nose. I think I've finally figured out the fragrance. It smells just like the bouquet of stargazer lilies Mom's boyfriend Gary sent her right before Jack and I came south.

She flashes that gleaming smile of hers. "I am sure they will find the necklace, and you and the Grannie can work some hoodoo magic."

My chest swells with gratitude. Clearly, I was wrong about her. She's not some wicked brother stealer—although she could lighten up on the intense public affection. She knows the stakes and just proved she's on my side. If it wasn't for her, I may not have convinced them to get the necklace. I owe her big time.

Thrilled by her assistance, I reach out and throw my arms around her. The sweet, cloying scent of those lilies overwhelms as my fingers register the ice-cold temperature of her skin. A shock of energy raises the hair on my arms, and my eyes fly open.

She jumps backward, out of my grip, and throws open the screen door. "I must be going now. I will see you soon, Emma Guthrie." She races down the steps toward the path that leads to the beach.

Chapter Twenty-two

The big yellow moon hangs low over St. Helena Island Sound, reflecting off its tranquil surface. Low waves lap at the shoreline in a meditative rhythm. It's a peaceful refuge from the curse craziness, illuminated by the bright summer stars. Because goodness knows, between Maggie's supreme and growing weirdness, The Creep inching up Jack's arm, and Cooper's doomed soul, I need a place to think.

Sitting on the beach, I sift the cool, powdery sand between my fingers and take in the balmy night air. There's so much to do in an ever-dwindling amount of time. It threatens to overwhelm me until I remind myself that Miss Delia's on my side, and now Maggie is, too. Soon we should have Lady Rose's necklace and, thanks to the *Psychic Visions*, the key to how Sabina worked The Creep. I've got to believe everything will work out, because the alternative is, well, unthinkable. I force the tension from my worried brow, then off my neck and shoulders.

Cooper's scent carries on the breeze, fresh and piney. I don't know how he found me or why, since I didn't tell anyone where I was headed. But my heart swells, anyway, happy just to be around him—for now—while he's still the Cooper I know and love.

"Emmaline?"

Slapping on a smile to hide any remnant of concern, I swivel to face him. "Hey, Cooper." I pray my voice sounds bright and normal. He's wearing fresh clothes. He must have taken a shower.

"I hope you don't mind my coming out here. I was in the living room in the Big House, and I saw you making your way down the bluff from the picture window. That shirt of yours kind of glows in the moonlight."

I look down at my white T-shirt. He's right, it is sort of luminescent in this light. "No, of course not. Why would that bother me?"

"Well, you're on the beach, alone and at night. That only happens when you've got trouble on your mind."

I love that he knows that about me. But will he remember after his change? Still, he makes me blush. "I'll admit I've got some stuff to work out, but I'm fine." I wrap my arms around my bent knees.

"I know you are. We're all under a lot of pressure. It takes a toll. I only came down because I don't like you being alone with everything that's going on. Mind if I stay?"

Although I thought I needed to be by myself to slip away from the gloom and find some clarity, now that he's here, I realize all I need is him. "Of course not. Have a seat."

He sits beside me and shakes the sand from his flip-flops. "You want to talk about it?"

Um, that you're about to turn dark and nefarious? No, not really. I'd much rather switch subjects. "How did your necklace scouting go? Any luck?"

He shakes his head. "No, Missy wore it all afternoon, even

in the hot tub. I'll work on getting it tonight after they've gone to bed."

"Good plan." I tilt my head to look at the brilliant Seven Sisters constellation, the one that kind of looks like an upside-down Little Dipper, and try to ignore how close his body is to mine. But all I want to do is rest my head against his big, broad shoulder and wrap my arms around him, offering what little protection I can against the Beaumont curse.

"You know, you're not in this alone."

I nod. "Yeah, I know." Actually, I sort of am.

Cooper grasps my arm. "No, really. I'm here for you." He strokes a few stray hairs off my face and tucks them over my shoulder. He's staring directly into my eyes. I'm pretty sure I've stopped breathing.

I nod, trapped in his consuming gaze. "Okay."

He draws a huge breath. "I've got a confession to make, Emmaline."

My chest tightens. I need to confess, too, but telling him about the Beaumont curse right now will definitely spoil the mood. I know I should tell him, but he's so beautiful, and he's never looked at me this way. The ethical debate rages, overloading my brain, so all I can manage in response is, "Uh-huh?"

He cups my jaw with his palm. "I'm worried for you."

That's so not where I hoped this was going.

"Oh?" My brow furrows, and I pull away from his muscular but comforting hands. "Look, I know I lost my cool earlier, but I'm fine. Really." My voice drips with irritation. Maybe I should tell him now.

He shakes his head. "No, that didn't come out right. What I mean is, I find myself worrying *about* you. A lot."

The sincerity in his voice soothes the anger in my chest.

"Thanks. I'll be okay."

He sighs, scratching his temple. "Aw, heck, this is harder than I thought," he says out loud, then clears his throat. "Um, what I'm trying to say is, you're pretty much on my mind every day. All day."

"Oh." Miss Delia and her stinking *Follow Me Boy* charm. That powder must have worked its way into his sinuses, because he's still feeling its effects. Which totally sucks. I'd give anything for this to be real. "Listen, I know that day in the museum was exciting, but believe me, it'll pass. Everything will go back to normal."

Deep creases mar his handsome face. "But what if I don't want things to be normal? I like thinking about you, worrying about your safety. Caring about you. From the moment you got here this summer, I knew I wanted things to be different between us." His eyes turn down. "I thought I sensed you did, too."

My heart seizes. "Um, did you just say, when I got here? Like, do you mean, when Jack and I came south from D.C.?" I can barely force the words from my constricted throat, afraid to hope it's true.

His lips curl into a hopeful half-grin. "Yeah. You were at your dad's, wearing that funky skirt of yours, and your hair was pulled up in a ponytail. I couldn't believe how pretty you were."

Holy. Sticklewort. Cooper Beaumont likes me.

I gulp, processing the words I've longed to hear for more than a year. This is way better than my fantasies. "Um, really?" My voice trembles with awe, and my hands quake. All other thoughts flee my brain. The only thing I focus on is what's happening here, in this moment, now.

He inches closer, his lips hovering near my mouth. "Was I wrong? Did I misread you, Emmaline?"

"N-n-no," I finally manage, then gush, "Gosh, no." My lids shut, and my mouth parts slightly, yearning for him. A moment later, his velvety lips are on mine, soft and gentle. He's smooth and so very kissable. Every inch of my skin sizzles.

His head tilts as he runs his cheek along my jaw, then plants another kiss in the hollow behind my ear. Tingles explode, reducing me to a hunk of jiggling, boneless jelly. The only thing that keeps me from collapsing back onto the sand are his strong hands that reach to caress my back. I melt, consumed by the electric inferno bubbling in my belly.

"You're amazing," he whispers. "Kissing you is better than I imagined."

My chest flutters with the knowledge he's been thinking about me. Maybe even dreaming about me. "You have no idea how long I've wanted this, Cooper. I can hardly even believe it now."

His brow quirks, and he pulls back to look at me. "Really? I had no idea."

I snort, shocked that I covered my crush so well. "Um, yeah. It's been a year." I roll my eyes in embarrassment.

A sly grin cracks his lips. "Wait, do you mean to tell me we could have done this last summer?" He leans in for another kiss, then nuzzles my opposite ear, shooting a shimmering charge through my body.

If he doesn't stop, I might have a heart attack. It's a risk I'm willing to take.

"Sorry," I giggle, then nudge his jaw so I find his lips again. This time it's my turn to direct the kiss. I've got a lot of lost time to make up for.

A few blissful minutes later, Cooper pulls back for air. "Yeah, I definitely don't want things to go back to normal." He grasps my hand and squeezes tight.

I laugh. "Me, neither." My heart pounds, then sinks as I realize how not normal he'll be if I can't find a way to save him.

That's not an option. I will save him.

Chapter Twenty-three

"Emma? Are you listening, child?" Miss Delia's voice jolts me from my thoughts. She places Bloody Bill's dagger on the kitchen counter. "I said the angry vibrations have calmed. It's ready to pull another memory."

"Huh? Oh, yeah, I'm totally with you."

No, I'm not. I've been up in my head all day, reliving what happened at the beach last night with Cooper. I barely remembered to take the cleansing bath Miss Delia prescribed. And then, when Cooper and Jack dropped me off this morning on their way to more Missy-necklace-stalking, Cooper secretly planted another kiss on me, giving me yet another thing to think about. But I can't dwell on his unbelievable hotness, or how giddy I am. I've got a *Psychic Vision* to cast.

Suppressing the idiotic smile that threatens to give me away, I reply, "Awesome. Let's do it."

She purses her lips and gives me a hard stare, sizing up my readiness. "All right, but you can't be dreaming about that boy of yours. You need your wits about you, especially since you're conjuring the charm yourself today. Do you remember the ingredients we used?"

How the heck does she always know what I'm thinking? Rather than admit she's right, I nod, hoping I do remember what goes into the potion.

I fill a kettle with water, set it on the stove to boil, and then assemble the earthenware crocks and vials I'll need for the spell. Before long, the homemade psychic tea bags are steeping, and the charcoal in the mortar is ready for the plants and roots. Feeling proud of myself for remembering all these steps without any help from Miss Delia or her spell book, I layer the acacia leaves and buchu, feeling the energy drain immediately. When they begin to smoke and crackle, I forge ahead to sprinkle some anise powder on top and reach for the myrrh.

"No!" Miss Delia grasps my hand. "You forgot the celery seed and dragon's breath."

I shake my cloudy head. "No, I didn't. They're right there." I point to the crocks on the counter. "I was going to add them next."

She wags her gnarled finger at me. "The order is as important as what you add. If you do it wrong, you'll have to start from scratch. And depending on how far you've gotten, you'll need to let the mortar rest before working another charm."

Jeez, that would've been good to know before I started tossing ingredients around. "Thanks for the tip."

I bite my lip and focus so I don't screw up. We can't afford to waste another three days. My arms are so weak, I can barely lift them to drop the celery seeds and dragon's blood on the smoking mixture. Somehow I manage to add the myrrh, frankincense, and mint. Soon the scents merge, evoking a dessert-filled church, so I know it's time for our tea. For luck, I rub my *collier* just like last time and *clink* my mug against Miss Delia's before gulping the

sour brown mixture. Clutching Miss Delia's hand, I lay my other .
arm against the rim of the mortar and fight the encroaching
drowsiness to grab hold of the bottom of the knife and share its
weight.

A gust of cold wind blows, encircling the house and yard, then
whips through the house, rattling the front and side screen porch
doors as it passes. The sunlight dims as the clouds collide and block
out the light. Rain pelts the roof, and thunder booms over the
forest.

"Ah!" The violent crash makes my heart skip and jolts me out
of my dreamy lull.

"Never mind that, child." Ms. Delia squeezes my hand. "It's
just the elements at work, helping us with the spell."

Oh, that explains a lot.

"Remember, since we already lifted the knife's last memory,
this charm is going to pull its second-to-last cut. We're moving
backward in time."

"Okay." I nod. Despite the crazy fatigue and life-and-death
circumstances, the thrill of doing this flutters in my stomach. Jack's
right, hoodoo is cool.

"Do you want to say the incantation this time?" Miss Delia
waggles her eyebrows. "You can change it up a bit if you like, to be
more specific." I freeze, my eyes wide, unsure of what to say. She
chuckles. "Don't fear, child. Remember the red and white beads
on that *collier* of yours give you the power of spoken word and
prayer. Just clear your mind. The words will come to you."

All four gas burners on the stove flare up. I gulp and try to
ignore them. It must be another elemental thing.

Focusing my dwindling energy, I close my eyes and inhale,
willing the dark space behind my lids to stretch and grow until it
envelops me. The words spring to my mouth just as the tea's fuzzy

effects begin to hit. "Smoke and mist, reveal the past, and how this object was used last. Reveal the truth about The Creep, so flesh and muscle Jack will reap." My speech is slurred, but I laugh, surprised it was so easy to come up with the charm.

Miss Delia squeezes my hand and chuckles. "You might want to open those eyes of yours."

Oops. One of these days I'll remember to look into the fog. I open my eyes to find the vision has already started. Bright images sputter on the thick smoke curtain, then pick up speed to create their own little movie. My head spins under the tea's power as I peer at the flickering light.

A large wooden ship with three tall masts sits anchored close to shore, its sails strapped down. The Jolly Roger, the pirates' calling card, hangs from the highest mast, its skull and crossbones flapping in the occasional breeze. The ship is quiet. A pirate dozes, slumped on a barrel on the main deck, a weathered spyglass in his limp hands and a tankard of grog at his side. A warm orange-pink glow hovers above the horizon in the east, promising a beautiful summer morning.

On the shore, scores of African men in tattered clothes work in silence, preparing to launch a small flotilla of canoes and long boats. One white man stands among them, dressed in a rich peach-colored silk coat and breeches and coordinating ivory waistcoat. He points his silver-tipped walking cane at the men and their boats, ordering them around in the early morning stillness. Within minutes, the men ease the crafts into the water, climb aboard, and row toward the pirate ship anchored just offshore.

The canoes surround the ship. Several Africans clamber up a rope ladder left hanging over the side, wooden clubs wedged under their strong arms. A man in a nearby boat heaves a long cable up toward the deck. It lands with a thump, waking the dozing pirate. He starts, scanning the quiet and still empty deck, then mumbles to himself as he crosses his arms and nods back to sleep. A moment later, a thin, wiry African ascends the top of the ladder, slips over the railing, and runs to secure the rope so others can follow. Several others climb aboard after him, stealthily catching and securing new lines of the thick, handmade cord so even more can come aboard.

A muscle-bound African with the thickest neck I've ever seen scales the side, hoists himself over the railing, and crashes with a deafening thud that rocks the ship. The pirate jerks awake and screams at the sight of the invaders.

"Captain! Captain, we be under attack!" The sailor's eyes are wide with terror as he sprints to ring the alarm bell. He manages to clang the clapper several times before the thick-necked man yanks him by the throat with one hand, lifts him off his feet, and tosses him overboard.

But it's too late to maintain the surprise. The pirates stream from the 'tween deck below, swords and daggers drawn, engaging the club-wielding Africans. Most of the seamen are dressed in filthy, ragged clothes, their greasy hair poking out from under grimy caps, but one stands apart from the rest. He's almost dashing in his scarlet brocade coat and matching breeches, and long, luscious carrot-red curls. But as fierce as the pirates are, they're no match for the Africans, who fight with fiery determination, besting the still groggy and probably hungover sailors. Every second, more dark-skinned men mount the ship, supplying reinforcements for the few who fall wounded by a pirate's blade. Soon the Africans outnumber the pirates at least two-to-one and easily restrain the few holdouts. The rest cower and drop their weapons on the deck with a *clank*.

The white man from the shore emerges at the top of the

ladder and boards the ship. "Good morning, Captain Ransom." A wry smile curls on his lips as he approaches the defeated leader, who, with his rich red coat, looks disturbingly like an Irish Captain Hook. Except he's wearing a sparkling camellia blossom necklace that glints in the early morning light. I try not to gasp and disturb the *Psychic Vision*. It's Lady Rose's ruby, the one Cooper and Jack are trying to steal from Missy at this very moment.

The pirate sets his jaw. "Lord Beaumont, what is the meaning of this attack?" As much as I try to stop it, a squeak escapes my mashed lips. It must be Lady Rose's husband, Edmund. I can't believe how much he resembles Beau. Well, Beau minus about three hundred pounds. The pirate continues, his eyes flashing with rage. "Surely we have no quarrel as we upheld our end of the bargain. As a gentleman, I expected you to do the same." His noble accent is jarring and completely unexpected from a scurvy pirate.

Edmund jabs the pirate's chest with the head of his walking stick. "Ah, but that is where we disagree, Bloody Bill." Edmund adds extra emphasis to his name. "You are in breach of our contract and therefore must pay."

Bloody Bill lunges toward him, but the huge African man leaps to Edmund's side and grabs the pirate by his throat, squeezing until his porcelain face turns purple.

Edmund taps the muscle-bound man with his stick. "Thank you, Jupiter. I believe that's sufficient to get the Captain's attention." Jupiter unclenches his fist. Bloody Bill drops to the floor in a heap and heaves for air. Edmund paces the deck, stalking each of the captive pirates. "I entrusted you with my property, and look what you've done." His voice bellows as he thrusts his stick toward the beach.

I squint into the distance and make out a crumpled, cloth-covered lump on the sand. A chill runs up my spine. I think it's a body. A dead one.

"But you said...we could..." Bloody Bill forces the words from his crushed throat.

Edmund charges toward him, glaring. "I expected to get her back." Spit collects in the corner of his mouth and flies from his lips as he speaks.

Bloody Bill cocks his head. "Surely you jest." His voice is thick and raspy. "Yours was the far better share of our bargain." He coughs and rubs his still-red neck. "I was daft to accept one measly slave girl, mesmerizing though she was, in exchange for not sacking High Point Bluff."

Edmund wields his walking stick like a golf club and lets loose, slamming Bloody Bill's legs. "She was *mine!*" The veins at the side of his head stick out.

"How dare you—"

Edmund snaps his fingers. Jupiter rushes toward Bloody Bill, landing a solid uppercut that snaps the pirate's head back. Edmund sneers. "Insolence will only increase your penalty, which, by my solemn oath, will be great."

The captain staggers to his feet, limping. "I daresay our poor barter was penalty enough, my lord. But if you insist, I shall gladly pay you for your trouble." He waves a hand, and a young cabin boy races to him, pulling an ornately carved wooden box from his coat.

It's the treasure box we unearthed at the tabby ruins. Bloody Bill grabs it, then leans toward Edmund, quirking his brow. "What, then, is a fair price? Not much, I venture." He pulls a few gold coins from the box and tosses them at Edmund's feet.

Edmund's cheeks flush crimson as he puffs his chest. "Oh, you'll pay, all right, but a few guineas won't come close." He jams the walking stick under Bloody Bill's chin. "Your pretty necklace might cover it, but I'll take your treasure box as well for good measure." Edmund yanks the box from Bloody Bill's hands and angles his head toward Jupiter, who lifts the ruby necklace off the pirate's neck and hands it to Edmund.

Bloody Bill sets his jaw and squares his shoulders, bracing himself. "Judging by the vengeful expressions of your servants, I know what you've got planned for me and my crew, and after all our many sins, 'tis a fate we richly deserve. Yet before we depart this earth, I beg one final observation."

A bemused smile creeps up Edmund's lips. "And what would that be?"

Bloody Bill sneers. "You my lord, are no more than a pirate yourself, masquerading in gentlemen's clothes."

Edmund chuckles and snaps his fingers. Jupiter cocks his colossal fist, preparing to land a blow. The pirate flinches and squeezes his eyes shut.

"No, Jupiter! This is mine to finish," a gravelly voice bellows in a thick foreign accent. A small, stocky figure with ebony skin and facial scarification emerges from behind a cluster of Africans. It's Sabina.

The Africans fall back, giving her a wide berth as she advances toward the captive captain, her eyes blazing with fury as she grinds a dark-colored root between her teeth. The pirates must sense her power because they gasp in unison and hunch even lower to the deck. Sabina raises her arm and points at Bloody Bill. He cringes, having lost all his bravado, and slinks back a few paces, nearly collapsing on his damaged leg.

Edmund glowers. "Sabina, what are you doing here? You should be back at High Point Bluff."

She turns her sights on him, her nostrils flaring. "Not till I settle my business, *Master.*" She bows to him, but even with her broken English, her tone is filled with unmistakable sarcasm. "A mighty wrong been done to my kinfolk. I'm here to see the guilty pay for their sins."

"Watch yourself, Sabina." Edmund points his walking stick at her. "I've allowed you certain latitude because of your healing powers, but I will not sanction such insubordination. You are not as exceptional as you assume."

Sabina cocks her head. "Oh, no?" She thrusts her hands above her head and waves them in a circle. "Hear the word of the Lord!" The wind swirls, howling as it whips around the ship and lifts Bloody Bill's long, luscious curls. The sea swells, churning choppy waves that slap against the hull, rocking the vessel. Sabina spins her hands. A waterspout forms just off the port side, spiraling upward in a tall thin column. She twists, and the waterspout responds, zooming toward the ship. Guiding it over the bow, she holds her hands still, allowing it to hover over the shocked and trembling passengers. Then she drops her hands, sending it crashing to the deck and dousing the pirates and Edmund but somehow avoiding the Africans.

Edmund and Bloody Bill freeze, paralyzed with fear as she thrusts forward, yanks a dagger off Bloody Bill's belt, and swipes it at his hair, slicing a huge hank off. She tosses his long orange curls at his feet, then reaches into her skirt pocket, retrieving a handful of beach sand and some black wool, and hurls it on the deck in front of him. She chants in a lyrical foreign language, then clicks her tongue against the roof of her mouth. Even though everything's soaked, the hair, sand, and black woolly stuff burst into flames. Edmund and the pirates scream, just as Jack did when he contracted The Creep. They clutch their stomachs and collapse to the floor, writhing in agony. The Africans flinch, shrinking several steps until they're nearly on top of one another.

Sabina erupts in crazed laughter and stalks the deck, stepping over Edmund and the crippled pirates. "Dem bones, dem bones, gonna walk around!'" she sings, taunting them with the lyrics to the haunting Negro spiritual. "Dem dry bones. Oh, hear the word of the Lord!" Then she darts to the side of the ship. Clutching the dagger with one hand, she grabs some rigging with the other to steady herself and jumps up on the railing. She pivots, revealing a maniacal grin. "This ship is cursed! And so are those with royal blood on their hands!" She leaps off the side and swims toward shore. Moments later, scores of others follow her, splashing into St. Helena Island Sound.

Vicious barks penetrate the quiet of Miss Delia's kitchen. Their staccato vibrations hammer against my chest and suck me back to the present. Groggy, I wrench away from the vision and scream.

Eight dead, fluorescent eyes glare at me from the backyard, just beyond the side porch. They belong to the four snarling *plateyes* that are poised to barrel up the steps and through the screen door to attack. The knife slips from my hand as the blood drains from my face and my muscles go limp. Too heavy for Miss Delia to hold by herself, the knife falls into the still-smoldering mortar with a *clank*, cutting off the vision.

Another thunderclap roars, this time closer to her house. The rain intensifies, accompanied by another blast of cool air that races through the kitchen and extinguishes the flames on the stove.

"Miss Delia?" My voice trembles, barely above a whisper. "I thought you said they couldn't come near the house." My instinct is to run and hide, but I'm so zonked, I can barely lift my head, much less haul myself off the stool.

"Maybe the rain washed some of the potions on the lawn

away. But don't worry about the house. Those charms are in place. They can't cross the thresholds." Although she tries to sound reassuring, Miss Delia's voice quivers even more than normal. She squeezes my other hand, but I'm not sure whether it's to comfort me or herself.

Growling, the *plateyes* advance, gnashing their jagged teeth and dripping with frothy saliva. They smell like wet dog. I don't care what she says about her protection charms, I've got to snap out of this stupor and get out of here. But Cooper isn't around, and neither is his car, so we're stuck in the house. Miss Delia doesn't have a basement, either. Her bedroom's the only option. It's not Fort Knox, but at least it doesn't have an exterior door.

My mouth is as dry as steel wool. I muster just enough energy to swallow hard and force out a few words, trying to convey my plan. "We've got to hide." My words are husky and thick. I slide off the stool, but my feet are as heavy as anchors, and my head is still fuzzy from the psychic tea. I stumble and fall to the floor.

"Emma!" Miss Delia screeches.

Splayed on my stomach, I struggle to right myself and strain to focus on the side porch. My eyes lock on an enormous black muzzle that's pressed against the screen door. The dog snarls and curls his lips into a vicious, serrated smile. It snorts, filling the kitchen with the sulfurous scent of brimstone. I shriek and scramble to get back on my feet, but those electric yellow eyes hold me like a tractor beam. A second *plateye* stalks up the porch steps, crams in next to the first, and howls. His deep, grumbling yelp shakes the floorboards.

That's enough to clear my mind and launch me to my feet. Desperate to stay as far away from the demons as possible, I wrestle out from under the fatigue and kick out my leg, catching the edge of the wooden exterior door with my toe and slam it shut.

Yowling and barking, the *plateyes* jump up on their hind legs and paw at the screen door. Their sharp claws rip gashes in the metal mesh, and they stampede through the flimsy barrier, crossing the side porch and slamming against the closed door.

"Come on, Miss Delia. I don't think those charms of yours are going to hold." I grab her arm as gently as I can and help her off her stool, then stumble through the swinging door into the living room, trying not to trip again.

Another scream leaps from my throat. Two of the *plateyes* have made their way around to the front porch. They launch into a fresh volley of barks, then crouch, readying to lunge through the screen. I gulp and consider trying to drag myself to the door to close it, but I'm not sure I'll make it. Besides, from the recoiled dogs' menacing expression, even if I could, it would be guaranteed suicide. We've got to get out of here before they pounce.

I tug on her arm. "Come on, Miss Delia. We've got to get to your bedroom. At least we can lock ourselves in there."

She juts out her jaw. "I won't hide in my own house."

What? She'd rather get eaten in her living room instead? "But they're coming!" My eyes are wide with fright as I thrust my finger toward the door. "Can't you see they're about to rip through the screen?"

She shakes her head. "My charms will hold them." Her voice is filled with certainty.

I steal another view of the *plateyes*. They're pawing the floorboards with their muddy, razor-sharp claws, gouging deep lines into the wood. In their frenzy, they shake their gigantic heads and fling their foaming spit everywhere. For a split second, I consider leaving Miss Delia here on her own and barricading myself in her room, but then I come to my senses. Or not. For better or worse, I'm her apprentice, and we're in this together. I just hope the end comes quickly, and it doesn't hurt as much as I fear.

I gulp. "We're going to die." My voice trembles.

"Not if I can help it. Go to the sideboard under the television and grab me a bottle of whiskey."

Chapter Twenty-four

I blink. Does she seriously think getting drunk will help matters?

She nudges me. "What are you waiting for, child? Get me some whiskey!"

The *plateyes* growl and spit at us from behind the screen.

Hauling myself across the room, I throw open the sideboard cabinet and reach for one of several bottles of dark brown liquid labeled "Southern Magic Whiskey." I didn't realize Miss Delia was such a drinker. Then I limp back to her and twist open the still-sealed bottle.

She grabs my hand. "Do you know the Lord's Prayer?" Her eyes bore into me as the barking increases.

Whew, at least she's thinking straight now. We are dealing with demon dogs, after all—asking for a little divine intervention can't hurt. As long as you know how. I search my memory for the prayer I learned when I was little but haven't recited in years. The first line runs through my mind, but I draw a blank on the rest. "Um?" I wince.

She scoffs. "Didn't anyone ever teach you about religion?"

I shake my head. "Not really."

She purses her lips. "Remind me to give you a lesson when this mess is over. We're going to have to do this together. Walk me to the door."

The dog-beasts stop digging into her porch and stare at us with their horrible, vacant eyes. They seethe, grinding their massive jaws and spewing that nasty white slobber. Then they butt their silky black heads against the screen and snort, shooting the revolting scent of sulfur into the living room. Miraculously, the mesh doesn't tear under the pressure of their massive weight. Miss Delia's charms must be having some effect, though they're clearly not enough to repel them, because their snouts are bulging into the room.

Gripping Miss Delia's arm, I override all sense of self-preservation and force my feet to move toward the door. My heart pounds. This feels like a march toward certain death, which is the last thing a normal-thinking person should do. But like so many of the crazy things that have happened this summer, this is *so* not normal.

As if they have some kind of telepathic abilities, the other two *plateyes* from the kitchen race around the house and bound up the porch steps. Together, all four bark in eerie unison. Their hollow yellow eyes glow as their furious intensity mounts.

Miss Delia points to the screen. "Shake the whiskey at them," she yells so I can hear over their barking, and points to herself. "I'll do the talking."

My hand shakes as I tip the bottle, and I try to ignore their snapping jaws and ear-popping snarls. As much as I'd love to turn tail and escape to Miss Delia's room, I know I can't. My pulse rages as I thrust the bottle toward the screen and watch the dark brown liquid splash through the mesh onto the *plateyes* and the porch floor.

Miss Delia recites the prayer, beginning with the one line I know, "Our Father, who art in heaven, hallowed be thy name."

The barking stops. And so does the rain. Encouraged by the sudden quiet, I toss some more whiskey, and Miss Delia continues with the rest of the prayer. Tilting their heads, the hellhounds sniff the air, then exchange blank fluorescent looks. One dips his head to the floor and laps up some liquid. A second follows him. I pour a third round of whiskey, and then a fourth. The alcohol pools in the deep ruts their claws carved into the floorboards. By the time Miss Delia's finished praying, all four *plateyes* are lapping the whiskey with as much frenzy as they used to attack us.

Gulping, I gather the courage to push open the screen door and dump the rest of the whiskey out onto the porch. The dogs lick the floor clean, then sit like normal pups and bark, but this time it's a lazy, appreciative yap. In unison, they pull back their lips and flash their jagged teeth in drunken smiles, then rise and stumble down the porch steps, wagging their long, wispy tails. They saunter into the yard, swaying and bumping into each other, but careful to avoid the bottle tree as they head toward the woods.

The silver clouds part, unveiling a bright azure sky and the warm South Carolina sun.

I guide Miss Delia to the nearby sofa, then slump onto the floor next to her, unable to stay on my feet. My chest heaves, sucking air, and my head lolls back onto the cushion. I'm so weary I'm surprised I haven't passed out. It's a good thing we've both got our *colliers* on, otherwise we'd be dead. "That was the scariest thing I've ever seen." My hands tremble in my lap.

She cackles. "Then you must not remember what's happening to your brother. His curse has certainly frightened the bejesus out of me."

I nod, willing my pulse to return to normal. "Yeah, but The Creep only affects Jack. Those beasts would've ripped us apart if they could. And they'd laugh as they were doing it." I suddenly realize how selfish that sounds—only worrying about my own bodily harm—but I can't help it. Those *plateyes* are terrifying.

She pulls a tissue from the box next to the sofa and dabs her moist brow. "You're right about that. But I knew my charms would keep us safe." She winks her cloudy eye. "Though I'll confess I was a little worried there for a minute."

"How'd you know the whiskey would work? And why didn't you give me a bottle for protection when we got your ancestors' mortar?"

She shrugs. "I didn't remember until those hellions came so close, sending that evil stench into my house. It reminded me of something my gran told me when I was a gal." She nudges my shoulder. "She's the one who told me about the power of whiskey and the Lord. Said it's the only way to defeat a rotten-egg-smelling *plateye*." She cackles. "All this time, I thought she meant *plateyes* went around, smelling rotten eggs, but it turns out they just stink like them. Funny, how a smell can bring back a memory like that. Thing is, the liquor and prayer will only turn them away, not get rid of them for good. But maybe the ancestors will have an idea. We'll contact them just as soon as the mortar rests. It'll be nice to see Ole Gran again." She pauses, staring out into the room, as if reliving a memory. "I loved her so. You see, she's the one who taught me about the wicked creatures I might have to fight with hoodoo. My *maamy*, she didn't think I should learn that young, but Gran didn't want to shield me from the haints and boo-hags."

I scratch my head, which is still spinning from the whole contacting-dead-people thing. "Um, I'm pretty sure I know what a haint is—it's a ghost, right?" She nods in response. "But what the heck's a boo-hag? And is it something we're going to have to worry about while we're fighting The Creep?"

She sighs. "Oh, child. It's just about the worst thing you'd ever encounter during a full moon. It sheds its skin and slips into your house, then climbs up on you, riding your chest while you're sleeping, sucking the life out of you. When it's done, it jumps into your skin and takes over your body. Evil doesn't come close to describing it."

I shudder as a chill runs up my spine. "Thanks. Now I won't be able to sleep in peace."

She laughs and waves me off. "I doubt you've got to worry about a nasty boo-hag. Remember it clothes itself in skin, and last time I checked, that's in short supply in your house."

True, but now that we've pulled that second memory from the knife, and seen how Sabina worked the curse, we should be able to break it. "But not for long, right? I mean, the *Psychic Vision* gave us everything we need to reverse The Creep, right?" I hope so, because I don't think I can take much more of this magic stuff. I'm so drained, I'm not sure I'll be able to get up off the floor anytime soon. Maybe she'll let me sleep over.

She shakes her head. "It did, but I'm sorry to say we're no closer to knowing what to do."

My chest sinks from the unexpected punch in the gut. "How can you say that?" My voice is faint as I lean my throbbing head against my hand. Just when I thought we'd gotten a break, this stupid curse crushes me. "We saw what Sabina did and watched her create the spell. Why isn't that enough?"

She reaches down and grasps my shoulder. "For two reasons, child. Those words she used when she cast the spell—I don't know what they mean. I've never heard anything like it. It's not Gullah, even an early version of it. And second, even if I knew what she said, I don't pretend to have her power. You saw the way she commanded the wind and water, created a funnel cloud, and then used the earth to create a fire. I didn't even know that was possible."

My mind races as it calculates the horrific implications of this latest revelation. Ever since I learned about the Beaumont curse, I sort of forgot about Jack and switched my concern to Cooper. I was so sure we'd be able to reverse The Creep, and Jack would be fine. But now, that seems impossible. Without a translation for Sabina's strange, lyrical words and some way to whip a whole lot of water and wind around, not to mention light a fire in the middle of all that, Jack's going to die. And then, my best friend—and now boyfriend—will lose his soul. And I'll be the only one who understands exactly what happened. Well, except for Maggie and Miss Delia, of course.

My throat tightens. "So you're saying he's doomed." My voice breaks. "Just like Cooper." My chest shudders as fat tears flow down my cheeks into my lap.

She pats the back of my bowed head. "Now, now, Emma. Don't lose hope. Those *plateyes* didn't show up for nothing. They multiplied because they knew we're getting close. If they thought we couldn't crack this, they wouldn't bother. There's got to be an answer we don't see yet."

I wipe the hot tears from my face and sniff the snot back up into my nose. "Really?"

She smiles. "Really. Now let me set to work on those words of hers." She chants Sabina's foreign phrase perfectly from memory, then nods and sucks her teeth. "That's the key, I'm sure of it."

"Do you think we'll figure it out in time to save Jack?" I bite my lip, afraid to hear the answer.

Her eyes soften. "I hope so, child. I hope so."

Chapter Twenty-five

After returning home and indulging in a two-hour nap, I'm feeling strong enough to check in with the guys. "So how'd it go? Did you get the necklace?" I plop down on the couch next to Jack and, because Dad's not home, put my feet up on the coffee table. Cooper and I have decided not to tell Jack about our relationship. He's got enough problems. He doesn't need to worry that Cooper will abandon him for me. We'll wait until after he's cured to break the news. Although now that we've hit another honking road block, that might take awhile.

"Nice of you to join us, Em." Jack nudges me in the ribs with his elbow. "I wondered if you were going to sleep clear through tomorrow. I guess all that non-curse breaking gets pretty tiring."

He has no idea.

Cooper kicks the sole of Jack's outstretched flip-flop. "Hey, be nice." He glances up at me and smiles. His powder-blue eyes gleam and send that delicious chill through my body. Memories of last night roll through my mind, flushing my cheeks with amorous heat.

I squelch a sigh. He's perfect. And if I have anything to do with it, he'll stay that way. The darkness will not swallow him.

Cooper winks. "You'll have to forgive your brother, Emmaline. He's grumpy from chasing Missy around all day."

"That's only because you haven't managed to swipe that necklace before now." Jack crosses his arms and turns to me. "Dang, Em, I've never known anyone to be so busy doing nothing. We followed her to the grocery store, the gym, a restaurant, and her salon."

I snort. "What'd you do, stalk her?"

Cooper shakes his head and smirks. "Nah, not really."

Jack kicks him back. "Of course we did. How else are we supposed to get the ruby and reverse this?" He rips off the glove, then lifts his arm and jerks up the rash guard sleeve. The moldy scent of decay floods the room. Cooper and I both groan and slap our hands to our noses. The end of his radius and ulna are bare now, and a new, wider band of flesh is red and bulging. It takes up half of his remaining forearm.

I silently chastise myself for making him believe the necklace is the key to breaking his curse and not Cooper's—which, of course, they don't even know about. But I can't reveal the truth. It'll crush Cooper to know I lied, and then we'll be over before we've even begun. It's better to change the subject. "Look, I'm sorry you guys wasted your time. What were you thinking, anyway? Don't you think she got a little suspicious with you two popping up everywhere she went?"

Jack glares at me through his long black lashes. "Do we look that stupid?" He peers at Cooper, who's chuckling at his annoyance. "We were discreet. Besides, she's not the brightest halogen. She wouldn't realize we were following her unless we strapped on neon signs and waved at her."

I can't help but laugh. But before his ego's boosted too much, I shrug my shoulders and try to bring him back to earth. "Yeah, but what was the point? Did you think she'd fall unconscious in the freezer aisle, and you'd get to rip it off her neck?"

He quirks his brow so hard the creases form an S. "No, but I figured she'd at least take it off while she worked out or when she had her massage at the spa."

Cooper nods. "Actually, I thought it was a good idea, too. We were ready to sneak into the women's locker room and go through her stuff." He mashes his lips together and scratches his temple. "Am I the only one worried about how easy it's getting to commit crime?"

Jack waves him off. "Don't stress, dude. It's only temporary." He turns back to me. "It was a great plan, except Missy wore the stinking thing the whole time. I mean, even during her yoga class and when she was on the elliptical."

I wince. "Ew, it must be crusted with sweat."

Jack shrugs. "Probably, but who cares, right? I'll take it any way I can, slimy or not." He lifts his arm. "This is already the grossest thing ever. A little sweat doesn't scare me."

A wave of sadness overwhelms me. He doesn't realize how bad it'll get before it's too late to save him. Hot tears build up behind my eyes and threaten to well over. *Normal, Emma, act normal.* Nothing's changed—Jack's still got The Creep, and Miss Delia's working on a cure—so there's no need to volunteer the news about our latest obstacle. I grit my teeth and gulp the rising sob back down my throat.

Cooper leans toward Jack. "So, genius, what's our next move? I tried to sneak in their room last night, but…"

"But what?" Jack knits his brow.

"It's just…well, you know." Cooper turns the most adorable shade of pink. "Their room isn't exactly quiet at night, if you catch my drift. I'd hate to walk in on something I shouldn't see."

A little throw-up lurches into my mouth. Beau. Missy. Then Beau and Missy. I shudder. On second thought, Jack was wrong. His arm isn't the grossest thing ever—this new picture in my head is. By a long country mile.

Jack crosses his arms and stares at his outstretched legs. "I was hoping she'd take it off at night, but after today, I wonder if she ever does. I think our best bet is to just keep following her. Who knows? Maybe Emma's right. Maybe she'll trip on one of those stilettos of hers and knock herself out. We wouldn't want to miss a perfect opportunity to grab it."

Cooper chuckles. "That would sure make it easy, wouldn't it?" Then his face falls. "You're not suggesting we trip her or anything, right?" He hitches a worried eyebrow. "Because stealing is one thing. Hurting people, even Missy, is another."

Jack cocks his head. "Don't be an idiot. Violence is only very rarely the answer. I'll figure something out. It just might take some time."

I stare at his arm and count the weeks between today and Cooper's birthday. Time is the one thing we don't have. Jack's disintegrating every couple of days. How can he be so casual about this?

I purse my lips and approach this gently. "Um, Jack, you need to figure this out soon. Actually, sooner than soon."

"Yeah, I know. I'm working on it."

I rub my throbbing forehead. "Really? Because you seem kind of laid-back about it."

"I got this. We're cool."

Heat rushes to my cheeks as words trip from my mouth. "No, we're not. We're running out of time."

Cooper leans forward. "What do you know, Emmaline? Did

something happen at Miss Delia's today?"

Jack's brow furrows. "Yeah, weren't you supposed to do another one of those *Psychic Vision* things? Did you see who created The Creep?" He winces and pinches the bridge of his nose. "Stupid headache is back again."

I exhale and try to figure out how to answer their questions. "Yeah, I saw it all right. It was pretty horrible." Launching into the story, I explain what I saw and stick to the facts, skirting all references to how Lady Rose's progeny was cursed because of the necklace. To reduce Cooper's and Jack's panic, I play down the *plateye* attack, putting as much positive spin on their presence as possible. Despite the guys' horrified expressions, I force a smile and act as if being attacked by four seething beasts is no big deal.

I shrug. "Really, Miss Delia said it's actually a good thing that so many showed up. They wouldn't multiply if we weren't getting close." Cooper strains to keep his cool, but after last night, I know no matter how I spin it, his protection meter is off the charts. To keep from tipping off Jack, I avoid eye contact with Cooper and try to stay focused.

"So while we work out the *Break Jinx*, I need you guys to get the necklace because—I don't know if you've noticed, Jack, but The Creep is moving faster up your arm."

He lifts his hand. "Duh. That's not a news flash." He drops his ruined arm. "Believe me, I understand what'll happen if we don't get the ruby."

No, he doesn't, because I haven't told them about the Beaumont curse. Images from both *Psychic Visions* fly through my head, and dread swells in my gut. There's still a slim chance Miss Delia and I will decipher Sabina's words and generate enough power to seal the elements together, but without the ruby necklace, Cooper will be lost.

A brutal concoction of despondence and fear churns my stomach. Who am I kidding? We probably won't be able to save Jack, either. I'll lose them both. Forever.

I suddenly feel so small, so battered from fighting Sabina's relentless twin curses. After watching the visions, I understand why Sabina wanted revenge. Bloody Bill and Edmund did a horrible thing and had it coming. But why do both curses have to exact so much havoc on the two people I love the most? What did *we* do to deserve this?

Maybe it's the pressure of hiding the lie, the post-traumatic stress from the *plateye* attack, or my anger toward Sabina for creating these horrific spells, but Jack's smug expression puts me over the edge, igniting a fury that explodes and travels from my heels to my hair. I clench my fists and shout, "You think you know everything, but you don't know squat."

Jack's eyes flash with as much surprise as anger. "Who do you think you are? I'm the one who's falling apart!" He slams his bony hand on the coffee table. The tips of his phalanges crack and splinter, and the top of the middle one snaps clean off.

Chapter Twenty-six

Cooper guides the station wagon down the country lane toward Miss Delia's house. We've driven this road several times since the museum heist, so the overgrowth is mashed down, making it easier to avoid the rocks and potholes. It's overcast and chillier than normal, so for once we don't need to blast the air conditioner.

Cooper glances at me in the rearview mirror, his eyes filled with concern. "I know you and Miss Delia think you can handle things on your own, but if those *plateyes* show up again, I want you to call us. Missy's meeting some friends for lunch in Beaufort, so we'll be nearby. It won't take us long to come and get you."

I wish I could sit in the front seat with him, holding his hand. But that would give Jack a giant clue that things have…evolved between Cooper and me.

Jack's lip curls. "Hey, speak for yourself. I didn't volunteer to fight those hellhounds. I've got enough problems." He raises his elbow to remind us that, if things proceed as usual, the rest of his forearm is likely to burst tonight. And that he's irretrievably lost the tip of his middle finger. He's soaked his phalanges in water and slathered them with moisturizer every night since, trying to keep them moist. I'm sorry for him, but the upside is, it's reduced his enthusiasm for flipping the bird. At least he was kind enough to keep everything covered up and the stink under his rash guard. He crosses his arms. "If you want to be a hero go right ahead, but count me out."

I roll my eyes, then turn my attention to Cooper. "Thanks, but Miss Delia's got plenty of whiskey. We'll be fine." I toss him a surreptitious kiss from behind Jack's back.

He smiles but then looks stern. "I'm serious, Emmaline." His voice drops. "Those things keep multiplying. At some point you won't be able to hold them back, no matter how much liquor you've got."

"Maybe, but we've got hoodoo magic on our side." I waggle my brows and grin, hoping he's thinking as much about our second and third beach dates as I am. "Besides, I don't want to take you away from your mission. We need the necklace."

He nods. "I know. I've got a good feeling about today. I overheard Missy planning a trip to a jewelry store with her friends. There's no way she'll keep the ruby pendant on if she's considering other necklaces."

Jack twists in his seat to face Cooper. "So, brainiac, how are we going to get it if we're outside the shop watching them?" He looks out the window at the silver sky. "Which won't be a lot of fun if it starts to pour."

Cooper shrugs. "Aw, what's the matter, you afraid you're going to melt? Trust me, you aren't that sweet." He laughs and steers around the last big hole in the road. "Besides, you'll be fine. There's an umbrella in the trunk. If we see her take off the necklace, we'll go in there, distract them, and grab it. Easy."

Jack blinks. "Right. Easy."

I laugh. "Let's hope so."

We round the bend in the lane. The bottle tree sways in the breeze, its multicolored glass the only bright spot on this usually gray morning. A tuft of white cotton lies on the ground under its gigantic canopy. I squint to make it out, then realize the dark green lump next to it isn't grass—it's a housedress. Unease crawls up my spine. I throw open the back door of the still-moving car.

Cooper's eyes widen in the rearview mirror. "What are you doing, Emmaline?"

"Stop the car!" I yell.

He slams on the breaks as I release the seat belt, bolt from the car, and charge toward the crumpled body lying on the ground. Miss Delia's features come into view. So do the crimson splotches that cover her face, dress, and legs.

No! No! No!

A surge of adrenaline charges through me, catapulting my heart into overdrive. I scream her name, then dive to the ground to grab her bloody hand. Pounding feet run up behind me.

"Miss Delia," I cry again. I gently jostle her soiled shoulder to rouse her, but she lies motionless with her eyes shut. Shock and fear swell in my chest as my trembling fingers search her broken body. She's been mauled and is covered with at least a hundred bite marks that have torn into her clammy skin and shredded her dress. Her tattered flesh hangs in places, slathered with frothy drool and slashed by the *plateyes'* jagged teeth.

I press a quaking finger to her neck. Her pulse is slow and weak, but it's there. The faintest moan slips from her lips. A glimmer of hope springs in me. She's not dead. Yet.

"Call an ambulance!" I shriek because I left my messenger bag and phone in the backseat. The guys reach my side and kneel next to her. Cooper flips open his phone and places the call.

Jack's eyes fill with panic. "Is she dead, Em?"

"What do we do?" Cooper asks at the same time.

"No, and I don't know," I answer as my eyes dart around, taking in the scene. An empty bottle of whiskey lies next to her, and her other hand clutches Bloody Bill's knife, which is splattered with blood. I'm not sure whether the sticky red substance belongs to Miss Delia or the *plateyes*, but I pray she hurt at least one of them. The ground is scarred with dozens of enormous paw prints, claw marks included. Her *collier* beads are strewn all over. My mind zooms, calculating what must have gone on here. One bottle distracted four dog-beasts the other day; based on the number of impressions and the extent of her injuries, she must have been attacked by at least eight. Judging from how bright the color of her blood is, she hasn't been here long. We probably just missed them. My gaze flies around us in a three-sixty, making sure the evil beasts aren't still lingering in the shadows.

Thick, stinging tears erupt as I imagine what she endured. Cornered by demons and armed with only one bottle of whiskey, the terror must have been overwhelming and the pain immeasurable. She didn't deserve to suffer this way.

As much as I want to wail at the cold gray sky and give in to hopelessness, I can't. I have to be strong, take charge of the situation, and care for her. Smearing the tears from my face, I swallow the lump in my throat, then clench my fists and mine an extra reserve of strength from deep in my gut.

Maybe I can work some hoodoo to help her. Sirens whirl in the distance, so I've got to work fast. *Four Thieves Vinegar* saved her the last time, but she's too far gone for it to make much of a dent now. Although it might help her survive until the ambulance gets her to the hospital.

Stained with her blood, I leap to my feet. "I'll be right back.

Stay with her, and make sure she doesn't die!"

I'm not sure how they'll accomplish that, but somehow they'll have to. I sprint to the front porch, shove open the screen door, and bolt through the living room into the kitchen. Scrambling up onto the counter, I scan the shelves for the potion, grab the little clear vial and a spoon, then run back out to the yard.

Jack's pacing under the bottle tree, his head in his hands, muttering to himself, "Who's going to fix me if she dies?"

Cooper strokes Miss Delia's forehead, the least bloody part of her body, and whispers soothing words close to her ear.

I wipe the sweat trickling down my forehead with my arm. "Here, Miss Delia, it's *Four Thieves*." My hands shake as I pour the spicy mint potion onto the spoon and lift it to her lips. "You've got to stay with us. Help is on the way." Her mouth doesn't open, so I nod toward Cooper. He pries her lips apart, and I insert the spoon. The vinegar slips down her throat, and her eyes twitch behind her closed lids. Maybe she knows what I've given her. At least I hope so.

The sirens grow louder, and multiple engines rumble as they round the turn. They'll be here in a few seconds. The last thing we need is for the sheriff to take the knife as evidence. I reach across Miss Delia's frayed and crippled body, uncurl her fingers from the handle, and hand it to Cooper. He snatches the knife and the empty whiskey bottle, then jogs to Beau's car and tosses them in the driver's-side window. The ambulance emerges from the turn in the road first and is followed by a sheriff's car.

I grasp Miss Delia's hand. "Help's here, Miss Delia. Hold on." When I squeeze, my fingers brush against something in her grip. A small square of folded paper. My scalp prickles. Whatever it is, it's important. I slip it into my back pocket just as the emergency responders climb from their vehicles.

An EMT with a nametag that says Briscoe jogs toward us. "What's going on here?" A deputy sheriff strides up to the tree after him.

Jack stops short. "Can't you see she's been attacked?" His eyes are crazed. "Stop asking questions and help her!" He thrusts his golf glove in Miss Delia's direction.

Cooper returns from the car and clamps Jack on the shoulder. "Sorry, he's just upset," he tells the paramedic. "She's very important to him."

Briscoe depresses the button on the walkie-talkie strapped to his shoulder. "Johnson, we're going to need the stretcher. This one's a real mess." He turns away from Jack, who's jerked out from under Cooper's grasp and gone back to pacing. Briscoe crouches next to Miss Delia to take her vitals.

The deputy pulls me aside. "Do you have any idea what happened to her? It looks like a bear attack. 'Course we don't have any in these parts. Whatever it was, it was big."

I gulp. "I think it was a dog. Or, actually, dogs. She's been having trouble with them coming out of the woods."

He rubs his chin and scans the surrounding trees. Between my seemingly ridiculous cover story and Jack's hair-pulling and murmuring panic, it's clear he's not buying it. I half wish a few *plateyes* would bound out of there to prove what I'm saying, but that would only raise more questions and require more hospital transports.

"We better get her out of here before Amelia arrives," Briscoe tells his partner.

Cooper and I exchange looks. I can tell he's wondering the same thing I am. Who the heck is Amelia? Probably a rival ambulance driver.

"I'm with you. I don't want to be out here any longer than I have to." Johnson pushes the stretcher under the tree, and he and Briscoe get to work on her. A few minutes later, Miss Delia's safe and secure in the ambulance. I try to go with her, but Johnson refuses, explaining that I can't because I'm a minor, plus she's so messed up and needs so much care, they don't want me to distract them. After the ambulance leaves, Jack continues his freak-out while Cooper and I do our best to answer the deputy's questions. Sort of. I mean, how do you explain that much damage to a little old lady? A couple bites are kind of understandable, but a hundred is a stretch. Plus I'm pretty sure he can smell the lingering scent of whiskey on the ground.

As soon as the EMTs and the deputy are gone, Cooper turns to me, exhausted. "So now what?"

I slip the note from my pocket and scan it. At first the jumbled letters don't make sense, but I sound them out phonetically and realize what it is. A chill zips up my spine. "I'm going to need that knife."

Chapter Twenty-seven

Jack rushes up to my side. "Why are you wasting time with the knife?" His face is drawn and yellow with panic. "I thought you already saw how The Creep was created."

"We did, but there was something we didn't understand. I found this in Miss Delia's hand"—I flash the paper in front of him—"so I'm hoping Miss Delia's figured it out." I dash toward the porch.

Jack follows me. "But what is it, and what does it have to do with the knife?" His voice is filled with a mixture of confusion and hope.

"She might have stabbed one of the *plateyes*. If she did, a *Psychic Vision* charm will tell me what she was doing just before the attack. It might be the answer we've been looking for." I offer a silent prayer that it will.

Panting, Cooper sprints up the porch steps with the knife.

I reach out and squeeze Jack's upper arm. "I'm sorry, but you know the drill. You can't come in."

His jaw tenses. "What are we supposed to do? We can't sit out here, not with those demons on the loose."

I look around for a suitable substitute. "Wait in Cooper's car. You'll be safe there."

Reluctantly, Cooper nods. He hands me the knife, and the guys turn and head for the station wagon.

I charge in the house and run to the kitchen, making a mental list of everything I need to do before conjuring the charm. No matter what, I've got to fight the weariness and stay focused. This spell has got to be right if I have any hope of seeing the knife's last cut. I hope Miss Delia plunged the blade into a *plateye*'s gut, or maybe carved a hole in a fluorescent dead eye, anything, so long as the scene it reveals isn't from three hundred years ago. I'm done with the scary history lessons.

I stack the ingredients on the counter in the order in which they'll be added, then sit on the stool for a few moments and breathe, clearing my head to prepare. I took a ritual bath this morning, just in case Miss Delia and I worked some hoodoo, but since her blood is on my clothes and skin, I'm betting that purification is ruined. A quick splash of citronella should be enough to set me straight. I wash her blood from my hands, then dab enough of the lemon-scented essential oil on my wrists, behind my ears, and down my neck to smell like a backyard barbecue. I rub my *collier* for luck and set to work on the *Psychic Vision* spell. Biting my lip and doubling my focus, I brew the tea and ignite the charcoal.

Just as I'm about to add the ingredients as Miss Delia taught me, the sky opens up, dumping a deluge. The familiar rumble of thunder rolls in the forest just beyond the house. Moments later, the temperature drops, and the rain transforms into hail, beating against the roof and window. Thunder claps again, this time just overhead, shaking the building. Almost instantly, a bolt of lightning

follows, zapping the ground in the side lot and scorching
Miss Delia's kitchen herbs.

Dodging the flying chunks of ice, Cooper and Jack run
screaming through the yard, then bound up the steps to the
kitchen porch and jump through the tattered screens.

I jump from my stool and race to meet them. "What are you
doing? You're supposed to stay in the car."

Jack's frantic. "I don't know if you've noticed, but it's hailing.
And there's thunder. And scary frigging lightning."

Cooper nods. "It almost hit us. If it strikes again, we'll be toast."

Don't they know that lightning almost never strikes in the
same exact place? But then again, this isn't normal lightning. It's
elemental magic.

I sigh, sensing they're probably right to want to get out of the
car. But that doesn't mean they're allowed in the house, either.
"Listen, you need to stay out here on the porch, okay? Jack can't
bring that curse inside, and you're not allowed to watch me work
the magic. They're Miss Delia's rules, and I'm not going to break
them."

They nod in unison. "Whatever you say," Jack says,
uncharacteristically compliant. "As long as I'm not stuck in the
yard." He plops down in a chair and pulls it as close to the house
as possible.

I turn to Cooper. "I'm going in there to work the charm.
Don't come in, no matter what you hear." I level my gaze at him,
anticipating his shining-knight impulse. "If you make me screw up,
I'll have to let the mortar rest for another few days."

He lifts his palms in surrender. "I understand." Then he sits
next to Jack as I shut the kitchen door to keep them from hearing
the spell.

Ten minutes later, as hail continues to lash the roof, I'm poised over the mortar, ready to begin again. I layer the ingredients in the mortar, fighting to keep my focus, but feel my strength drain nonetheless. Resisting the weariness, I unfold the paper and sound out the strange words scratched in Miss Delia's shaky handwriting. Even with my horrible American accent, I can tell it's the foreign incantation Sabina spoke on the ship. I wrap the paper around the knife handle, then clutch it in my hand and rest my arm on the mortar's carved lip.

This is it. My first official, solo hoodoo spell. I hope my spirit guide is with me, because I'm not sure I can do this on my own. My heart pounds as I swig the rusty brown psychic tea in one giant gulp. The cherry-spinach flavor is just as disgusting as before, but that's a good thing because it means I brewed it right.

Another clash of thunder breaks the air above the house. A sharp pain twists my stomach, and I lurch forward on my stool, doubling over. The energy seems to seep from my limbs, only to coalesce and swirl in my gut. I retch but clamp my mouth shut to keep the tea down. As much as I want to puke this all out, I can't. I've gone too far with this charm to turn back now.

Exhaling to center myself as best I can, I rub the *collier* once more and trust the red and white glass beads will help me find the right words. The tea's woozy effects take hold, spinning my brain as the spell leaps from my lips. "Smoke and mist reveal the past, and how this object was used last. Reveal the truth behind this verse, and guide my way to break the curse." The words are mumbled, but they make sense and seem to do the trick.

Dark images flicker on the smoke screen: nightfall, water, a ship, candlelight. I knit my brow. This isn't a memory from this morning. It's *The Dagger*. I grunt. The blood on the blade didn't belong to a *plateye*. It must have been Miss Delia's. Too bad she didn't get to stab even one of those heinous creatures.

I'm about to drag myself out of the vision when a menacing voice jeers, "Come now, be a nice little flower."

The scene zooms closer to reveal a pack of ravenous pirates circling and taunting a bound girl. I assume she's the slave Edmund gave them in exchange for not sacking High Point Bluff. The fabric of her dress appears finer than that of the other enslaved people I've seen in earlier visions, but the bodice is torn, hanging ragged in several places. Her hands are tied behind her back, and a sack covers her head. The pirates pace around her, laughing as they jab their swords and daggers in her direction.

Bloody Bill claps his hands to interrupt them. His carrot-red hair glows in the candlelight. "Now, now, you're pirates, but there's no need to be such rotten scoundrels. Have you learned nothing while under my tutelage?" Despite his aristocratic accent and words, his arched brow and smirk reveal his insincerity. "Why, the maiden is our guest, courtesy of Lord Beaumont, so it's our duty to provide her with the very best accommodations. Show her some manners, won't you?" He flashes a sinister grin. "After all, even Shakespeare advocated killing with kindness."

The pirates erupt in peals of hearty, lusty laughter.

Through it all, the restrained girl stands square shouldered and motionless, her head held high under the burlap cover.

Bloody Bill steps close and fiddles with a long lock of fuzzy black hair that peeks out from under the sack. He ducks down and sniffs it. "Hmm, as sweet as any flower I've ever smelled." He licks his lips. "What say you, boys? Shall we meet our guest?"

"Aye!" they cheer in unison and hoist their daggers and swords in the air as he yanks the cover off her face.

I suck in a huge mouthful of air. It's Maggie. Our Maggie. *Jack's* Maggie. My exhausted mind spins. How could she have been on the ship?

Bloody Bill smiles and takes a deep bow. "Good evening, miss. Welcome aboard my humble vessel, *The Dagger*. 'Tis a pleasure to make your acquaintance."

Maggie juts out her jaw and narrows her gaze but says nothing in response.

He grabs her chin and stares hard at her features. "Your master spoke the truth, love. You are the most beautiful creature mine eyes have gazed upon." He snickers. "This may have been a fair barter, after all." She snaps her head away, out of his grasp. His face hardens. "Oh, you wouldn't want to disappoint your master, now would you? He promised you'd be of good use. I know most of this lot is ragged and infested with scurvy, but I assure you, they'll be perfect gentlemen. You won't even notice their bloody gums or open sores." He roars with laughter.

Her nostrils flare, and she spits in his face. "I care not what my master thinks. Kill me. I am through doing his bidding. And I certainly won't do yours." Her accent is thicker and more foreign than I recognize, but it's definitely Maggie's voice.

Bloody Bill's chest puffs up, exposing his giant ruby necklace, and his eyes fill with rage. He pulls his fist back and pounds her hard in the face. The crew cheers again, lunging for her, but Bloody Bill holds up his hand to keep them back.

Maggie sways, then falls to the deck with a *thud*, her bound arms preventing her from breaking her fall. She glares at him.

He wags his finger. "See what you made me do, poppet? If only you'd been a bit more agreeable. Now you'll have a bruise as big as a cannonball on that pretty eye." He drags her up from the floor and leans close to her ear.

"Get away from me, vermin."

He sighs. "Very well, have it your way." A malicious smile creeps across his lips as he paces around her. "Though I suspect you'll change you mind after spending some time in the brig." He howls with laughter. "Take her below, mateys!"

The pirates charge, like starving dogs racing for scraps, and scoop her up. Her expression turns blank as they carry her down the steps to the 'tween deck.

The vision flickers to a stop, and the smoke dissipates. Just as quickly, the hail ceases.

My heart rages in my chest, and my fingers tremble as I try to make sense of what I just saw. Maggie was on *The Dagger* with Bloody Bill. How is that possible? I grab my bleary head to make it stop spinning. A thousand scenarios race through my rattled mind. Maybe the girl was one of her ancestors. But Maggie doesn't just resemble the girl in the vision. She looks and sounds *exactly* like her.

A chill runs up my spine. Maggie *is* the girl.

Chapter Twenty-eight

Suddenly it all makes sense—her weird accent and strange cadence, appearing out of nowhere and then vanishing to find her non-existent grandmother, even the cold temperature of her skin. She's not alive and hasn't been for almost three hundred years.

I grunt. How did I not see this earlier? It's so obvious, I'm embarrassed I missed it. But I have an idea of how we were so easily fooled.

Knife in hand, I work to lift myself off the stool. My legs are thick and lazy, refusing to obey my command to cross the kitchen. Forcing each foot to lift and walk across the floor, I finally manage to make it to the side door. Pulling it open, I stumble past Cooper and Jack, ignoring their alarm, and cross the porch, heading for the ragged screen door. Tripping down the porch steps, I drag my depleted body out into the side yard and stand in the scorch mark left by the lightning.

Jack and Cooper scramble after me, dodging the herbs and other plants in Miss Delia's garden.

Squinting at the sky's harsh silver light, I bellow, "Magnolia

Akan! Show yourself now!" The scent of the storm hangs heavy in the air. A cool breeze blows through the garden, swaying the bottles on the tree.

Maggie's got a lot of explaining to do. After everything I've been through today—actually, make that the whole summer—it better be good.

Cooper's brow knits. "What's going on?" His voice is tense. "What did you see?"

"What does Maggie have to do with this?" Jack asks. "And why are you yelling at her? She's not here."

My chest heaves as I strive to stay upright. "You'll see in a second." My pulse throbs at my temples as I stare at the woods. My finger flicks at the edge of Miss Delia's note. It's still wrapped around the knife handle, which feels like it weighs twenty pounds. The inscription is too important to risk losing, so I unravel it and shove it into my pocket.

The trees rustle in the wind. Just as I expected, Maggie emerges from the forest, barefoot and in a flowing white dress, her shoulders thrust back and a broad smile on her face. She approaches with an unmistakable air of calm and dignity. "Congratulations. You have done well, Emma Guthrie." The scent of stargazer lilies floods the cool air around us.

I fail to see how this is something to celebrate. From where I sit, it's pretty awful. One half of me wants to run to her, scoop her up in my arms, and console her for all she's endured, but the smarter half keeps a safe distance. No matter how much sympathy I have for her, I can't forget that our lives were normal, even boring, until we met her.

Even though my brain is working at half-speed, I'm still quick enough to realize she's the one who goaded Jack into searching for the treasure. If it wasn't for her, Jack never would have opened the box and gotten The Creep. His hand and arm would be whole, and instead of conjuring hoodoo spells, I'd be worried about getting close to Cooper on his boat. She couldn't leave us alone, and now things are beyond freaky. I don't care what happened to her all those years ago. She can't be trusted.

I set my jaw. "Thanks, but after the *Psychic Vision* I just watched, I don't think I'd be smiling." My body trembles. I'm talking to a ghost. Even though I know it's true, it doesn't seem possible. I scan her flawless face for some evidence of the past, maybe a mark where Bloody Bill punched her, or some other horrendous scar, but there's nothing. She's so real, so present, so… alive. How?

Her smile falters, but only slightly. "It was a long time ago. Old wounds heal. Even the worst of them. Eventually you barely notice they exist at all."

Of course she has to make this all about her. This has all been about her, hasn't it? She endured something truly evil, but that doesn't make up for what she's done to my brother. I scoff and mine every last morsel of energy to confront her. "I'm glad you've had plenty of time to get over the trauma. But I doubt Jack *barely notices* his bony hand and arm, since you know, he hasn't had almost three centuries to heal."

Cooper scratches his head. "Um, I'm totally confused."

Jack nods. "Yeah, Em, you want to clue us in here?"

I cross my arms, careful not to cut myself with the blade. "I wish I could, but it seems Maggie's been keeping a lot of secrets from us," I answer, not taking my eyes off her. "Haven't you, *Magnolia*?"

The sky tinges green, and a few scant drops of rain fall.

"Hey, take it down a notch, Emo. Just because you're upset about what happened to Miss Delia doesn't mean you get to take it out on my girlfriend." Jack steps to her side, and she clasps his good hand.

"Ha! That's a good one! Yeah, your girlfriend. Uh-huh. A real, live person who's honest and trustworthy." My eyelids droop as I fight to keep them open.

His lip curls. "What's wrong with you?"

I stagger toward him, ignoring the pain that still burns in my gut. "Wake up, Jack. She's not what she appears to be. Haven't you ever noticed how she just arrives and disappears? Or how cold she is?"

He cocks his head. "Huh?"

He doesn't get it. How can he miss her icy touch? I felt it the split second I hugged her on Dad's porch. Yet she practically crawls over him, and it's never occurred to him? Unless…I turn to her. "Or is that something you've magically blocked from his mind? That is one of your powers, right? Mind control? That's how you got Jack to go after the treasure, even though we thought it was a giant waste of time."

Jack grimaces and rubs his head. "What are you talking about, Emma?"

Cooper reaches for my arm and pulls me back a step. "I hate to say it, Emmaline, but you sound a little crazy," he whispers in my ear, just loud enough for me to hear over the strengthening breeze.

I yank free of his grasp. "Believe me, I know exactly what's going on, and so does Maggie. Don't I?" I struggle to lift the blade and point it at her.

She nods, the broad smile still spread across her face. "I cannot deny that Emma is correct."

What's wrong with her? Doesn't she realize what she's done to us? To Jack? I don't care what happened to her, I want to smack that stupid grin right off her face. If I wasn't about to fall on the ground, I just might.

Cooper's face falls. "What are you saying?"

"Maggie's the flower!" My voice echoes across the garden. "The one Bloody Bill's crew plucked."

Jack's lip curls. "What?" He laughs. "You're insane." Maggie shudders and rubs her arms at the sound of the pirate's name. Jack's eyes widen, and he turns to her. "But...you can't be the flower." Her gaze shifts down to her toes. He shakes his head. "That's...impossible." His voice trails off as he stares at her.

"No, it's not," I answer. "The magnolia tree produces a gorgeous, aromatic flower. You can look it up in any botany book."

"Who cares about that—Maggie, how?" Jack shivers. He drops her hand and pulls away from her. Finally he must have felt the chill.

Shaking his head, Cooper takes a step back as well. "That means you're a..." His voice trails off.

She moves toward Jack. "I can explain—"

I lean in, narrowing my gaze. "It better be the truth. I'm sick of your lies."

She levels her stare at me and juts out her jaw. "I didn't have a choice."

Heat boils from my gut, overflowing in rage, giving me the strength to stand my ground. "That's crap!" I flick my wrist at the ground, sinking the knife deep into the rich soil with one fluid movement. Cooper takes another frightened step back, but Jack just stands there, dazed. I force myself forward to grab hold of his arm. "You had a choice, Maggie! You didn't have to drag us into your drama. I don't care what happened to you. It doesn't make up for what you've done to Jack!" I yank up his sleeve, exposing his bones and releasing the God-awful smell of death. "Not very pretty, is it?"

She winces and turns away, but I don't care. I'm riled up and going for the throat while I still have the energy. "You did this to an innocent person. You know what that means? You're just as bad as Edmund and those pirates." The words shoot from my mouth like bullets as I stagger backward, pulling him toward Cooper and me.

She trembles and casts her eyes down. "Emma, you don't understand. I didn't want this to happen, but it was the only way." Her voice is small and weak.

I huff. "Really? You had to hurt my brother? That's fascinating."

She nods. "Yes, I needed him, needed all of you. I cannot break the curse by myself."

I cock my head. "Oh, so now you want to break it. That's funny, considering you unleashed it on us!"

"Emma!" Her voice booms. "Can't you see I want to be free?"

Blinded with anger, I prepare to yell some more, but her words register, and I stop short. "What's that supposed to mean?" I teeter on my weary feet.

"My soul cannot pass on until the curse is broken." Her voice sounds small and desperate.

"How's that?" Cooper crinkles his brow.

She sighs. "My grandmother Sabina was a powerful root doctress, but she made a tragic mistake. In her rage, she burned my hair with that of the pirate's, thinking it would condemn him and his crew for my murder, but instead, she forever entwined my fate with the curse."

So that's what the black woolly stuff was on the deck of *The Dagger*. Yet another clue that I missed.

Maggie's eyes turn down. "So long as The Creep is unbroken, my soul remains here with my spirit on the shores of this island."

"So you've been stuck here for almost three hundred years?" Jack asks.

She purses her lips. "Yes. It has been a very lonely existence." She reaches out to him, but I shoot her the evil eye, and she drops her hand. I don't care what happened to her, or how much she needs us. She's not going to work any more magic on my brother.

Squinting in the dull gray morning light, Cooper drags his fingers through his hair, then raises his hand as if he's in class. "Hang on. How can your soul pass but your spirit stay behind? Aren't they the same thing?"

She opens her mouth, but I rush to answer, in case she decides to explain a little too well, using his scenario as an example. He's having enough trouble absorbing the whole Maggie reveal— finding out about his own soul's impending departure would probably kill him. And then he'd kill me. "The Gullah believe the soul passes on when the body dies, but the spirit stays behind to help its loved ones."

She flashes a wry grin. "You have learned much about the Gullah, Emma Guthrie. The Grannie has taught you well."

"Thanks," I snap, unmoved by her compliment. "But you haven't explained why you needed to hurt Jack to free your soul."

Her shoulders sink. "The curse is too powerful to break on my own. I have tried, believe me, but it is impossible." She looks off toward the bottle tree and blinks. "I came close once, more than a hundred years ago, with a human assistant. He worked a powerful charm, one I was certain would work, but was missing the key ingredient, and at the last moment, it failed. He was severely injured, and the first High Point Bluff was destroyed." She shuts her eyes and shakes away the images.

Jack breaks out of his stupor. "So that's all I am, your assistant?" His voice cracks as he pinches the bridge of his nose.

She nods. "You all are."

The magic's effects dissipate enough to allow me to plant my hands on my hips. "Um, maybe you don't understand the concept, but you're supposed to guide your assistant, not kill him."

Her eyes flash with anger. "I have been guiding you, every step of the way."

Jack's olive cheeks flush magenta. "Really? How? Because so far, all I can see is how you got me jacked up."

"I brought you to the Grannie"—she takes a small step toward him—"and you found my grandmother's mortar easily, did you not? Did you think it was a coincidence that it remained on Sa'leenuh all this time?" She points to the dagger handle sticking out of the ground. "And that knife, the one that has allowed your sister to see into the past." She hitches her brow. "Cooper might have overlooked it at the museum, had I not helped him see it." Then she turns to me. "And you, Emma, may never have picked it up without my urging."

My mind flashes back to how my hand itched and burned, and how badly I needed the cooling touch of the polished knife handle. "But I thought my spirit guide made me take it."

She scoffs. "She is far more subtle than that. I had to be forceful to ensure you took it. You needed to see all it could show you." She raises her brow and shoots me a knowing look. "*Everything* it knew. So you can right what is wrong."

I gulp. The Beaumont curse. She's right. If Miss Delia and I hadn't worked a psychic charm on the knife, we'd never have known how the curse was created, and I wouldn't have a chance to save him.

I ball my fists, reminding myself to stay strong and not lose sight of what's important. "You lured us into finding the treasure." I already know it's true, but I need to hear her admit it.

She nods. "Yes. I saw you and your brother on the beach that morning and was certain you were the right ones to break the curse."

Cooper shakes his head. "Even though you knew it was laced with The Creep, and at least one of us would get it?"

She swallows. "How else could I motivate you to help break it?"

My brow crinkles. "Um, how about just asking?"

She bats her long black lashes. "Ask? Really, Emma, humans are not as accommodating as you wish to believe."

Jack shakes his head. "No, she's right. We would've helped you. I'm sure of it."

She scoffs. "Why? Because of my beauty?"

"Uh," he scratches his scalp, seeming a little embarrassed, "I can't deny that would have helped. You're the most gorgeous girl I've ever seen." His cheek raises in a half-smile. "But that's not why we would've helped you. We'd have done it because you needed it."

She laughs ruefully. "Ha! And you would have believed I was dead, and my claims about a vicious, flesh-eating curse?"

He nods. "Yeah. I think we would have."

She mashes her lips together and bats back a tear. "I wish I could believe that, but I have had too much experience with humans. And too much disappointment."

Jack sets his jaw. "So rather than trust us, and tell us the truth, you manipulated us —manipulated *me*—instead."

She stiffens. "Yes. I am sorry, but it was the most expedient thing to do."

Cooper puts his hand on Jack's shoulder. "Well, I hope you're satisfied. He's my best friend, as close to a brother as I've got. Thanks to you, he might die."

She shakes her head. "No, he won't. Emma has been an excellent student. She will set things right. I am sure of it."

I cross my arms. "Um, I'm not sure if you're up to speed on things, but Miss Delia was attacked by a pack of *plateyes* this morning." The gruesome image of Miss Delia lying under the bottle tree, bloody, torn, and unconscious, flashes across my mind, choking me up. I wince and force back tears. "She's barely alive. Hopefully she made it to the hospital, and they can save her." My lip quivers.

She nods. "The curse demands many sacrifices."

"What?" The words burst from my mouth. "She didn't deserve to be mauled by a bunch of hellhounds! She was only trying to help me save Jack!" My voice breaks. "How can you be so coldhearted?"

"Because I have faith in you and know all will be well. For Jack. For the Grannie. For *everyone* who is doomed because of what happened so many years ago. You can do it, Emma. I am sure you can."

Great, no pressure there. Now on top of trying to save Jack and Cooper from two completely different curses, Miss Delia's fate and Maggie's soul get thrown into the mix. Hasn't anyone noticed I don't know what the heck I'm doing?

My cheeks flush, and my temples throb from the impossible stress. I rub my pounding forehead. "How can you say that? I'm only an apprentice. I can't do this alone." Aside from being dead, she's nuts.

She waves me off. "Nonsense. I have shown you everything you need to break the curse. Be resourceful, and you will succeed."

"No, you haven't." I shake my frazzled head, tired of her cryptic crap. "We're still missing the most important piece. I'm pretty sure Miss Delia was working on it when she got attacked."

I snatch Miss Delia's note from my pocket and charge toward Maggie, slapping it into her hand. Cold jolts my fingers, shooting straight through my flesh and into my bones. She's more frigid than I remember. My hand snaps backward.

She opens the crumpled note and scans the cryptic words. "What is this?"

"You tell me. Sabina said it when she cast The Creep, but Miss Delia had no idea what it meant."

Jack and Cooper lean toward Maggie. "What's it say?" Jack asks.

She chuckles. "My grandmother was very dramatic. This is ancient Akan. It means, 'I bind the blood of the sun and the moon, the day and the night, to bring you darkness and shorten your life.'"

The guys recoil, but I knit my brow and hold my ground. "What the heck is that supposed to mean?"

She shrugs. "I cannot say."

"You can't say, or you won't say?"

She smiles. "My grandmother based many of her spells on nature, just like your Grannie. Rest assured, it is the key to reversing the curse."

That's the worst non-answer answer I've ever heard. She hands me the note, and her icy fingers graze mine, sending a frozen shiver up my arm.

I shake off the chill and stuff the note back into my pocket. "Well, that's just awesome, considering I'm just as clueless as before you translated it. Thanks for nothing."

"It will come to you. I am sure of it. Listen to your spirit guide." She tilts her head toward Jack. "If I am right, and Emma succeeds in reversing the curse, will you ever find a way to forgive me?"

His shoulders sink. "I don't know." His voice is small and sad. "I didn't deserve this." He lifts his gloved hand.

Her eyes fill with contrition. "No, Jack Guthrie, you didn't. And you didn't deserve to suffer the headaches, either, but they are an unfortunate side effect of being influenced."

He gapes and clutches his skull. "That was you?" She nods, and he shakes his head. "Thanks for telling me. I guess. It's nice to know I don't have a brain tumor." Then he squares his shoulders. "I hope Emma can break the curse, but if she can't"—he swallows hard and clears his throat—"my whole arm will be gone soon, and then, God knows whether it'll hit my chest or my head next, or maybe both at the same time. I don't think I can live with my guts spilling out of my abdomen." He shakes his head and swallows again, but it doesn't stop the tear from running down his cheek. "You might have killed me."

"I am sorry." Her voice breaks with heart-wrenching sorrow.

He nods. "Yeah, me, too." He kicks at the long, spindly legs of an oregano plant. "Maybe you should leave us alone now."

Her breath hitches as she swallows a sob. Her body shimmers in the gloomy light, then grows fuzzy and thins, as her image breaks up and evaporates into mist. The wind kicks up, gusting through the garden and shaking the surrounding trees.

Cooper blinks. "Did that just happen?"

I nod, my eyes wide. "Uh-huh." Drained, I crash against him to stay upright.

Jack slumps to the ground. "You know what this means?" He lays his head in his hands and doesn't even notice I've fallen into Cooper's arms.

"What?" Cooper and I ask at the same time.

"I made out with a ghost."

Chapter Twenty-nine

The radio crackles with static as we drive home from the hospital after checking on Miss Delia. By some miracle she survived the surgery but is still in a coma. With her lying there unconscious, there was no sense in hanging around, especially after the last festering section of Jack's forearm exploded right there in her room. Luckily, we grabbed some gauze from a supply closet and wrapped up his radius and ulna before anyone caught sight of his exposed bones.

The music cuts off abruptly. "We interrupt this program to update you on Hurricane Amelia's progress." The disc jockey's voice sounds controlled but strained through the electrical interference. "Storm winds have taken an unexpected and sudden turn and are now projected to reach one hundred fifteen miles per hour, and are on course to make landfall on St. Helena Island in a little more than twenty-four hours."

A chill runs over my body. Amelia is a *hurricane*. Craning my neck out the window, I peer at the thick gray sky.

"Turn it up," Jack calls from the backseat. I'm finally riding shotgun next to Cooper, so I get to control the radio.

The DJ continues. "The Sea Islands haven't seen a hurricane this strong since 1893, when twenty-foot waves bashed the shore and claimed the lives of more than two thousand people. We urge you to take proper precautions and get to high ground if possible."

My ears tingle, suddenly growing warm. I rub the cartilage, wondering why they're feeling so weird. The lobes heat next, swelling enough to make my earrings feel uncomfortable, like maybe they've been in too long or are getting infected.

A faint buzz resonates deep in my ear.

Jack shakes his head. "Dang."

"How the heck did we miss this?" Cooper asks, scratching his temple.

Jack rubs his chin. "Though now that they mention it, the weather has been kind of crappy the last few days."

Fat raindrops splatter the windshield.

It suddenly dawns on me: maybe Miss Delia and I actually caused this from working too much elemental magic.

The buzzing slowly increases and expands, dampening other sounds. I jam my finger inside and pull at the outer ear, attempting to shake loose whatever's going on. But nothing stops it. Between the radio static and the zapping sound in my ear, I can barely think straight. I shut off the radio, but the internal hum persists.

Suddenly, I remember how my burning hand longed for the cool dagger at the museum, and wonder whether Maggie's doing something to tip me off. Yanking my ear, I call out, "If this is you, Maggie, you can knock it off and just tell me what I need to know." Since I can't hear myself, I'm probably speaking louder than I think.

The buzzing continues, and my skin blazes.

Cooper's eyes expand. "What's going on?" He reaches over

and strokes my arm.

Jack lunges forward, popping his head between the two front seats. "Is Maggie here?"

I shake my head. "I don't know. My ears are ringing, and they're hot, so I thought she might be trying to tell me something."

"Is the feeling as strong as you had in the museum?" Cooper asks, keeping his eyes on the road.

I consider his question. There isn't any urge or deep longing. "No. It's just a weird physical thing. Why?"

Cooper shrugs, dropping his arm from mine and grasping the steering wheel. "Didn't Maggie say your spirit guide was more subtle than she was?"

"Do you think my spirit guide's talking to me?" I ask.

The buzzing stops, and the heat drains from my ears. A chill runs up my spine as I lean back in the front seat.

"What is it, Em?" Jack asks. "You look kind of weird."

I turn my head toward him and stare, amazed by the clarity of his voice when just a second ago it was fuzzy and warped. "It stopped. Everything. The buzzing, the hot feeling. Everything's back to normal." I rub my ears again.

Cooper smiles. "I think you just learned to hear that spirit guide of yours."

Jack nods. "Dang."

"Okay, but what is she saying?" I push a strawberry-blonde lock behind my ear. "I mean, it started as soon as that DJ finished reading the news."

Jack quirks his brow. "Come on. You heard a report, and your ears started acting up. Duh, put them together."

My ear buzzes, and the heat spikes for just a few seconds, then cuts off again. Okay, it's definitely my spirit guide, and she wants me to pay attention to what the weatherman said. I gnaw the inside of my bottom lip and stare at the dash, pondering. Disparate pieces from the last few weeks come together, illuminating the path I should follow.

A jolt of realization zaps me. "It's the hurricane. It'll give us the wind and water we need to break the curse."

"But what about the other stuff? Don't you need earth and fire, too?" Cooper asks.

I grab Miss Delia's spell book from my messenger bag and clutch it close to my chest. "Leave that to me and my spirit guide to figure out. In the meantime, we've got to get that necklace from Missy."

"But—"

I cut him off. "Listen, we've only got twenty-four hours to get this right. I don't care if you have to rip it off her neck while she's sleeping, you have to get it."

• • •

Dad's sitting at the kitchen table when we walk in, his head in his hands. "Where have y'all been? I've been calling you all day. Amelia bent eastward early this morning and is nearly here." His face is creased with worry.

My stomach sinks. We had to turn our cell phones off in the hospital. I reach into my bag and fumble with my phone. There they are, six unread messages. Jack's phone probably has the same amount. "Sorry, Dad."

He nods, then squints at Jack's gauze-wrapped hand and arm. "What happened to you, son? Are you okay?" He goes to stand up, but Jack jumps to explain.

"Yeah, I'm fine." He chuckles and waves Dad off. "Just a little poison ivy incident from when we were hiking. That's where we were, when you couldn't reach us, probably out of signal range." He points to his bandaged arm. "Anyway, I asked Emma to wrap it for me so I won't scratch it up." He forces another laugh. "It's probably overkill, but you know how gross poison ivy can be."

Dad's shoulders relax. "Good, you had me worried. This storm's likely to do some damage, and I'm going to have my hands full. The last thing I need is to be searching for you two or tending to a serious injury."

"Do you want us to help you board up the house or High Point Bluff?" I ask, knowing how much work it'll take to protect the plantation.

"We can take care of this house in the morning." He shakes his head and huffs. "But we're not touching the Big House."

"Why?" Jack asks.

Dad sighs. "Because rather than following the mandatory evacuation order, Missy's decided to go ahead with her Fourth of July party, only she's making it a hurricane-watching party. She'll have a full house of her fancy friends tomorrow night, and they want a clear view of the Sound."

Jack's lip curls. "That's the dumbest thing I've ever heard."

Dad scoffs. "You said it, son. But that's not the worst of it."

"What is?" A tingling feeling creeps up the back of my neck.

"She wants me to bartend, and you two to do the serving."

Chapter Thirty

I mash my lips together and try not to yell, remembering he's now the requited love of my fourteen-year-old life. "What do you mean you didn't get the necklace?" My hands fly to my hips.

Why doesn't Cooper get how important this is?

Cooper winces and backs away from me on Dad's screened porch, so I'm confident I've conveyed my frustration. He holds up his hands. "I tried, Emmaline, I swear. But my dad never went to sleep, so I couldn't go in there."

Jack plops down on the swing. "How do you know? What'd you do, stay up all night watching them?"

Cooper squares his chest and narrows his eyes. "Actually, yeah. I hung out in the hall, crouched in the dark like a frigging maniac, listening at their door all night. I don't know what he was doing in there, but he was laughing, moving things, and making all sorts of noise. And Missy was snoring the whole time. Believe me, if he ever quieted down, I was ready to sneak in there and unhook it from her neck."

Jack rakes his new glove through his jet-black hair. He's lucky

Cooper's got a bunch of unused golf equipment lying around. A tinge of panic fills Jack's eyes. "So what are we going to do? Emma, are you sure you can't skimp and work a spell without the necklace?"

My stomach drops. Sure, I can try to break The Creep, save Jack, and free Maggie's soul without the necklace, but that would leave the Beaumont curse in place and Cooper doomed. That's not an option.

I shake my head. "No, I need the necklace, and we've got to have it before the hurricane passes."

The rain's already begun, and the wind's kicking up, too, which is why we spent the morning boarding the windows of the caretaker's cottage. The screen porch is the only open area left in the house.

I turn and watch fat droplets spatter onto the screen and cling there. I'm still not exactly sure how to use the necklace, but thanks to my improved communication with my spirit guide, I'm hoping it'll hit me when the time is right.

I could also use a clue as to how I'm supposed to bind the blood of the sun and moon, the day and the night. Overnight, I scoured Miss Delia's book and my own notes and came up with a whole lot of nothing.

Cooper rubs his forehead and slouches into the settee. "So how are we going to get it? It's not like we can just ask her to hand it over."

A spark ignites in my brain, and I take a quick breath. "Maybe we can." I dash into the house to grab Miss Delia's spell book, feeling suddenly less resentful of our forced employment at tonight's stupid hurricane-watching party.

"What are you talking about?" Jack asks when I come back to the porch.

Cooper eyes me suspiciously. "What's that for?"

I settle into the settee next to him and thumb through the book, searching for a few entries I only skimmed over because I didn't think they applied. A plan forms as I review the entries. "I think we can confuse her enough to get her to hand it over tonight at the party."

Jack's brow quirks. "Right, she's just going to take it off and give it to us in front of Beau and all her friends. And no one's going to notice when we take it and ditch the party."

I nod. "Exactly."

Cooper scratches his temple. "But how?"

"We'll work a *Mind Confusion* charm on everyone there." I grin, proud of my awesome advancing hoodoo skills.

Cooper's gaze turns dark. "I don't like the sound of that. It's not right to make people do things against their will, no matter what your reason."

My brain throbs. He's going to get all moralistic on me now? After we've stolen from a museum and lied to our parents, sheriff's deputies, and hospital officials? After half of Jack's arm has fallen off and we've been chased by seething dog-beasts, the same demons that almost killed Miss Delia yesterday? Not to mention hiding our relationship from Jack. *Really?* I pinch the bridge of my nose, squeezing back the headache that's gripping my skull, and search for the words to convince him.

Jack beats me to it, leaning forward on the swing. "You're kidding, right?" I sigh, thankful we're on the same page. For once. Jack lifts his arm, which is covered by another of his rash guards. "We're talking about my life here, Coop. This morning, I woke up to find it's already moved halfway up my bicep. I'm running out of time, and you're worried about making Missy give us the necklace?"

Cooper clasps his hands and looks down at the floor. "That's not what I'm saying." His lips form a straight line. "You know I want that necklace more than anything. Heck, I was ready to crawl across my dad's bed to get it." He shakes his head. "I just don't like the idea of brainwashing anyone."

Jack rakes his good hand through his jet black hair. "It's Missy, for God's sake. You hate her, I know you do."

Cooper shuts his eyes tight. "I don't hate her." His words are stilted and forced. He looks at Jack. "I may not like her, but that means I have to be even more careful with what happens to her."

"Huh?" Jack and I tilt our heads and ask in unison.

Cooper sits up straight. "I have to treat her fairly and with respect. Otherwise, I'll question my motives."

Jack shakes his head. "I'm sorry, I still don't get it."

Cooper takes a deep breath. "It would be too obvious to do something bad to her. I can't stand the way she bosses everyone around and thinks she's something she's not. And I hate the way my father lets her get away with—even encourages—her behavior." He turns to me and gently grasps my hand. "Don't you see, Emmaline? I'd love to ask you to work some horrible hoodoo spell and sic a pack of *plateyes* on her, then watch her run screaming in those stilettos off this plantation. But that's the easy way out. As much as I can't stand her, it won't change the important things. It won't bring my mother back, and it won't make my father a decent human being."

I gasp. His words land like a punch in the gut, but only because he doesn't know how right he is about his father. A *Mind Confusion* charm won't change Beau, but it will help ensure that Cooper doesn't morph into someone like him. It'll keep Cooper the kind, loving, soulful person that he is. The Cooper I love.

I can't keep the secret from him any longer. If our relationship means anything to me, I have to tell him the truth.

I clear my throat and place my other hand on top of his. "Um, Cooper, I understand where you're coming from—"

He nods. "Right, so there's got to be some other way to get the necklace. Another spell."

I shake my head. "I'm sorry, but I don't know enough, and we're out of time. This is it."

"No? Are you sure?" His pale green eyes search mine for a different, more ethical answer.

"There's something I haven't been able to tell you, but you need to know," I say, bracing myself. "Maybe it'll help you be okay with what we have to do." I bite my lip.

He tilts his head, and his eyes narrow with alarm. "What is it?"

Gripping his hand, I squeeze my eyes shut and concentrate on forming the words. "Sabina was really angry at what Edmund and the pirates did to Maggie."

Jack huffs. "Yeah, hello, she created The Creep." He thrusts his arm in our direction.

I shake my head. "That's not all she did."

Cooper's brow knits. "What are you talking about?"

"When Edmund died, his wife, Lady Rose, needed a midwife to help her give birth to their son. Sabina was brought in to help, but when she saw the pirate's necklace around Lady Rose's neck, she freaked out." My heart thuds in my chest, and a sick feeling swirls in my stomach. These are the last words I want to utter, but I don't have a choice.

Cooper's face turns ashen. "And?"

"The necklace proved that Lady Rose had some connection with what happened on *The Dagger*. Sabina said it was a blood stone, purchased with Maggie's life. As punishment, she placed a curse on the Beaumonts, starting with Lady Rose's baby, that would be passed down to every generation."

Jack sneers. "How can the Beaumonts be cursed? They're rich."

Ignoring him, Cooper shakes his head. "What's that supposed to mean?" He grabs my arms and peers into my eyes. "Emmaline?"

I swallow hard. "You're going to lose your soul when you turn sixteen." Even though the words came out of my mouth, they sound impossible.

Cooper releases me, then stumbles off the settee as the color drains from his skin.

Jack looks stricken, as if Sabina herself had just punched him in the gut. "Whoa, that woman was hard-core."

Cooper's eyes search the room as he struggles to find words. "Lose my soul? How's that possible?"

"The curse dooms all of Edmund and Lady Rose's male progeny to lose their souls when they come of age. In Sabina's time, that was sixteen. It's happened to every generation since their child was born, including your dad. It's why none of the Gullah ever come up to High Point Bluff or work for your family. They can sense the darkness here."

Deep creases etch Cooper's brow. "No. I won't give away my soul. It can't happen if I don't agree."

I rush to him, gather up his hand, and try to impart some measly sense of comfort and support. "I'm sorry, but it's been this way for almost three hundred years. It's going to happen unless we get that necklace and break Sabina's spell. It's the only thing that links the Beaumonts to Sabina's original curse."

He draws his hand from mine. "So I have to do something wrong to make something else right. That's what you're saying?" He staggers backward toward the screen door.

"Duh, yeah." Jack jumps off the swing and meets him at the door. "This is your soul we're talking about. You can worry about hurting Missy's feelings later."

"Cooper, I know this is a lot to take in"—I gingerly step toward him—"but Jack's right. Your soul, the thing that makes you the kind and wonderful person you are, is way more important than the method we use to make Missy hand over that necklace." My voice cracks under the weight of the enormity of Sabina's curses, and the stress of finally telling him. "You're our best friend. We can't lose you." My throat constricts, and my cheeks flush hot. "*I* can't lose you."

Cooper tenses his jaw and balls his fists. His mind must be spinning, trying to sort all this out—the explanation for his father's disgusting behavior, the fear for his own life and future, and the horrible fact that I've deceived him. His chest heaves.

Jack goes to him, patting his upper arm in a gesture of tentative guy-affection. "Come on, you don't want to end up like your dad, do you? What's a little *Mind Confusion* charm when you can save yourself?"

Cooper snaps his gaze to mine. "How long have you known this, Emmaline?"

I gulp. It's the question I dreaded but knew he'd ask. "Since Miss Delia and I worked the first *Psychic Vision*." My stomach churns.

His eyes narrow. "You knew? Even before…" Knowing he's referring to our first night on the beach, I nod, unable to speak as tears well in my eyes. His mouth hangs ajar. "I can't believe you kept that from me." Shaking his head, he unknowingly grinds salt into my already weeping wound, but I deserve every ounce of pain coming to me. "You should have told me earlier."

I swallow hard to keep from puking all over the porch.

Cooper turns his back to me and addresses Jack. "Fine, what the heck. We'll do this *Mind Confusion* spell and anything else we need to break these curses. Find out what she needs from us to set things up. I'll be in the car. I can't be here anymore." He throws open the screen door and tromps down the steps into the rain.

I've been reduced to a 'she.' He might as well have plunged a dagger into my heart.

Chapter Thirty-one

Before heading to the Big House to set up for Missy's hurricane party, we take a torturously quiet trip to Miss Delia's so I can whip up a few potions and get things ready for tonight. The windshield wipers provide the only sound as Cooper drives in stony silence, his square jaw set and fingers clenched around the steering wheel, fighting the increasingly strong winds. Jack ignores me, too, but my twin sense tells me he's not angry with me, just supporting Cooper. I can't fault him. I just rocked Cooper's world, and not in a good way. He may be done with me as a girlfriend, but I hope he'll find a way to forgive me, so at least we can still be friends.

When we get to Miss Delia's, Jack and Cooper wait in the station wagon while I rummage through her kitchen, assembling everything I'll need tonight. Luckily, Miss Delia's already stockpiled some of the white magic charms I'll need to counteract Sabina's black magic, but there's one I have to blend myself in the ancestors' mortar. Miss Delia's spell book lists several *Mind Confusion* recipes with similar ingredients, so I figure it can't hurt to combine them all to create an extra strong concoction. We have to befuddle everyone at the party.

Even though I took a cleansing bath this morning, I dab my wrists and neck with the citronella oil and rub my *collier* for luck before getting started. It's impossible to avoid sniffing a little of the powder as I grind the red and black pepper, mustard seeds, salt, and dauber dirt together. The spicy mixture burns my nose, and I sneeze, then cough up a little of the gray powder. It's not until I add the poppy seeds and sulfur powder that the fatigue kicks in and I start to feel woozy.

Disoriented, I survey the kitchen. What am I doing here? And why am I so incredibly tired? My gaze settles on a list in my handwriting. I focus hard, trying to make out what I've written. Hmm…a *Mind Confusion* spell.

Scratching my head, I sense it means something important. But what? I sink onto a stool, lay my head on the counter, and battle the drowsiness to search my memory. As I sneeze a few more times, a faint idea glimmers, then sharpens until the whole mission floods back.

I shake my head and sit up straight. Holy cow, this is powerful stuff! It'll be perfect as long as I can get out of this house without losing my mind or zonking out. I'll have to remember not to get too close to it tonight.

Yanking my shirt up over my nose to keep from breathing in the potion, I find a plastic container and resealable lid to transport it. After I've tidied the kitchen and wiped down the mortar with a wet cloth, I toss the spells and other equipment I'll need into my messenger bag and head out.

Ducking my head, I jump off the front porch steps, dodge the increasingly heavy rain and blustery winds, and rush toward the car. Racing through the garden, I nearly trip on Bloody Bill's dagger, which is still stuck in the ground, a sad reminder of our argument with Maggie. My right hand twitches, vibrating with a subtle electric current. I stop short, getting drenched, and focus on my hand to make sure I didn't imagine the odd sensation. It zings again, this time, stinging a little as it radiates through my palm. Okay, okay, I get it. Yanking the blade from the dirt, I chuck it in the bag and dart to the car, throw open the back door, and dive into the backseat.

"Got everything?" Jack asks.

Cooper's staring out the front window, a blank expression on his face.

I wipe my soaked hair off my face. "I've got the spells, but we need the ancestors' mortar."

Jack huffs. "Are you kidding me?"

"No, I'll need a tarp from Dad's workshop, too, and we'll have to set them up on the dunes between the beach and the tabby ruins. If that's not too much to ask."

"That thing is way too heavy for me to carry," Jack whines. "Plus I'm not allowed in Miss Delia's house, remember?"

I shrug. "You're not the only one who can carry it, are you?"

Seriously, I might have broken Cooper's heart, and we might not be on speaking terms, but he's still got to help.

Without a word, Cooper throws open his door and slams it behind him, then runs through the garden, up Miss Delia's front porch, and into the house.

"He's pissed," Jack says.

"You think?" I can't worry about it now. There's too much to do and too little time. I'm just glad we never told Jack about us. It saves me a lot of explaining.

A minute later, Cooper crosses the porch, the granite mortar gripped between his strong hands, and staggers back to the car. I open the back door, and he heaves it onto the seat next to me.

After making the trip out to the ruins to drop off the tarp and mortar, we finally arrive at High Point Bluff. It's later than we expected, but there's still plenty of time to set up for the party. Missy meets us in the grand foyer as we're drying off. She's less than pleased.

"Where've y'all been?" She crosses her arms over her canary-yellow tube dress and smacks her gum behind cherry-red lips, which are the exact same color as the ruby necklace. "My guests will be arriving soon, and I expected your help."

Cooper steps in front of Jack and me. "We had a few errands to run. But we're here now, and everything will be fine." He forces his lips into a smile.

She taps her stilettoed foot, which matches her dress perfectly. I didn't know they could dye shoes that shade of yellow. It's so… electric. She hitches her brow. "I hope so. This'll be the party of the summer, and I don't want it messed up."

Jack nods. "It'll be great, ma'am. I bet people will be talking about it for years." His eyes twinkle as he nudges Cooper in the side.

"Yes." Cooper suppresses a grin. "Why don't you go and get ready, Missy? We'll take it from here."

Her eyes narrow in disdain. "I am ready, sonny boy." She tosses her platinum hair and rolls her heavily made-up eyes. Her gaze settles on Jack and me as she fiddles with the enormous stone around her neck. "You're not wearing that to my party, are you?"

Jack and I look down at our clothes. He's thrown a polo shirt over his rash guard and dug out his khaki shorts. They're the nicest summer clothes he's got. My peasant blouse and bohemian skirt aren't exactly rags, either. We're wet, but we'll dry soon enough.

"Um, is there something wrong with these?" I ask.

She chomps her gum. "Not if you're a guest, but you're the

help." A wry grin creeps across her face. "I figured we'd run into this problem, so I had the caterers drop off some uniforms for you. You'll find them in the kitchen along with the food." She snaps her fingers twice. "Come with me, Ella, and I'll show you what needs being done."

Cooper glares. "Her name is *Emma*." Our eyes meet, and his soften as his mouth turns down. My heart soars. Maybe he doesn't completely hate me.

Missy laughs as she spins on her heels. "Uh-huh, whatever, Cooper. Bring your little friend into the great room so he can help his daddy set up. Then he needs to change, too. And for God's sake, tell him to take off that nasty swim shirt." She then curls her finger, motioning me to follow as she sashays down the hall like a giant swaying banana.

She brings me to the kitchen where caterers have dropped off trays of Mexican food and points to a white, long-sleeved, button-down shirt and black polyester pants. "Put those on, then set up the chafing dishes for the fajitas. I want them to be nice and hot when the guests show up. And don't forget the *queso*. My Beau loves his spicy cheese." She walks to the kitchen door but pauses before leaving. "Thanks, Edna." She winks.

Oh, it'll be hot, all right. The peppers, mustard, and poppy in the *Mind Confusion* powder should add more than a kick to tonight's menu. With the rain pounding against the kitchen windows, I change into the waitress costume, then cover my mouth and nose as I mix the potion into the dips and hot sauces and sprinkle it on the fajitas. The only thing spared is the tortilla chips.

A bowl of blood oranges is tucked into the corner on the kitchen counter. The sun's blood could mean orange juice, specifically the juice of a blood orange.

I hover my hand above the oranges. It doesn't tingle. My spirit guide must not be interested. But I'm nearly out of time, and it's the best idea I've got. I might as well make some juice in case it comes in handy later. I pull Bloody Bill's knife from my bag, wash off the dirt from Miss Delia's garden, then slice into the dark red flesh and squeeze enough juice to fill one of the empty vials in my bag. I'm still not sure what to do about the blood of the moon. Maybe it's got something to do with the tides. If so, we can always collect a little seawater.

Jack enters the kitchen as I'm cleaning off the knife. He parks himself in front of the food and drools. "Oh, man, I'm starved. You mind if I grab some?" He snatches a plate and reaches for some grilled steak.

"No!" I drop the knife in the sink and lunge for the fork in his hand. "You can't eat that. It's got the…you know." I waggle my brows.

He stares at me, rubbing his growling stomach, then finally catches on. "Oh, yeah. Right. I didn't want any of that, anyway. I mean, who eats Mexican food at a Fourth of July party?" He leans in and whispers in my ear. "Is that stuff safe to eat?"

I wince, biting my bottom lip. "Um, most of it. Probably." He laughs as I dry off the knife and return it to my bag. A little clear vial at the bottom catches my eye. "Hey, what kind of drinks is Missy serving?"

"Margaritas, why?"

I grab my trusty *Four Thieves Vinegar* and hand it to him. I remember that one of its side effects can be confusion. Perfect. "Slip this into the tequila while Dad's not looking. It should help speed things along."

I put some *Mind Confusion* powder in my pocket, then leave him to change into his uniform while I set up the buffet in the great room. I pass through the library with a fajita tray, sprinkling a little powder as I go, and avoid Lady Rose's portrait as usual. Her eyes cling to me as I cross the room, beckoning and making my neck itch, until I can't resist a peek. Yep, those bug eyes still stare out from her ghastly gray skin and super high forehead. But for the first time, I notice something deeper in the portrait. She's not freaky in a look-at-the-scary-lady kind of way. She's haunted, traumatized, and now I know why. She watched her husband fall apart from The Creep, then witnessed Sabina's prophecy come true as her only child lost his soul and turned dark and corrupt. After all that, I'd probably look that bad, too. Maybe worse.

I round the corner to the great room and pause to take in the impressive view of St. Helena Island Sound. Normally the golden South Carolina sun hangs in a dazzling blue sky, dancing off the tranquil inlet waters. Not today. The sky's a harsh slate gray, and the churning Sound is nearly black. The tide's higher than I've ever seen it, with choppy swells that break in chaotic white caps far off the shore. Rain pelts the huge panoramic windows, and squalls bend the surrounding trees. Battery-operated lanterns line the room for when the electricity inevitably cuts off.

Dad's at the bar, wearing a similar uniform, but his includes a black vest and bow tie. "Hey, Em, how's it going? You need some help?" His brow is creased as his gaze shoots toward the windows. I know he'd rather they be boarded up with plywood, or at least secured with duct tape, but that would ruin Missy's majestic view of the storm.

I shake my head and set the tray in a chafing dish. "Nah, I got it." As much as I hate including him in this spell, there's no getting around it. I just hope he doesn't have any food or drinks. Missy's probably already banned him from having some, anyway.

Jack walks into the room in his uniform and golf glove.

Dad laughs. "Well, look at you! I don't believe I've seen you dressed alike since you were babies." He chuckles. "Of course, Emma isn't wearing that silly glove you've grown so fond of."

"It's only because of my poison ivy, remember?" Jack says. "I didn't think Missy would want me oozing all over her guests."

Dad winces. "Yeah, that wouldn't be best. Well, glove or not, you two look great. I ought to take a picture of you."

I roll my eyes. "Right, because we want to immortalize this hot fashion trend." Jack and I laugh.

"I'm serious." Dad pats his pants pockets. "Where's my cell phone? Oh, it's in the other room. I'll be right back. You two stay put."

As soon as he's gone, Jack darts to the bar and empties the *Four Thieves Vinegar* into the nearly full bottle of tequila while I keep watch.

Cooper carries in another fajita tray and sets it in the second chafing dish.

The doorbell rings, heralding the arrival of the first guests.

"We ready?" Cooper asks, but doesn't make eye contact with me.

I nod. "Ready as we'll ever be."

Chapter Thirty-two

Before Missy brings in the first of her guests, I click the salsa playlist on her iPod, then race to the kitchen to get the rest of the food and set it up in the great room. I'm in charge of the buffet, and Jack's the drink runner, so he'll spread most of the powder.

A gaggle of wind-blown Missy clones and their decrepit husbands saunter in just as I've finished. Cooper sits in a corner chair, doing his best to ignore them while Jack takes their drink orders. Beau grunts his way to a sofa and slaps his lap. Missy jumps at his cue, perching herself on his enormous thigh and twiddling with the ruby necklace.

"It's going to be a fantastic night, y'all!" Missy gleams in a sparkly red-white-and-blue top hat. She gestures toward the windows and cracks her gum. "While everyone else is huddled in a horrible evacuation shelter, we're partying in style. There's plenty of food for our fiesta, so eat up!" She snaps and points to Jack. "Jake, I'm parched, and my hand's empty!"

Jack grabs a margarita from the bar and places it in her outstretched hand. We exchange worried glances as she sips, but rather than spitting it out, she smiles. "Mmm, that's tasty! Keep them coming!"

Between taking orders for the waves of arriving guests and delivering drinks for those already here, it doesn't take Jack long to spread his potion around the room. I make a few unnecessary trips as well to empty the spell from my own pocket. Soon every guest has a drink, and most have moved through the buffet line, taking a heaping plate of hoodoo-laced Mexican food. Before he sits down to eat, Beau pulls one of the men off to the side. The man nervously downs his drink in one gulp. I motion to Jack to get him a refill.

Missy pouts. "Now, Beau you promised not to talk business tonight."

Beau smiles. "I'll only be a second, possum. Mr. Johnson and I have some important matters to discuss."

She cocks her head and crosses her arms. "What could be more important than our friends, sweetness?" She huffs. "No one wants to hear about your boring land deals."

His eyes narrow into snake-like slits. "Those land deals afford the lifestyle to which you've so quickly become accustomed, my dear." He flashes a menacing smile. "Without them, you'd be back in that lovely double-wide. But you needn't worry, I won't be bothering my friend about a Beaumont Builders' development." He slaps the man's shoulder. "Mr. Johnson runs the King Center which was robbed this summer. As one of their largest donors, I'm interested in their security upgrades. We can't have people carting off valuable artifacts willy-nilly, leaving us no clues to catch them, now can we, Johnson?" Beau lumbers down the main hall, into his private study, with his anxious party guest in tow. Beau slams the door shut.

My heart skips a beat as Jack and I exchange nervous looks.

Cooper slumps in his chair and covers his face with his hand. I offer a silent prayer that Beau's right, and there isn't any way to link us to the crime.

One of Missy's friends, an equally blonde and bejeweled twenty-something, gasps. "A burglary? At the King Center? What's next, our houses?" She swigs the last of her margarita. Jack rushes to replace it.

A few guests get up from their seats and wander around the room, staring at pillows, a lamp, and the terra cotta wall paint. One plays with the stereo, increasing the volume and drowning out the howl of the beating wind and rain. I swallow a snicker, delighted the charm's kicking in.

Missy nods. "I hope not, Bunny. As you can see, we've got so many valuables here at High Point Bluff, we'd be a natural target for robbers." She downs her margarita and shakes her empty glass. "Oh, Jared, where's my refill?" Jack springs up to replenish her glass.

Bunny empties her plate, then comes up to the buffet for more salsa and chips. "Of course you would, Missy. They'd especially love to steal that gorgeous necklace of yours." She scratches her head and surveys the buffet table, her eyes filled with uncertainty.

I spoon an extra large serving of salsa on her plate. She scoops it up with a chip and swallows it whole, then walks aimlessly to a different couch and plops down, draping her arm around another woman's husband. Several more guests shift in their seats, their eyes filled with vacant stares.

Missy swallows the last of her fajita and rubs the ruby. "You're right, Bunny. I never thought of that." She gulps her second margarita in one long mouthful, then sways on the couch and grips her forehead. "You know, I never take it off." Her eyes stretch wide, and her voice quiets to a whisper. "If a robber wanted it, he'd probably kill me to get it." She rakes her acrylic fingernails through her hair, mussing it, and slides off the couch onto the floor.

Since no one seems to notice the hostess's condition, the potion's got to be in full force. Everyone is in their own confused world, including Dad, who's drooped on a stool behind the bar, his head propped in his hands and muttering to himself. It's time to strike.

I nod at Jack, then Cooper, who rises from his chair in the corner and scooches next to Missy on the Oriental carpet. "You're right, Missy," Cooper says. "That necklace is putting your life at risk."

She tilts her head to the side and nods. "Yes. Bad guys. Danger." She grabs her plate off the end table, scoops a handful of hoodoo guacamole with her fingers, and shoves it in her mouth.

Cooper forces back a laugh. "I'd hate to see something bad happen to you because of that silly ruby."

Missy sticks out her tongue and laps at the green dip that's smeared around her lips and cheek. "Me, too." Then she crawls on her hands and knees to the coffee table to down someone else's margarita. "What do you think I should do?" she whispers.

Cooper balls his fists, undoubtedly still uncomfortable with what he's about to do, but forges ahead. "You should put it away for safekeeping."

She nods. "Yes. But where? They'll take it if it's at High Point Bluff." She wrenches the chain around and fumbles with the clasp. It falls open, dangling from her swerving hand.

He gulps and opens his palm. "I'm sure I can find a good place for you."

"Thanks a lot, Coopie." She drops it in his waiting hand, then pokes the tip of his nose. "You're cute." Then she lies down, rubbing her guacamole-caked cheek against the silk carpet. "Don't let the bad guys get me."

Cooper slinks back toward the door while Jack crouches next to her. "Remember, it's a secret hiding place, so you can't tell anyone what you did with the necklace."

"Uh-huh." She nods, tracing the rug's pattern with her finger. "What necklace?"

Jack snorts. "Never mind. There is no necklace. Forget I said anything." He backs up, grabs one of the lanterns, and joins me and Cooper at the archway to the foyer.

"Okay." She hums to the mariachi music on the stereo.

Jack turns and slaps Cooper's arm. "Come on, Coopie. Let's go bust some curses."

Chapter Thirty-three

I duck into the kitchen for my bag of supplies and meet the boys at the door. We don't bother with raincoats, since they won't do us any good, anyway. We'll be drenched no matter what.

Beau's locked the cars in the garage for the duration of the storm, so we've got no choice but to use the golf cart. Racing to the cart in the dwindling light, I struggle against the driving wind and rain, which knock me back toward the Big House. I've come too far to be beaten by the wind. Tucking my head, I trudge forward, determined to make it out to the tabby ruins and with any luck, the end of these curses.

Cooper inches the cart down the driveway. If the ruins weren't so far away, we'd probably be better off walking. The gusts are more powerful than before, rocking the vehicle and dumping what feels like gallons of water on the flimsy roof. Without doors or a windshield, we're assaulted by storm debris as small branches and dead pine needles whip through the air, smacking our bodies and clinging to the car. There are no headlights, so it's nearly impossible to see through the heavy rain and mist. No one says a word, allowing Cooper to concentrate amid the lashing wind and rain.

Lightning strikes, sending a giant pine branch flying in front of the cart. Cooper yanks the wheel to the side, just missing the tree missile as it lands on the opposite side of the driveway. A moment later, another tree lining the drive bends so far over, it topples, its roots pried out of the ground.

Cooper floors the cart to get off the tree-lined entrance to High Point Bluff. The driveway is majestic in beautiful weather but a certain death trap in a hurricane. The back tires skid on the slick pavement, but he corrects the wheel and guides us toward the dirt path that leads to the tabby ruins. Off the asphalt, the cart sinks into the soaked forest floor. Just as I'm sure we're stuck in the mud, the rear tire catches and propels us out of the muck.

Minutes later, we've dodged a few more fallen trees and arrived at the ruins without major damage. Cooper snatches a flashlight from our supply bag while Jack and I dash through the clearing to where we've left the mortar and other equipment propped on a tabby stump and wrapped in Dad's blue plastic tarp to stay dry.

Even though it's the height of summer, the air is cool, infused with the salty scent of the angry sea and the thrashed earth. I peer out at the Sound. The roiling water's nearly as dark as the dusky sky, making it difficult to tell where one ends and the other begins. But I can tell how close the water is. It's risen so much, the crashing waves almost crest the bluff. If it gets much higher, the murky water will flood the ruins.

Jack sets the lantern next to the mortar and clicks it on. "What do you want us to do?" he yells over the howling wind. Cooper jogs up next to him.

I wipe the pelting rain from my face. "I need you two to hold the tarp like a canopy so I can stand underneath it and light a fire in the mortar." My hair whips my face, stinging my eyes.

Cooper shakes his head. "There's too much wind. You'll never get a flame going."

"Let me worry about that. Just give me some cover." I grab my hair and tie it in a knot at the back of my head to keep it from slapping my skin.

Cooper hands me the lit flashlight and helps Jack unwrap the mortar. I toss my bag over the open vessel to keep the inside as dry as possible. They clutch the tarp's ends and hoist it above their heads. The wind catches the plastic, snapping it like a sail. It billows, nearly flying out of their hands.

"I don't know if I can hold this, Emma!" Jack shouts, digging in his heels and pulling the tarp against the gusts. "My hand isn't strong enough."

I shake my head, and my hair falls out of its knot. "You'll have to, Jack. Try to make your good hand do most of the work." I glance at his white golf glove as my hair whips around again. "You should take that off. And undo the button on your sleeve. If we break the curse, and your skin comes back, it should be as free as possible."

The last thing we need is for it to grow back all weird, like if his skin enmeshes with the glove and shirt. That would be grosser than what he's got now. He jams his hand into his mouth and rips the glove off with his teeth, exposing his brittle bones. Then he thrusts his arm at me. I tuck the flashlight under my elbow, reach my waterlogged fingers to undo the button on his long-sleeved waiter's shirt, and roll it up over his swollen and blistered bicep.

With Jack's radius and ulna unobstructed, I duck under the makeshift shelter, which flaps like a parachute in the gusting wind. Cooper holds the end of the tarp behind me, and Jack's in front, watching my every move. The tarp blocks the brunt of the blustery rain, but it doesn't keep all the weather out. There's still plenty of air and water to propel the spell.

Crouching next to the ruin, I scoop up a little dirt and dump it into the mortar. Then, slinging my bag across my shoulders, I pull out two cups of charcoal chips from a Ziploc and pour them in, dousing them with one of Miss Delia's paraffin-based unjinxing oils. If lamp oil won't burn in a hurricane, nothing will. Bracing myself for the inevitable fatigue, I strike a match and drop it into the mortar's deep belly, then watch as it flickers to life. The flame is small, though determined in the dampened breeze.

Rubbing my *collier* for luck, I grab Miss Delia's spell book from the bag and, keeping a firm grip, flip to a passage I found while sitting on her hospital bed. Ever since the first *plateye* arrived, she insisted we needed her ancestors' help. Since she's not here to explain what she meant, I've got to trust she was right and invite them here. Maybe they'll tell me the secret to Sabina's incantation, since I'm not at all convinced blood orange juice and seawater are the answer.

The hurricane's power bears down on Cooper and Jack, drenching them and blowing hard against their strained bodies. Their sopping hair clings to their heads, and the rain whips their faces. Jack especially struggles against the gale, relying on his one strong hand. He grunts. "Emma, I don't know how much longer I can do this."

Thunder booms nearby, making us all jump.

After my heart stops racing, I call, "We're almost there, Jack," and hope he hears me over the wailing wind. I sprinkle one of Miss Delia's premade white magic charms into the crackling mortar, a mixture of althaea root, myrrh, frankincense, and copal, which is supposed to attract well-meaning spirit helpers. It smokes, releasing a rich, aromatic, and slightly chemical smell.

The exhaustion slams into me like a ten-ton truck, and I struggle to stay on my feet. Every ounce of energy seems to drain from my limbs, amassing in my core, this time centering in my chest. The pain and tiredness has never been this bad, but then again, I've never attempted to conjure a spell this big before. Miss Delia said magic was energy, and this particular charm is going to require nearly all I've got.

I close my eyes, do my best to quiet my mind, and force out the words I copied from Miss Delia's spell book. "Benevolent spirits reveal your existence, present to us now, we need your assistance." Another verse leaps to my lips, probably influenced by my *collier*, so I add it even though I can barely afford the effort to speak. "Miss Delia's ancestors are the ones that we need, but only the ones who'll help us succeed." Because there's no way I want to meet Sabina. Not today. Not ever.

A sharp pain jabs in my chest, causing my knees to buckle. I crash to the muddy ground.

"Emma!" Jack calls, his voice brimming with alarm.

I wave them off and muster the strength to stand. As long as I don't breathe too deeply, the sting isn't too bad.

Two giant bolts of lightning strike the woods behind the clearing.

The clearing's perimeter glows as bright orbs of light float in the air, then stretch and elongate into person-shaped entities and settle onto the ground. Gawking, Cooper and Jack wrench around to see what's happening. I gulp and grip the sides of the mortar to help me stay upright. So this is what it means to see dead people.

The figures sharpen and come into focus, then morph into sixteen very real-looking women, all with skin in varying shades of brown and wearing different periods of dress. A few have scarified faces and wear cloth that appears as if it was spun in Africa. Others seem to have lived in the Americas, their clothes ranging from simple coarse slavery garments to more modern dresses worn in the early twentieth century. Maggie is among them. Our eyes meet, and she nods with a grin. The women turn to one another and smile, then walk toward us and join their outstretched hands to form a perfect circle around the ruins.

The ground rumbles. From the corner of my eye, I catch a glimpse of something on the beach, just beyond the dunes. I turn my head and squint to make it out.

It's sort of a tannish-gray cloud that hugs the shoreline. It's billowing. And growing closer.

Holy sticklewort, it's a sandstorm! A pain stabs in my chest. In my shock, I must have inhaled too much air.

Within seconds, the storm rolls up the dune, churning up a hazy fog of sand and prowling toward us. If we don't do something—or move—it'll envelop us all.

Yellow energy grows from the ancestor's clasped hands, stretching toward the sky and forming a bubble above the clearing. Like a giant sieve, it shields us from the brunt of the biting gusts and blasting sand but still lets in enough of the storm's power to maintain the spell. The shield glows a bright amber, illuminating the darkness as if it's midday and warming the area under the bubble by at least ten degrees. It suddenly smells like a giant botanical garden as the scent of roses, gardenias, lilies, peonies, even honeysuckle, infuses the ruins.

My pulse pounds slow and deliberate in my ears, which I can hear now because the shield has dampened most of the storm's noise. If I wasn't seeing this with my own eyes, I'd be sure it's a dream. An amazing but incredibly freaky dream. A calming wave rolls over me, reassuring me we're safe.

Exhausted, Jack and Cooper drop their arms and clear away

the tarp, then twirl around to gaze at the supernatural spectacle. Maggie delinks from her celestial sisters and steps forward as the two women at her sides join hands to maintain the circle.

"Emma Guthrie, you have come very far indeed." She smiles. "You have combined the elements. You are nearly there."

What is she talking about? I'm miles away from making this work. I shake my dazed head and strain to keep my head up. If I didn't know better, I'd say my blood pressure was dropping. "I'm trying. I've got unjinxing oil, but it's not enough." My voice cracks. "I don't know how to bind the blood of the sun and the moon, the day and the night."

"Yes, you do."

"No, I don't. Why can't you just tell me what to do?" Desperation swells in my gut. I thought these spirits were supposed to be benevolent. Why won't they help?

"Because I cannot. You must find the answer on your own." She hitches her brow, and her gaze bores into me. "It is one of the fundamental laws of hoodoo."

Light-headed, I ignore the pain, then clutch at the sharp twinge in my side. Righting myself, I push a long hank of tangled hair off my face and forge ahead with the mission.

"Is it the juice from a blood orange?" I manage to mutter. "Because I've got some here in my bag. And the moon regulates the tides, so maybe the moon's blood is water?" My mind spins, unsure of how I'll have the energy to break through the ancestors' protective barrier and claw through the flying sand to get some seawater. The deadpan expression on Maggie's face tells me I'm way off.

She purses her lips. "Look within you and without you. The answer has always been before you."

What the heck is she talking about? Her stupid riddles make

no stinking sense.

I sip shallow mouthfuls of air, my head throbbing as I peer at the fire in the mortar. It's dwindling. I don't have more charcoal, and the wood in the clearing is soaked. It'll never light, even if I use another whole bottle of paraffin oil. We're out of time.

My gaze cuts to Jack, who seems as clueless as I am. I don't have to tell him how frightened I am. I know he can sense my panic and anxiety.

His mouth turns down, and he grasps my hand. "It's okay, Em. You tried your best. Maybe it's time to accept that I'm going to die like Edmund and the pirates."

Cooper shakes his head. "Don't say that. There's got to be something we can do."

"I don't think so." Jack grimaces.

My stomach seizes, and the tears roll down my cheeks. "No!" I wail as I collapse into him and bury my head against his wet shoulder.

He wraps his arms around me and rubs my back with his bony hand. "Shh," he whispers. "It's okay."

Sobbing against his damp shirt, I hyperventilate as I imbibe his Jackness, the same boy-scent I've smelled our whole lives. I can't imagine life without his piles of dirty clothes, his unmade bed, or his nasty soccer cleats lying around. Life without my other half. My twin.

I squeeze his unfairly skinny midsection tight, wanting to keep him here in this protected clearing forever, but it's no use. He's right. He's going to die. And it'll be a horrible, grotesque death that he doesn't deserve. The flesh on his upper arm will fall off next, and then The Creep will inch up his shoulder and crawl over the rest of him, destroying his body one part at a time.

Pulling away from his now-slimy shoulder, I blink through

burning tears and gaze at his face, wanting to etch it into my memory. This is the Jack I want to remember—young and strong, loving and fearless, and bravely resigned to face the horrors of The Creep. I reach my feeble hand to stroke his cheek. Soon he'll become a terrifying walking skeleton, stripped of this glorious olive skin, his brilliant blue eyes and thick jet-black hair.

Suddenly, a shooting pain rockets through my chest, squeezing the last reserve of air from my lungs. I try to inhale, but my side refuses to budge. It's like being caught in a vacuum. I may not know what I'm doing with magic, but I do know one thing: I can't last long without breathing. Panicked, I tug at my weary muscles, but they're limp and refuse to draw oxygen.

A shock charges through my body, shooting from my toes all the way up to my scalp. I don't know where it came from, but it's an energy boost I desperately need. Sucking in a breath, I ignore the jabbing ache and revel in the glorious, life-preserving air. My hand vibrates, shaking against Jack. His eyes bulge. He must have felt it, too. I stare hard at my hand and try to discern what it, or my spirit guide, is trying to tell me, but all I see is my pale hand on Jack's golden cheek. It pulsates again, this time with more force.

And then, like a wave crashing down on me, I suddenly realize what's been in front of me all along: Jack is dark, and I am light. Twins, but polar opposites. Standing there in our white and black waiter's uniforms, we're the human embodiment of a yin and yang symbol.

Maggie's reference to the universal law of hoodoo reverberates through my mind, echoing what Miss Delia stressed about the importance of balance in hoodoo. Good defeats evil; day breaks night; love conquers hate. And most importantly, only a white magic spell can reverse a black magic charm.

Suddenly, it all makes sense.

Chapter Thirty-four

I turn to Maggie, my heart swelling with hope. "Within me, and without. That's Jack and me, isn't it?" I rasp.

"Huh?" Cooper asks.

"What are you talking about?" Jack asks, his brow furrowed. He's probably afraid to hope I've figured it out for real.

Maggie beams. "You have done well, Emma Guthrie. Just as I knew you would."

I look at the ancestors, who nod and smile as one. A surge of joy shoots through my body, thrusting off the iron yoke of dread that's crushed me for weeks. I finally know what needs to be done. My chest eases, allowing me to draw air again. Elated and empowered from the sudden rush of knowledge, I throw open my bag, and whip out Bloody Bill's dagger.

Cooper steps forward, his face tense with alarm. "What are you doing with that, Emmaline?" Great. Now he wants to talk to me, but only because I've got a weapon.

"You must act quickly. Your fire is dwindling," Maggie urges. "Save your brother and free my soul."

There's no time to explain and quell Cooper's fears. Knife in hand, my strength grows as I step toward Jack. "Give me your good hand."

"Emmaline!" Cooper calls.

Jack takes a step back. "You're freaking me out."

"Give me your hand!" I repeat.

He retreats another foot. "Seriously, Emma, you look crazy. What are you doing?"

"Isn't it obvious? We're the sun and the moon."

"W-w-hat?" Jack asks.

Taking advantage of his confusion, I lunge forward to catch his hand, but he pulls it away. I huff. "We have to bind our blood to break the curse."

His eyes dart toward Maggie. "That's crazy talk."

She rolls her eyes. "I can see I picked the right twin. You would not make a good root doctor, Jack Guthrie. You lack imagination." She turns to me. "You must find a way to convince him, Emma, before it's too late."

Jack's eyes narrow. "Why should I believe anything you say, Maggie? You lied to me and gave me those horrible headaches."

Her gaze turns down. "Jack—"

I cut her off, because this is no time to rehash the past. "Fine, I'll prove it to you." I lift my left hand and bear down, slicing the knife across my open palm. It burns like hellfire as bright red blood trickles down my skin and drips on the ground. I swallow a sob. If I'm right, and we're really this close to breaking the spell, he's about to get all the proof he needs.

Cooper screams, "No! Don't hurt yourself!"

A low growl rises up from the forest. Even though the hair on the back of my neck rises, I exhale with relief at the terrifying, though welcome, sound. It's exactly what I was hoping for.

Cooper and Jack spin around, terror etched on their faces as the rumble grows, increasing in volume and intensity as it draws near. The vibrations rattle my chest. A moment later, a giant horde of *plateyes* emerges from the surrounding forest in all directions, their evil yellow eyes glowing and their jagged fangs bared. They stalk toward the ancestors.

Uh-oh. We don't have any whiskey.

Maggie smiles. "Do not fear. Delia was correct. The ancestors will protect you."

The *plateyes* stop, then launch into a brutal volley of barks and claw at the sodden dirt. As if on command, they break out into a full-on run, each one sprinting toward an ancestor, intent on breaking the protective barrier. Their thick legs move so quickly, they almost fly over the ground. I wince, anticipating their vicious attack, and pray there's some way to prevent it.

Steps away from the ancestors, they dive headfirst but slam into an invisible blockade. The demon-dogs bounce off the spectral women then crash into the dirt, skidding across the mud. Snarling and filthy, they narrow their cruel fluorescent eyes, dip their enormous heads, and barrel toward the ancestors again. The wall holds strong. A few of the beasts are knocked unconscious by the collision's force. The rest of the hellhounds yowl and snap their massive jaws in frustration as they pace the perimeter.

Emboldened, I square my shoulders. "See, Jack, I'm right. The *plateyes* wouldn't show up unless we're close. Now give me your hand."

He nods, his frightened eyes bulging, and extends his good palm. I yank him to the mortar and hold his hand above the shrinking flame. Then I remember Missy's ruby pendant and pause. Although I'm not sure how, I'm certain I should incorporate it into the ritual to save Cooper, too.

"Cooper, give me the necklace." I thrust my bloody palm at him. He digs into his front pocket and slaps it in my hand, the sharp gold leaves digging into my wound. Wincing, I drape the chain over my fingers and clutch the ruby pendant. I turn back to Jack. Staring into his petrified eyes, I try to reassure him. "This won't hurt, I promise." It's a total lie, but it's better than dying from The Creep.

He squeezes his eyelids shut. My heart thumps as I drag the blade across his skin and draw blood. He whimpers and presses his lips together to hold back a yowl.

"Grab hold," I urge, entwining our fingers and palms. Clutching tight, I lift our hands above the mortar. Aided by the extra pressure, my blood pumps, oozing over the ruby and its gold setting, and mixes with his. The slick red fusion seeps down our fists, over our thumbs and dribbles onto the flame.

A flash bursts in the granite mortar, and a fireball leaps into the air, shooting cherry-red flares into the sky. Blazing, they speed toward the ancestors' shield.

Jack shrieks and falls to the ground, convulsing.

Shocked, I scream and drop Bloody Bill's dagger, just missing Jack.

Cooper starts toward him, but Maggie holds up her hand. "Do not interfere."

Cooper shakes his head. "I've seen this before. It wasn't good then, and I'm sure it can't be good now."

She presses her hand against the center of his chest. "Have faith. All will be well."

Jack thrashes, kicking his legs wildly, and screams like a torture victim. He crunches into a fetal position, then flips so his head grinds into the muddy ground.

The fire plumes blast through the top of the dome, then arc

back toward earth like heat-seeking rockets aimed straight at the *plateyes*, which incinerate on contact, leaving only piles of demon-shaped ash in their place.

Jack wails, clutching his bony arm close to his chest. The skin on his upper arm repairs as the blisters shrivel and shrink, and the redness and swelling calm. Within seconds, it's normal. Then the regeneration inches down from his bicep, creating flesh where there is none. The bright red muscles, ligaments, and tendons unfurl first, followed by a layer of fat, and finally skin. On and on the process repeats itself, making its way down his upper arm, over his elbow, then onto his forearm. It crawls down into his wrist, then his palm, and at last, over his fingers. When his arm is whole, Jack howls once more, then falls over onto his side, exhausted, and weeps.

Thank goodness. It's over. Finally. He's safe.

My shoulders crumple with relief, and joy surges through my body.

Maggie runs to him, crouching in the mud. "You are saved, Jack Guthrie!" His tears carve tiny rivers in his muck-caked skin. She strokes his forehead, pushing his dirt-matted hair off his face. "I hope you can forgive me. I am sorry. But without you and your sister, I would not be free."

He reaches his now nearly perfect but shaking hand up to her smooth brown cheek. The tip of his middle finger is missing and shorter than the others. "It's okay, Maggie." His voice is raspy and thick. "It sucked, but it's over now, and I forgive you." He takes a couple ragged breaths, then adds, "I'm glad you can move on. You deserve some peace."

She leans down and kisses his grimy lips.

When they part, Cooper reaches down for Jack's now-healthy hand and hoists him to his feet. "You're back, Jack!" Eyeing the stump, he adds, "Well, mostly." Laughing, he offers his palm for a high-five.

Overjoyed, Jack smacks it back. Hard. It's the most he's been able to do with that hand in a while, and he's clearly relishing the opportunity. He gazes at his restored flesh and flexes his fingers, then pumps his fist. "Amazing," he whispers. His eyes flicker to me. "And it's all because of you, Emma. If it wasn't for you, I'm not sure how much longer I'd have. You saved me." A grateful tear rolls down his cheek.

Overwhelmed by his sincerity, my throat tightens, and I bat back a couple tears of my own. But as good as all this feels, I know I didn't do it alone. "Thanks, but Miss Delia deserves the credit. She taught me everything. And of course, there was my spirit guide."

Cooper grabs my arm. "Are you kidding? You did it!"

Full of pride, his classic Cooper grin gives me the shivers. I thought I'd never feel that again. Stunned by his renewed attention, I try to respond, but the words are locked in my throat.

Cooper ducks his head to peer into my eyes. "Did you hear me, Emmaline? You might have gotten some help, but when it came down to it, *you* saved Jack!" He yanks me into his embrace and squeezes, then twirls me around in a circle.

Giddy from his exuberance and the nearly impossible accomplishment, I squeal with delight. He's right, I did do it. The Creep is gone, my brother's going to live, and I won't lose my other half.

Jack embraces Maggie, clutching her tightly with his rebuilt arm. His capacity for forgiveness is astounding. The world would have been a darker place if he left it.

Cooper releases me and runs his thumb across my jawline. "I'm so proud of you." The earnestness and intensity of his gaze reminds me of how things were between us before I betrayed him and he hated me for lying about his soul. Which I'm not entirely sure has been saved.

I grab his thick forearm. The sticky, bloody ruby pendant is still in my palm and clings to his skin. "But I don't think I saved you. The necklace hasn't buzzed in my hands or anything."

"Wait—how can Cooper still be in danger?" Jack asks, happiness slipping from his face. "I thought Emma just broke the curse."

Maggie strokes his cheek. "'Tis true she broke The Creep, my grandmother's punishment for how Edmund and the pirates ended my life. But her second curse remains, the one imposed for the Beaumonts' greed." Clicking her tongue, she shakes her head. "If only Edmund had not given his wife the pirate's ruby."

My hand burns, but considering the cut has been contaminated by dirt, Jack's blood, and goodness knows what else Missy may have put on this necklace, it's likely the start of a colossal infection.

Before Cooper can respond, Maggie releases Jack and holds up her hand. "Please, friends, my time is near." She steps to me and clutches my shoulder with her frosty fingers. "Thank you, Emma Guthrie, for all that you did. Please tell your root doctor that my gratitude has no bounds." She glances into the mortar at the smoldering embers and hitches her brow. "Your flame is nearly extinguished and before long will grow quite cold." She stares at me for an uncomfortable moment. My earlobes prick. She turns toward Cooper, her eyes filled with sorrow. "You are a fine young man, Cooper Beaumont, nothing like your forefathers. I regret you are destined to suffer their bitter fate. You do not deserve such a frigid and lonely existence." She steals a furtive glace at my hand. "A blood stone, indeed."

My outer ears burn and swell, then pulse with energy. With a grunt, I rub at the pain.

"What's wrong?" Cooper asks.

"My ears hurt."

Maggie backs away, a smile on her lips. "Follow your instincts, Emma. The answer lies within your grasp." She turns and walks toward the ancestors.

Okay, it's clear my spirit guide wants me to pay attention to something, and Maggie's talking in her jumbled code again, so I better pay attention. My brain zooms, reviewing her words, most of which had something to do with the fire. My left hand vibrates, and a chill emanates from my palm and leaks into my fingers. I look down at the ruby necklace, which is covered in Jack's blood and mine. It's literally a blood stone, and it's also literally within my grasp. But what does it have to do with the dwindling fire in the mortar?

Beau's words slam to the front of my brain. For as long as I can remember, he's always described the necklace as "eighty carats of pure fire." Sabina cast the Beaumont curse because Edmund stole it for his wife after he'd delivered Maggie to the pirates. Every Beaumont wife since Lady Rose has worn the ruby pendant, and every Beaumont child has been stricken with the curse since her son was born.

That's it! The curse resides in the stone itself. The only way to reverse it is to destroy the ruby. With fire. I yelp with realization. I have to act now before the flames die.

"What's going on?" Jack and Cooper cry in unison.

My palm turns icy and vibrates violently. I fling the necklace at the mortar before I suffer freezer burn.

With the necklace in midair, Maggie whirls around, halfway to the ancestors. "No, Emma!" She shrieks and bolts toward us.

The ruby finds its target, falling into the belly of the mortar and clanking against the granite. A volcanic explosion ignites, generating intense heat as centuries of hate and revenge combust, then shooting sparks of unjinxing oil out of the mortar.

Cooper, Jack, and I run for cover behind a tabby stump. Maggie joins us as we watch the mortar shake. Something gold and shiny bubbles up over the rim and drips down the side. It must be the chain and leaf setting. Suddenly, loud pops and bangs erupt from the mortar like a hundred firecrackers going off at once. The mortar quakes, gaining momentum until it wobbles too far and tips over on its side. Three broken pieces of ruby bounce out, roll across the pedestal, and drop over the edge to the ground.

We stand up from behind the tabby and tiptoe to the mortar.

My stomach drops as dread slinks up the back of my neck. Something tells me I just made a colossal mistake. I'm too afraid to ask, but Jack's twin sense kicks in.

"What just happened?" Jack asks.

Maggie's face is ashen and drawn. "Emma misinterpreted my clues."

"What's that supposed to mean?" Cooper asks, his voice tight and strained.

"Fire was not the solution. Ice was."

I break into a sweat, and my mouth fills with sour saliva as my palms turn clammy. Of course, the hoodoo rule of balance! I remembered it long enough to break The Creep, but I was so caught up in trying to save Cooper too, I charged ahead without thinking.

"C-can we still fix it?" I stammer, eyeing the three red stones lying in the dirt. "We've still got the pieces. Maybe we can work another charm."

She shakes her head. "I do not think so. I am not a root worker, but I would guess it must be whole to reverse the curse."

My body shudders, and my chest heaves as thick, fiery tears flow down my face. Cooper's still doomed, and it's all my fault. I've destroyed the only thing that could've saved him. Now he'll be as corrupt as his father, and there's nothing we can do to stop it. I've ruined everything.

I peer into his still perfect and innocent face and wail, "I'm so sorry!" Then because I can't bear to see him, I slap my quivering hands over my face and weep.

"Hey now, Emmaline," Cooper coos and gently pries my hands away. "Shh, don't cry." He envelops me in his strong arms, drawing me close against his broad chest, and rubs my back.

Even though I don't deserve this kindness, I sob against his shoulder. He's got every right to yell and scream, to push me down into the mud and stomp off in a rage. But that's not Cooper. Yet. I'm sure that's only a fraction of what he'll be capable of after he loses his soul because of my unthinkable screwup. Tears flow in a torrent, soaking his already wet shoulder.

He pulls back and lifts my chin with his palm. "Hey, it'll be all right. I'm sure of it." He smiles, his eyes filled with compassion.

How can he say that? Doesn't he understand what just happened?

My throat constricts, and a tear streams down my cheek. "No, it won't. You'll still lose your soul on your birthday."

He shakes his head. "I don't think so."

I gulp. The trauma must be too much for him to bear. He's lost his mind.

I clutch his arms. "Cooper, maybe you don't get it, but breaking the stone was a huge mistake. I can't use it to reverse the curse."

He wipes away my tears. "Don't sell yourself short, Emmaline.

You saved Jack when I was sure it was hopeless. My birthday is a month away. That's plenty of time to figure something out."

Time. I hadn't considered that. Maybe he's right.

"Really?" My voice cracks with a sliver of renewed hope. "I know you hate me for lying to you, but will you still help break the curse, and—"

"Shhh." He places a finger on my still-moving lips. "I don't hate you, Emmaline."

"No?" I sniffle, wishing it's true. I accept that he'd never want to be with me again, but losing our friendship would kill me.

"I wasn't happy with you, but I could never hate you." He pauses for a moment, scanning my face. "Don't you realize that I love you?"

I gasp. The world spins around me, then narrows down to the small space separating us. "You do?"

He grins. "I always have."

My jaw hangs slack as I fumble for something to say. He's forgiven me, even though I haven't saved him and may, in fact, have sealed his fate.

But I don't get a chance to even utter a thank-you before he scoops me up in his crazy strong arms and tenderly lays his lips on mine, kissing me deeply once again. Chills surge, icy and hot at the same time, and race over my skin. My heart pounds as he slides his hands around my back and tugs me close. Intoxicated by his closeness and his crisp, summer-rain scent, I wrap my arms around his broad back so I don't collapse.

The world slips away, all sound and thought muted by this amazing sensation. The dampened wind and rain are silent, Maggie and Jack are as good as invisible, as are the ancestors who still light up the clearing. The cut on my hand doesn't burn and throb anymore, and I don't care that my blood is dripping down

Cooper's back. The only thing that matters is Cooper's forgiven me.

Jack clears his throat. "Ahem. PDA much?"

I start and regretfully pull away from Cooper, but he clutches my right hand, anchoring me. Oh, Jack. I forgot he didn't know about us.

Cooper punches his shoulder. "Look who's talking, bro."

Maggie's image flickers and fades. "I am free, my friends! Finally and forever." She sighs as centuries of burden appear to slip from her incandescent shoulders. She looks as if she might break out in tears of joy. Her visage flashes and sputters again. "My journey is about to begin. Remember to care for one another and have faith in yourselves. Hold fast to the small spark that binds you as one. Together you will find a way to break the curse and save Cooper."

She turns and joins the ancestors. At once, a deep, resonant chord echoes throughout the clearing as their perfect harmony vibrates the ground beneath our feet. They unclasp their hands, drop their shield, and let in the hurricane's gusts and rain. The sandstorm retreats toward the Sound, and the *plateye* dust mounds blow away. The ancestors dematerialize, evaporating into radiant orbs of light, then float up into the stormy night sky.

Jack drags his gaze from where Maggie disappeared. "I know it's weird, but I'm going to miss her." Even though he has to yell to be heard over the wind, his voice is wistful.

I shake my head. "It's not so weird."

Cooper turns to me. "She's right, you know. As long as we stick together, we can do anything." He wraps his arm around me, gripping me close.

I hope he's right and it'll be that easy. The creeping sensation itching at my scalp tells me otherwise. But that's a worry for another day.

Threading my arm behind his back, I cling to Cooper, knowing I can stand on my own two feet, but having him here is so much better. The howling wind and rain bear down on us, but it can't hurt me. Nothing can. Because Cooper Beaumont loves me back.

 Epilogue

The sun streams through the windows of Miss Delia's hospital room. From the brilliant blue sky, it's hard to believe a hurricane blew through here yesterday. The Big House was damaged, but it's nothing Dad can't handle.

Miss Delia is propped up in her bed, looking spry and not at all like she's just woken from a coma. Except, of course, for the bandages and stitches that pretty much cover her body.

Her face lights up. "Good morning, children!"

Cooper smiles. "You're looking fine this morning, Miss Delia."

"Funny thing. I woke last night smack in the middle of a hurricane. I figured you three had to have a hand in it." She adjusts the new *collier* I draped around her neck when we visited before the storm hit.

Jack waves his right hand as he leans against the windowsill. "Hey, Miss Delia, notice anything different?" His stump is obvious, but it's a thousand times better than his funktastic bare bones.

She winks her cloudy eye. "Good girl. I knew you could do it."

I sit in the chair next to her bed and scoot close, her praise warming me from the inside out. Cooper pulls the other chair next to mine and tucks the bag we've brought underneath. I reach out to pat Miss Delia's bandaged hand. "I was able to break The Creep, but only because I found the note you were holding, when you, well, you know." My voice catches at the thought of those evil monsters attacking her.

She shakes her head and squeezes my hand. "Shh now, we needn't speak on that."

I nod. "Yeah, we got a...translator. It was ancient Akan, the language some of the Africans spoke when they came here. It means, 'I bind the blood of the sun and the moon, the day and the night to bring you darkness and shorten your life.'"

She rubs her chin, pondering the phrase, then laughs. "How long did it take you to realize you and your brother there were the sun and moon?"

I gape, astonished it was so obvious to her. "Um, awhile, actually. I almost didn't." I gnaw my lip.

"She was awesome, Miss Delia." Jack beams at me.

I'm used to sarcastic Jack, and his unfettered gushing makes me uncomfortable. His euphoria over being saved should pass soon enough. Then he'll snap back to his normal, annoying self.

Miss Delia claps her hands. "Very good, you bound the elements and remembered what I taught you about the importance of balance. Sacrificing for love is the strongest white magic around. Definitely the fix for Sabina's black magic."

I wince, ashamed of myself for forgetting that rule when it came to Cooper's curse. "I didn't remember it long enough."

Cooper reaches over and squeezes my hand. "We promised not to dwell on that."

Miss Delia's eyes narrow. "What are you talking about?"

I exhale and drop my gaze to my flip-flops, afraid to meet her eyes and her disappointment for messing up. "I threw the blood stone into the fire when I should have frozen it."

"Don't be too hard on yourself, Emma." Her voice is soft and not at all angry. "You're still an apprentice. With me in here, you were bound to make at least a few mistakes."

Her words are comforting, but they don't erase the guilt I feel. A little mistake is understandable, but she doesn't know the epic nature of my screwup. "The stone broke into three pieces."

We each dig into our pockets and pull out a glistening red rock. We divvied up the pieces as souvenirs, since we can't exactly hand them back to Beau and Missy without getting killed for real.

Cooper chuckles, but it's a nervous laugh. "I'm not sure how we'll keep it from my dad." He bounces his broken ruby in his palm. "We're hoping he won't notice it's not hanging around Missy's neck."

Not wanting to dwell on Beau's inevitable wrath, I focus on the more immediate problem. "Since the stone's not whole anymore, I don't know how to break the curse. So Cooper's soul's still in danger."

Tilting her head, Miss Delia looks at Cooper. "If I recall, your birthday is about a month away, right, son?" Cooper nods. Miss Delia stares out the window and ponders something for a few moments. She sucks her teeth, then turns back to us. "It's not long, but we might be able to work up another cure."

"See, Emmaline? We've got plenty of time." Cooper wraps his arm around my shoulder and tugs me close, kissing my temple.

Miss Delia's brow furrows. "I didn't say that, boy. This curse has hung on for three hundred years, a month may not be enough."

Cooper's shoulders slump as if he's finally comprehended the severity of his situation.

I can't let him slip into despair. I've got to try and keep up his hope. "We'll figure it out." I clutch his hand and lean my head against his shoulder.

Miss Delia chuckles. "Seems you didn't do everything wrong, Emma. Perhaps you gained a little more than a broken ruby for your trouble?" She smirks.

Cooper pulls his lips into a half grin. "Yeah, doomed soul aside, I'm the luckiest guy on St. Helena, now that Emmaline's my girlfriend."

My cheeks flush with heat, and my chest heaves. I still can't believe that, even after all that's happened, we're officially together. Squeal! Now we've really got to save his soul.

Jack snorts. "Aw, man, are you guys going to be gross?"

Cooper winks. "No grosser than you and Maggie were, bro."

Jack's olive cheeks flush.

I wipe the stupid grin off my face and clear my throat. "Um, okay, can we show Miss Delia what's in the bag?"

Cooper laughs and removes his arm, then leans down to grab the paper sack. "Sure. We're hoping you could do us a little favor." He pulls out Bloody Bill's treasure box. "We dug it up this morning after the hurricane blew through. Now that The Creep's been destroyed, it's harmless."

Her snowy brow knits. "What do you want me to do with that, boy? It looks an awful lot like that pirate's dagger."

Jack steps to her bedside. "Nothing, really. We just want you to let us donate it to the King Center in your name."

I nod. "It would make us feel better about stealing from them."

Jack leans over and takes the box from Cooper. "Plus we're guessing this'll make you one of their biggest donors ever." He lifts the lid to reveal about a hundred shiny gold doubloons.

She squints through her cataract. "So I'll only be donating the box and treasure?" We nod. "What happens to the knife and my ancestors' mortar?"

Cooper scratches his temple. "We'll find a way to dump the knife off at the museum. Maybe leave it in a bathroom or something." He laughs. "'Course we might need some of that *Semi-Invisibility Powder* to get back in there."

Jack crosses his arms. "The mortar's yours. They're not getting it back."

Miss Delia smiles. "Okay, what do you need me to do?" Cooper takes the donation papers out of the bag and hands her a pen to sign on the dotted line. She scribbles her signature, then chuckles. "I'm glad we didn't have to fight over that mortar. I'm going to need it to continue Emma's training. There's no telling what we'll face breaking the Beaumont curse, and she needs to be prepared."

Three sets of eyes land on me. The enormity of the task weighs heavy on my chest.

I gulp as a chill runs up my spine. Something tells me Miss Delia's right. Breaking the Beaumont curse could be even more freaky and dangerous than The Creep. I'll need all the help I can get. With Jack and Cooper at my side, I know we'll find a way.

Acknowlegments

Thanks first and foremost go to the Gullah people of the South Carolina and Georgia Sea Islands, for whom I have a deep and abiding respect. I hope you feel I've done Miss Delia justice. I love her fiercely.

The seeds of this book were planted two decades ago while I was an undergraduate history student at Georgetown University. Dr. Marsha Darling introduced me to the Gullah, and Dr. Marcus Rediker taught me about pirates. Your classes were the highlight of my undergraduate experience and left an indelible impact. It was an honor to be your student.

The following books have been invaluable in researching the Gullah and hoodoo magic: *Hoodoo Herb and Root Magic: A Materia Magica of African-American Conjure* by Catherine Yronwode, *Hoodoo Medicine: Gullah Herbal Remedies* by Faith Mitchell, *Lowcountry Voodoo: Beginner's Guide to Tales, Spells and Boo Hags* by Terrance Zepke, *Gullah Fuh Oonuh (Gullah for You): A Guide to the Gullah Language* by Virginia Mixson Geraty, *Hoodoo Mysteries: Folk Magic, Mysticism & Rituals* by Rev. Ray

T. Marbrough, and *Blue Roots: African-American Folk Magic of the Gullah People* by Roger Pinckney as well as his essay, "Burying Miss Louise," which appeared in the January/February 2004 issue of *Orion* Magazine. The pages of these texts are well worn, highlighted, and layered with sticky notes. Although I have taken some artistic license, I could not have written this book without this outstanding scholarship. Finally, I would be remiss if I didn't mention the premier resource on Gullah culture, St. Helena's own Penn Center and its York W. Bailey Museum. I wish I had a treasure chest full of gold coins to give you.

Debut books are molded by many hands, and this one is no exception. The following people trudged through early rough drafts with great fortitude and enthusiasm: Theresa Fuller, Susan Hatler, and my fellow students in Rebecca John's Advanced Novel Workshop at the University of Iowa's Summer Writing Festival in July 2010, especially Kevin Smith, Jon Stonger, and Joan Burda. The following people graciously read the entire manuscript and offered invaluable critiques: Veronica Blade, Regina Gramss, Laurel Wanrow, and my three favorite teenage beta readers: Conor Dougherty, Rachel Lefkowitz, and Alyssa Reiman.

Thanks also to Nicole Resciniti, who plucked me from the slush and believed in this story even before it was finished. Your comments and suggestions shaped and strengthened this book for the better, and the experience taught me never to think, *I can't,* because I've proved I can. I am eternally grateful for the journey we walked together and all I learned along the way.

To Madison Pelletier, who beta-read this book before acquisition at Entangled Publishing and demanded that her mother buy it: I'm sending you a big, squeezy hug and your very own *Follow Me Boy gris-gris* bag. Use it wisely. And to Madison's mother, Liz Pelletier, editor and publisher extraordinaire, who "got" this action-adventure-romance story and knew exactly what to do with it: you have my undying gratitude and affection. Thanks for pushing me to make the magic bigger. As usual, you were spot on.

Writing can be a solitary endeavor, making support and writing partners all the more necessary. The Romance Writers of America and several of its affiliated chapters—the Young Adult Chapter of RWA, Fantasy, Futuristic and Paranormal, and the Maryland Romance Writers—have provided extraordinary education, kinship, and community.

So, too, have several of my writing sisters: Amanda Carlson, Marisa Cleveland, Jen Danna, Amanda Flower, Marianne Harden, Melissa Landers, Cecy Robson, Julie Ann Walker; the Honestly YA girls: Carey Corp, Lorie Langdon, Kim MacCarron, and Jennifer McAndrews; as well as the Maryland Vixens: Christi Barth and Stephanie Dray.

But chief among all is Laura Kaye, my best friend and partner in literary crime, with whom I bounce plot ideas and write every day, critique, freak out, cry, and laugh. You are the sister of my heart, but I hardly have to tell you that.

Finally, this crazy writing life could not be possible without the sustaining love, support, and patience of my devoted husband Patrick, who makes it possible for Mommy to work late nights and weekends to meet my deadlines. I know it isn't always easy, but you pull it off with aplomb. I swear I'll buy you a forty-foot sailboat someday. And to Gillian, Riley, and Lila, my little pies: I write these stories for you, so you'll believe in the power of magic, love, and your very own brilliant minds.

Keep reading for a sneak peek of Rachel Harris's

my super sweet
Sixteenth Century

> *"Prepare yourself for a Renaissance-shaped treat!* MY SUPER
> SWEET SIXTEENTH CENTURY *is a fun, romantic romp among*
> *deliciously dressed and cultured people. But it goes a bit deeper, too.*
> *It's also a chance to witness Cat experience things that will*
> *change her forever. Don't miss Rachel Harris's debut. It's a totally fun*
> *and totally satisfying read."*
> - Lisa T. Bergren, author of the River of Time Series

On the precipice of her sixteenth birthday, the last thing lone wolf
Cat Crawford wants is an extravagant gala thrown by her bubbly
soon-to-be stepmother and well-meaning father. So even though
Cat knows the family's trip to Florence, Italy, is a peace offering,
she embraces the magical city and all it offers. But when her
curiosity leads her to an unusual gypsy tent, she exits . . . right into
Renaissance *Firenze*.

Thrust into the sixteenth century armed with only a backpack
full of contraband future items, Cat joins up with her ancestors,
the sweet Alessandra and protective Cipriano, and soon falls for
the gorgeous aspiring artist Lorenzo. But when the much-older
Niccolo starts sniffing around, Cat realizes that an unwanted
birthday party is nothing compared to an unwanted suitor full of
creeptastic *amore*. Can she find her way back to modern times
before her Italian adventure turns into an Italian forever?

Chapter One

I'm trapped.

I concentrate on the monitor in front of me and scan through the in-flight entertainment, attempting to tune out Jenna. Like that's even possible. When my dad's bubbly fiancée gets this excited, I swear sometimes only dogs can hear her.

We've been on this plane for over six hours. I woke up less than an hour ago, cramped, cranky, and carb-deprived, and yet the woman insists on being perky. It's as if she were born with caffeine in her veins.

"Cat, do you know what this means?!?"

I quirk an eyebrow at Dad, but judging by his all-consuming interest in the newspaper, his stance of neutrality is in full effect. To tell you the truth, it's not his impartiality that hurts. It's knowing that by staying out of it, what he's really doing is taking her side.

And moving further away from mine.

I settle for a crappy rerun and decide to throw the evil step-witch-in-training a bone. I lean forward and look across the aisle, catching a glimpse of her flying fingers on her BlackBerry—thank goodness they have in-flight Wi-Fi, or she might've actually wanted to bond. "No, tell me, Jenna. What does it mean?"

"It means your party is practically a shoo-in for the show!"

My party. Right. As if anything about this is for me. If Jenna really cared about me, you'd think she'd have clued in to the fact that anything involving crowds, paparazzi, and scrutiny isn't exactly my thing. She refuses to grasp that while I might be a daughter of Hollywood, it doesn't mean I'm a product of it. If anything, this party is for *her.*

Jenna's too excited by her coup to notice my lack of reaction. She leans over Dad and gushes, "The buzz on this is absolutely unreal. Your party is going to be the biggest, flashiest event I've ever put together!"

Yay, me.

I turn back to the television and pick up my headphones.

Unfortunately, that does nothing to deter her. "You can even sketch caricatures of the guests as they come in the door if you want." She flashes a brilliant smile, like she's doing me a huge favor. "Adds a fun, kitschy element to the whole thing, don't ya think?"

No, I don't think. I'm an artist, not a street performer.

She kisses Dad on the cheek, then rubs her thumb over the coral lipstick stain, and I watch him turn to mush. He's so whipped. "Order me a Diet Coke if the cart thingy comes by, 'kay?" Jenna says. "I'm off to brave the bathroom line!"

I shake my head as she haltingly maneuvers down the aisle and stumbles into a woman's lap. Jenna turns on her hundred-watt grin, tosses her poufy blond hair, and apologizes profusely. Then she plops herself on the woman's armrest, abandoning all thought of bathroom trips in lieu of getting better acquainted with her new bestie.

Whatever. At least her ADD works for me, I think as I slide into her vacated seat, lay my head against Dad's shoulder, and inhale the familiar scent of his spicy aftershave and Armani cologne. He wraps an arm around me, and I snuggle closer. It's quiet moments like this when I can imagine things are back to normal. Before he fell in love with someone completely wrong for him.

Dad kisses the top of my head. "Thank you."

I lift my head slightly, not willing to move out of his embrace just yet, and shoot him a puzzled look. "For?"

"For letting Jenna throw you a Sweet Sixteen. You may not believe it, but she has the best of intentions."

Sure she does. I glance forward to see her slap the armrest and let out a high-pitched squeal. The only intention Jenna has is having her event-planning business showcased on MTV. Date someone famous, get his daughter on television, and generate mad buzz for your business—not bad for nine months of work.

I glance back at Dad. Why can't he see how fake she is? It's like ever since she came into the picture, he's had blinders on, only seeing this giggly blond happy person—who is *nothing* like me.

"Jenna had one when she turned sixteen," he continues. "She said it was, and I quote, 'the highlight of her adolescent experience.'"

He rolls his eyes and grins, and the pressure in my chest lessens. He hasn't changed. We're still us, even with her around. Then his forehead wrinkles and he shifts uncomfortably, and that guilty look creeps back into his eyes.

Crap. Here it comes.

"Peanut, I know you're always trying to take care of me, but I'm the grown-up. And it's my job to look out for you. I want you to have at least *one* normal childhood experience."

I snort. "Normal. Right." With a teasing grin, I lean back a little and lift my eyebrows in disbelief. "Dad, I hate to break it to you, but we live in Beverly Hills. And while having your birthday party and private life broadcast around the world for entertainment purposes may be an unfortunate reality for media-obsessed brats, I don't think anyone would call that behavior normal."

Dad chuckles, and I gift him with a confident smirk. "Besides, when have we *ever* done anything like the rest of Hollywood?"

And the defense rests, I think, sitting back with a nod. Dad can't argue with that logic. If it weren't for our zip code and my fancy, overpriced education, you'd never know we had money. Although he's a well-known film director and has a handful of Golden Globes, Dad has this thing about "normalcy." I've never missed a day of school in my life, and he rarely takes on projects during the summer. That's time for family and vacations, but none of that "private jet to remote locations" stuff for the Crawfords. Nope, we go to good old Disney World and the beach, with the occasional stop at a film set in Canada to spice things up. We don't even have a maid or a cook.

Dad squeezes me tighter. "You're right, we're abnormal. But I still think it's a good idea." My head lolls against my seat, and he smiles. "It's a party; it'll be fun. Plus, I'm already doing a major suck-up job bringing you to Italy. Doesn't that earn me any negotiating cred?"

I have to admit, if everyone has a price, a trip to Florence would be mine. I've been obsessed with my Italian heritage—the only thing I accept from Mommy Dearest—and the Renaissance ever since I saw Bernard van Orley's *Madonna and Child with Apples and Pears* painting in fourth grade. Since then, I've inhaled every art book and novel on the time period or on Italy that I can find.

As bribes go, the trip is a good one.

Still, there's no way I can let Dad off the hook that easily. What he's asking of me is huge. Maybe things would be different if I were just a normal girl from the Mississippi countryside or the Cape Cod beachfront, or if people didn't take one look at me and assume they knew my whole life story. If I could just be me, Cat Crawford, without any expectations or preconceived notions, then maybe I'd be bonding with Jenna over napkin samples and color swatches right now. But that's not reality. So I shrug, affecting the confident, blasé image I've perfected for school and the media, and move back to my own seat.

I immediately reach in front of me for my backpack. Just holding it makes me feel better—more in control of my crazy life. I peruse the contents: my makeup kit and toiletry bag; my wallet, camera, iPod, and funkadelic purple iPhone; my art supplies and color-coded binder filled with tour packages and historical information; and finally, my reading material, including the copy of *The Hunchback of Notre Dame* I'm reading for English. I brought it to work on whenever I needed a Jenna break.

By the time this trip is over, I'll be a freaking Victor Hugo expert.

I pull out the book and zip my bag before leaning down to slide it back under the seat. As I sit up, I spot a familiar woman's face out of the corner of my eye and freeze. My hands slick with sweat. My heart pounds, and the roar of the jet engine beneath me intensifies.

It's just a picture, Cat, I tell myself. But it doesn't help.

Splashed across my seatmate's tabloid is a beautiful, smiling face and yet another jilted lover with the headline, CATERINA ANGELI DOES IT AGAIN.

"Another one bites the dust."

The words are out of my mouth before I can stop them. The

owner of the tabloid takes a break from her engrossed reading to sneer at me, but then a hint of recognition dawns on her face. She quickly turns to compare the picture of my mother on her cover to the downgraded, non-airbrushed, soon-to-be-sixteen-year-old version next to her.

I want to sink into my seat and look away, pretend I have no clue why she's staring, but I can't. So I force myself to meet her gaze head-on with a confident smile. Casually, I turn back to my book, open it to the dog-eared page, and pretend to read. I feel the woman's eyes on me—watching, waiting for me to do something scandalous—and fight the urge to fluff my coffee-colored hair or gnaw off a nail.

Soon enough she'll stop looking at me, expecting to see my mother. She'll grow bored, go back to her gossipmonger ways, and forget all about me.

They always do.

To read more of Cat's epic adventure, pick up

my super sweet Sixteenth Century

online or in a bookstore near you!